DATE	BORROWER'S NAME	

Books by Kim Vogel Sawyer

FROM BETHANY HOUSE PUBLISHERS

Waiting for Summer's Return

Where the Heart Leads

My Heart Remembers

In Every Heartbeat

Where Willows Grow

A Promise for Spring

Fields of Grace

A Hopeful Heart

Courting Miss Amsel

A Whisper of Peace

Song of My Heart

When Hope Blossoms

A Home in Drayton Valley

Sweet Sanctuary

SWEET SANCTUARY

Kim Vogel
A Novel by
Sawyer

BETHANY HOUSE PUBLISHERS
a division of Baker Publishing Group
Minneapolis, Minnesota

Published by Bethany House Publishers
11400 Hampshire Avenue South
Bloomington, Minnesota 55438
www.bethanyhouse.com

Bethany House Publishers is a division of
Baker Publishing Group, Grand Rapids, Michigan

Printed in the United States of America

Library of Congress Cataloging-in-Publication Data
Sawyer, Kim Vogel.
Sweet Sanctuary / Kim Vogel Sawyer
pages cm.
ISBN 978-0-7642-0789-1 (pbk.)
1. Christian fiction. 2. Love stories. I. Title.
PS3619.A97S94 2013
813'.6—dc23 2012040436

All other Scripture quotations are from the King James Version of the Bible.

This is a work of fiction. Names, characters, incidents, and dialogues are products of the author's imagination and are not to be construed as real. Any resemblance to actual events or persons, living or dead, is entirely coincidental.

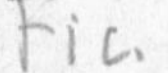

The internet addresses, email addresses, and phone numbers in this book are accurate at the time of publication. They are provided as a resource. Baker Publishing Group does not endorse them or vouch for their content or permanence.

Cover design by Lookout Design, Inc.

13 14 15 16 17 18 19 7 6 5 4 3 2 1

For *Kaisyn Faith*

Right now you are so at peace in your little world.
As you grow, and your "world" becomes larger,
may you always find your peace and security
in the arms of Jesus.

"From the ends of the earth I call to you,
I call as my heart grows faint;
lead me to the rock that is higher than I."

Psalm 61:2, NIV

1

Queens, New York
July 1944

Micah Hatcher scanned the letter a second time, his pulse beating at twice its normal rhythm. *A joke . . . This has to be a joke.* Yet there was nothing funny about it.

Someone bumped him from behind, and he apologized, moving away from the rows of mail cubbies to lean against the opposite wall, where he wouldn't block the foot traffic. Half the population of Queens seemed to be retrieving mail right now. He scratched his head, trying to understand why this letter had come to him.

He checked the signature. *N. Allan Eldredge.* Scowling, he pressed his memory. Eldredge . . . Eldredge . . . The name seemed familiar. Then he slapped his forehead, remembrance hitting like a wave.

Lydia Eldredge. The nurse from Schofield Station Hospital. The one who had left Oahu early because of a mysterious emergency. An emergency that was no longer a mystery, thanks to the letter.

Micah's gaze dropped to the letter again. Yes, now he understood. Small wonder Lydia had been in such a hurry to get back to the States—halfway through her tour of duty, as he recalled. He released a huff of disgust. He knew Lydia had been rather . . . well, flighty . . . and somewhat self-centered. But despite Lydia's faults, he would never have taken her for a liar. How could she make up such drivel about him? He didn't have time for this kind of nonsense now—not with Jeremiah depending on his help.

Tucking his other mail into his jacket pocket, Micah left the crowded lobby and plunked down on a wrought-iron bench outside the post office. With the noonday sun heating his head, he flattened the letter against his pant leg and read it once more. Slowly. Concentrating on every word and searching for hidden meaning between the lines.

Dr. Hatcher,

I am sure by now you feel certain that your responsibility has been fully avoided, and this letter has come as a surprise. It has taken me some time to locate you. But this is a matter of extreme importance. A child's life has been impacted. As the child's grandfather, I cannot allow him to grow up wondering why his father has chosen to abandon him.

Therefore I request that you honor your responsibility toward your child. He and his mother are living with me in Boston. I will allow you two weeks to contact me. If by the end of that time, you have not chosen to honor your duty to your son, I shall be forced to take legal action. I assure you I have the wealth and influence to see that you do not continue to neglect your responsibility. I encourage—no, I insist—that you come with all due haste to Boston to settle this matter in an honorable fashion.

N. Allan Eldredge

"My son?" Micah muttered, his frustration growing. He had no son—it was impossible! Why on earth would Lydia tell her parents he had fathered her child? He folded the letter and shoved it roughly back into its envelope.

Going to Boston wasn't out of the question, he realized. It would be at least another three weeks before his brother's package arrived in New York. He could spend some of his hard-earned money on a train ticket and be there in less than two days. But to go might acknowledge the accusation held merit, which was ridiculous. Still, could he allow this farce to continue? And what of this boy—Lydia's son? He must be between three and four years old, certainly old enough to understand a father's absence. What had the child been told?

The questions tumbled in Micah's head as haphazardly as a tumbleweed blowing across the Texas prairie of his childhood. And then another childhood remembrance—a welcome one—intruded. His mother's voice tiptoed through his mind: *"Son, whatever comes your way, the good Lord knew it was comin' and has a solution in mind. Trust Him to guide you."* The letter might have caught Micah by surprise, but nothing came as a surprise to God.

Right there on the bench in the open, he closed his eyes and communicated silently with his Heavenly Father. He offered the situation into God's keeping, and a feeling of peace settled in his heart. "Thank You," he whispered, opening his eyes and focusing once more on the busy noonday traffic. He'd made his decision, and he trusted it was the right one. He would travel to Boston, confront Lydia and her parents, and insist that she tell the truth. Micah was not the father of this child. A twinge of sympathy pinched his conscience for the little boy, but it was not his responsibility no matter what Lydia's father might think. The sooner the man realized it, the better off they would all be. Especially Micah. Being caught up in his brother's travails was responsibility enough.

He pressed his hands against his thighs, pushing himself to his feet like an old man. The situation left him feeling much older than his thirty-six years. But hadn't the burden he and Jeremiah carried aged them at least ten years for each of the past two? Another deep sigh set him in motion toward his small, lonely apartment. He'd make a couple of phone calls and arrange for a temporary replacement at the clinic. He couldn't hand off the other responsibility. He'd have to be back to take care of Jeremiah's package himself. But as soon as possible he'd knock on Lydia Eldredge's door and bring an immediate end to this nonsense.

Micah thanked the taxi driver with a generous tip and a smile before slamming the door. The taxi departed, leaving him standing on the cobblestone street of Boston's prestigious Back Bay neighborhood outside a tall, narrow, ostentatious brownstone crunched side-by-side with several other tall, narrow, ostentatious brownstones. Micah whistled through his teeth—apparently Mr. Eldredge had been accurate in his description of his wealth.

Micah stepped onto the ridiculously tiny yard fronting the house, and not until he was nearly to the steps leading up to double front doors did he see the small boy, crouching in the shadows next to a bush under an overhanging bay window.

Micah stopped, staring. This, then, must be the child in question—the one Lydia had said was his son.

Micah froze in place, observing the silent child. The little boy hunkered on his heels, his bottom hovering above the neatly trimmed grass, his elbows tight against his ribs and his hands clasped in front of him. His hair—dark and soft-looking—curled upward at his collar and around his ears. He was obviously intent on something in the grass, his face studious even in shadow.

Curiosity overwhelmed Micah, and instead of climbing the stairs he crouched beside the boy. "Whatcha lookin' at?"

In slow motion, the child placed one finger against his own lips. "Shhh. Bug."

Micah peered into the sparse blades and spotted what held the child's attention. A shiny black beetle dug busily in the dirt between the boy's feet. Micah's lips twitched.

The child peeked sideways at Micah, his thick lashes nearly shielding his brown eyes from view. With a stubby finger, he pointed at the beetle. "I named him Buggy. I'm gonna keep him for a pet, if Mama will let me."

"Buggy is a good name." Micah looked the boy over. He was a handsome lad, small but sturdy, with soft features and expressive eyes. Micah recalled Lydia had brown eyes, but other than that he didn't see much resemblance between the child and his mother.

"Think he'd be happy in a shoebox? That's all I got to put him in." The little boy turned his gaze fully upward.

Somehow it pleased Micah that the child trusted him enough to ask his opinion. He scratched his head thoughtfully, considering the boy's question. "We-e-e-ell," he finally answered while the child waited patiently, still unmoving from his position, "seems to me that bugs are happier when they've got some grass an' dirt to scurry in. A shoebox seems a rather gloomy place to live."

The child's face fell. "You mean he'd be sad in a box?" He looked wistfully at the beetle, his fingers working up and down against his knuckles. "I don't want to make him sad. It's not fun to be sad."

Micah wondered briefly what sadness the child had experienced to make him so empathetic to a simple beetle. "Most creatures are happier in their natural environments."

The little boy wrinkled his forehead. "Nat'ral en—en—what?"

Micah stifled a chuckle. "Natural environment," he repeated, enjoying this exchange more than he could understand. "You know, the place where God planned for them to live."

The child nodded with a serious expression, then stated, "You talk funny."

Micah laughed. "I do?"

The little boy nodded, making the lock of hair falling across his forehead bounce. "Yes. Your voice goes like this—*lee-uv*. How come you don't say 'live' like I do?"

Again, Micah scratched his head. He exaggerated his southern twang just for the boy. "Well, I reckon because my natural environment was Texas when I was growin' up. Most ever'body there talked just like me."

The boy's eyes danced with glee. "Lahke," he repeated, mimicking Micah's accent. "Lahke tha-et." He grinned, dimples appearing in his apple cheeks. "I *lahke* the way you talk."

Micah felt smitten. What a charming little boy. Whoever his father was, the man was certainly missing out, not being a part of the child's life. Micah stuck out his hand. "I'm Micah. What's your name?"

The boy placed his moist, grubby hand into Micah's. "Nicholas Allan Eldredge the Third. Mama calls me Nicky." He leaned toward Micah, cupping his hand next to his mouth as if telling a secret. "I'm small for my age."

Micah struggled against a chuckle. He forced a serious look. "Hmm, let's see. Stand up for me, partner."

The boy straightened, revealing one untied Oxford and two sagging socks. Micah looked him up and down, stroking his chin thoughtfully. "Well, now, Nicky, 'pears to me you're just about right. Your feet reach the ground an' everything. That's about all a boy could want."

Nicky laughed, his face crinkled with delight. "I like you."

The compliment warmed Micah right down to the soles of his feet. *Whoa, be careful. This one could grow on you.* Micah straightened, too, his height much greater than young Nicky's. The little boy tipped his head back and looked up at Micah, a grin still dimpling his cheeks.

Micah realized he needed to get down to business. "So, partner, is your mama inside?"

Nicky nodded. "Uh-huh. And Grammy and Poppy."

Micah assumed those must be Lydia's parents. It was good they were all here—he could get this situation righted with everyone all at once. "Could you show me?"

Suddenly Nicky's mouth dropped open and he clapped a hand to his cheek. "My bug!" He fell to his knees, his fingers parting the grass blades in a frantic search.

Micah dropped to one knee to search, too, but the beetle was gone. He looked at the bereft child. Two plump tears hovered on Nicky's lashes. They nearly broke Micah's heart.

"He left." The boy's chin quivered. "And I was gonna make him my pet. Not in a shoebox." He placed one dirty hand on Micah's upraised knee. "I was gonna build him a little fence out here so he could be in his nat'ral en—envire—" He huffed.

"You know, where God planned him to be. Right out here in the grass and dirt." A huge sigh heaved Nicky's narrow shoulders. "But now he's gone."

"Aw, don't be sad." Micah wrapped his broad hand around Nicky's sweaty neck. "You know, Buggy probably went on home to his mama. He's probably tellin' her right now, 'I met me a boy who was real nice an' let me come home again.'"

Nicky tipped his head, considering this. "You think so, Micah?"

Micah liked the way his name sounded on the child's lips. "I do."

Nicky stuck out his lower lip, his eyes on the grass. Then he nodded and stood up. "I want him to happy. He's prob'ly happier with his mama than he would be in a little fence all by himself."

"Good boy."

Lydia had done a fine job with Nicky. He was articulate, obviously bright, polite, and kindhearted—a wonderful little boy. For the second time Micah warned himself: *Be careful.*

Nicky reached out and grabbed Micah's hand, tugging. "Come on, Micah. I'll take you to Grammy and Poppy."

Micah rose slowly, his knees popping.

Nicky smirked. "Poppy's legs do that, too. But you're not old like Poppy."

Micah certainly felt old some days. But somehow this child had lightened his heart, taking years away. He smiled, sending Nicky a wink. "Let me give you a word of advice there, partner," he said as the boy led him toward the stairs. "Don't tell your poppy he's old. Most folks don't like to be reminded of that."

Nicky's shoulders lifted in a carefree shrug. "Okay." He released Micah's hand to scamper up the steps. Micah followed more slowly, using the hand rail. Nicky waited beside the door, clutching the door handle and bouncing on his toes while he waited for Micah to catch up. But before Nicky could turn the knob, the door was pulled open from the inside, and framed in the doorway stood Nicky's mother.

Micah stopped, one foot on the last riser and one on the porch floor, as Lydia's gaze met his. She scowled momentarily, as if trying to place something, and then her jaw dropped in shock. Her hand flew to her chest and color climbed her cheeks.

Micah took the final step onto the porch, pushing his hands into his pockets. "Hello, Lydia."

2

M-Micah?" Lydia stared, unable to believe she wasn't imagining his presence. On the island of Oahu four years ago, this man had flooded her dreams, but when she'd left the army base she'd assumed she would never see him again. What brought him to Boston? How had he found her?

"That's right," Nicky chirped, swinging his arms and smiling up at his mother. "He's Micah. And he's my friend. Micah-my-friend. And he talks lahke thee-us."

Though aware of Nicky's words, Lydia felt strangely distanced from them. She placed a trembling hand on her son's head, her gaze never wavering from Micah's. "That's nice, Nicky."

Micah took another step forward. "May I come in?"

"What? Oh! Yes, certainly." Lydia stepped back, heat searing her face. She gestured jerkily for him to enter. "Please . . . come in."

Nicky darted through the long corridor, calling, "Grammy! Poppy! We have comp'ny!" The child disappeared around a bend, and Micah looked after him, a smile playing at the corners of his lips.

Lydia used two hands to close the door and stood with her

palms pressed against the solid wood, hoping to gain strength from the sturdy oak. If she were to make a list of the people least likely to show up on her doorstep, Dr. Micah Hatcher would top the list. Having him so near, after the years that had passed since they'd worked together at Schofield Station Hospital, completely disoriented her. Her knees quaked. Her body tingled with awareness. And her tongue stuck to the roof of her mouth. Which was just as well, because she had no idea what to say.

She turned to find Micah waiting patiently behind her, hands still in his pockets, his face expressionless. "I suppose you knew I'd come."

Lydia frowned. What did he mean? Before she could phrase a response, her father appeared at the end of the corridor and strode quickly toward them, his hand extended to Micah.

"Dr. Hatcher?"

Father's bearing—chin raised, shoulders square, eyes slightly narrowed and gleaming with arrogance—cowed most people. But Micah didn't shrink. He grasped Father's hand. "That's correct."

"I am Allan Eldredge, Lydia's father. It was good of you to come." He kept his chin raised, peering at Micah in the superior manner Lydia knew well.

Micah raised one sardonic eyebrow. "You didn't give me much choice."

Lydia looked from one man to the other, questions racing through her mind. Choice? What was Micah intimating?

"Let's step into my den." Her father glanced at her. "Lydia, have your mother prepare some tea." He turned back to Micah. "Or do you prefer something stronger?"

Micah shook his head. "Don't bother on my account. I don't need anything, thank you."

"Very well." Father lifted a hand, indicating a wide doorway to the left of the corridor. "Then let's get better acquainted."

Lydia tried to follow, but her father abruptly closed the pocket doors in her face. She considered opening them, demanding to be included, but she decided she wasn't up to an argument. Sighing, she turned and headed to the kitchen, where she found Nicky at the table, swinging his feet and chomping an oatmeal cookie. Her mother hovered uncertainly behind him, a glass of milk in her hand. When Lydia entered, Lavinia Eldredge placed the milk on the table in front of Nicky and busied herself with some cut flowers on the dry sink. Lydia knew she'd get no information from her mother, assuming she knew anything.

"Hi, Mama!" Nicky's cupid's mouth was ringed with crumbs. "Do you lahke Micah, too?"

Oh yes, at one time she'd liked Micah. To the point of infatuation. But she wouldn't admit it. She seated herself next to Nicky and reached for his foot, bringing it up to rest on her knee and tying the loose shoelace. "So you made a friend, huh?"

Nicky nodded, a grin lighting his sweet face. "Micah-my-friend. He's nice, Mama. He said I'm just right 'cause my feet reach the ground. And Buggy is prob'ly with his mama being glad I didn't put him in a shoebox."

Nicky and his whims of imagination. Lydia couldn't follow the little boy's line of talk, but she nodded anyway. She rested her chin in her hand, watching fondly as Nicky finished his snack. Her mind carried her backward to the last time she'd seen Dr. Micah Hatcher.

Under the sun on idyllic Oahu, standing beside the Pineapple Express . . . He hadn't spoken to her as she'd waited to board the train. She hadn't spoken either, caught up in worry about Eleanor. As much as she'd admired Micah and wanted his attention, she hadn't sought it that day. And she wasn't certain she should seek it now, even though he was only a few yards away.

Voices exploded from the den. Mother turned from the sink, her fingers covering her mouth. Nicky sat up straight. His head turned toward the sound. Then he gave Lydia a worried look. "Mama, Poppy is yelling at Micah-my-friend."

How odd Nicky would express loyalty to a man he'd only just met rather than the grandfather who had helped raise him, but then Lydia listened again and understood. It wasn't angry *voices* they were hearing, but only *one* angry voice—Allan Eldredge's.

Nicky jumped up as if to run to the hall, but Lydia caught him and eased him back into the chair. "Stay here, Nicky."

Mother crossed to the table and placed her hands on the boy's shoulders. "Yes, Nicky, stay here with Grammy. Finish your milk. Micah and Poppy will be fine—men are just noisy sometimes."

Nicky looked up at his grandmother, his expression innocent. "Like boys are noisy, Grammy?"

"Yes, my little noisemaker, like boys are noisy." Mother smiled and bestowed a kiss on the crown of Nicky's head. "Your mama will make sure they quiet down," she added, giving Lydia a meaningful look.

Lydia rose and hurried to the pocket doors, but she jumped back as they burst open and Father charged into the corridor. His neck and cheeks were mottled, his jaw clenched. The question on Lydia's lips remained unasked in light of the rage on her father's face. She swung her gaze to Micah, who looked equally grim. Father kept his back to Micah, his arms crossed, the anger palpable.

Micah spoke to Father's stiff back. "Mr. Eldredge, I appreciate your concern. But you must understand this situation is between Lydia and me. She and I will need to be allowed to find the solution."

Lydia looked from one man to the other, hoping for a clue. What kind of situation existed between Micah and herself? She hadn't seen the man for over three years.

Father whirled, his finger pointing at Micah, but before he could speak, Nicky came racing down the corridor with Mother on his heels. He slid to a stop and wrapped his arms around his grandfather's knees. Nicky's bangs flopped across his forehead as he peered upward. "Poppy, I heard you yelling. Why were you being so noisy?"

Father looked down at the boy, and his expression softened. He cupped the back of Nicky's head with a tender hand. "Did I frighten you?"

Nicky nodded, his little forehead puckered. "You yelled at Micah."

A brief look passed between the men. They seemed to reach a silent agreement to do whatever necessary to prevent upsetting the little boy. Father stroked Nicky's tousled hair. "I'm sorry, Nicky. Poppy is a big man, and sometimes big men make big sounds. But I won't yell anymore."

Micah crouched to Nicky's level, a warm smile lighting his eyes. He was obviously touched by Nicky's concern, and Lydia's heart lifted as she watched him interact with her son. Placing a hand on Nicky's small back, Micah said, "I won't yell either, partner. Deal?"

"Deal." Nicky grinned and then released Father's knees to turn and lean backward against his poppy's sturdy frame.

Micah rose, his gaze on Lydia. The warmth in his expression drained away. "We need to talk." The quiet tone seemed ominous.

A prickle of trepidation made the fine hairs on the back of her neck stand up. She swung her confused gaze on her father.

Father, his hands now on Nicky's shoulders, jerked his head in the direction of the door. "I suggest you take a walk."

Nicky angled his head nearly upside down as he tried to see his grandfather's face. "Can I go, too?"

"No, you stay with me," Father said.

"But I want to take a walk with Micah-my-friend."

Micah reached out and lightly tapped the end of Nicky's nose with one finger. "Tell you what, partner. I'll take a walk with your mama first, and then when I get back, I'll take a walk with you. Sound good?"

"You and me take a walk alone?" Nicky's wide brown eyes begged.

Micah glanced at Lydia, and she nodded her approval, her heart turning strangely in her chest at Micah's kindness to Nicky.

"Yep, just you an' me, partner."

"Hurray!" Nicky suspended himself happily from Father's hands. "Poppy, Micah and me are gonna take a walk!"

"Good." Father looked at Lydia, his expression carrying a warning. "Go on now."

Winging a quick, wordless prayer for strength heavenward, Lydia pressed her trembling palms against the hips of her trousers and raised her shoulders. "Well, let's go then."

Micah followed her out the door.

Micah's anger had been stirred in his brief encounter with Nicholas Allan Eldredge the Second. Had he ever been part of such a one-sided, accusatory conversation? The man's angry—and inaccurate—allegations still rang through Micah's head. He needed to gain full control of his temper before he asked Lydia why she had named Micah as her son's father. She walked slowly, purposefully, each step measured and stilted. Her gaze stayed straight ahead, not even acknowledging his presence. He sensed her tension, but why should she be tense? She'd started this mess with her untruths.

Micah looked up and down the street. Square patches of grass formed emerald carpets leading from the sidewalk to the bricked faces of four-story-high houses. An abundance of flowering bushes and patches of flowers reminiscent of those his mama planted in her garden—geraniums, poppies, daisies, and bachelor buttons—created eye-catching splashes of color that helped soothe the frayed edges of his nerves.

Lydia's neighborhood was certainly different from the one where he lived in Queens. Her corner of the world seemed much more tranquil than his, few people and fewer vehicles around. A bird sang cheerfully from a snowball bush growing next to the railed stairway of one house. The lilting melody further quieted Micah's irritation.

They were well away from Lydia's home, and Micah had calmed enough to address the issue. *Help me keep my anger in check, God.* He cleared his throat to speak, and Lydia jumped at the sudden noise. She turned in his direction, her brown eyes wide and apprehensive. The expression in her eyes brought to mind little Nicky's pensive gaze, and he had to fight against a smile that threatened. He didn't want to smile at Lydia. Not yet.

"Is Nicky the reason you left Schofield?"

She looked forward again with a defensive thrust to her jaw. "Yes."

"Why didn't you tell anyone?"

Lydia reached out and picked a daisy from a cluster growing near the sidewalk. She twirled the bloom as they continued ambling side by side. "I didn't believe it concerned anyone else."

Micah sent her a sidelong look, irked by her indifferent response. "Your father obviously doesn't agree with your opinion." He paused, his hands clasped behind his back, lest he give in to the temptation to throttle someone. "Why did you tell him I'm Nicky's father?"

Lydia came to a dead halt and spun to face him, her mouth hanging open and her eyes wide. "Why did I—?" She threw down the daisy with force. "I did no such thing!" The denial was adamant and—unless Micah was a poor judge of character—truthful. He remembered her expression when she'd found him on her doorstep earlier. Her shock had seemed genuine. Could she be innocent of creating this muddle?

"Do you have any idea why your father would make that assumption?"

"Father couldn't possibly believe such a thing."

Her indignation was real but misguided. Micah reached inside his jacket and removed the letter he'd received from Allan Eldredge. He handed it to Lydia and watched her read it. Her face slowly drained of color as her eyes scanned the written script. Finally she raised her gaze, her dark eyes wide. She held out the letter as if it were a poisonous snake and shook her head.

"I can't believe . . ." She swallowed, glancing once more at the letter, her face pale. "I had no idea. Oh, Micah, no wonder you came. I'm so sorry."

Micah took the letter from her unresisting fingers, folded it, and returned it to his pocket. In the brief time he'd visited with N. Allan Eldredge, he'd been given the impression Lydia's father was a man few people crossed. He suspected his daughter didn't cross him, either. He gave Lydia's arm a gentle squeeze, his anger with her completely gone in light of her very real distress. "Lydia, I'm sorry, too. I thought you knew why I was here and that you had told him to contact me."

She shook her head, her chin-length dark hair lifting in the slight breeze. "No, he didn't say a word to me." She placed one hand along her jaw as if she had a toothache. "But where would he have . . . ?" Then her shoulders slumped, comprehension dawning, the hand falling to her side. "About two months ago, I noticed my diaries had been moved. I didn't think much about it at the time—I thought perhaps the maid had shifted them when she dusted my shelves—but now I wonder . . ."

Micah could have made a teasing remark about her writing about him in her diary, but he didn't feel much like teasing right now. "You think he read your diary?"

She flipped her hands outward. "He must have. It's the only explanation. I've never mentioned you in conversation. The only place he could have found your name would be my diaries." She ran her hands through her hair from temples to nape, sweeping it into appealing wings away from her face. "I can't believe he would violate my privacy this way!" She spun and stomped up the sidewalk, her heels clacking.

Micah trotted to keep up. He had no difficulty believing that her father had read through Lydia's private thoughts. Allan Eldredge struck him as a ruthless man, intent on having his own way regardless of the cost. "Did you write about Nicky's real father in your diaries?"

Lydia stopped again, dropped her head, and gave a slight nod.

"Then he must not have read everything."

Lydia slowly brought up her chin and looked ahead, giving Micah a view of her profile. He found it just as appealing as he had the first time he'd spotted her across the mess hall at Schofield. Oh yes, he'd been interested. Until he'd discovered she had no interest in Christianity. He wouldn't pursue a faithless woman.

She spoke, her voice flat. "Father has no need to read my diary to discover the identity of Nicky's father. He's known all along."

"Then why would he—?"

Lydia turned her gaze to Micah. Her eyes appeared much

older than her years. "He's afraid. *I'm* afraid. He did it for me—and for Nicky."

Micah crunched his brow, completely confused. "Lydia, I don't understand."

"Of course you don't. You'd have to know the whole story. . . ." Turning away again, she sighed. A tired sigh. A sad sigh. She ran a hand through her hair once more—a thoughtless gesture—then blinked rapidly, biting down on her lower lip. "Micah, you came in answer to a letter that should have never been sent. The least I can do is tell you about Nicky. But not in the open, on the sidewalk where anyone could overhear." Her eyes begged him to listen and understand. "Can we go somewhere private?"

Micah shrugged. "I'm new in town. You'd need to pick the place."

"We'll take a drive," she said. "I have my gas ration coupons for three weeks saved up—we'll drive to Manchester-by-the-Sea, where there's no chance of being overheard." Such secretiveness set Micah's teeth on edge. "Of course, you'll have to take a walk with Nicky first." A small smile appeared on her face.

Micah chuckled. "I promised him. I won't break the promise."

Lydia nodded, giving him an approving smile. Yet her eyes still seemed sad. "Let's head back, then." She turned, took one step, then stopped. Her expression turned desperate as she caught hold of his arm in a surprisingly strong grip. "Micah, what I share with you this evening must stay between us. Nicky's safety depends on it."

A jolt of fear struck as firmly as a fist to Micah's belly. He nodded, making a silent vow. She began walking, and he fell in step beside her. They didn't speak, but his mind raced, his questions taking on a prayerlike quality. *God, this has got me spooked. What kind of secret does Lydia harbor?*

3

The sky had changed to a dusky pink by the time Lydia parked her Hudson at a high point overlooking a steep decline to the ocean's expanse. Micah looked out the window, whistling softly at the view. Manchester-by-the-Sea stretched behind them like a twinkling blanket, electric lights shining in countless windows. On the opposite side, stars shimmered in a clear night sky, sending dappled reflections across the gently rolling waves. God had outdone Himself when He created this corner of the world.

He cranked his window open to allow a breeze, and the sound of a cricket singing its night song intruded. The air was a bit cooler here, but certainly not cold. Sweet scents—fruits, flowers, and damp earth—drifted in, competing with the tang of sea air. He glanced at Lydia. Her gaze was turned outward, but he suspected she wasn't really seeing the view. The fingers of one hand ran idly across the steering wheel, and her puckered face indicated she was lost in thought.

"Are you ready to talk?" Although he spoke softly, she gave a start.

Slowly she faced him, her hand stilling on the steering wheel and curling around the varnished wood as if in need of security.

She released a breath, then set her jaw in a familiar, determined way. "Yes." She shrugged slightly, the shiny fabric of her blouse rippling like the ocean waves with the movement. "But I'm not sure where to start."

Micah shifted, bringing up one knee to prop his heel on the edge of the seat. He wrapped his arm around his knee in a casual pose he hoped would reduce the tension in the vehicle. "How about starting at Schofield, when you left."

She tipped her head, seeming to considering this, then nodded briskly. "All right. Do you remember I asked permission to go to Honolulu?"

He nodded. He'd been given instruction to drive her to the train station, and he hadn't been pleased. Her penchant for flirtation made him uncomfortable. But she hadn't been flirtatious that day.

"I desperately needed to get away. You see, for weeks I had been struggling with a problem, and I just couldn't find a solution. I had gotten a letter from a friend, Eleanor . . ." She paused again, grimacing. "Micah, I'm sorry. For all of this to make sense, I'm going to have to go farther back—to when I took the Red Cross classes and agreed to a year of army service at Schofield. Please bear with me."

Micah reached out and gave her arm a reassuring squeeze. "Take your time."

She gave him a grateful look, then continued. "Eleanor and I were lifelong friends. Our fathers worked together. Father is in crating—"

Micah frowned in confusion, and Lydia laughed softly before offering a brief explanation. "His business is to make crates. The crates are used for shipping everything from oranges to machine gun parts. It's been a very lucrative business and the war has only made it more so."

Micah nodded. Considering how many things were being shipped overseas these days, Eldredge had no doubt amassed a small fortune.

"Eleanor's father was the foreman of the plant, so our relationship was multifaceted. Our parents worked together, socialized together. . . . Since we were both only children, we became like surrogate sisters. Eleanor and I practically lived together."

She fell silent for a few moments, apparently reliving childhood memories. Micah waited, allowing her the time to sort her thoughts. Eventually, she resumed the story.

"About six months before I left, Eleanor's father hired a new worker—a man named Nicolai Pankin. He was missing one arm—the result of an auger accident when he was a teen—but his remaining arm had more strength than most men possess in two good arms. Oh, he was handsome." Lydia's eyes slid shut, and she drew in a deep breath, as if savoring something sweet. Then she fixed him with a serious look once more. "Despite his handicap, he was very rugged and roguish, which only added to his masculinity. And charming . . . He could coax an apple tree to bear orange blossoms. I found him very attractive, and the first time Eleanor spotted him, she was instantly besotted. But, unlike me, Eleanor was shy. She was too afraid to approach Nic."

Although the dim light made it difficult to make out Lydia's features, Micah heard a change in her voice. A tightness, an underlying anguish.

"One time when Eleanor and I went to visit with her father, I saw Nic following her with his eyes. It bothered me at first—I liked him, too. But I realized that after I completed my Red Cross training, I would leave for nursing duty somewhere. Time with Nic would be short-lived. Additionally, I knew Nic was below my station—no matter how attractive I found him, my parents would never approve."

She lifted one shoulder, a flippant gesture that fell short of being convincing. "So I thought, if I can't have him, then my best friend should." She sighed, crossing her arms across her stomach. "I dragged Eleanor over to where he was working and introduced them. It was my only attempt at playing matchmaker, and it proved to be one time too many. They had a whirlwind romance, and I stood up as Eleanor's maid of honor four months before leaving for Schofield."

She dropped her chin. "Of course, we didn't know until after the wedding that Nic was addicted to morphine. Apparently, when he'd had his accident, the doctor had prescribed it for the pain, and he grew dependent on it. He'd hidden it well, and afterward, it was too late. When Eleanor got pregnant, Nic was furious. He didn't want the worry and burden of children, he said. He found someone who would terminate Eleanor's pregnancy."

Micah grimaced. Although he knew only a bit about Nicolai Pankin, he held no respect for the man.

Lydia continued her story. "Eleanor ran away from him. She went to her parents, but they refused to help her. They hadn't been pleased with her marrying a common laborer, and they told her she'd have to deal with the problem herself. So Eleanor wrote to me, begging for help. She didn't know where else to turn. Besides, I had linked her with Nic, which made me partly responsible. It was her letter that created my emergency.

"I wrote and told her to go to my parents and I would be home as soon as I could. My parents were afraid of taking Eleanor in—they didn't know what Nic might do, and they knew it would create a serious rift in their friendship with her parents, which would also affect Father's business. So they arranged sanctuary with a midwife, and they paid for Eleanor's keep until her baby was born."

Lydia paused, and Micah, now certain he knew Lydia's secret, interjected with a gentle question. "Lydia, Nicky isn't really your son, is he?"

"Not my son?" Lydia choked out a single sob. She pressed a fist against her mouth, gaining control. "Nicky has been mine from the moment the midwife placed him in my arms." The fervency in her tone pierced Micah. "He couldn't possibly be more mine if I'd given birth to him. He *is* my son, in every way that counts."

Micah contemplated her answer. He understood Lydia's love for the boy. He'd only just met Nicky, and he already felt the stirrings of fondness. "Why isn't Eleanor raising Nicky?"

"Eleanor died three days before I got back from Schofield." Deep sadness colored her tone. "Nicky came early. The midwife said there were complications—there wasn't anything she could do because Eleanor refused to go to the hospital. Eleanor had instructed the midwife to give Nicky to me—she trusted me to come. The moment I held him, I knew I would keep him and raise him as my own. With God's help, and the support of my parents, I've been Nicky's mama ever since."

Micah shook his head in wonder. It seemed the self-centered Lydia had changed a great deal since her time at Schofield. And it was hard to think of that hardheaded man he'd just met assuming responsibility for someone else's baby. "How did you convince your parents to take Nicky in?"

Lydia raised her chin. "I didn't give them much choice. If they wanted me, they had to accept Nicky, too. I was stubborn." Then she shrugged, her tone softening. "And I was lucky my parents were much more accepting than Eleanor's parents had been. Of course, it didn't take long before they loved Nicky as much as I do. We all think of him as my baby."

"And where is Nicky's father?"

While Lydia talked, the moon had sneaked high into the sky, painting a golden pathway across the water and sending a soft glow into the car, illuminating Lydia's silhouette. Her chin began to quiver. "Nicky's father is hanging over our heads like a hangman's noose."

A chill eased down Micah's spine.

"Shortly after Nicky's birth, he somehow found out where Eleanor had been hiding. He visited the midwife, demanding the baby. The midwife told him the baby had died with Eleanor. But Nic didn't believe her. He told her he'd found a family that wanted the baby—a family willing to pay for the baby—and he wanted 'the kid.' That's what he called Nicky—'the kid.' Not 'my son' or 'Eleanor's child,' just 'the kid,' like Nicky was nothing." Lydia's voice quivered with indignation, and anger swelled in Micah's chest toward the unfeeling man. How could anyone see his own child as merchandise to be placed on an auction block?

"For nearly two years, he periodically went to the midwife's home, badgering her for information. With Father's help, she finally moved to escape his constant visits. And it worked. For a while. It's been almost a full year, but recently he found her again. She said he acted wild and desperate. She was afraid—for herself and for us. He wants Nicky."

Micah stared at her. "Surely he can't still be hoping to sell Nicky?"

"Why not? Nicky is young. Someone would surely take him." Lydia's voice rose passionately. "Nic moves in circles we would rather didn't exist. If he didn't sell Nicky to a family, he'd find some other way to make money from him. If he didn't have a plan for selling him, he wouldn't be trying to find him. We know he doesn't want to be Nicky's father. If he legitimately loved him and would care for him, I'd probably give Nicky up.

It would be hard, but I would do it because I believe as Nicky grows older he's going to need a father. I won't be enough." She uttered the last sentence in a harsh whisper. "But I can't let Nic take him only to sell him to strangers, or—or—whatever he has planned. I can't, Micah!"

Without conscious thought, Micah pulled Lydia against his shoulder and rubbed her back. Her muscles quivered beneath his palms and he sensed she battled tears. But she didn't allow herself the privilege of completely breaking down. After a few moments, she pulled away, offering a weak smile.

Embarrassment welled. Why had he embraced her? He didn't need to give her ideas. Years ago, Lydia had harbored affection for him, he knew. It wouldn't do to encourage those old feelings to blossom. Yet, oddly enough, knowing how unselfishly she had turned her world around for her friend's baby had ignited something within his own heart. But he had no time for such thoughts. His patients and Jeremiah needed him.

Micah squared his shoulders and assumed a businesslike tone. "How many people know Nicky is really Eleanor's baby?"

"Four." Then she grimaced. "Well, five. My parents, the midwife, of course I know—and now you."

"You're sure the midwife hasn't told anyone?"

"Father pays her well to keep silent. She depends on the income. She won't tell."

"Eleanor's parents don't know?"

Lydia shook her head. "Shortly after Eleanor's death, they were in an accident. Her father was drunk and ran off the road. Both he and Eleanor's mother were killed."

So much tragedy. "And no one has ever questioned how you came to have this child?"

Lydia turned her gaze to the lights of the city glittering below. "Father said to let people believe Nicky is my child. Father is well respected, and since I had been away, the story was plausible. I'm sure there are those who disapprove, believing I had him out of wedlock, and they no doubt whisper about me behind my back, but Father's standing in the community keeps them from being openly judgmental."

"In other words, you're living a lie."

"Only to protect Nicky."

Micah didn't respond. A lie was a lie, and someday—maybe quite soon—this one was going to trip her up. "What does it say on Nicky's birth certificate?"

"He doesn't have one."

Micah shook his head, certain he hadn't heard correctly. "Doesn't have one?"

"There hasn't been a need for one. Father thought—" She paused for a moment, as if trying to decide whether or not to trust Micah with the rest. Finally she sighed, threw her hands outward, and said, "Father thought eventually I would marry, and when I did, we'd get a birth certificate made with my husband's name listed as the father. There!"

Micah blew out a breath. "Your father is really full of plans, isn't he?" He couldn't hide his sarcasm.

"I'm sure Father hoped, from what I wrote in my diaries, that the feelings I had for you were reciprocated and perhaps some affection still remained. I'm sure he also hoped once you met Nicky, you'd be taken with him. Nicky is rather hard to resist."

Micah couldn't refute that—Nicky was a very likable little boy. But he wouldn't validate what Allan Eldredge had done. "It was wrong of him to bring me here, Lydia. It was deceptive, and it only served to create another problem."

Tears trembled on Lydia's eyelashes. "Micah, what you have to understand is we've lived in fear for the past three years that somehow Nicky would be taken from us. Father should not have dragged you into this, but his having done so only proves to me how frightened and desperate he is. He loves Nicky as his grandson. He can't bear to think of losing him. Neither can I." Her voice broke.

Instinctively Micah reached for Lydia's hand. He linked fingers with her, offering comfort. "I understand your fear and worry. But, Lydia, you can't continue to mislead everyone." Micah shifted slightly on the seat, his knee bumping against hers. "If nothing else, Nicky deserves to know the truth. Do you ever plan to tell him about Eleanor and the sacrifice she made to bring him into the world? And you're going to need help from legal authorities if you're going to protect Nicky from his father. You've got to go to the police if this man is making threats."

"I can't!" Lydia yanked her hand free. "Don't you understand? The courts will take Nicky from me if we admit I'm not his mother. I won't risk losing him."

"But all of this will eventually unravel, and you could end up losing him because of your deception."

Lydia ran both hands through her hair, then held the strands, her elbows splayed outward. "No one can find out Nicky isn't really mine. The only solution is for me to provide a father for Nicky. If I have a legal document—a birth certificate—stating I am Nicky's mother and another man is Nicky's father, then Nic will have no claim to him." She dropped her arms, clasping her hands together once more. "So I have to do this, Micah. If I don't, Father will never forgive me." She brought her hands beneath her chin in a prayerful position. "Micah, will you marry me?"

4

"Have you completely lost your mind?"

Lydia cringed at Micah's incredulous outburst. She'd expected it, but she had to ask the question, nonetheless. She would never forgive herself—and her father would never let her forget it—if she didn't at least ask. She sighed, her chin low. "Yes, I suppose the fear of losing my son has finally driven me over the edge."

Her quiet admission seemed to remove Micah's indignation. He slumped into the seat, leaning his head back. A long sigh heaved from his chest. "Lydia, I apologize. That was uncalled for. You just took me by surprise there."

The word "surprise" held his Texas twang, and Lydia smiled, remembering Nicky's imitation of Micah's accent.

"Well, I suppose then we've both gotten a surprise today. You just now, and me when you showed up." She touched his arm, and he rolled his head sideways, meeting her gaze. "I am truly sorry my father pulled you into this."

"Aw, it's okay, Lydia. I understand why he did it. Just wish I could really help you."

Warmth flooded Lydia's frame at his kind acceptance and forgiving attitude. She removed her hand, finally relaxing a bit.

"You are a nice man, Micah. I remember that about you. You were always a nice man."

Micah chuckled lightly. "Is that why you proposed?"

Lydia laughed, finding sweet release in letting her amusement escape. The teasing also reminded her of the Micah from Schofield. She looked outside, noticing for the first time that night had completely fallen. She'd been so caught up in her tale, she hadn't paid attention to the lateness of the hour. As if on cue, Micah yawned.

Lydia grimaced. "I'm sorry—I know you're tired from your trip. May I offer you our guest room?"

"I got a room at the Parker House. My travel things are there. But thank you for the invitation."

Lydia started the engine and pushed the button to turn on the headlights. "I'll take you to the hotel."

"Just head back to your house. I can get a cab."

"No, it's the least I can do." She pressed the clutch and shifted into gear, expertly guiding the Hudson down the road. "You know, we could pick up your things at the hotel and cancel your room—get your money back."

Micah yawned again, shielding his gaping mouth with his palm. "Naw. Actually, I kinda like the idea of sleepin' in a place with some history. The bellman told me John Wilkes Booth stayed there."

Lydia shook her head, smiling. Micah was something else. But then her thoughts turned serious. Micah had paid for a train ticket at her father's prompting—no, at her father's threat. They should cover Micah's hotel bill. She'd address the situation with Father when she got home. She glanced at Micah. A grin crept up her cheek when she saw he slept with his face turned sideways against the seat and his mouth open.

What a nice man. What an incredibly nice man . . .

When Lydia arrived home, she let herself in quietly through the back entrance—the servants' entrance, her father called it, although the only servant was a cleaning lady who came once a week to tidy up and do laundry.

The light above the kitchen sink burned, and she pushed the off button, blanketing the room in darkness. She stood in the gray shadows, her mind playing over the suggestion Micah had made before he'd gotten out of the Hudson to enter the hotel. Shame washed over her. Why hadn't she thought of it herself?

She moved to the stairway in the dark, navigating the familiar surroundings easily even without light. Upstairs, she cracked open Nicky's door and peered in, smiling fondly when she spotted his sweet face illuminated by the gentle glow of his nightlight. He lay on his back under a rumple of blankets, his battered teddy bear tucked under his arm. She tiptoed in, then leaned down to kiss his cheek and smooth the dark curls from his forehead. He stirred slightly, and she murmured, "Shhhh." Instantly he quieted, pulling the bear closer, his eyelids quivering. After giving him one more kiss, she sneaked out, quietly closing the door behind her.

Across the hall, the double doors leading to her parents' suite were closed, but a thin band of light shone from the crack along the floor. She crossed to the doors and knocked lightly. Mother's voice called, "Come in."

Lydia turned the crystal knob and entered. Both of her parents were awake, the bedside lamps on, books in their hands. Mother turned her book upside down in her lap and worried her lower lip with her teeth. Lydia crossed to the foot of the canopied bed and seated herself near her mother's feet.

"We waited for you," Father said gruffly. "Will he do it?"

Lydia crossed her arms and raised one eyebrow sardonically. "You mean, will he marry me?"

"That's what I mean."

"Of course not. Did you really expect him to?"

Father slapped his book closed and plopped it on the marble-topped table next to his side of the bed. "So I brought him here for nothing." His tone held disgust. "Couldn't you have convinced him? Do you know how hard it was for me to track him down? It's taken weeks. Now it's all lost time."

Lydia placed her hand on her father's foot. "Father, you can't honestly believe Micah would be willing to marry a woman he doesn't love and assume responsibility for a child who isn't his, just because you want him to."

Father jerked his foot, his nightcap slipping sideways. "He could do worse. He's a fool not to want Nicky—the boy is already crazy about him. And you love him. What more could he want?"

Heat climbed her cheeks, and she fought the temptation to turn her face away. Instead she raised her chin in a silent challenge. "What makes you think I love Micah?"

Father's neck became mottled with color as Mother sent him a disapproving look. "I have my reasons."

"Father, you read my diaries, didn't you?" Lydia was careful to keep resentment from her tone. She knew a reasonable front was the best offense with her father.

Father cleared his throat, his thick brows coming together in a fierce scowl. But a hint of embarrassment glittered in his eyes. "How else was I to find a likely prospect? You don't talk to your mother or me. And it was the best solution to keep that . . . that insane Pankin away from Nicky."

Lydia sighed. "Father, I understand why you did it. Truly, I do. And Micah does, too. But bringing him here . . ." She shook her head. "We're lucky he's a forgiving man. I think we need to pay for his room at the Parker House and also his train ticket home. He was brought here under false pretenses. You made an unfair accusation, knowing full well it was fabricated."

Father went on as if she hadn't spoken. "What if you were to quietly marry—not a real marriage, but a marriage in paper only. Long enough to file for Nicky's birth certificate. Then, when the document is in hand, you could quietly divorce. Do you suppose he would be willing to do that much, at least?"

"Oh, Father." Lydia hung her head. "There's been enough deceit surrounding Nicky. Let's not make it worse."

Father huffed and thumped the bedcovers. "Well, young woman, do you have a better way of handling this problem?"

Lydia recalled Micah's parting words. Strength filled her frame. She raised her head and met her father's gaze. "Yes, Father. I think we need to pray."

"Pray?" The word came out like a rifle shot. "What can that possibly do?"

Lydia leaned back, resting her weight on one hand. "Father, when I got the letter from Eleanor, begging for my help, I felt absolutely powerless to help her. I was filled with guilt for having introduced her to Nic, and I was angry that I couldn't repair the damage. I was lucky to have found friends who believed in prayer, who prayed for me even when they didn't know what my problem was. I felt those prayers, and when I acknowledged Jesus as my Savior, I became a child of God." Lydia watched her parents' faces closely. Mother seemed receptive, as she had been in previous times of discussing spiritual matters, but Father remained dour and doubtful.

Lydia continued. "All the way back from Oahu, every day on the ship, I prayed for a way to help Eleanor. I prayed for Eleanor's baby—for its health and safety—and for it to have a happy home. Of course, I envisioned the happy home with Eleanor and Nic, but my prayer was answered in a different way. Nicky *was* safe—with the midwife. He *was* born healthy, even though he came too soon and his mother didn't live. And he *has* had a happy home—with us. All of my prayers were answered. And look at how we've been blessed by having him here." Lydia pressed her hand once more against her father's foot, stressing her point. "Father, I know God heard my prayers. And if we talk to Him now, He'll listen and He'll help us."

"I've always taken care of things myself," Father insisted.

"Yes, you have. And I love you for it. But things are falling apart. I can hardly believe we've resorted to accusing the wrong man of fathering a baby and that I had the audacity to suggest marriage to him."

Her parents exchanged glances, and Lydia was gratified to see contrition pinch her father's face. She continued gravely. "Micah said something tonight that has bothered me for a long time. He asked me if I never planned to tell Nicky about his real mother. Eleanor made such a sacrifice for Nicky—he deserves to know what she did. But if I tell him about his mother, I'll have to tell him about his father. And I don't think I can look into his innocent face and lie to him." Tears gathered in her eyes, distorting her vision. "I don't want to lie anymore."

Father, always uncomfortable in the face of emotion, harrumphed. "We should continue this discussion tomorrow, when you aren't tired."

"I'm not tired, Father, I'm upset. And guilty. And confused." Lydia squeezed her father's foot. "You said I never talk to you, but when I try to talk to you about what's important, you turn me away. We need to talk about this now."

"Later, Lydia." Father reached over and turned the key to extinguish his lamp. "Tomorrow morning I'll make arrangements for the cost of Hatcher's hotel room and I'll contact the train station about billing me for his ticket. Good night." He rolled over, pulling the cover up to his chin and effectively shutting himself away.

Lydia turned to her mother. Although Mother's face creased with sympathy, she remained silent. Mother would never cross her husband. Lydia stood, her shoulders slumped in defeat, and left the room. In her own bedroom—her place of solitude for as long as she could remember, she moved to the window seat looking out over the backyard. She sank onto the pile of pillows and lifted the shade to peer skyward. The lights of the city made it difficult to see stars, but Lydia knew they were there, even if she couldn't see them. She knew God was there, too, even though He held no physical presence.

"God, Micah believes You have the answer to this problem," she whispered, her voice husky with unshed tears. "I'm afraid. I'm afraid of losing Nicky. I love him so much, God. You have a Son, too, so I know you understand my love for Nicky. I still believe keeping him with me is the best thing for him. You protected him and kept him safe before he was born, and I'm trusting You to keep him safe now. Keep him safe from Nic Pankin. Help us find a way to let Nicky stay with us without this threat hanging over our heads. Please, God."

Her voice drifted off, but her heart continued begging, crying for comfort and strength. In time she calmed, comforted by her Lord's presence, and she dressed in her nightclothes. But before turning down the covers and slipping between the sheets, she knelt beside her bed and offered one more brief prayer. "God, thank you for Micah's concern and support. He truly is a nice man."

Nic Pankin paced the foul-smelling alleyway. His soles echoed on the damp concrete, the sound reverberating from four-story-high brick walls. The *drip-drip* from a leaky waterspout several yards ahead pierced his ears. His flesh prickled beneath his dirt-encrusted clothes, and he clawed at his chest with his remaining hand. No amount of scratching ever erased the endless itch and tingle of need, and when it ceased to bring relief, he spun and kicked a trash bin. He groaned at the clatter of tin colliding with the solid brick wall.

From behind one of the windows, a woman screeched, "Be quiet out there!"

Nic shouted a curse in reply. Pain shot through his gut. He wrapped his arm across his ribs, panic sending his pulse into galloping beats. He wouldn't last much longer before the writhing began. Where was that wretched Murphy and his magic dust?

A familiar *scuff-clop, scuff-clop*—the footsteps of someone who dragged his heels—intruded. Nic sucked in a breath and whirled toward the sound. Murphy's bulky form materialized from the deep shadows at the other end of the alley.

Nic bolted forward and grabbed the man by his coat lapel. "Where've you been? You said eleven o'clock, an' it's past midnight."

Murphy jerked loose from Nic's hold. In the darkness, his scowl looked menacing. "You ain't my only customer, Pankin. An' truth be known, the others come before you 'cause they always have cash in hand."

Nic jammed his hand into his jacket pocket and withdrew several crumpled bills. "I got cash, too. So gimme my stuff."

Murphy snatched the bills from Nic's trembling grasp and held them to the weak glow of the corner streetlamp. He counted aloud, his scowl increasing with each number's announcement. "Six dollars?" He crushed them in his fist, then thrust the wadded bills at Nic. "You gotta be kiddin' me. I can't give you nothin' for six measly dollars."

Nic pushed the money back at Murphy. "It's all I got right now. You don't hafta gimme a full packet—just a pinch. C'mon . . ." The desperation in his tone shamed him, but need overcame pride.

Murphy huffed but then flapped his jacket open and pulled out a folded square of paper from an inside pouch. "I must be nutty as a loon to keep meetin' you, Pankin. But I deserve somethin' for bein' out here instead o' in my warm bed. Gimme the money."

Nic slapped the bills into Murphy's big paw and watched as he pocketed them. He sucked in shallow breaths as Murphy shook the little packet, distributing the tiny particles of white powder into opposite corners. Finally, while Nic nearly wriggled out of his skin in agony, he tore the packet in two and handed half to Nic.

Nic wrapped his fist around the precious packet and turned away, eagerness making him clumsy.

Murphy grabbed Nic's empty dangling coat sleeve and pulled. Nic stumbled in a circle. Murphy pointed at him. "This's my last time meetin' you. Ain't worth my time when you only spend a pittance. You understand me, Pankin?"

Fury roared through Nic's chest. He gritted his teeth. "You ain't the only dealer, Murphy. I can take my business to—"

"Nobody's gonna want your piddly business." Murphy spat on the filthy pavement, then swiped the back of his hand across his lips. "Word's out on you. Next time you put out a call for the goods, you better be prepared to buy more'n a pinch or won't any of us bother with you again." He spun and strode away, the *scuff-clop* of his heels echoing through the alley with the finality of nails being hammered into a coffin lid.

Nic pressed his fist to his chest. Sweat broke out across his back, making the prickle increase in intensity. What would he do if all the dealers in town cut off his supply? He'd die. He *had* to have his magic dust. Heart pounding, he made a silent vow. Whatever it took, he'd get the midwife who'd taken care of Eleanor to tell him what she'd done with their whelp. The fancy man and woman in Weston with only a pony-sized poodle instead of kids—they'd pay. Pay big. And once he had their money in hand, he could satisfy the sellers, as well as his own deep need.

Holding the little packet securely in his fist, he turned eagerly toward home.

5

Micah lay in the unfamiliar bed, his hands folded beneath his head, staring at the plaster ceiling. He was incredibly tired, but sleep eluded him. He couldn't stop thinking about Nicky and the story Lydia had shared. What a mess! A morphine-addicted father seeking to sell his child, a family claiming a child to whom they had no legal right, a little boy growing up in an entanglement of falsehoods and half-truths. But Micah well knew the world was not a perfect place, and far too often innocent children suffered. He might not be able to keep all the world's children from pain and anguish, but he desperately wanted to help this small, tousle-haired boy who worried about bugs being happy.

He wanted to help Lydia, too.

Strange how quickly they had lapsed into comfortable conversation. At Schofield, when they'd seen each other on a nearly daily basis, their conversations hadn't been as open as the one they'd shared this evening after a three-year separation. He'd always been on edge, fearful of giving the wrong impression, since he knew she held a fondness for him that he hadn't reciprocated. But tonight that hadn't been a concern.

Her face, pinched with worry, appeared in his memory, and a rush of protectiveness rolled through him. Lydia had always been beautiful. He reflected on her shiny black hair that fell in silky layers around her heart-shaped face; her velvety brown eyes surrounded by thick, curling lashes; her full lips, which today wore a pale coral rather than the bright lipstick she'd preferred when at Schofield. Her physical beauty would capture anyone's attention, and he was amazed men weren't lining up to offer marriage proposals.

Although it had seemed finding a husband was her main focus three years ago, her focus was now on Nicky, rather than on herself. Which only served to increase her beauty in Micah's eyes. When he'd brought the idea of prayer into their conversation, he'd expected her to rebuff him, but instead she'd welcomed the idea. She'd even appeared shame-faced for not having mentioned it herself. Her response spoke of another change in Lydia's heart and gave Micah hope this whole situation could be ironed out in time. He felt honored that Lydia trusted him enough to open up to him—much the same way he had felt honored by Nicky's immediate trust.

A smile tugged at his lips as he remembered his walk with the boy. Nicky had held tight to his hand, pointing out flowers and telling him who lived in which houses, jabbering incessantly the entire trek through the neighborhood. When they'd returned to the house, Nicky had thrown his arms around Micah in an exuberant hug, proclaiming with a full-fledged Texas accent, "I lahke you, pardner!" It was the best compliment Micah had ever received.

If Micah stuck around for any length of time, he suspected he'd grow attached to Nicky, but Micah didn't have time for attachments. He needed to get back to Queens as soon as possible. But before he went, he wanted to offer assistance. How could he ignore the fact that a ruthless, desperate man might hurt the innocent little boy? The world Lydia had built for Nicky was about to collapse. He'd told Lydia to look to God for guidance—to pray, and to listen. So Micah prayed fervently, his eyes closed tight, his hands clasped against his chest. Then he listened, waiting. And in time, an answer came.

"Thank You, God. Thank You," Micah breathed, his soul rejoicing. And finally, blessed sleep followed.

Lydia turned from the icebox, milk pitcher in hand to fill a glass for Nicky, when the door chime sounded. Since her parents and son were seated at the breakfast table, she said, "I'll get it." She plunked the pitcher on the table next to her mother and made her way through the corridor to the front door. Swinging the door open, she found Micah Hatcher, dressed casually in a blue plaid shirt and twill dungarees, standing on the tiny porch. Her pulse leaped into double-beats at the sight of his handsome face, and she froze, stupidly staring for a few silent moments, willing her pulse to settle into a normal rhythm.

"May I come in?" Micah asked, just as he'd done yesterday.

Lydia's face flooded with heat at her breach of etiquette. "I'm so sorry." She gestured for him to enter. "I didn't expect to see you so early. We're breakfasting. Would you care to join us?"

Micah smiled, the familiar Micah-smile she remembered, with the left side of his lips tugged slightly higher than the right. "A cup of coffee would be good, if you have it."

"I'm sorry. No coffee, but we have Postum."

Micah lifted his shoulders in a shrug, his grin intact. "That'll do."

Lydia smirked. "With extra cream?"

Micah laughed, his white teeth flashing. "Now how could you possibly remember I like a little coffee with my cream?"

Lydia remembered quite a lot about Micah Hatcher, but she kept most of it to herself as she led him toward the kitchen at the back of the house. The moment they entered the room, Nicky's face lit.

"Micah-my-friend!" The little boy raised his arms for a hug.

Micah took the two steps needed to reach Nicky and wrapped his arms around the child, seemingly unconcerned by the sticky fingers and jelly-smeared face. Then he straightened and turned his attention to Lydia's parents with his hand resting on Nicky's head. "Good morning, Mr. and Mrs. Eldredge. I apologize for intruding on your breakfast." While he spoke, Lydia crossed to the stove and poured Micah a cup of the grain substitute for coffee they'd learned to drink in place of the real beverage.

Father put down his fork and gave Micah his full attention. "You aren't intruding. Please have a seat."

Micah took the only open chair, which happened to be Lydia's. She placed the coffee cup in front of him, pulled the cream pitcher close to his elbow, then leaned against the counter as he took up the cream and poured a healthy serving into his cup.

Mother offered, "Dr. Hatcher, would you care for some toast and eggs? I can make a fresh batch for you."

Micah shook his head. "No, thank you, ma'am. I had a sweet roll at the hotel this morning. Some Postum'll do." He took a sip, smiled, and nodded. "Mmm . . . perfect."

Nicky waved a piece of toast in the air, ignoring the clump of jelly that fell onto the table. "Are we going for another walk, Micah-my-friend?"

"Not today, I'm afraid, partner." Micah guided Nicky's toast-holding hand over his plate. "This morning I need to talk to your mama and grandparents. An' then I'm going to head for home."

Two plump tears appeared in Nicky's eyes. He rubbed a fist

across his eyes, smearing jelly from one port to another. "Why do you have to go?"

Micah leaned on an elbow, bringing his face close to Nicky's. "Know how we talked yesterday about Buggy bein' happy to get home to his mama?" The little boy nodded. "Well, I reckon Buggy's mama was pretty happy to have him home 'cause she depends on Buggy. I have people at my home who depend on me. So I need to go back."

"Oh." Nicky looked at Micah, his expression somber, the tears still quivering on his lashes. "What's 'depend'?"

Lydia was accustomed to such questions, but Micah reared back slightly as if startled. He rubbed a finger under his nose, then pooched out his lips in thought. Nicky waited patiently, his eyes never leaving Micah's face. After several seconds had ticked by, with Micah crunching his face in silence, Lydia came to his rescue.

"'Depend' means people are trusting Micah to come back and help them. Micah is a doctor, Nicky, so lots of people come to him to get help when they feel sick or hurt."

"That's right," Micah chimed in, sending Lydia a brief, grateful look. "We didn't want Buggy to be sad, did we? And I can't let my patients be sad, either, so I have to go home."

Nicky considered this, his elfin face puckered. Finally he sighed. "I reckon you better go, then." He placed a sticky hand on Micah's forearm. "But it makes me sad for you to go away. I lahke you, Micah."

"I like you, too, Nicky."

At Micah's sincere words, Father and Mother exchanged a meaningful glance, and Lydia's heart rose to lodge in her throat. To cover her unsettled feelings, Lydia stepped forward and touched Nicky's back. "Nicky, hop down, and let's get you cleaned up. Then you may go to your room and play for a bit. Mama needs to talk to Micah."

Mother rose. "I'll take him."

Lydia appreciated her mother's offer—Nicky would probably be up and down the stairs, interrupting their talk, without someone to entertain him. The pair left the kitchen hand-in-hand. Lydia quickly cleaned the area where Nicky had been sitting, then joined her father and Micah at the round table.

Micah drained his coffee cup, plunked it down with a smile of thanks, and linked his fingers on the edge of the table. "Mr. Eldredge, Lydia, I did some thinking and praying last night. I think I might have found a way to solve your problem."

Father leaned forward, his brows coming together in a serious expression. Lydia's ear perked up, as well, ready to hear Micah's idea.

Micah turned a pensive look in Lydia's direction. "You said Nicky's father—this Nicolai Pankin—wants Nicky because he wants the money he can gain. The man isn't interested in parenting Nicky, so his custody will be short-lived, no matter what. He'll be handing Nicky off to someone. So why not arrange to have him handed off to you?"

Father frowned. "I'm not sure I follow."

Micah worked his thumbs back and forth, his forehead wrinkling. "What if you two, with the midwife, visited an attorney. The midwife can verify Nicky has been in your care since his birth at his mother's request. The attorney could draw up adoption papers for Nicky." Micah grimaced, flicking an apologetic glance at Lydia before facing her father. "It's likely they would prefer for you and your wife to be recorded as the adoptive parents—"

Lydia's heart jumped. "But I'm Nicky's mother!"

Micah touched her arm in understanding. "I know, but you're also unmarried. If you want the court to work in your favor, you will probably need to bend on this issue. It would only be on paper—it wouldn't change your relationship with Nicky. He could continue calling you the familiar names."

Lydia opened her mouth to argue, but Father's stern expression silenced her protests. When she dropped her chin, Father nodded at Micah.

"Continue with what you were saying, Dr. Hatcher."

"Your next step would be to locate Pankin and find out what his other connection has offered in the way of purchasing"—he made a sour face as he spoke the reprehensible word—"Nicky. Let him convince you to pay him instead, but insist he sign papers relinquishing Nicky to your custody before you actually give him the payment."

Lydia stared at Micah in shock. "You want *us* to buy him?"

"Truthfully, Lydia, in the eyes of the law, what you've done up to this point is kidnap him." The words were harsh, but Micah's gentle tone softened the reprimand.

"But to give that man money . . ."

Micah held up his hand. "Let me finish, please? Your attorney will be notified of your intentions and the reason you're doing it. Once Pankin has taken the money from you, you can go to the authorities and alert them to what has transpired. They can pursue the legalities of the whole situation. If you have forewarned a legal authority of your intentions, as well as Nic's reason for wanting his son, I'm certain they will work in your favor. Plus you will have a legally binding document saying that Nicky is yours. You won't have to fear Pankin anymore."

Lydia silently digested Micah's words. Father stood, poured himself another cup of Postum, then returned to his seat and bracketed the cup between his palms without drinking. Releasing a heavy sigh, he said, "Don't think I haven't considered offering that lunatic money. What's kept me from doing it is the fear that he'll just come back for more, like a leech, until he's drained me dry."

Micah nodded. "If you do it on your own, it's very likely Pankin will see you as an unlimited source of income to feed his habit. That's why you can't do it on your own. You've got to involve the proper authorities."

"Do you really think Nic would be arrested and Nicky would be free of him?" Lydia hardly dared to hope that Micah could be right.

Micah shrugged. "Obviously, I can't guarantee anything. I don't know the laws of the state of Massachusetts. But it only seems logical that if you go to an attorney, armed first of all with the midwife's verification that Eleanor wanted you to have Nicky and secondly with the proof Nicky's father only intends to use his son—a child who has been in your care his entire life—in a money-making scheme, I can't imagine the law turning its back on you."

Lydia shifted to Father, who sat with a frown of concentration on his face. "What do you think? Should we try Micah's idea and contact an attorney?"

Father leaned back in his chair, examining Micah, his brows lowered and his chin thrust forward. "I suppose we could approach an attorney—I know one who would be discreet. We'll need to ascertain Mrs. Fenwick has all of her facts straight before we make an official visit."

At Micah's puzzled look, Lydia explained, "Mrs. Fenwick is the midwife who cared for Eleanor and kept Nicky for me until I arrived."

Micah nodded. "Yes. Hopefully she will have a written record of the babies she delivers to prove the date of Nicky's birth. A note written by Eleanor giving you custody would be best, but even the midwife's testimony as to what was said before Eleanor died will be important."

The pitter-patter of little feet carried from the corridor, and all eyes turned toward the intrusion. Nicky pounded into the kitchen, his stocking feet slapping the floor and his hair bouncing across his forehead. Mother followed closely, her face twisted into a disapproving moue contrasting with Nicky's beaming smile.

"Micah-my-friend is still here!" Nicky threw himself into Micah's arms. Micah scooped him up and settled the little boy in his lap. Nicky leaned against Micah's chest, crossed his arms, and beamed triumphantly at his grandmother. Lydia suspected a battle of wills had taken place upstairs, and Mother had lost. But looking at Nicky snuggled in Micah's lap, she couldn't find the means to scold him. Strange how quickly Nicky had taken to Micah. Nicky was a very personable little boy and he liked most people, but he had seemed to form an immediate attachment to Micah—much more quickly than he'd ever attached himself to anyone before.

It pleased Lydia yet saddened her at the same time. Nicky's affection for Micah solidified the knowledge that Nicky needed a father, but what man would willingly marry a woman who had given birth to an out-of-wedlock child? Carrying the stigma—a stigma she and her father had intentionally perpetrated—would make it nearly impossible for her to provide what Nicky needed.

Despite her gloomy thoughts, a smile tugged at her lips as she watched Nicky engage Micah in a finger game. *God, have our deceptions created a situation that will someday hurt Nicky more than it helps him?* She recalled Micah saying that the courts would be more willing to name her parents as Nicky's adoptive parents, and as much as it pained her, perhaps she should consider allowing them to assume the roles of mother and father. At least then Nicky would have a father in his life.

"Mama?"

Lydia gave a start. Nicky and Micah were looking at her

strangely. She released a light, self-conscious laugh. "I'm sorry, sweetie, Mama was daydreaming. What did you say?"

"I *said*," Nicky repeated slowly, "Micah-my-friend has time for one more walk before he has to go be a depend. Do you want to come, too?"

Lydia looked at Micah. His blue eyes, expectant, pulled at her heart. She knew it wasn't a good idea to spend time with Micah—it brought back memories of a time when she wanted him to be much more than a friend. But he'd be leaving soon, and there would be no more opportunities. She should grasp this brief happiness while she could. She offered a warm smile, answering Nicky but addressing Micah, "Yes, I would like to come."

Micah stood, scooping Nicky from his lap and swinging the giggling boy to his shoulders. "Up and down the street we'll go, partner, and then Micah-your-friend must catch a train."

Nicky grabbed two handfuls of Micah's hair as Micah headed for the door. The boy called out, "C'mon, Mama!"

Lydia fell into step with Micah, and they ambled along the sidewalk under the morning sun. From his perch, Nicky waved and called greetings to neighbors. So this, then, was how it felt to be a family. For one brief moment, she believed her heart smiled. And then a tightness built in her chest. She should memorize the moment, because it could very well be the only time this pleasure would be hers.

6

Micah leaned back into his seat, still shaking his head. *That Allan Eldredge does enjoy managin' things for people. . . .* What a surprise to check out from the hotel and be told the bill was already paid in full. Then to receive his train ticket with the message that Mr. Eldredge would be billed for the expense. Of course, Micah wasn't unappreciative of this interference—to be truthful, this little side trip was a stretch for his budget. He sent every spare nickel he earned to Jeremiah in the shape of food staples and articles of clothing.

The train chugged into motion, creating an uncomfortable rolling in his stomach. As always, thoughts of Jeremiah brought an instant prayer to his heart: *Lord, watch out for that brother of mine.* After contracting polio as a young boy, Jeremiah depended on braces and crutches to walk, and his heart was weaker than most, but he didn't allow any of it to slow him down. Jeremiah had more determination than the other four Hatcher boys put together. Which is precisely why he had willingly placed himself in the path of danger in Russia and Poland.

Micah released a sigh. Oh, he was proud of this brother. Jeremiah was making a difference in the lives of war's most vulnerable victims—the children. But pride didn't keep the worry at bay. Micah closed his eyes, his heart groaning another silent prayer. *Lord, why must the innocent suffer?* He continued to ask the question, even though he knew there was no real answer for it. Man's sinful nature would always create sorrow.

He had witnessed man's sinfulness too vividly when the Japanese dropped their bombs on Pearl Harbor. Micah and the other medical personnel had worked around the clock on those victims. His heart still carried a burden for the men and women who had died. But God had opened his heart to a ministry in the midst of the attack. Micah's lips twitched as he recalled the biblical admonition that "all things work together for good to them that love God"—there was a rainbow after the storm, his mother always said, if one would only look for it. Still, the sorrow of the storm itself was hard to accept.

He shifted slightly in his seat, folding his arms across his queasy stomach—how he wished the train wouldn't rock so—as he remembered Nicky's sorrowful face when he'd hugged the little boy good-bye. Funny how that tousled-haired imp with the drooping socks had worked his way into Micah's heart. This morning, walking with the boy's weight on his shoulders and those small hands on his hair, he'd felt . . . fatherly.

His thoughts flitted to Lydia, who hadn't appeared any happier than Nicky at his parting. He'd enjoyed having her walk beside him in her graceful, feminine way, smiling up at Nicky on his perch and then letting her smile drift to Micah. He bit the inside of his cheek, recalling how *she* made him feel. It sure wasn't fatherly.

He squelched the thought immediately. Micah had committed himself to serving the immigrant population of New York and to helping with Jeremiah's cause. There wasn't time for anything more than those two commitments. Besides, Lydia lived in one state while he lived in another. A relationship was out of the question.

Micah remembered berating Lydia for her deception where Nicky's parentage was concerned, and guilt twined through his middle. Though he had never been forced into telling deliberate lies, he had intentionally kept secret his involvement in Jeremiah's work. Secrecy was necessary—the more people who knew, the more likely Jeremiah's life would be in danger. The posters hanging in most public buildings—"Loose lips can sink ships"—weren't displayed as a tool for amusement. Information overheard by the wrong ears spelled trouble. He supposed, in a way, he was also living a deception.

Lord, I reckon there's a fine line between the truth and the whole truth. Help me find a way to do Your service without breaking any of Your commandments. Help Lydia find a way to be open and honest in her relationship with Nicky, and keep a watch over both of them as they try to put to rest this threat from Nicky's dad. Please don't let anyone ever ask a question that might tempt me to lie. I want to be honest in all of my dealings. But I am pretty worried about my brother. . .

Lydia stood aside as Father knocked on the apartment door. No one answered. She waited until he'd knocked again. Then she braved a question. "Are you sure this is the right address?"

He blew out his breath and shot her an impatient look. "I have been sending monthly payments to this woman for almost four years. I chose this apartment for her myself. Yes, I'm certain it is the correct address."

Lydia experienced a twinge of resentment at her father's brusque tone. "Well, apparently she isn't home. We may need to come back another time."

"We don't have the luxury of coming back another time. If we're to convince a lawyer our claims are not manufactured, we need her testimony." Father raised his fist and pounded on the wood door once more, the solid booms echoing through the hallway.

"Father, perhaps we should—" Lydia began, but an irritated voice interrupted.

"Hey, why don'tcha stop that racket? Those of us who work nights need our sleep."

A woman, her hair hidden by a knotted kerchief, peered out from a doorway down the hall. Father strode briskly toward her, and at his commanding presence she withdrew slightly, clutching her ratty robe closed at the throat.

"Madam, we are seeking Mrs. Fenwick. Do you know where we might find her?"

The woman shrugged. "Had ya asked a week ago I'da said right there." She pointed to the apartment. "'Cause she didn't go no place much, just waited for ladies who needed her services to come to her. But she took off a couple o' days ago—had a suitcase in hand. Ain't seen her since."

"Suitcase?" Lydia's heart raced with alarm. "Did she say when she'd be back?"

Again, the woman gave a shrug, the worn fabric of her robe pulling across her chest with the movement. "I don't figure she'll *be* back. That feller finally run her off for good."

Father scowled. "What fellow?"

The woman lowered her voice to whisper. "Don't know that I should say—don't want him comin' after *me*."

"Madam, I can assure you no one will come after you." To Lydia's relief, Father also tempered the volume of his thunderous tone. "Please explain your meaning."

After giving a furtive glance up and down the hallway, the

woman spoke, her voice so soft both Lydia and Father leaned forward to hear. "Some feller—big, wild-eyed man missin' one arm—came round and said he wanted his kid. Mrs. Fenwick kept tellin' him, 'I don't know nothin', leave me alone,' but he wouldn't believe her. He come by here three days in a row"—she held up three fingers to emphasize her words—"and each day he was more wild than the one before, hollerin' he was goin' to the cops and they'd make her talk." The woman nodded her head, the knot in her scarf bobbing with the movement, her eyebrows high. "She was real scared, I can tell you that."

Father asked, "How long ago was this?"

"Week. Maybe week an' a half." The woman bit her lower lip, her gaze zinging up and down the hallway as if she expected Nic Pankin to step out of the shadows. "He come back here yesterday, too, banging on the door just like you done. But I didn't tell him nothin'."

Lydia's stomach rolled. Just as Micah had feared, they were already too late. She clutched her hands together. "Do you have any idea where Mrs. Fenwick might have gone? Perhaps to the home of one of her children or another relative?"

The woman crunched her brows. "Well . . . I know her man was killed in the Great War. She an' him didn't have children. S'pose that's why she liked helpin' bring other people's babes into the world—always glowed for a day or two after the births. 'Cept if somethin' went wrong. Oh, how she'd mourn if somethin' went wrong. . . ."

Father drew in a deep breath, his warning sign for an imminent explosion. Lydia stood poised, ready to stave off her father's verbal attack if necessary, when the woman's face brightened.

"Say! She got postcards now an' then, from her sister, she said. She was right proud of those postcards—always showed me the pictures on the back."

Lydia's heart rose with hope. "Did you ever see an address? Do you know where this sister lives?"

"She never showed me the word side, an' I didn't ask," the woman said, a rather defensive edge creeping into her tone. Then she shrugged once more. "But the last one that come had a picture of the big statue France gave the U.S. of A.—the Lady of Liberty, I think it's called."

Father and Lydia exchanged a glance. Lydia's mind raced. The Statue of Liberty—might Mrs. Fenwick have gone to New York?

"Thank you for your time, madam," Father said, and the woman closed the door. His hand on Lydia's back, he steered her toward the staircase leading to the lower floors.

Halfway down the hallway, Lydia glanced at her father. "Why do you suppose Mrs. Fenwick left without any word to us?"

"My guess is she was afraid if she contacted us, somehow Pankin would find out." Father practically growled, "Imbecile! If I get my hands on that man—"

They stepped out of the dim apartment building onto the sidewalk and made their way to Father's waiting vehicle. Tears pressed behind Lydia's eyelids. So much of Micah's plan hinged on Mrs. Fenwick's validation of why they had Nicky. "How will we be able to prove Eleanor wanted me to have Nicky if Mrs. Fenwick isn't here to verify it?"

Father pulled his door shut and started the engine with a vicious twist of the key. His mouth formed a grim line. "We can't." He clasped his hands around the steering wheel so tightly the knuckles appeared white. Then he slammed his palms on the steering wheel twice and released a mild oath. He turned an accusing gaze on his daughter. "So much for your prayers."

"Father, you aren't giving up, are you?" To her own ears, her voice sounded unnaturally high.

Father's brows came down in a fierce scowl. "I'll not give up.

I'll locate Mrs. Fenwick if I have to go to New York myself. I'll not let Pankin have Nicky."

"Maybe," Lydia said pensively, "we won't have to worry about it since he can't bother Mrs. Fenwick anymore. How will he find out where Nicky is living?"

Father released a huff of irritation. "Lydia, think! Pankin is a raving lunatic, but he isn't *stupid*. He knows Eleanor and you were best friends. I'm reasonably certain he suspects Nicky is with you, but he has been too fearful to approach us. Instead, he terrorized a defenseless old woman, figuring she would ask for help from whoever had the child if he finally frightened her enough. Now that she's gone, he's left with no choice but to come after us."

Lydia's breath came in short, frightened spurts. "Do you really think so?"

"Yes, I really think so." Father pulled into the traffic.

Lydia gazed straight ahead, her pulse racing. "What I can't understand is why Nic's interest in Nicky seems to come and go. He allows months to pass between his inquiries to Mrs. Fenwick. He bothers her for days or weeks on end, then disappears for even longer periods of time. There's no pattern."

Another snort made Lydia feel foolish. "Obviously he only needs the money that can be made from his son when he's between jobs. My supposition is while he is able to hold a job, he can fund his own vile habit. But eventually the habit costs him the job—just as it cost him the job at my plant—and then in desperation he seeks his son."

"That makes sense, I suppose," Lydia mused. For long moments they rode in silence through the busy streets, the whine of rubber tires against the winding street and the occasional ring of a cable car's bell the only intrusions.

As he turned the Studebaker onto the avenue that would lead

to their home, Father spoke again, but Lydia had the impression he was thinking aloud rather than addressing her directly. "We have no legal standing now to go to the police. They won't help us. Mrs. Fenwick may or may not be in New York, among a milling throng of residents. No doubt Pankin will eventually show up on our doorstep, demanding his son. . . ."

Helplessness washed over Lydia, and she wished Micah were still here. Micah would be able to look at the situation logically rather than emotionally. He would pray with her and remind her God was in control. She closed her eyes and wove her fingers together in her lap, praying inwardly for God's comfort. Another muttered oath from her father forced her eyes open.

Lydia looked at her father's white face. The veins in his temple stood out as darkly as if drawn by the broad stroke of a pen. Under his breath, he vowed, "When he comes, I'll be ready. He'll regret the day he tries to remove Nicky from under my roof."

Fear roiled in Lydia's stomach, and she broke out in a cold sweat. *Heavenly Father, what does Father mean?* She didn't ask the same question of her earthly father. She was afraid of the answer.

7

Nic paused on the brick portico fronting the enormous Georgian Classic home situated on six rolling acres of landscaped lawn. The fancy words—*portico, Georgian Classic*—rolled through the back of his mind and created a sour taste on his tongue. The home's mistress had thrown the words around on Nic's last visit as if her personal worth increased by residing in such a stately house. He'd had to work hard to keep derision from his expression and tone when speaking with her.

He raised his hand to make use of the brass lion's-head door-knocker and caught a glimpse of himself in the door's full-length leaded-glass window. Even in his best clothes—tan trousers, cambric shirt, and duck jacket—he looked out of place here. But he had something these people wanted. Wanted desperately. So they'd welcome him the same way they'd welcome a visiting dignitary. He squared his shoulders and raised his chin, a wry grin climbing his freshly shaven cheeks. Then he gave the door-knocker two solid whacks.

Moments later the door swung wide, and a uniformed maid ushered Nic inside without so much as a moment's hesitation. "The missus is in the south parlor. Please follow me."

Nic plodded across the marble floor through an arched doorway. The moment he entered the parlor, the maid discreetly disappeared. The mistress of the house—Mrs. Darwin Thaddeus Bachman the Third—sat in a velvet tufted chair beside a scrolled round table, a China teacup in her pale, slender hands. But he'd gotten a whiff of the cup's contents on his last visit. Mrs. Bachman wasn't drinking tea.

When she spotted Nic, she set the cup aside and rose, hands outstretched, to greet him. "Mr. Pankin, how lovely to see you." She clasped his hand between hers. Her lips formed a smile, but her eyes remained cold. Distant. Tipping sideways slightly, she peeked behind him. "You're alone?"

Nic knew what she was asking. He cleared his throat and tugged his hand from her clammy grasp. "Yeah." He stifled the curse that rose in his throat. The midwife's disappearance had thrown a roadblock into his plans. But he'd find his kid. He had to. Too much rested on it. "Came to tell you there's been a little delay. But don't worry—the kid'll be yours soon."

The woman sank back into the chair. "Mr. Pankin, please understand, I'm trying to be patient. But Darwin and I have been alone for eleven years." Her brows puckered. "Eleven . . . years . . ." She swept her hand, indicating the surroundings. "This house is longing for the presence of a child. Every generation of Bachmans before us has provided an heir. It is imperative my husband not be the one who breaks with tradition. I *must* secure a child."

Nic fidgeted in place. The woman's high-pitched voice grated on his nerves, but he wouldn't bark at her. Deep down it pleased him to hold the upper hand. Hadn't taken him long on his previous visit to understand why she'd turned to him. No judge or decent person would give her a child. Her unnaturally rosy cheeks, slightly slurred speech, and trembling hands betrayed her weakness. If an uneducated bum like him read the signs, decent people would, too. Which made her dependent on the likes of him. He nearly laughed. She seemed to have everything—a fancy home, servants, nice belongings, money—yet she needed something from *him*. Such power he held. Almost made him want to prolong the sale. But he needed the money now, and he might lose out to somebody else if he didn't produce the kid soon. Worry clawed at him.

"You ain't looking elsewhere, are you? Thinking of buying a baby?"

Mrs. Bachman cringed. "A squalling infant? Oh, mercy, no. Diapers and nighttime feedings hold no appeal to me." She lifted her shoulder in a lazy shrug. "A child of three, already fully trained, able to speak and understand directions yet young enough to be molded into Darwin's expectations—that is precisely what I desire."

Leaning forward, she fixed him with a steady look. "And it's precisely what I expect from you. But I need to know, Mr. Pankin, if you're able to deliver. You made a promise to me nearly a month ago and I've yet to receive anything more than excuses. Do you or do you not intend to allow us to adopt your child?"

Her words—*be molded into our expectations*—echoed in Nic's mind. For one brief second something at the center of Nic's being caused a stir of apprehension. Would this woman love the kid and treat him right, or would she just hound him to become someone like herself—uppity and spoiled? He pushed the odd feeling aside. Why did he care what she did as long as he got what he wanted most?

Narrowing his gaze, he ground out, "'Course I do. And the age'll be just right for what you're wanting. Just gimme another week. I'll be back, and you won't be disappointed."

Lifting her teacup, she drank until she'd emptied it. Then she clattered the cup onto its saucer and fixed Nic with a haughty glare. "I hope not, Mr. Pankin. Because yours isn't the only available child in the city."

Nic puffed his chest and glowered at the woman. "Maybe not. But I reckon I'm the only one willing to deal with . . ." He allowed his gaze to flick to the discarded cup then back to her flushed face. "The likes o' you."

She blanched. Shifting her face sharply away, she set her chin at an arrogant angle. "Just bring me the child, Mr. Pankin, without any further delays. I'll have your money ready."

Micah gave a big smile to the little boy slumped on the edge of the examination table. The boy, flushed with fever, managed a wavering smile in return, then lowered his head. Micah tapped the youngster on the shoulder. When the child looked at him, he pointed to his own mouth, then opened it as wide as he could. His mouth still gaping, he touched the boy's chin and nodded, trying to give the message to open up. Micah had played this game of pantomime many times before. He had it down to an art.

The boy dropped his jaw, and his dark eyes widened when Micah placed a wooden depressor on his tongue and pressed gently. But, bravely, he didn't try to pull away. A peek at the child's throat gave Micah all the proof he needed—tonsillitis. He removed the depressor and offered it to the boy, who took it with a weak smile of thanks.

Micah would have liked to treat the infection with a dose of penicillin and then schedule the child for a tonsillectomy once the illness had cleared. But neither were an option. He had no penicillin on hand in the clinic, and no hospital would take this child without advance payment, which Micah already knew was an impossibility. So the best he could do was give the child's mother a gargle for the boy to use to ease the pain, show her how to keep his temperature down, and let the infection run its course. It was frustrating to know what to do but be unable to carry it out.

With a sigh, he turned to the boy's mother, who perched on a chair in the corner, her brow furrowed with worry. In her arms, she held another, smaller child. Micah suddenly envisioned the ill child playing "doctor" with the younger one and infecting the little one with germs from the tongue depressor. He reached into his pocket, found a penny, and offered it in trade for the stick. The child made an immediate swap.

Micah winked, then turned his attention to the mother again. He showed her the directions of how to mix the gargle, then demonstrated rinsing a rag in cold water and placing it on the boy's sweaty head. The mother nodded as if she understood. She took the items and replayed Micah's actions.

Micah smiled broadly and patted the woman's shoulder. "Good." He nodded exuberantly. "Yes, that's right."

The woman nodded, too, patting Micah back. "Thanks you. Good man. Thanks you."

Micah sighed as the trio left the clinic. He needed to learn Russian, German, Italian, Polish, Yiddish, and Dutch just to communicate clearly with the people in his neighborhood. And, he thought with a self-deprecating chuckle, according to Nicky, he had difficulty just spitting out English. What a disadvantage these people had, living in a country where they couldn't speak the language. Yet they were safer here than in their homelands, what with the Nazis marching across Europe, wreaking their havoc. Micah was grateful for each "foreigner" who came in—it meant one less to be mowed down in Hitler's quest for power.

He washed the table where the child had sat, using a disinfectant solution so potent the vapors stung his eyes. Yet it wouldn't do to spread germs. Some people were uneasy enough, blaming the immigrants for all types of illnesses. He would do whatever he could to keep diseases from spreading. As close as these people lived to one another, a simple illness could turn into an epidemic.

The task finished, he walked to the dirt-streaked window and looked out onto the street. Things here were so different from his own small hometown. The sky nearly blocked by towering buildings, grass only growing in parks, people constantly teeming . . . There were times Micah longed for the open spaces and blue skies of Texas. Yet he knew he was exactly where God wanted him to be, and he would stay until God uprooted him.

Micah had never planned to live in a big city, but when he'd volunteered for service in Schofield, everything had changed. The attack at Pearl Harbor, specifically, had brought the change. One of the injured men had said, in gratefulness for Micah's care, "Boy, we could sure use you back in Queens, Doc. You're a great doctor." The simple statement had refused to leave his mind. When he'd read about the immigrant population and how many of them were without medical care, his heart had ached over their plight. As soon as he'd finished his duty at Schofield, he'd packed his bags and come directly to New York to work at this medical clinic established by a missions group. The elderly doctor running the Queens Free Clinic had willingly handed the reins of service to Micah. The mission paid him a small but decent salary, and he'd been right where he needed to be to assist Jeremiah in his work. God had known what He was doing when He planted Micah in Queens.

Local doctors who believed in the work of the clinic—those with flourishing practices and homes in Brooklyn, away from the industry and noise—offered supplies, medicines, and occasional monetary donations to keep the clinic running. Micah suspected a few of them supported him to prevent the immigrants from coming to them for help. Whatever their motivation, Micah was grateful for their offerings, as they allowed him to treat the people who needed him most.

He was also grateful for the three volunteers who rotated through each week to help with cleaning and to give rudimentary first aid. He frowned, checking his watch. In fact, Stan should have arrived an hour ago. He sighed. Stan was notorious for being late. He'd show up eventually.

A young boy paced outside the open window. He held a stack of newspapers under one arm, and with his free hand he waved a paper above his head. "Island of Saipan falls to U.S. forces! Another victory for our brave fighting men! Island of Saipan falls! Read all about it!" Two men traded coins for papers, and the boy moved on, continuing to shout his message. Micah watched him go, wishing for the hundredth time for a headline that didn't bring immediate images of death and destruction.

Lord, keep Your hand of protection on Jeremiah.

As much as Micah abhorred the war and all its evils, it had brought about one positive: jobs. Ten years ago, he'd heard, grown men haunted New York's street corners, shining shoes for a nickel a pair just to get by. But factories had sprung up across the country and manufactured everything from rubber to airplane parts. If a body was willing to work, there was something waiting to be done.

Women, whose men had left to fight, were even taking up tools and working in factories. Micah couldn't help wondering what would happen when the war was over and the men came back. Would the women be reluctant to relinquish their positions? What kind of domestic battles might be waged when this ugly war was finished?

His attention turned to a cluster of boys who dashed from an alleyway to the street. They quickly organized a ball game, using a rock and a wooden slat in place of real equipment. He shook his head. So many of New York's children went unattended during the day while their mothers worked and their fathers fought overseas. It broke his heart to see them using a dirty street or sometimes the roofs of their apartment buildings as their playground. What kind of place was that for a child to play, with no grass to rumble through, no wildflowers to pick, or no trees to climb? When he was a boy growing up outside of Arlington, he and his brothers had the run of acres of ground. The fun they'd had . . . He sighed. Again, the children suffered. When would it end?

As had happened frequently of late, thinking of children brought Nicky to mind. He pictured the little boy hunkered in the shadow of that bush, watching a shiny-backed beetle, hoping to make it his pet. A smile pulled at his heart. Tenderhearted little soul. He'd be good with a pet. Had his mama considered getting him a puppy or kitten?

He tried not to let Lydia sneak into his thoughts. She'd been doing that too much the past two weeks. Especially when the lights were low and it was time to be sleeping. Instead of sleeping, he'd be thinking. Thinking of Lydia's earnest, blazing eyes as she proclaimed her love for Nicky. Thinking of her determined vow to protect the little boy. Thinking of her shame-faced, penitent expression when he reminded her to pray. Thinking of her warm smile when they'd walked with Nicky.

He pushed his hand against the window casing, spinning himself around. *Knock it off, Hatcher. You've got more important things to think about.* As if to prove it, the door to the clinic opened and a bearded man entered, cradling his arm against his rib cage. Blood soaked through his sleeve.

"Doctor, I have injured myself." He spoke through gritted teeth, his face contorted with pain.

"Come with me." Micah guided the man to the examination table in the back. His thoughts of Lydia were pushed aside. Again.

8

Lydia stepped from the steel-and-glass hall encasing Pennsylvania Station onto Seventh Avenue. She clutched her purse tightly in one hand and her suitcase in the other. People jostled her, but Lydia was accustomed to crowds, and the milling throng didn't intimidate her. She moved with the masses until she reached the open sidewalk. There, she found a spot next to a three-story limestone building with advertising posters nearly covering the plate-glass windows. She placed her suitcase on the concrete as close to the building as possible, stepped in front of the case to guard it with her legs, then opened her purse. It took her only a moment to locate the folded paper with Micah's address on it. Her father had added a brief, terse message to the bottom: *Be careful*.

Lydia shook her head. Father hadn't been happy about her boarding the train and coming to New York City to find Mrs. Fenwick. It had taken almost a week to convince him that if Nic Pankin showed up at the house, Father would be a better defense against the man than two women and a little boy. Eventually, Father had seen the truth of Lydia's statement. So, with his typical modicum of grumbling, he had purchased her train ticket and sent her on her way.

Now here she was, in Manhattan, and she needed to make her way to Queens. She glanced up and down the street, her gaze sweeping across buildings that nearly blocked the gray-blue sky from view. A niggle of apprehension attacked. Up close, the city was a rather intimidating place, after all—and so big! How would she ever find Mrs. Fenwick among the vast number of people who lived here?

She reminded herself of a Bible verse she'd read the morning before she'd boarded the Union Pacific train. The verse had stated that nothing is impossible for the one who believes. Well, it was too important for Nicky's safety for her *not* to believe. She *would* find Mrs. Fenwick. She was depending on God's help—and an earthly assistant, Micah Hatcher.

Two men walked past, their gazes roving openly from the toes of her sling-back pumps to the top of her freshly brushed hair. Their unabashed appraisals sent a tingle of trepidation down her spine. *Be careful*, her father had admonished, and it seemed good advice at the moment. She stood with her most confident bearing until the men had gone by, then slumped with relief. The sooner she found a taxi driver who could transport her to Micah's clinic, the happier she would be.

A boy rounded the corner. He appeared around fifteen years old and was rather scruffy in attire, but Lydia thought he had an honest face. "Excuse me!" She hailed the passing youngster with a wave of her hand.

He came to an abrupt halt, then looked up and down the street as if seeking someone before his focus came back to her. "Yes, miss? You callin' me?"

Lydia nodded. "Could you tell me the best place to catch a cab?"

The boy grinned. "You must be new in town, miss. You're *at* the best place in Manhattan to catch a cab. Comin' an' goin' all the time from the station. Just step up on the curb an' watch. One'll be by."

"Thank you." Lydia retrieved a coin from her purse and held it out.

The boy looked at the coin, his eyes wide. His hand began to reach for it, but then he shrugged, shoving his hand into his pocket instead. He gave her a broad grin. "Nah, miss, keep yer change. No charge for common sense." And he galloped on down the sidewalk.

Chuckling to herself, Lydia pinched her purse beneath her elbow, gripped the slip of paper in one hand, and grasped the handle of the suitcase with the other. She stepped up onto the curb. Just as the boy had claimed, within minutes a jitney screeched to a halt not twelve inches from her feet.

The round-faced driver hollered through the open window. "Needin' a ride, are ya?"

"Yes, sir. I need to go to Queens, the corner of Armstrong and Twenty-seventh."

The man scratched his head. "That's a far piece o' drivin', miss. Goin' to cost ya a pretty penny."

"Whatever it costs is fine," Lydia said, then added, "within reason. I won't be taken advantage of."

The man broke into a grin, revealing a broken tooth in the front. He jammed his thumb toward the backseat. "Climb in, miss. I'll git ya where ya want to go. An' I'll be fair an' reasonable in my charge o' the ride."

"Thank you." Lydia opened the backseat door, swung in her case, then settled herself beside it. The moment her door closed, the driver pulled from the curb, blasting his horn to warn others of his approach. Fear rose in her belly at his aggressiveness. Lydia grabbed the seat and held on tight as he wove through the other traffic. Closing her eyes for just a moment, she whispered a quick prayer for safety. She wanted to get to Queens in one piece.

To Queens—and Micah.

The thought brought a rush of feeling that had nothing to do with fear. Micah would no doubt be surprised to see her, but she knew he wouldn't turn down her request for help in locating Mrs. Fenwick. His affection for Nicky, and his knowledge of their dire situation, would make it impossible for him to refuse. Guilt pricked as she considered taking advantage of Micah's kind heart, but she really had no choice. Nicky was too important to not use every advantage she could find.

"Mr. Jensen, you did a fine job on your arm." Micah shook his head.

"*Ja,* was a stupid thing to do, I know." The man grimaced as Micah forced the needle through his flesh. "I will be wiser than to put my arm through a window next time."

"Let's not put anything through a window, okay? No arms, legs, heads . . ." Micah tried to make light of things. He knew he inflicted pain on his patient, but distraction was a good antidote to discomfort. "You know, my mama was in a quilting group when I was a boy. I used to stand by the frame and watch those needles go in and out, in and out, creating pretty patterns in the fabric. I just never figured I'd need the skill for myself. But look at this—I bet Ma would be proud of the stitch job I'm doing here."

The man's face was white, but he managed a weak laugh. "Ja, I'm sure your mama would be proud. My own mama, she could make such tiny stitches. Fourteen to the inch, she would say. But I think I would rather you did not try so many on me."

The cowbell Micah had hung above the clinic door clanged,

and a loud, wild wail filled the room. Both men jumped. Mr. Jensen said, "You better go see what is wrong."

Micah placed a wad of bandages on Mr. Jensen's arm. "Keep that covered and hold still. I'll be right back." He moved from the curtained examination area to find a mother and child standing just inside the door, both crying loudly. The child had several scrapes on the side of her face. Her hair was matted with blood, and she clung tenaciously to her mother, making it impossible for Micah to examine her. The mother's distraught wails did nothing to calm the child.

Where was Stan? Micah couldn't handle both patients unassisted. The cowbell clanged again, and Micah glanced up, expecting to see Stan rushing forward with an apology on his face. Instead, Lydia Eldredge, wearing a butter-yellow skirt and jacket and holding a suitcase, stepped through the door. He blinked rapidly, certain he was hallucinating, but the thud of her suitcase hitting the floor and the clack of her heels across the scuffed hardwood dispelled the theory.

"What's the problem here?" Lydia spoke with the lyrical yet determined tone Micah knew well. The howling of the distraught mother and child increased in volume. Micah had to raise his voice to be heard above the din.

"I'm not sure. The mother won't release the child to let me examine her."

"Let me try." Lydia placed an arm around the mother's back, patting her shoulder. She smiled in a warm, encouraging manner. "Ma'am, I want to help you. Are you hurt?"

The mother shook her head so hard she nearly dislodged her scarf. "My baby. My baby, she is hurt."

Micah again reached for the child, but the woman snatched her back, and the child screamed in fear.

Lydia resumed patting the mother's shoulder. "Come sit over

here with me and let me look at your baby. I will help her." Lydia gently guided the woman to some chairs in the corner. Micah watched, dumbfounded, as Lydia took over. She settled the mother on one chair, sat down next to her, and eased the little girl from the mother's lap onto her own. Lydia glanced up and met Micah's gaze.

She waved a hand of dismissal. "We'll be fine. Go finish whatever you were doing." She looked pointedly at his bloodstained hands. "I wouldn't have let you touch my baby, either, with those awful hands. Clean up. By the time you come back, we'll be ready for you."

Micah stood rooted in place for a moment, staring stupidly as Lydia turned her attention back to the mother and child and continued soothing both of them. The wails died down to mild, hiccupping sobs. He shook his head and returned to Mr. Jensen. While he finished stitching the man's arm, he kept an ear tuned to the other side of the curtain. An occasional giggle carried over low-toned conversation. The stitching done, Micah carefully bandaged the arm and fished in his supply cupboard for some aspirin. He found it difficult to stay focused on the task at hand with Lydia on the other side of that curtain, whispering with the frightened mother and child.

Micah assisted Mr. Jensen from the table, and the man gave him a knowing look.

"That lady who is out there, she is a pretty one."

Micah straightened his spine. His ears went hot. "Well, yes, I suppose she is."

"She is your friend?"

Micah considered the question. Then, somewhat uncertainly, he gave a nod. "Yes. She is my friend."

Mr. Jensen winked. "You are a lucky man."

Micah frowned. That waited to be seen. Then he smoothed

his forehead and handed the packet of aspirin to Mr. Jensen. "Take these when the pain is too much. You'll need to keep the wound clean and dry. Come back each day for a new dressing. In a week, we'll take those stitches out. In the meantime, no using that arm."

Mr. Jensen's brows raised in alarm. "No using arm? No working? But I must to work. My family—"

Micah stopped the man's worried protests with a gentle hand on his shoulder. "I will speak to your foreman and make sure he understands why you can't be there this week. And when you come tomorrow, I'll have a box of food for you to help your family through until you're working again."

Mr. Jensen's jaw clenched. Micah held his breath, waiting for the man to refuse his help, but then tears appeared in the man's eyes. Brokenly, he said, "You are a good man, Dr. Hatcher. I thank you for your kindness."

Micah squeezed Jensen's shoulder. "You take care of yourself. Watch out for windows."

The man managed a smile, and then he headed out, holding his wounded arm against his rib cage. Micah returned to Lydia and the other patient. Although the child's cherubic face was tear-streaked and apprehensive, she sat quietly on Lydia's lap.

Micah squatted down next to Lydia's chair, smiling at the little girl. He asked Lydia, "What have you determined to be the problem here?"

Lydia stroked the child's hair. "She fell from the stoop of her apartment. She has several scrapes and one minor cut above her ear. It bled a lot, as head wounds are prone to do, but I don't think it requires stitches."

Micah checked. The child whimpered softly when he placed his hands on her head to part the grimy hair at the site of the cut, but Lydia soothed her, and the little girl remained still.

Micah sagged in relief when he determined Lydia was right. He could hardly bear to think of pressing a needle into this little one's scalp.

Micah turned to the mother. "She'll be fine. We'll clean her up and put some bandages on her wounds. Come with me." The mother stood and Micah reached for the little girl, but the child wrapped her dimpled arms around Lydia's neck.

Lydia stood. "I'll bring her."

A strange pressure built in his chest. Lydia cradling a child was an arresting sight. He shook his head to clear it, then gestured to the curtain. "Back here." He led the small parade to the examination area, where he saw to the child's wounds. As soon as the mother and child departed, Micah turned to address the question he was sure Lydia was expecting.

"What in the world are you—"

The cowbell sounded, and Micah threw out his arms, his gaze raised heavenward. What now? But instead of a patient, Stan rushed in. Finally. Micah started to berate the man for his late arrival. Before Micah could speak, the man blurted, "Hey, Micah, I have a message for you. Some dockworker said to tell you there's a package for you due in on the next Red Cross ship. Said it would be in around ten this evening."

9

Micah's sudden change in demeanor left Lydia feeling strangely unsettled. He seemed to blanch at hearing the message, then straightened and deliberately assumed a nonchalant pose. When he spoke, his voice was even and held no hint of anxiety, yet Lydia sensed he was hiding his true feelings.

"Thank you, Stan. Now suppose you tell me where you've been. You're more than an hour late."

Stan ducked his head and dug the toe of his boot against the wooden floor. "Aw, I'm sorry, Micah. I lost track of time. I was shooting billiards with some of the boys, and—"

Micah waved a hand. "Never mind. I can guess." He dropped the subject, but Lydia imagined it would be brought up again, when Micah no longer had an audience to overhear the conversation. Micah held out his hand in her direction. "Stan, let me introduce Miss Lydia Eldredge from Boston, Massachusetts. She arrived just in time to help with an emergency."

Lydia smiled and offered her hand.

Stan took it and held it longer than was polite, grinning foolishly above the shaggy beard. "Well, hello, Miss Eldredge. I'm Stan—Stanley Forrester. Nice to make your acquaintance.

What brings you to New York? I don't imagine you came just to help Doc Hatcher here with his emergency."

Lydia forced a light laugh and withdrew her hand from Stan's massive paw. She resisted the urge to wipe her palm on her skirt. "No, actually, I'm here on business." She felt Micah's querying look and had to fight to keep from turning to him and begging for his help. She didn't want to say anything in front of a man about whom she knew nothing more than his name.

"Business?" Stan's bushy eyebrows rose. Lydia thought it looked as if he had as much hair growing across his forehead as he did on his chin. "Now, you're much too pretty to be concerned about business. Since you're new in town, maybe I could—"

"Stan, Miss Eldredge has said she's here on business." Micah's tone carried a hard edge. "To me, that intimates her social time is limited."

Stan took a step backward, still grinning. He held up both hands. "Okay, okay, Micah. Don't get your dander up. Couldn't pass up the opportunity, ya know?"

He swung his gaze back to Lydia, and she experienced a sense of discomfiture as real as when the two men had ogled her outside the Pennsylvania Station.

"Have a good time in New York, Miss Eldredge." He winked. "But don't expect too much attention from ol' Doc Hatcher here—this boy is all work and no play."

"Thank you. I'm sure my time here will be well spent."

"Stan, I'd appreciate it if you would clean up, and then lock the clinic on your way out. I need to take Miss Eldredge to her lodgings."

Stan waved a hand, a smirk still creasing his face. "Sure. Okay, Micah."

Micah walked behind the curtain and emerged a moment later with a brown felt hat pulled low over his eyebrows and a brown jacket in place of the apron he'd been wearing earlier. He picked up Lydia's suitcase with one hand, took hold of her elbow with the other, and ushered her out the door.

Lydia knew that to anyone looking on, he would appear the perfect gentleman, but his fingers dug into her arm. He seemed to be simmering with controlled fury. She bit down on her lower lip—it hadn't been her intention to make him angry. Perhaps she should have wired ahead that she was coming. But it was too late for that now, she told herself as she was forced to walk faster than she preferred to keep up with Micah's longer stride. When her heel nearly caught in a crack of the sidewalk, she lost patience and jerked her arm loose.

Micah swung around, her suitcase banging against his knee. "What's wrong?"

"Do you mean, what's wrong that brings me to New York or what's wrong that I suddenly decided I didn't care to have my arm pulled from its socket?" She rubbed her elbow where it felt as if his fingers had imprinted her flesh.

At her outburst, Micah plunked the suitcase on the sidewalk and sat on it, propping his elbows on his knees and resting his face in his hands. She stood silently until he raised his chin, dragging his hands along his cheeks and creating temporary jowls with the movement. He sighed. "I'm sorry if my pace was too . . . brisk."

"Brisk? Micah, I felt as if we were running from the law!"

A grin threatened—she saw the left corner of his lips twitch. It pleased her, but still she admonished lightly, "And you haven't even asked after Nicky."

Micah's head came up. "Is he okay?"

The obvious concern in his expression nearly melted Lydia's heart. She hastened to assure him. "Nicky was fine when I left. He sent me with a drawing which I'm to give to Micah-his-friend." She smiled. "You left quite an impression on that little boy. He talks about you every day."

Micah's eyes softened at that news, and he dropped his gaze to the sidewalk near his feet. When he stood, she noted the tenderness that had appeared at the mention of Nicky had slipped away. "Lydia, are you really here on business?"

Lydia gave a quick nod. "Yes. Very important business. Micah, do you remember when you said—"

Micah held up a hand. "I do want to hear about your reason for being here, but I have to be honest. I've got some important business of my own that needs immediate attention." He glanced at his wristwatch, grimaced, and looked beyond her shoulder for a moment, a frown creasing his handsome face. Finally he looked at her again. "Do you have a hotel yet?"

She shook her head. "No. I came straight to the clinic when I arrived."

"Well, I believe the apartment across from mine is empty right now. The older couple who lived there moved closer to their daughter's workplace so they could watch her children while she's at work. Let me see if the landlady would allow you to camp out there while you're in town. It's only a studio apartment, but it will be more spacious than a hotel room. Would that be all right with you?"

Lydia tipped her head. "Do you think the landlady would be willing to do that?" Housing in Boston rarely lasted more than a few hours between tenants.

"She might." Micah smirked. "She thinks I'm cute."

Lydia frowned. "Micah, really." An improper rush of jealousy followed.

He shrugged, his lopsided grin causing her heart to turn over. "She's also old enough to be my grandma. But I look out for her, so I think she'd do this for me. Come on." He took her arm again, but much more gently. He also tempered his stride to match her shorter one. As they walked along, he glanced at her and offered a smile. A real smile. His Micah-smile. It warmed Lydia all the way to the open toes of her shoes.

Heavenly Father, guard my heart, Lydia willed even as she returned Micah's smile with a tremulous one of her own. *I'm here to save my son, not give my heart away.*

To turn her attention elsewhere, she allowed her gaze to scan the area. She wrinkled her nose. Did nothing green grow in New York? A few sad flower boxes hung on apartment windows, but the poor plants growing there drooped and sagged as if blooming were too much effort. Happy squeals reached her ears and she looked upward, spotting a group of children playing on a rooftop. *A rooftop?* She thought of Nicky in such a location, and her heart nearly stopped. Never would she allow such a thing! But when one considered the traffic, perhaps a rooftop was safer than the streets. . . .

They reached a block of solid, brown-brick apartment buildings standing four or five stories high. Sets of concrete steps every fifteen feet or so either led one below sidewalk level or up to a square landing. Micah guided her to the third upward set. He opened the door for her, and she preceded him into a dimly lit hallway that stretched toward another door at the back. An iron-railed stairway led to the upper floors. She didn't have a chance to explore further, because Micah stopped at the first apartment and knocked. They waited a moment. Then he tapped again.

A sour voice came through the door. "I'm comin', I'm comin', no need to break down the ever-lovin' door!"

Lydia would have taken a step back, but Micah blocked her. The door swung open and a wrinkle-faced old woman in a wrinkled, faded housedress, bare legs, and—of all things—men's boots with no laces, stood scowling in the opening. She fixed

Lydia with a harsh glare. "Yeah, missy, what do ya want? I ain't buyin' nothin', if yer sellin'."

Micah leaned over Lydia's shoulder. "Mrs. Flannigan, me old darlin', I wouldn't dream of sellin' you a thing."

The woman's face lit when Micah came into her view. To Lydia's amazement, she even preened, lifting her hand to touch the frizzy gray curls above her left ear. "Ah, Micah, m'boy. Didn't see ya there in the shadows. What can I be doin' for ya today?"

Micah tipped his head to indicate Lydia. "This is Miss Lydia Eldredge, a friend of mine from Boston. She's here in New York on business, and she needs a place to stay." The woman shook a ferocious finger at Micah, her blue eyes snapping. Micah rushed on. "Now, you know I'm not suggestin' she stay with me, Mrs. Flannigan. You know me better than that!" The woman's face relaxed, the warmth returning to her faded blue eyes. "But I was wonderin' if Kelsey's apartment was rented yet. Thought perhaps she could stay there. Might be only a day or two, but I'd pay for the whole month."

Lydia shot him a startled glance. She hadn't intended for him to pay her room bill!

Mrs. Flannigan scratched her knobby, whisker-dotted chin. "Well, now, Micah, ya know I've got a waitin' list for that apartment. Could call today an' have it filled, just like that." She snapped her bony fingers. Then she tucked her chin downward with a flirtatious smile, causing her double chin to triple. "But, for you, m'boy, I'll put off that call for a day 'r two. Yer friend can stay." Finally the woman's smile swept to include Lydia.

"I thank you, Mrs. Flannigan. You're a real darlin', ye are!"

Lydia never expected to hear an Irish brogue combined with a Texas twang. Her ears might never recover.

"Now, can I be trustin' you to get Lydia settled? I've got some business I must attend to."

Lydia's heartbeat increased its rhythm. He wasn't going to leave her here with this crusty old woman, was he?

Micah dropped the suitcase by Lydia's feet, touched her back lightly, and whispered, "You're in good hands with Mrs. Flannigan. Turn in early, rest well, and I'll take you along to the clinic with me tomorrow morning. We'll talk there." After a broad wink in Mrs. Flannigan's direction, which caused the woman to titter like a young girl, Micah spun on his heel and dashed out the door.

Lydia propped a hand on her hip. She turned to Mrs. Flannigan, who still wore a glow from Micah's attention. The older woman sighed, patting the soiled bodice of her dress, then glanced in Lydia's direction. She gave a start, dropping the hand and fussing with a torn corner on her pocket in a self-conscious gesture.

"Yes, well, come along now, Miss . . . Eldredge, did ya say? From Boston, eh? I imagine yer tired from yer journey. Mrs. Flannigan will take good care o' ya, yes she will. Grab yer case there, m'dear, an' follow me." The older woman herded Lydia to the staircase and began grunting her way upward, tugging at Lydia's hand.

Lydia followed, but she looked between the stairway railing toward the doors where Micah had disappeared. How she wished she knew what business had caused such a state of urgency.

10

Micah hoped Lydia would forgive him for dumping her on his landlady, but he knew Mrs. Flannigan would get her settled in. He chuckled, fondness for the older woman warming his chest. She was a feisty old bird, but she possessed a heart of gold. Even so, she might turn up her nose in distaste if she knew of his package retrievals.

He moved along briskly, glancing once in a while at his watch. He had to reach the synagogue before seven if he wanted to speak with Rabbi Jacowicz. He could make it in plenty of time if he drove, but he'd made it a habit to save his gas ration coupons for emergencies—such as making Jeremiah's deliveries. Walking was good exercise, anyway. If he increased his pace, he'd get there in time.

Arms swinging, heels pounding the pavement, he blew out a breath of frustration. What was the dockworker thinking to pass that message off to Stan? Micah had given all of the men strict instructions to give every communication directly to him. Anger propelled by worry rolled through his chest as he considered the possible consequences of the breach of confidence. Anger faded to guilt when he remembered taking his frustration out on Lydia. He shouldn't have been so abrupt with her.

He turned a corner and was forced to slow his speed as he weaved between evening shoppers returning home with their supper fare. The sight of food in baskets made his stomach growl. He hadn't had his supper yet—getting Lydia settled had taken the place of eating. Of course, she hadn't eaten, either, to his knowledge. Maybe he should pick up something—sandwiches from a deli and fruit from one of the vendors—and take it to her when he returned to the apartment. It would be a gesture of goodwill after his grumpy attitude earlier.

What on earth was she doing here? She'd never mentioned her father having business associations in New York. He would get to the bottom of her "business" later. For now, making arrangements for his package took priority.

He jogged the last few steps to the solid doors of the synagogue. The hinges released a low-pitched moan as he pushed the door inward. Micah entered the cool, dark interior. Two men with long beards, skull caps, and black sidelocks framing their cheeks, looked up from a table where they read together by candlelight. They nodded in a solemn fashion and went back to their book. Micah passed them and entered the small room at the back where he knew he'd find Rabbi Jacowicz.

"Hello, Micah, my friend," the rabbi greeted when Micah entered the room.

The combination of words brought Nicky fleetingly to mind. Micah swallowed a smile and focused on the purpose of his visit. "Package arriving this evening. Should be here around ten."

"So you will bring it here by eleven?"

"Between eleven and twelve," Micah corrected. "Can you be ready?"

"How many?" the man asked.

Micah shrugged. "I'm not sure. At least two, probably. To be safe, we should make preparations for twice that number."

A single nod acknowledged Micah's request. Then the man smiled, his beard lifting at the corners and his eyes crinkling. "I will be ready."

"As will I."

Lydia washed down the last bite of her sandwich with a swallow of milk, then wadded the empty wax paper wrap. She tossed the crumpled paper onto the table, releasing a sigh. Her tummy was now comfortably full thanks to Micah's delivery of a cheese sandwich, two wrinkled apples, and a pint-sized bottle of milk half an hour ago. But the empty room closed around her.

Why hadn't he stayed to eat with her? She would have liked his company at the scarred kitchen table. This aloof, seemingly uncaring Micah was not the man who had sat across her own kitchen table and presented a way to help Nicky two weeks ago. He hadn't even questioned her reason for being in New York. His preoccupation raised a dozen questions in her mind.

Picking up the coarse white sheets Mrs. Flannigan had loaned her, she moved to the corner of the room. She flicked the sheets, one at a time, onto the contraption masquerading as a bed. Nothing more than a worn, sagging mattress on a rusty iron frame that folded up on itself, the bed promised to be very uncomfortable. But she wouldn't need to spend too many nights on it. Father had warned her to prepare for a lengthy stay in New York, claiming there was no way to know for certain how long it would take to find Mrs. Fenwick. But Nicky needed rescuing *now,* and Lydia trusted God to guide her quickly to the woman.

Her hands paused in their task and she drew in a slow breath, a smile twitching at her lips. How wonderful to rest confidently in the assurance of God's attention to her need—especially since Micah's attention seemed sorely lacking. She had pulled out her Bible and read some passages in Matthew while eating her simple supper, and she reflected on a section of Scripture. The words *"If ye have faith as a grain of mustard seed . . . nothing shall be impossible unto you"* had nearly leaped from the page onto her heart. Bending forward, she smoothed the wrinkles from the sheets as she reminded herself even if right now her faith was small—no bigger than a mustard seed—it was still sufficient. And just as a mustard plant grew from a tiny seed, her faith would continue to grow as she placed her trust in God. The thought brought a pleasant rush of peace.

A breeze pressed in through one of the windows, riffling the back of her hair and carrying a mildewy odor. Crossing to the closest window, she pushed the simple off-white curtain aside. Palms resting on the dirty sill, she leaned out slightly and gazed left and right. The army-ordered dim-out resulted in the city resting beneath a muted glow, but the dimming of lights seemed to have little effect on activity. The afternoon's busy traffic had slowed with the descent of evening, but groups of people loitered on the sidewalks, talking and laughing.

At the corner, a pair of teenage boys leaned on the iron light pole, cigarettes dangling from their lips, while they jostled one another and whistled at any young woman who wandered by. While Lydia watched, one of the boys lifted his head and fixed his gaze on her. He punched his buddy, pointed, and then both boys leered at her. Lydia withdrew and closed the window as the boys' raucous laughter filtered to her ears. She whisked the shades downward on both windows, sealing herself away from any other prying eyes. Then she busied herself emptying the contents of her suitcase.

Shelves tucked into a cubby near the tiny kitchen held most of her belongings, but her suits required hanging. A search of the apartment revealed no closet, so she made use of a series of pegs along one wall. She slipped out of her yellow travel suit and hooked it carefully over a wooden peg. A smear of blood marred the lapel of her jacket. Lydia slid her fingers across the brownish stain, and an image of the frightened little girl she'd held filled her mind. How quickly the child's countenance had changed with gentle attention. What a wonderful service Micah provided, seeing to the needs of the city's immigrant population. She nibbled her lower lip, pondering. Might the package he needed to retrieve be supplies? If so, why did he seem upset rather than grateful?

Reaching for her pajamas, she started to dress for bed. But an inner restlessness changed her hands' direction. Instead, she donned a pair of trousers and a blouse. Despite the bedtime hour and her long hours of travel, she wasn't ready to turn in. Perhaps a few minutes of taking in the night air would clear her mind and allow her to sleep. Leather slippers on her feet and the key Mrs. Flannigan had given her in her pocket, she left the apartment.

On the stairway, she passed a couple locked in a rather ardent embrace and an older woman who muttered insults at the unconcerned couple. Her slippers slapped softly against the concrete stairs, her shadow creeping along beside her. She moved quickly to the double doors that led to the street, stepped outside, and seated herself on the top step. Pulling up her knees, she wrapped her arms around them and looked skyward, hoping to see stars.

Her thoughts worked their way across the states to Boston, where Nicky was probably already asleep. She missed him. She'd never been away from him before. He had cried when she left, nearly breaking her heart, but she'd told him he should look out the window at the stars before going to sleep and know that Mama was looking at the same stars. So she searched the smoke-smudged expanse overhead for stars, thinking of Nicky doing the same thing. The idea comforted her.

The squeak of the door hinges caught her attention, and she looked over her shoulder, prepared to move out of the way if necessary. To her pleased surprise, Micah stepped onto the stoop.

He whisked a glance up and down the street, his brow puckered. "What are you doing out here?"

His flat tone chilled her. She hugged her knees more tightly. "Just sitting. Taking in the night air. I often do that at home before turning in."

Micah descended two steps, then lowered himself beside her with his legs stretched out in front of him. "Lydia, this isn't your neighborhood. This is a Queens ghetto. It isn't safe for you to be sitting out here alone."

"Then sit with me." She offered a smile, hoping to remove the scowl from his face. "Let me tell you why I've come. And you can tell me all about your clinic work."

Micah flicked an impatient glance at his watch. "I can't right now. I have an appointment."

Lydia drew back, startled. "At this hour?"

"Yes. But I won't feel comfortable leaving until you're back in your apartment. Please go back up."

A muscle twitched in his cheek, and he repeatedly clenched and unclenched his fists. The nervous gestures raised an alarm in her mind. Surely just finding her sitting outside on a stoop wouldn't create this much anxiety. She touched his knee. "What's troubling you, Micah?"

Instead of answering, he took hold of her elbow and assisted her to her feet. He led her to the door, opened it, and applied gentle pressure to her back to ease her through the opening. "Uncle Micah says it's time for bed." His voice quavered, and his attempt at humor only served to increase her trepidation.

"I'll take you to the clinic with me in the morning and we'll talk there, but for now you need to turn in. Good night, Lydia."

Without giving her a chance to respond, he turned and trotted down the steps, then headed up the street. Lydia stepped back onto the stoop, hands on her hips, staring after him. Curiosity twined through her middle. What kind of business would require his attention at this hour of the evening?

He reached the corner, paused, looked both ways, then turned right. She bit her lip, her thoughts rolling erratically. He'd told her to go up to bed, but she wasn't sleepy, and she wouldn't be able to rest, wondering what he was doing. Without a thought to the ramifications, Lydia dashed down the stairs in pursuit.

11

Micah breathed in short, nervous spurts. Someone tailed him. The hairs on the back of his neck had been tingling for the last three blocks. The person walked with a light step, but the steps had dogged him relentlessly since he'd left the apartment. His heart beat in his throat. Who was it? The police? Someone who had discovered what he was doing and wanted to stop him?

Fists balled so tightly his fingers ached, he forced himself to keep moving, circling blocks and forming a meandering path meant to confuse his pursuer. This was exactly what he'd feared would happen when Stan came in with that message. Whoever followed was certainly up to no good, and Micah couldn't afford to have his plans disrupted. What would happen to the package if he didn't retrieve it? None of the dockworkers knew how to reach Rabbi Jacowicz.

He set a deliberate pace—not so fast as to alert his pursuer he knew of his presence, but fast enough to make the follower work to keep up. Every fiber of his being strained to break into a run, but he didn't dare—if the person following was armed, he might be antagonized into shooting. Micah wouldn't risk anyone being hurt. He clung to hope the person would tire of following him if he continued an aimless journey. But he couldn't keep it up forever—he needed to go to his vehicle and then to the docks.

Micah turned another corner, making careful note of street names so he'd be able to bring himself back on course. In and out of the soft glow cast by hooded streetlamps he went, his shadow running ahead and then falling behind, his ears constantly tuned and alert, his pulse pounding in worry. The mysterious follower turned wherever he did. How long would this continue?

Then Micah's heart leaped in his chest. Ahead, a gloomy alley opening beckoned. If he ducked in there, might he be able to hide long enough for the person to give up and leave? If so, he could get to his coupe and the ship docks. He maintained his same brisk pace as he approached the alley. Then, sending up a silent prayer for success, he abruptly dove into the dark passageway between towering buildings.

He paused, disoriented. The absence of streetlamps left him temporarily blinded, but after a few seconds his eyes adjusted and he spotted a haphazard stack of wooden crates leaning precariously against the side of one building. He dashed behind them, then peeked out to watch the alley opening, his heart threatening to burst through his chest.

In less than a minute he was rewarded with the appearance of his follower. Micah couldn't make out the person's features in the shadows, but the pursuer was slight in build—shorter than Micah—and very slender. The person paused, tipping at the waist and peering into the alley, apparently hesitant to enter it. Micah held his breath. *Go away. Please go away.* But the shadowy figure took two slow steps forward, head swinging back and forth, seeking. One hand came up, and it appeared he scratched his head. Micah stifled a satisfied snort—he'd managed to bamboozle the mysterious tail. Now if he'd just leave . . .

Micah watched, hoping, as the person's hands went to his hips. In a rush, recognition dawned. Fury roared through Micah's middle. He burst from his hiding spot. "What do you think you're doing, Lydia?"

Lydia let out a strangled yelp and leaped backward. Her hand flew to her chest and she released her air in a whoosh. "Oh! Micah! Thank goodness it's you! You frightened me out of a year's growth!"

"You deserve it." He spoke through gritted teeth. His fingers itched to shake the daylights out of her. "I had no idea who trailed me. Don't think *I* haven't been scared."

"Well, I didn't *intend* to frighten *you*. You needn't have jumped out at me that way." Defensiveness colored her tone, which only added to Micah's ire. She stepped closer. "What are you doing out here?"

"None of your business." He grabbed her arm and ushered her into the light, where he could check his watch. Not enough time to return her to the apartment and then get himself to the dock before ten. He'd have to take her with him. He nearly growled in aggravation.

Hand still curled around her elbow, he marched her toward the garage where he stored his coupe. "Listen, I've got a package to pick up, and as much as it irks me, you're going to have to come along. But you're going to stay in the car, and you aren't going to ask questions. Not even one. Do you understand?"

She looked at him, her slippered feet slapping the concrete as he pulled her along. Her wide brown eyes communicated unease. "Micah, you aren't involved in something illegal . . . are you?"

Well, Lord, there's one of those questions I didn't want to have to answer. He ground his teeth together as he entered the parking garage. At his coupe, he assisted her none too gently into the passenger's seat, slammed the door with more force than was necessary, and stomped around to slide behind the wheel. Not until the car was in gear did he offer a terse response. "Never mind. Just sit there and be quiet."

Lydia, to his great relief, leaned into the corner and sat in stony silence while he drove the familiar streets to the docks. The ship's outline loomed ahead, and he prayed Jonesy had waited for him. He'd never been late before.

He parked the car in his usual spot and turned to Lydia. She slumped in the seat, arms crossed and mouth set in a firm line. He fought the urge to roll his eyes. She had no reason to pout. "I'll be back soon. You stay here."

Her chin lifted. "I heard you the first time."

He still wasn't sure how he was going to explain all of this to her later. "Just stay put," he said once more, ignoring her huff of irritation. He closed his car door and trotted to the dock. The gangplank met the dock, and Micah trotted onto the ship's deck.

Two men looked up at his approach, and the first one broke into a smile, nudging the second. "See, told ya he'd be here. Never misses a pickup." He grinned at Micah. "Tucks thought we was gonna hafta care for your delivery ourselves, but I told him you'd turn up. Get waylaid, Micah?"

Micah managed a wry grin. "You might say that, Jonesy. Where is it?"

Jonesy gestured with his head, since his hands were full. "Over there. Three of 'em this time. I took good care of 'em on the way over."

Micah recognized the hint. He reached into his pocket and withdrew several bills, which he held out to the sailor as Tucks turned away, busying himself with moving boxes.

Jonesy shoved the bills into his pocket without counting them.

"Got a letter for you, too." He handed over a rather damp, crumpled envelope. "Got it from Jeremiah himself."

"You saw Jeremiah?" Micah's pulse skipped into eager double beats. "How was he?"

Jonesy's brow furrowed for a moment. "He's thin. Don't think he hardly eats. Don't know how much longer he can keep this up."

Tucks looked over his shoulder, his narrow face creased with worry. "He's gonna get us all in trouble, Micah. You gotta tell him to stop."

Micah shook his head, a sad smile tugging at his lips. "You've met my brother, Tucks. You know he won't stop as long as he still draws breath."

"Well, from the looks of 'im, that might not be much longer."

Tucks's gloomy words sliced straight to Micah's heart. But Jonesy gave Tucks a firm smack on the shoulder. "Oh, get on with you. It weren't that bad." He swung his gaze back to Micah, his expression brightening. "Sure he's thin, an' his legs are botherin' him—limp is worse'n ever—but his spirits was good. He said to tell you not to worry."

Warmth flooded Micah's frame at Jeremiah's strength. How typical of his brother, telling Micah not to worry. Micah had the easy part, though, and they all knew it. He asked, "When will you head out again?"

"Be here a week, the captain said. Got more supplies to send to that brother of yours?" Jonesy stood in the wide-legged pose of a seasoned sailor, his arms crossed on his chest. "I'll make sure we got room."

"Thanks. I have six crates, at least. I'll be in touch to arrange a time with you to leave them here. But"—he lowered his voice to a whisper—"you've got to make sure the messages come directly to me from now on. The last one came through one of my clinic volunteers. He didn't ask any questions, but you never know. . . ."

Jonesy frowned. "Don't know how that happened, Micah. Everybody involved knows they're not to share any of our work with someone new. Not without your go-ahead. I'll check into it. It won't happen again."

"Good." Micah slipped Jeremiah's letter inside his shirt. "I better get my package out of here before someone else comes along."

"Take care, Micah," Jonesy called as he turned back to his work.

Micah moved toward the stack of crates Jonesy had indicated. Behind the pile, three children sat in a silent row. At Micah's approach, they crunched together. The one in the center—a girl who appeared to be about ten—wrapped her arms around the other two. Three pairs of eyes widened in obvious distress, and the littlest one tucked a finger into his mouth. Although they huddled mostly in shadow, Micah could make out their haunted faces and fearful poses. Tears stung behind his eyes. Jesus had told His disciples, *"Suffer little children to come unto me."* So why did God allow cruelty to touch innocent children? He'd never understand. But he'd do whatever he could to help.

He approached slowly to avoid frightening them, a smile quivering on his lips. He stopped a few feet away and went down on one knee, reaching his hand out to them and offering a simple message of welcome. *"Witajcie, dzieci."*

The children exchanged glances. Micah knew his Polish was poor, but he hoped they understood. He kept his hand extended and assured them they were safe. *"Jesteście tutaj bezpieczni."* The oldest child tipped her head inquisitively, as if trying to ascertain if he spoke truth. Her large, dark eyes appeared much older than her years. He repeated the words, noticing how the girl looked beyond him to the ship, then back at his face. She made not a sound. Her thin arms tightened around the other two.

Micah finished with the last of his memorized Polish phrases. "*Proszę ze mną.*" Would they heed his invitation to come with him?

The littlest one must have decided Micah wasn't a threat, because the child slipped away from his siblings and placed his hand in Micah's. Tears stung behind Micah's nose. After everything the child had been through, he still found the courage somewhere inside himself to trust a stranger. Micah curled his fingers around the tiny hand and gave the child a warm smile. He lifted his gaze to the other two. After a moment they, too, rose and came to him, although much more slowly.

Micah stood, continuing to instruct them to come with him, assuring them they were safe. He moved slowly across the dock toward the walkway leading to his coupe. He held the littlest one by the hand, and the other two followed obediently, clinging to each other. Micah wondered if they were brother and sister, and he winged up a brief prayer that if they truly were siblings, they would be able to stay together here in the States. When he reached the coupe, he realized Lydia stood beside the vehicle. Irritation built. Hadn't he told her to stay put?

At his approach, she stepped forward. Her gaze swept across the children, and her eyes widened. "This is what you call a package? Micah—"

He held up one finger. "Huh-uh. Remember? No questions."

12

Nic hunkered near the bushes at the edge of the Eldredges' Back Bay property. Even at half past ten, lights glowed behind several windows—some upstairs, some down. So somebody was awake in there. Probably high-and-mighty N. Allan Eldredge himself. Nic released a grunt of derision. A man who never toiled with his hands didn't need the rest required by those who did his bidding. Resentment pricked as Nic recalled the day Eldredge had issued Nic a pink slip and told him to never show his face at the factory again, taking away his dignity and his means of providing for himself.

And if Nic's suspicions were right, the man had also squirreled away Nic's most prized possession: Eleanor's child. Nic swallowed, eagerness to burst through those doors and see if his instincts were correct nearly turning him inside out. It'd please him beyond words to see shock and fear on Eldredge's face. To take something from him that mattered. And as soon as those lights went out, he'd do it.

Crouched low, his full focus on the house, he nearly jumped out of his skin when a hand clamped over his shoulder. He jolted upright and spun, squinting against the bright glare of a flashlight.

"What're you doin' out here, mister?"

The stern voice was unfamiliar, so he hadn't been spotted by Eldredge. The relief made his knees weak. Nic held his hand in front of his face. "Turn that wretched thing off, would ya? You're blinding me."

The bright beam lowered, illuminating the sidewalk, and Nic blinked into the unsmiling face of a street cop. The man tapped the flashlight against his blue-striped pant leg, the circle of light bouncing. "I asked you a question."

Nic cocked his weight on one hip, assuming a lazy pose he hoped hid his underlying nervousness. "Lost my dog. Just lookin' for it."

The policeman scowled. "Oh yeah? What kind of dog?"

Searching for a believable description, Nic rubbed the underside of his nose with one finger. "Brown. 'Bout knee-high. Kind of shaggy." He shrugged. "Just your regular dog."

The man flicked a glance at Nic's hand. "Where's his leash?"

Nic thought fast. "On him. He's draggin' it." He gestured to the bushes. "Thought he might've got tangled up, but . . ."

For a moment, the officer's brow crunched and he examined Nic's face, as if seeking the truth. Nic remained square-shouldered and untwitching beneath the glare, his legs aching with the desire to turn tail and run. Finally the man took a backward step. "Well, your dog isn't here, so keep movin'. Where do you live?"

Nic scowled. "Why you wanna know?"

The cop raised one eyebrow. "If I find your dog, I'll bring him on home for you."

"Oh." Nic sought another lie. He bounced his hand in the direction of the second house down the street. "Just put 'im inside the fence there. Thanks." Pushing his hand into his jacket pocket, Nic scuttled up the sidewalk. He muttered a curse. Why'd that fool cop have to come along and foil his plans?

Now he'd have to come back another night to claim what was rightfully his.

Lydia thought she might explode. The questions pressed against her lips like water straining against a dam. Who were these children? What were they doing on that ship? What was Micah to them? Why was he keeping them a secret? He had accused her of hiding the truth—it appeared he was just as guilty as she. He had said no questions, and she would honor it. Until they were alone. But then he'd better prepare for a barrage, because she wanted answers.

She looked over her shoulder at the three silent children wedged together in the center of the backseat. Two boys and a girl, all solemn with dark eyes full of fear and thin cheeks that spoke of hunger. Young children, yet there was something distinctly *old* in their appearance. While Lydia watched, the girl opened her arms and pulled the boys close against her sides in a protective gesture. The action raised a mighty lump in Lydia's throat, and she turned forward again.

They drove through silent streets with minimal traffic. Micah seemed to take a winding route, and Lydia wondered if he knew where he was going. It seemed hours before Micah pulled the coupe into an alley and glided to a stop behind a beautiful building Lydia recognized immediately as a place of worship. The back door opened the moment Micah turned off the engine, and a man wearing a long robe and a black skull cap over gray hair emerged. The long gray curls of his beard lifted slightly as the night breeze swept around the building. A Jewish rabbi—so this must be a synagogue. Her curiosity mounted as Micah stepped out of the vehicle and the two men greeted each other warmly with smiles and clasped hands. They obviously knew each other well.

Micah guided the old rabbi to the car and opened the back door. The children still huddled together, but the two little ones now slept on the girl's shoulders. The rabbi reached in and lifted the smallest one from the backseat, and the child continued drowsing in his arms. He spoke softly to the girl in a language Lydia didn't understand, and she shifted the head of the other sleeping child to the backrest of the seat before sliding across the seat. Micah then reached in to pick up the third child. The boy startled awake, looked at Micah with wide, frightened eyes, and began to wail.

Lydia started to get out, but Micah shook his head. "Stay there." He cradled the child close, rubbing his back and murmuring, "*Jesteœ tutaj bezpieczny.* You're safe." The child quieted, but he clung to Micah as if he would never let go.

The rabbi turned toward the synagogue, the girl trailing him with her sparrowlike hand clinging to his robe. Micah followed. All went inside the building. Lydia sat, drumming her fingers on the armrest and watching the door, until finally Micah emerged. She sat up eagerly.

But instead of climbing into the driver's seat, he went to the back of the coupe and opened the trunk. He rustled around back there and then slammed the lid, and he headed back into the synagogue with a bundle of some sort in his hands. Worry, curiosity, and an unnamed fear made Lydia wish to crawl right out of her skin. Seconds turned into minutes while she waited, watching the door, heart pounding and palms sweating.

At last the synagogue door opened and Micah came out again and climbed into the car. She sat, biting her tongue, while he turned on the lights, started the engine, and reversed out of the alley. Once he was on the street, Lydia's dam broke.

"I know you told me not to ask questions, but you certainly can't expect me to pretend I didn't just witness you taking three foreign children from a ship and carting them to a rabbi in the middle of the night." The muscles in Micah's jaw clenched and he grasped the steering wheel, his eyes straight ahead as Lydia continued. "Micah, are you involved in some—some sort of international child market?"

He swung his gaze in her direction. His blue eyes were like granite. "Is that what you really think? That I could be loathsome enough to sell a child?"

Lydia bit her lip, shame rising in her chest. She didn't want to think ill of Micah, but his actions—so secretive, under the cover of darkness—brought images of espionage and illicit dealings. "I don't know what to think. Why are you sneaking around at night, pretending to pick up packages, when clearly you are involved in something much . . . much bigger?"

"'Much bigger' doesn't begin to describe it."

"Is the clinic involved?"

"No! The clinic is not involved, and I want to keep it that way! If someone thought the clinic was involved, they might shut it down, and then hundreds of immigrants would go without health care. Lydia, don't even mention something like that."

Stung by his tone, Lydia shrank into the corner. "But, Micah, it's just the two of us right now. No one else is listening."

Micah groaned, his distress breaking her heart. "You don't understand. . . ."

"Then help me understand. Who were those children? What are they doing here? Why did you take them to the synagogue?"

Micah gripped the steering wheel and remained silent, his teeth clamped together so tightly the muscles in his jaw bulged. He drove to the parking garage and pulled the coupe into the slot it had occupied earlier. His hand trembling, he turned off the engine, then slowly swiveled his face to meet her gaze.

"Against my better judgment, I'm going to answer your

questions." The anger had fled, and in its place a sad resignation resided. For reasons Lydia couldn't understand, she preferred the anger. He sighed. "Do you recall asking me to keep private your situation with Nicky?" She gave a quick nod. "I'm now asking you for the same favor. This must remain between us. It's crucial."

His face, shrouded in shadow, carried such an expression of desperation her blood seemed to chill. She hugged herself. "Is someone in danger?"

"Yes." Micah's grim tone sent a tingle of apprehension down Lydia's spine. "Several people could be in danger. My brother Jeremiah is at the top of the list. Do you promise not to repeat what I'm about to tell you?"

"I promise."

He paused for a moment, his gaze boring into hers as if he were still trying to decide if he could trust her. She met his gaze head-on without flinching. Finally he gave a small nod, took a deep breath, released it, and found his voice. "Lydia, those children are Polish Jews. They're either orphans or they've been separated from their parents by the war. My brother is a minister who has served as a missionary in Russia for the past four years. He worked out a deal with the crew of an American Red Cross ship to sneak children into America. I take them to Rabbi Jacowicz, and he places them with Jewish families here in New York."

Lydia frowned, almost disappointed. After the tense night of secrecy, the explanation seemed anticlimactic. "But why must this remain a secret? Other countries have been providing sanctuary to German children."

Micah shook his head. "You're not paying attention. America has chosen not to allow European children of the Jewish faith to come into the country. In fact, according to Jeremiah, we've tightened the immigration laws to the point that it's almost impossible to enter America legally if you're a Jew."

Lydia nodded. "That's not surprising. Think of all the anti-Semitism. It's probably wise not to allow more of them in."

Micah dropped his head against the seat's back. A long, anguished sigh heaved from his chest. He angled his face to meet her gaze, and the stark pain in his eyes made Lydia catch her breath. "Do you realize Hitler is trying to eradicate the entire Jewish race?"

Despite his serious tone, Lydia released a little snort of disbelief. "I know there's been some trouble over there, some real mistreatment, but—"

"Haven't you read anything of the number of Jewish deaths in Europe?"

"Yes, of course. But there's a war waging. As deplorable as it seems, there are always civilian casualties in war."

Micah leaned toward her, his low tone taking on a fervency that she found chilling. "Lydia, this is beyond civilian casualties. Hitler and his henchmen are systematically rounding up groups of people who don't meet with Hitler's Aryan standards and taking them to their deaths. This includes Jews, Gypsies, anyone with a handicap . . . My own brother could be included in the last group. Jeremiah depends on leg braces and crutches to walk. He is crippled. Only his title as an American minister has protected him thus far."

Lydia shook her head. There was always propaganda during wars. Surely Micah had been misinformed. "It's beyond the scope of reasoning that a country's leader would deliberately kill off his own countrymen. It's got to be a mistake."

"That's what everyone wants to believe. But my brother is there. He's witnessed it in both Russia and Poland. He's heard about it happening in other European countries—wherever Germany has overtaken the area. Entire communities of Jews, gone overnight. Or marched through the center of town and loaded on trains, carted away to who knows where."

"But they have to be somewhere."

"Yes, somewhere." Micah's white face appeared grim in the muted shadows. "To what Jeremiah calls death camps. Or graves. Jeremiah talked to a farmer who hid in the trees and watched a group of soldiers force twenty to thirty Jewish men and boys to dig a pit. Then, when the pit was done, the men and boys were lined up in front of it and the soldiers shot them down like—"

"Stop!" Lydia covered her ears. "I don't want to hear it!"

"I don't blame you." Bitterness filled Micah's tone. "I didn't want to know about it, either. No one in their right mind would *want* to know about it. If we don't know, then we can't be blamed, can we? But Jeremiah knows, and he told me. And I can't go on knowing without helping. Because knowing and not helping makes me just as guilty as those who are doing the killing. So I'll keep on doing whatever I can to bring Jewish children to safety."

Lydia broke out with gooseflesh, fear turning her mouth dry. "But you and Jeremiah can't do this alone. Why doesn't America help? You said the children were on a Red Cross ship—can't the Red Cross do something? They help the prisoners of war—I know they do."

Micah sighed tiredly. "Red tape, Lydia. The Red Cross is allowed to help prisoners of war. But the Jews have been declared people without a state and are therefore banned from receiving humanitarian assistance."

"But that's ridiculous! They are obviously citizens of their own countries."

"Not according to Hitler. And Jeremiah thinks no one is willing to force the issue for fear we'll be banned from helping our own military men who are held in prisoner-of-war camps."

Lydia's mind reeled with this knowledge. She hugged herself tighter, shivering despite the warm summer night. "But where do you find these children? Does Jeremiah break them out of the . . . the death camps?" She shuddered, never imagining that such words would come out of her mouth.

Micah shook his head. "Jeremiah discovered that a group of Polish Baptists living along the Styr River were hiding a few Jewish children. The Baptists told him about some other area farmers who dared to do the same. Imagine—children living underground in root cellars, or in tiny attic rooms or barn lofts, never seeing the sunshine or breathing fresh air. Hiding—just hiding in fear."

Lydia didn't want to imagine it. Suddenly children playing on a rooftop didn't seem so terrible.

Micah continued. "First he asked me to send food and clothing so he could provide assistance to the families who harbored Jewish children. Just like here, people are rationed on what food supplies they can purchase—having those extra mouths to feed is a real burden. But after a while, he realized that the longer the children remained in hiding, the more likely someone would find out and turn them in. There are rewards offered for turning in Jews or anyone harboring them. And the punishment for helping a Jew is death."

Lydia gasped. "Micah, this frightens me! I'm not sure I want you involved—"

Micah gave her a look so full of disappointment, heat built in her cheeks. "'Whosoever shall receive one of such children in my name, receiveth me.'" Micah's soft recitation was a knife in her heart. "Jeremiah included that reference from Mark in his letter when he asked if I would help. Would you be able to say no to such a plea?"

Lydia shook her head, her chin quivering. "But . . . but what exactly *is* your part in all of this?"

"I find people in the United States willing to take in a Jewish child, and Jeremiah finds a way to sneak them out of Europe. He's never told me how he arranges it. He's trying to protect his sources over there."

Lydia ran her hands through her hair. Micah's ugly descriptions left her unsettled. Tainted. Would she ever feel safe and secure again? "How many children have you and Jeremiah brought out?"

"Only twenty-two. In almost two years, that's all. He has to limit himself to those who speak fluent Polish. If the child spoke Yiddish and someone overheard, the whole group would be in danger. It's nearly broken Jeremiah's heart to leave so many behind." Tears glinted in the corners of his eyes. "Only twenty-two of the hundreds of thousands who have been rounded up and forced into horrible places where they aren't fed properly or cared for the way children should be—or worse. It's not enough. It's not nearly enough. . . ."

They sat in silence, the darkness of the parking garage surrounding them. Lydia had never been afraid of the dark, but with this new knowledge forcing its truth into her resistant conscience, she wanted to escape to a sunlit field or a beach or a mountaintop.

Lydia reached through the quiet shadows and touched Micah's arm. "How can I help?"

Micah whirled on her with a look so fierce she instinctively shrank back. "You can help by not telling anyone what I've told you about what Jeremiah is doing over there. The more people who know, the more likely we put Jeremiah's life—and the lives of those helping him—in danger. If Hitler's conspirators found out what my brother is doing, his life would be worthless, American minister or not. There are dozens of places for a man like Jeremiah to disappear, a dozen ways for a handicapped man to die without anyone questioning it. And if he dies, his cause dies with him. No more lives saved."

She closed her eyes to ward off tears. A longing to return home—to cradle Nicky—washed over her. She opened her eyes to find Micah staring blankly ahead, lost in thought. She touched his arm again. The muscles were hard, his body tense, but he didn't withdraw from her gentle touch.

"Micah, I know you're angry at me for following you. I shouldn't have done it, but I'm not sorry. I won't tell a soul what you've told me. You must be silent to protect your brother. How well I understand that." She thought again of the secrets of Nicky's parentage. Micah nodded, and she sensed his thoughts aligned with hers. "But whatever you need—money, clothing, food, medical supplies—you tell me, and I'll get it for you. Father gives me a monthly stipend that well exceeds Nicky's and my needs. Please let me help you and Jeremiah."

Her voice quavered and tears blurred her vision, but she refused to give in to emotion. With her hand on Micah's arm, she kept her gaze aimed at his, awaiting his answer.

At last Micah released a sigh, his chin dropping. Then he raised his face, and his brow furrowed. "Lydia, what are you doing here?"

13

Lydia tipped her head, scowling. Micah rephrased his question. "What business has brought you to New York?"

"Oh." She slid her hand from his arm and shifted in the seat to face forward. "We can discuss it tomorrow. You said you'd take me to the clinic and we'd talk there, remember?" She glanced at him, her expression apprehensive.

An unexpected wave of relief rolled through Micah. He was too tired to think straight right now. "Okay, let's talk tomorrow morning." He peeked at his watch and grimaced. "Or, rather, later this morning. It's already tomorrow." He pulled himself out of the car, then went around to open her door. Lydia curled her hand around his forearm, and they left the garage together. After the intense evening, he found it healing to stroll along empty sidewalks, yellow lamplight glinting on Lydia's dark hair, silence around them.

At his apartment building, he waited for her to retrieve a key from her pocket, then took it and unlocked the door for her. "Sleep well. I'll knock on your door around eight thirty. I need to be at the clinic by nine." She crossed the threshold, and he started to move on. Then he remembered something and turned back.

"We'll walk to the clinic, so wear something comfortable on your feet." He looked at her slippers. "The sidewalks will wear out those flimsy things. I trust you brought something else?"

A weary smile graced her face. "Good, serviceable Oxfords. Any other directions for my apparel?"

Micah shrugged, hiding a yawn with his hand. "Wear whatever you'd like if you plan to be an observer. If you'd like to get your hands dirty, however, and perform a few nursing duties, dress accordingly."

"Fine, although I'm sure my nursing abilities will be a bit rusty. I've only practiced them on Nicky since returning from Schofield."

"You did just fine with the little girl who came in."

To his gratification, color bloomed in her cheeks.

She offered one more timorous smile. "Good night, Micah. Thank you for a—" The blush on her cheeks exploded into a bold red. Micah's face heated, as well. They hadn't been on a date. Her voice faltering, she finished, "For an . . . enlightening evening."

He nodded, and she closed the door. He scuffed to his own apartment, let himself in, kicked off his shoes, and fell facedown across the bed without undressing. Jeremiah's letter pressed against his rib cage. He rolled onto his back and reached beneath his shirt to remove the envelope. Sliding his thumb under the flap, he opened the envelope and pulled out the single handwritten sheet. Jeremiah's brief message shared that he was well and he planned to collect more "souvenirs," so Micah should expect another "package" when shipment could be arranged—he would be in touch.

Micah sighed and placed the letter on his chest. He closed his eyes and whispered a prayer for safety for his brother. Then another thought followed. "And, Lord, please allow me to do more than collect packages for Jeremiah. Give me a bigger task." A feeling of fulfillment touched him, and he scowled, trying to sort out the emotion. But before understanding could be reached, tiredness took control and he fell asleep.

Lydia lay wide awake on her side on the lumpy mattress, her fists beneath her chin. She'd never been so tired, yet she couldn't close her eyes. Pictures flashed through her mind—of those three older-than-their-years children in the backseat of Micah's coupe; of Nicky, safe and warm in his bed at home while Nic Pankin prowled the city, trying to find him; of the children Micah had mentioned who survived hidden in cellars away from the sun; of death camps and guns and burning buildings and families ripped apart.

What a task Micah and Jeremiah had undertaken. She searched her memory for news articles pertaining to Jewish deaths. She knew she'd seen a few sporadic articles, usually tucked toward the back of the newspaper, but none of them had impacted her the way Micah's words had. Perhaps it was hearing the horrors spoken aloud, seeing the faces of the innocent ones who had been impacted, that had made the difference. She didn't think she would ever look at a newspaper again without seeking information on this topic. How could anyone ignore the situation once they'd been exposed to the reality of it?

In an anguished whisper, she prayed aloud. "Oh, Lord, what can I do to make a difference?"

You'll know in time. Be patient and wait.

Lydia sat bolt upright in the bed, the springs twanging with the sudden movement. She searched the dark room. Her heart pounded so hard she could scarcely breathe. She had *heard* a voice as clearly as if the person stood next to her. Yet she was alone. Grasping the sheet in both fists, she braved a question. "Who . . . who is there?"

Only silence greeted her ears, but a feeling of calm flowed from her head to her toes. Tears filled her eyes. She knew Whose voice she'd heard. She looked to the cracked plaster ceiling. "I will do whatever You ask. I will welcome the task, in Your name."

The distressing visions cleared, no longer haunting the darkness behind her eyelids. Curling into a ball, she fell into a deep, dreamless sleep.

At half past eight in the morning, Micah tapped lightly on Lydia's door. If she still slept after their late night, he didn't want to disturb her, but almost immediately the door swung wide. His eyebrows flew high, and he blurted, "What are you wearing?" He couldn't hide the laughter in his voice.

Lydia glanced down her own length, attempting an innocent look that developed into a knowing smirk. "What? You've never seen a woman in coveralls before?"

"Well, sure, on the posters of Rosie the Riveter." Micah chuckled. "But Lydia the Riveter? Never would have expected that."

She gave a feminine shrug that contradicted the masculinity of her apparel. "I would think you'd know by now to expect the unexpected where I am concerned." He snorted, and she plunked her fists on her hips. He held up a hand in apology, and her forbidding demeanor melted. She smoothed the legs of the coveralls. "I'm just glad I thought to bring them along. I wear these when I go to the plant with Father. They should be perfect for 'getting my hands dirty' today, as you said last night."

Micah stood in her doorway, unable to turn his gaze from her. Her flashing eyes and the trim-fitting uniform painted a more beguiling picture than he could have imagined. Would he be able to walk down the street beside her and not take her hand?

Stay focused, Hatcher. You've got enough on your plate without adding a romance with Lydia Eldredge to the mix.

"Do you know a good laundress?"

Micah blinked, uncertain he'd heard her correctly. "What?"

"A laundress." She disappeared for a moment, returning with a folded yellow skirt in her hands. "I got blood on my suit, and it needs to be laundered."

Micah took it from her. "There's a laundry service around the corner. We can drop off your suit on the way." He glanced at the smudge of dried blood. "I'll pay to have it cleaned."

"Micah . . ." Her tone held mild reproof.

Firmly, he said, "It was soiled at my clinic helping with one of my patients. I'll cover the bill, and that's final."

She clicked her tongue on her teeth, shaking her head. He braced himself for an argument, but she sighed. "Very well. Thank you, Dr. Hatcher."

"You're welcome. Now let's go." He gestured toward the staircase and she locked her door, clipping along beside him with an eager bounce in her step. Just to be on the safe side, he slipped his hands into his trouser pockets.

They stopped at a bakery and purchased sweet-smelling sticky buns for their breakfast, munching on them as they walked. When they rounded the corner leading to the clinic, Lydia pointed to a woman and two children waiting outside the doors. "Customers already."

Micah nodded. "Let's get busy."

Customers, as Lydia had called them, kept them occupied for most of the morning. Micah appreciated Lydia's assistance. She stepped in without direction to clean and bandage scraped knees, take temperatures, and—after only brief instruction—file the records for each visitor. Remembering her prissy demeanor when he'd worked with her at Schofield, he marveled at her willingness to do anything that was asked of her.

At one o'clock, Micah left the clinic in the hands of a volunteer and walked Lydia to a small café, where they sat outside under a striped awning. Lydia refused to go inside the way she was dressed, and Micah didn't argue. He preferred the outdoor setting to the smoky interior anyway.

They feasted on towering roast beef sandwiches dipped in a rich juice that dribbled down his chin and speckled his trouser legs. But what were a few juice drops when he had the chance to sit across the table from Lydia and gaze into her pretty face? The pleasure of their sunshine-splashed lunch contrasted with the shadowy activities of last night, and Micah discovered a real joy in basking in today's bright moments.

When they'd finished eating, Micah leaned his elbows on the table and prompted, "Okay, it's been long enough. Now you have to tell me what you're doing here."

Lydia swallowed, wiped her mouth with her napkin, and fixed him with a somber look. "I came to ask for your help."

Micah raised one eyebrow. "You had to come all the way to New York to ask? A letter or telephone call or telegram wouldn't suffice?"

Lydia released a wry laugh. "I suppose it does seem odd, doesn't it? But I didn't want you to have to handle it all alone—so I'm here to do my part, too."

Micah laced his fingers together and rested his chin on his knuckles. "Suppose you tell me what the two of us are in cahoots about." Again, last night's mission tripped through his brain. How quickly she'd become entangled in his life. And he discovered he was eager to entangle himself in hers.

Lydia leaned forward and assumed a conspiratorial air.

"Father and I went to see Mrs. Fenwick—the midwife who delivered Nicky—as you suggested. We intended to ask her to testify that Eleanor wanted me to take Nicky. But she wasn't there. A neighbor said she had packed her bags and left out of fear of Nic Pankin, who had been coming around and threatening her."

A swell of sympathy tightened Micah's chest. "Poor lady. It must have been awful for her."

Lydia grimaced. "She left without leaving word for Father. The neighbor told us Mrs. Fenwick has no husband or children, but she does have a sister. And the only clue to this sister's whereabouts was a picture of the Statue of Liberty on a postcard she had sent to Mrs. Fenwick."

"So you came here hoping to find Mrs. Fenwick?"

Lydia nodded eagerly. "Yes. I know it will be rather like hunting for a needle in a haystack—"

Micah gave a brief snort of laughter.

"But the Bible says that if we have faith like a grain of mustard seed, nothing will be impossible for us. So I'm stepping out in faith that I will find Mrs. Fenwick, and I'll be able to take her back to Boston. Then, with her help, I'll gain legal custody of Nicky."

Micah peered into Lydia's flushed, expectant face. "What is the name of Mrs. Fenwick's sister?"

"I don't know."

"In what borough does she live?"

She shrugged, lifting her hands in a gesture of defeat. "I don't know that, either. I'm not even completely sure she's in New York. The sister might have just visited and sent the postcard. But we have to start somewhere."

Micah whistled through his teeth. He wasn't one to stomp on someone's faith, but this plan of Lydia's seemed doomed to fail. Lydia's reference to a needle in a haystack was accurate. He didn't even know where to begin looking. But with Lydia's dark-eyed gaze aimed hopefully in his direction, he couldn't find the heart to voice his gloomy thoughts. "I suppose we could ask around. Make some phone calls to apartment buildings—"

Lydia's face lit. "Then you'll help me?"

"Sure I'll help, but I can't guarantee we'll be successful. How long were you planning to stay?"

Her expression clouded. "Not long—no more than a week, if possible. I miss Nicky terribly."

Micah's heart turned over. "Well, then we'd better get started right away." He dropped two crumpled bills and a few coins on the table and stood. "You're done getting your hands dirty for the day. I'll sit you down with the telephone and a number directory. You can start calling apartments."

Lydia dashed around the table and threw her arms around Micah's neck. "Oh, thank you, Micah! I knew I could count on you."

For a moment, Micah stood with his arms at his sides, stunned by the impulsive embrace, but then he awkwardly patted her back and nudged her aside. He smiled into her upturned face. "It's just a telephone, Lydia. I'm not sure it warrants this much gratitude." His gaze darted across the curious café patrons.

She looked, too, at the number of people watching, her cheeks turning a becoming shade of pink. She brushed nonexistent crumbs from her thighs in a self-conscious gesture. "Sorry. I forgot myself for a moment." An impish grin climbed one cheek. "I bet you've never been hugged by Rosie the Riveter before."

Micah guffawed, but then quickly stifled it. "Not in broad daylight." He winked, and he and Lydia shared a laugh. The joined laughter felt good. Warming. Then she locked her gaze on his once more. A soft smile tipped up the corners of her full lips, and a desire to lean forward and place his lips against hers rose from deep within.

The busboy hurried over and began to clear the table with a noisy clattering of silverware. The desire scooted for cover. Micah breathed a sigh of relief as normalcy returned. He held out his arm. "Let's head back."

Lydia slipped her hand into the curve of his elbow, and he escorted her in proper fashion back to the clinic. Without talking. Without looking at her. But very aware of her presence.

14

Mr. Pankin, I am very quickly losing my patience with you."

Although the woman spoke softly, her tone even and mild, Nic bristled. Rich or not, she had no business talking to him the way she would a snot-nosed child. He balled his hand into a fist inside his jacket pocket. "Yeah, well, I'm getting pretty impatient myself. Don't you think I'm eager to get my kid settled here?" Until he accomplished it, he wouldn't receive his promised payment. "The delays can't be helped."

Mrs. Bachman crossed her legs. Her skirt inched up, revealing her silk-covered calf. Nic had a hard time not staring. She dressed so nice, and the way she smelled—a floral scent filled his nostrils every time she moved. When was the last time Nic had enjoyed the pleasure of a quality woman? Not since Eleanor.

"Mr. Pankin?"

He gulped, his body jolting. "What?"

The woman pressed her lips into a tight line. She rested her linked hands on her knee. "How much longer?"

Nic threw out a guess. "Another week."

Her lips pressed so tightly they nearly disappeared.

He blurted, "Could be sooner if I had some cash. My old

truck, it needs repairs. So I've been afoot. Or I hafta hire a cab. Slows me down."

Mrs. Bachman drew in a slow breath, her nostrils flaring slightly. She peered at him from beneath the fluff of yellow bangs. For long seconds she held him captive with a penetrating stare while the ornate grandfather clock in the corner ticked out each second. At last she sat upright, curling her hands over the carved lions' heads on the chair's armrests. "If I give you funds to repair your truck, you'll deliver the child to me within a week's time?"

Nic swallowed, then bobbed his head in a brusque nod.

"One week?" She held up a slender finger, its nail painted the same pale pink color as the suit that fit her frame as snugly as a potato wore its skin. Oh, she was a woman of quality. Too bad she'd chosen to spoil herself by spending her day sipping spirits. Of course, if he ever caught her fully soused, he might be able to have some fun with her.

Caught up in his daydreams, he missed what she said. He scowled. "What?"

"You'll deliver the child by August fourth. Is that correct?"

Nic licked his lips, gathering his thoughts. "Yes. That's right."

"Very well, then. Wait here." She rose and strode from the room, leaving Nic in the middle of the parlor sofa with his hand twitching inside his jacket pocket and his scalp tingling. Anticipation sent his pulse into hopeful gallops. How much would she give him? Enough for half a dozen packets? If he didn't have to spend his nights pilfering items to pawn to feed his habit, he'd be able to put his full attention on getting his kid. In no time at all, he'd be rolling in money. Five thousand dollars! As much as he could make in two years at the packing factory. Saliva pooled in his mouth as he thought about the freedom the money would bring.

Footsteps alerted him to her return. He stood and turned, but instead of Mrs. Bachman, the butler—a dour-looking man with thick gray hair and a handlebar mustache—approached. He stopped several feet from Nic and extended a crisp fifty-dollar bill between two fingers. Nic stared at it, nearly groaning in disappointment. He'd hoped for at least twice that amount.

The man's gaze traveled from Nic's uncombed hair to the worn toes of his boots and back again. Disdain twisted his lips. "The mistress wishes me to remind you the delivery is due no later than August fourth."

Nic snatched the bill and jammed it into his pocket. "I know."

"And you shall be here as expected with delivery in tow?"

Nic narrowed his gaze, glowering at the man. "Yeah."

"Then allow me to see you out." He spun on the heel of his highly polished black lace-up shoe.

Nic charged past him, deliberately brushing the man's shoulder and pushing him off-balance. "I can see myself out." He gave the door a slam behind him.

❧

Crack!

Micah jumped when the front door slammed into its casing. He raised his head from the order blank he'd been completing. Lydia stormed into the clinic and flopped into the chair facing his desk. She slumped forward, her dark hair hiding her face, and rested her forehead on the desktop. He rose and rounded the desk. Placing a hand on her shoulder, he asked, "No luck?"

Lydia sat up straight and ran her hands through the silky strands of her hair, leaving it looking disheveled. "I feel like I've visited every apartment manager in Queens, Manhattan, and Brooklyn. No one has a Mrs. Fenwick on their resident list."

Micah crouched beside her chair. "Well, you didn't expect to find her quickly, did you? Searching out a needle in a haystack is a rather cumbersome prospect."

Lydia gazed in his direction, and it grieved him to see two bright tears glittering in her dark eyes. "I suppose I need to be patient. But it's been three days. I miss Nicky so much. And I'm worried about him. Finding Mrs. Fenwick is so important. What if I never find her?"

"Whoa, hold up a minute there." Micah fixed a stern look on his face, although he really wanted to wrap his arms around her and offer sympathetic comfort. "That's a defeatist attitude if I ever heard one. And I never thought I'd hear it from you. What happened to the brave lady who chased me through the dark streets of New York a few nights ago?"

Lydia's lips quivered as she considered Micah's question. "She's tired, I suppose."

Micah squeezed her shoulder, resisting the urge to lift his hand and smooth her hair. "I think I know what you need. You need a dose of Nicky." He picked up the telephone receiver and placed it in her hand. "Call him. Talk to him. Remind yourself why you're here and how much he's worth all this fuss and bother. Then when you're done, we'll have a little chat about that mustard seed of faith you mentioned, okay?"

"Oh, Micah, calling Boston would be so expensive!" But she didn't put the phone aside.

Micah offered a grin. "Dial. Doctor's orders." He returned to his order forms while Lydia followed his direction. He tried not to listen, but he couldn't help smiling when she laughed over something Nicky said. Hearing the joy in her voice gave his heart a lift. He rose to locate an envelope for his order, but Lydia interrupted.

"Micah? Nicky would like to say hello to you. Do you have a minute?"

"I sure do." He reached across the desk and took the telephone from her. "Howdy, partner. What are you up to?"

"Micah-my-friend!" Nicky's high-pitched voice came through the static on the line and straight to Micah's heart. "Guess what! I was lonesome for Mama, so Poppy buyed me a pet! A bird! It's a yellow bird and it sings when it wants to! I named it Buggy!"

Micah laughed. Nicky's animated face appeared in his memory, bringing forth a rush of affection. "That's a wonderful name for a bird, Nicky. I hope I get to meet him sometime."

"When Mama comes back, you come, too, an' you can meet him. He'll sing for you, prob'ly." While Micah searched for a way to respond, Nicky rushed on with a change of subject. "Can I talk to Mama?"

"Sure, Nicky, I'll hand you over. You take care of Buggy, okay?"

"Okay, Micah. Micah?"

Micah paused. "Yes?"

"I love you."

The simple, honest, innocent statement created a warmth that moved from the center of Micah's chest outward until his whole body felt aglow. He clutched the telephone receiver with two hands and managed to answer in a voice hoarse with emotion. "Right back atcha, partner. Now here's your mama."

Micah handed the telephone to Lydia and settled back in his chair. He might have been floating on a cloud rather than seated in a warped, slatted wood chair. His heart beat hard and his chest tightened with pleasure. The little boy's sweet voice played itself again and again in his mind. *I love you.* Were there any more beautiful words than those?

God, I thought I had too much to do to be lovin' this child and his mama. But Lydia's seen what I'm doing with Jeremiah, and she accepted it. Even offered to help. Do You reckon she might be willin' to be my permanent helpmeet?

His breath came in little spurts as he considered where his prayer had just led him. Nicky and his too-pretty mama, whose inner beauty was becoming more apparent each minute he spent in her presence, had already wormed their way into Micah's heart. He shifted to watch Lydia as she finished her conversation with Nicky. A reluctant smile teased his lips. How he would miss her when she headed back to Boston. Because she'd have to go back. It was her home, and Nicky waited for her. She would only be here for a short time on this visit. But maybe . . .

He made a snap decision. It might not be a sensible decision, but sometimes love overstepped the bounds of being sensible. As soon as she finished her conversation with Nicky, he'd ask.

15

Lydia sighed as she placed the receiver on its hook. "I sure miss that little scamp."

Micah smiled, and something lingering in his eyes set her heart aflutter. "Bet you do," Micah said. "I hardly know him, and I think I miss him, too."

Lydia forced a light laugh, seeking a grasp on her emotions. "Nicky does have a way of growing on you." Then she paused, puzzled. "Why do you suppose he chose the name Buggy for a canary?"

Micah threw back his head and laughed. "Oh, I know, but I'm not tellin'. You'll have to ask him yourself when you get back."

Lydia sent him a chastising look intended to get to the truth, but he was in one of his teasing moods—he winked at her and pretended to lock his lips. She pushed up from the table and shook a finger in his direction. "Sometimes you're as much a little boy as Nicky, Dr. Micah Hatcher." But the smile in her voice ruined the insult. Micah just grinned back at her, and her foolish heart set up such a clamor she thought she might swoon.

"Lydia, did you bring a dress-up outfit with you?"

Lydia had reached to shift the telephone back into its original position, but Micah's question stilled her hands. She angled her head, meeting his gaze. Her emotions turned so topsy-turvy she wasn't sure she could form an answer. So she drew on her own teasing as a cover and threw her arms wide. "You mean dressier than my Rosie the Riveter coveralls?"

Micah offered the expected chuckle. "Yes, somewhat dressier than coveralls."

Lydia lost her ability to tease. Something in his eyes . . . She swallowed. "Yes. The traveling suit I was wearing when I arrived. Why—" Her dry throat made her voice husky. She coughed delicately and tried again. "Why do you ask?"

He shrugged, moving away from the desk and taking measured steps in her direction. Her pulse increased its tempo with each inch closing between them. "You've had a few rough days, and I thought I'd take you out this evening for a little relaxation."

"Y-you don't have to do that." Her tongue became clumsy in response to her racing heartbeat. Such an effect this man had on her senses! She thought she'd set aside her infatuation with Micah Hatcher when she left Schofield, but apparently those feelings had lain dormant beneath the surface, waiting for an opportunity to come to life. And now they burgeoned beyond reckoning.

"But I'd like to. We could drive into Manhattan to the Plaza Hotel. Have you seen it? It's a masterpiece of architecture. I think you'd enjoy it."

Lydia tipped her chin downward and raised her eyebrows. "The Plaza?"

"Yes." He advanced one more step, bringing himself close enough to touch if she stretched out her hand. "They have a tea room—called the Palm Court." A grin crept up one cheek. "Palm trees—Hawaii. Might make you feel less lonesome."

Memories flooded her mind, all of which included Micah.

Lydia drew in a steadying breath. "But I don't miss Hawaii. I miss my son."

He shrugged, a sheepish gesture. "Well, I don't know of any 'Nicky' tea rooms, but I can do my best to get your mind on other things so you're not so homesick for him. Would you like to go?"

Lydia licked her lips. Yes, she wanted to go. Not to see the Palm Court Tea Room and the Plaza Hotel as much as to spend time in Micah's company. Which, of course, was folly. But how could she look into his handsome face and expressive blue eyes and refuse? She gave a quick nod before common sense took control. "Yes, I would like to go."

Micah clapped his hands together. "Good! I'll lock up. We'll clean up at the apartment, and I'll find us a cab. It should be fun."

Lydia watched him remove his smock, her lower lip caught between her teeth. *Fun?* She shook her head, stifling a self-deprecating huff. *Fun to fall helplessly, hopelessly, foolishly in love with you?*

Lydia sat across from Micah at a small, round, linen-shrouded table. A young woman in a long Grecian-style dress ran her fingers expertly across the strings of a harp, creating soothing background music as flickering candlelight illuminated his face and brought out the deeper rim of his irises. Without asking her opinion, he had ordered orange pekoe tea and a variety of sandwiches—watercress and egg salad on rye, salmon on ficelle sprinkled with fresh basil, and prosciutto on carrot bread. The waiter also delivered a plate of fresh fruit. Lydia's mouth watered as she gazed at the neatly arranged melon slices, grapes, and strawberries, and without warning a memory surfaced.

"Oh, Micah, remember the little café at the beach? Where

was that?" She wrinkled her brow, pressing her memory. Then she brightened, holding up one finger in a gesture of success. "Haleiwa! Remember they brought out an arrangement of fruit so pretty we hesitated to eat it?"

"I remember that evening well." Micah picked up a bright red strawberry between his thumb and forefinger and lifted it to his mouth. "It was the first time Holden and I spent time with you and Callie away from the hospital."

Lydia nibbled a skinless grape, replaying the evening in her mind's eye. Did Micah recall how childishly she'd behaved when Micah chose to escort her roommate, Callie, and she'd been stuck with Micah's friend, Holden? She decided not to ask.

The harpist finished a tune, and restrained applause broke out across the room. Micah and Lydia joined in briefly. The music began again, and Lydia allowed her gaze to move around the tea room, taking in the tapestries and gilt and tall columns. And of course the potted palms.

She released a sigh of satisfaction and faced Micah again. "This is a beautiful room. A very relaxing, enjoyable spot. Do you come here often?"

"I've been here twice—both times with special ladies."

She raised her eyebrows at him, hiding the rush of jealousy his statement evoked.

He chuckled softly, reaching for one of the slivered ham-on-carrot-bread sandwiches. "When my parents came to visit me shortly after I arrived, I brought my mama. And now, you."

Heat filled Lydia's cheeks as she realized he'd called her one of his "special ladies."

Micah continued. "So, no, I don't come often. I don't get away from the clinic much."

Lydia swished the silver-plated tea-leaf spoon through the hot water in her hand-painted, footed teacup. "How long have you been at the clinic, Micah?" She placed a watercress sandwich on her plate then lifted her eyes to his face.

"Well, let's see . . ." He puckered his lips, eyes rolled upward. "Almost two years now, I guess. I stayed a little longer at Schofield than I'd originally been commissioned, to help with the cleanup after the attack, and then I spent one month in Arlington with my family before moving here."

Lydia nodded, taking a small bite of the sandwich. She swallowed before speaking again. "And do you plan to go back to Texas someday?"

"I plan to follow God's leadin'."

Lydia smiled, noting the twang sneaking into his voice. Being in New York must have softened it somewhat—it had been much more noticeable at Schofield—but when he was very relaxed, or in a teasing mood, the Texas twang made itself known.

"Wherever He sends me, I'll go. Right now I know I'm supposed to stay here. God planted me here, and it's the perfect spot to be helpin' Jeremiah. I can't even consider leavin' as long as I still have packages to retrieve."

Micah's reference to "packages" brought to mind once more the three little children they'd delivered to the rabbi. Lydia leaned forward and whispered, "Do you suppose those children are in homes right now, sitting down to supper?"

"I hope so." His tone deepened with emotion. "They deserve normalcy after what they've been through."

Lydia nodded, then tried to set aside thoughts of the Jewish children. She really didn't want to focus on anything negative this evening. It was so nice to be with Micah in this pleasant atmosphere, enjoying simple but tasty food. Being with Micah was intoxicating—having his blue eyes focused on her whenever she spoke, watching his strong features relax into the familiar lopsided smile that tugged at her heart, admiring his broad shoulders encased in a neatly tailored black coat. . . . The mere action of looking across the table at him caused her pulse to increase and her mouth to go dry. It gave her reckless ideas, too. She dropped her attention to her flute-edged plate and picked up her sandwich once more.

"What about you, Lydia?"

Her gaze bounced upward to meet Micah's.

"What are your future plans? Other than being mother to Nicky, I mean. Will you use your nursing training in Boston?"

Lydia gave a gentle shrug. "To be honest, Micah, because Father does so well, I haven't had to think about doing anything except take care of Nicky. In the past few months, Father has been encouraging me to consider becoming plant foreman." She grinned. "Or, more accurately, fore*woman*. He'd like for me to know how things operate so I can keep the business going, and then eventually give it to Nicky."

She could have sworn Micah's face pinched in disapproval, but as quickly as the expression appeared, it cleared and a gentle smile replaced the frown.

"That's a fine offer. There are so many women assuming roles they wouldn't have had before the war. And as bright as you are, you'd probably be a terrific businesswoman."

Lydia laughed softly, pleased by his compliment. "I don't know if I'm interested in taking over the business, but Father has no other children. I feel obligated."

"Have you prayed about it?"

The question caught Lydia by surprise. It seemed so obvious that she would inherit Father's business. Why should she pray about it? "Actually, no. It didn't seem necessary. What other choices do I have?"

Micah's gaze softened. "Lydia, you have many choices available. The question is finding where God wants you to be. He has a plan for your life, and you should be actively seeking His plan."

Lydia considered his words, but before she could form an answer, the waiter came around and asked if they'd care for dessert. Micah tipped his head and asked, "What would you recommend?"

"If you want to sample something unique, I suggest the fig preserves on currant scones. If you prefer a more traditional dessert, then the custard tarts with fresh peaches are quite well received by most patrons."

Micah looked at Lydia, one eyebrow raised. Lydia pressed a hand against her stomach and shook her head. "Nothing for me, Micah. I've had quite enough."

Micah turned back to the waiter. "I suppose we'll pass on dessert. Thank you." The waiter placed a bill on the table next to Micah's elbow and disappeared. Micah picked up the bill, then smiled brightly at Lydia. "You know, as long as we're here, we should take a peek in the lobby of the hotel. It's quite somethin'. Then, if you're up to it, we could take a stroll through Central Park."

Imagining walking arm in arm with Micah on a summer evening sent a shiver of delight up Lydia's spine. "That sounds lovely."

Micah paid the bill, then escorted her with a hand resting lightly on the small of her back around the corner to the Fifth Avenue lobby. Micah held open the glass door for Lydia to precede him. She took three steps into the massive lobby and stopped, completely enthralled.

"Oh, Micah, it's beautiful!" She looked up at a recessed ceiling at least twenty-four feet above her head. Plaster moldings with gilt accents ran the full circumference of the ceiling. Square flowerlike decorations dressed each corner. A crystal chandelier hung from a gold chain, the light from its two dozen lamps reflecting on the highly polished wood floor. Tiny crystal teardrops ran like rain from the chandelier, creating hundreds of tiny prisms around the room.

The suited elderly man behind the counter glanced up, smiled, and invited, "Step on in, miss. Welcome to the Plaza."

Fire seared Lydia's cheeks. "Oh, we're not staying. I only wanted to look."

The man chuckled lightly. "That will be easier for you if you step all the way in."

Lydia laughed at herself, flashing an embarrassed look in Micah's direction. With his warm fingers anchored on her spine, he propelled her forward. Her heels clicked on the marble floor, then abruptly muted as she stepped onto a large Oriental rug. The rug created an island in the center of the room, so she remained there, turning in circles until her eyes had drunk their fill of the gilt-touched plaster moldings decorating the walls and front of the desk. The white-and-gold décor offered eye-pleasing elegance.

Chinese urns larger than Nicky stood sentry at the sides of every doorway, feather-like fronds splayed from the open tops. Unique arrangements of Louis XIV furniture upholstered in wine velvet invited one to sit and bask in the hotel's beauty.

"You're right, Micah. This is quite something." She shook her head, awed by the grandeur of the hotel. "I'm so glad New York hasn't been bombed. I imagine many fine buildings like this have been destroyed in Paris." The thought tarnished the edges of her pleasure.

Micah's hand returned to her back. "Let's not talk about the war tonight, Lydia. Tonight is for . . . well, for building happy memories. Okay?"

Lydia stared into his eyes. Building happy memories. What a

wonderful idea. Yes, she wanted happy memories to carry away from here. She nodded.

He raised his brows. "Are you ready for a walk through Central Park now?"

"Oh yes." She turned toward the door, but before leaving, she lifted her hand to wave at the man behind the counter. "Good night, sir. And thank you."

"You're welcome, miss. Enjoy your time in New York."

Lydia took Micah's arm as they stepped out of the hotel and moved to the curb. They waited for a clearing in the traffic, then dashed across the street, their feet clattering against the pavement. Once on the other side, she giggled. "Thank you for checking your stride to match mine! It's very hard to take big steps in this skirt."

Micah looked her up and down, causing her cheeks to heat again. How she hoped the falling dusk hid her blush. When he'd finished his perusal, he grinned. "I didn't mention this earlier, but you're quite fetchin' in that yellow suit. Probably as pretty as Nicky's canary."

Lydia burst out laughing. "Oh, Micah, what other man would dare to compare a woman to a canary and think that he was paying a compliment?"

"Do you mean I insulted you?" He assumed a hurt air, a hand on his chest.

Lydia shook her head, her hair lifting in the light breeze. She smoothed the strands back into place with her fingers. "Of course not. You just have your own brand of speech. Frankly, I find it refreshing."

"Good." Micah took her hand and slipped it through his elbow. He began moving her forward at a snail's pace. "Let's enjoy a leisurely stroll around the park. I'm sorry you missed the lilacs in bloom. Stunnin' to see. And the perfume of those blooms! Quite heady."

Lydia found it heady enough simply walking beside Dr. Micah Hatcher.

"But I do believe a few peonies might be hanging on, and the roses should be in full bloom, as well. So we'll see flowers."

Ahead, a bench waited beneath an arbor laden with thick vines covered in an abundance of deep green leaves and red roses in various stages of bloom. Micah pointed to it, and Lydia nodded in approval. Her sling-back white pumps, though stylish, were a far cry from walking shoes. Her aching feet welcomed the opportunity to rest.

Micah sat sideways on the bench, laying his arm across the back so his fingers rested right above her shoulder. His fingers didn't touch her, but her awareness of his presence was so acute she felt a tingle in her flesh. They sat in silence, breathing in the scent of the roses and listening to the traffic noises and the soft-toned conversations of other people walking through the park.

Lydia rolled her chin to face Micah, who gazed upward, seemingly admiring the darkening night sky. How handsome his profile appeared in the soft light. Micah's strong features gave an appearance of self-assurance. And he had such a giving heart. Admiration swelled in her chest, but then collapsed against a feeling of insignificance. She examined her own life. Still living with her parents, no real plan other than to learn her father's business, her only responsibility to care for Nicky . . .

As she recalled Micah's question concerning whether she'd prayed for God's plan for her life to be revealed, the words she'd heard the night after returning from the parking garage winged through her mind. She'd been clearly directed to be patient and wait—she would know in time what she was to do. She held no doubt the message came from God, and she also knew she needed to continue to pray and listen for God's leading. If she shared her experience with Micah, might he pray for her, as well? She turned to ask, and at the same time his head swiveled to meet her gaze.

"Lydia!" His eagerness dispelled the question quivering on the tip of her tongue. "I think I know how you can find Mrs. Fenwick!"

16

Micah caught hold of Lydia's shoulders, excitement coursing through him with such force he had a difficult time staying seated on the bench. "How did your father locate Mrs. Fenwick in the first place? When Eleanor needed help."

Lydia blinked a couple of times, as if awakening. "I believe—if I remember correctly—he found an advertisement in the newspaper, offering her services as midwife."

Forming a fist, Micah punched the air and let out a hoot of elation. "Of course! So doesn't it make sense that she will need to support herself in New York, if she's here?" He bounded to his feet. "She's probably still working as a midwife."

A slow smile crept up Lydia's cheek. "Her neighbor told Father and me how Mrs. Fenwick got a 'glow' from helping bring babies into the world. It does seem reasonable she would try to continue that work."

"And if she advertised in a newspaper before, it's logical she would choose the same means of alerting people to her services here." Micah slapped his forehead, laughing. "Why didn't I think of it before?" He held out his hand to Lydia. "Come on.

Let's go purchase every paper printed in New York and look through the advertisements."

Lydia bounced up, placing her hand in his. As his fingers closed around hers, his happiness suddenly dimmed. Once they found Mrs. Fenwick, Lydia would have no reason to remain in New York. The realization weighted his heart with sadness. Her responsibilities were in Boston, and his were here. The world was at war. This was no time for romance.

"This is no time to be squeamish." Nic held tight to Bosco's soiled shirt collar, their noses inches apart. Sweat dribbled down his forehead despite the late hour and the coolness of the dark alley. "I can't show my face over there again after that copper spotted me the other night. He'd recognize me right off."

Bosco's watery eyes crinkled with his grin. "Yeah, you're pretty hard to miss with that empty sleeve flappin' in the wind."

Nic gritted his teeth, battling the urge to release his pal's shirt long enough to plant his remaining fist in the middle of Bosco's whiskered face. "Never mind about that. Will you go or not?"

Bosco rubbed his hand up and down his cheek, stretching the skin and sending his oil-smudged corduroy cap askew. His callused fingers scraping across two days' growth of whiskers made the same sound as sandpaper on a board. "Dunno, Nic. Like I already told ya, it's a mighty big risk. Somebody sees me a-gawkin' in them windows an' calls the coppers? I end up in the clink for bein' a peepin' tom. Ain't too keen on spendin' another night on one o' them cots. Hard on my arthur-itis."

Nic rolled his eyes. "Didn't I say I'd bail you out if you got caught?" Not that Nic had money to squander for bail. But Bosco would turn yellow and run if he knew all Nic had in his pocket was the five dollars he'd promised in return for the alley rat's help. "So don't worry about sleepin' on a jailhouse cot. You'll be warm in your own bed no more'n an hour after you've done the job."

Bosco squinted at Nic. "An' you'll pay me five dollars? Just for peekin'?"

"Five dollars for five minutes of work. Just look for anything that would tell me if a kid lives in there. Toys. Little shoes, or a small-size jacket." Desperation crawled like lice across Nic's scalp. He was running out of time. If his kid wasn't with the Eldredges, he'd have to set his sights elsewhere. Maybe even kidnap someone else's kid. And he'd do it, if it came to that. He gave Bosco's jacket a yank. "You game?"

Bosco's lips stretched into a foolish grin, exposing yellowed teeth. "I'm game. Let's go."

"How many do you have on your list?"

Micah finished writing the last phone number and looked up at Lydia. He squelched a grin. She must have run her hands through her hair one too many times—it was a disheveled mess. Upon their return from dinner, they'd changed into comfortable clothes and met in her apartment to search the newspapers he'd purchased. In a wrinkled, untucked shirt and faded trousers, her hair flying wild, she was still too pretty for good sense to prevail.

He shifted to a seated position on the floor so he could look eye to eye with her where she lay on her stomach across the end of a swaybacked cot. "I have nine so far. How about you?"

"Nine, too." Lydia bent the corner of her list up and down with her thumb, her forehead creasing. "Do you really think Mrs. Fenwick will be one of these midwives?"

He reached out and tapped her knuckles with his pen. "Hey, what happened to that faith you were telling me about?"

She bounced to her knees, the cot springs complaining with the sudden movement. Her lips pursed for a moment, then she sighed. "I'm sorry. You're right. It's a good idea to search for her here. Of course, it would be simpler if they would put their names in the advertisement!"

"Ah, but I do enjoy a good challenge." Micah sent her a crooked smile intended to lighten the mood. To his pleasure, she grinned at him in response, then turned back to her paper.

Micah flipped to the front page of the *Long Island Daily Star* and checked the lead articles. An update on Operation Cobra caught his eye, and he eagerly scanned the columns of print. Germans had been forced to retreat as Sherman tanks and the armored infantry of the U.S. Second Armored Division broke through their defenses southwest of St. Lo. His heart tripped in excitement at the news. Anytime the Germans had to retreat gave reason for celebration. Micah prayed daily for the Germans' defeat, for liberation of the Jews held in captivity, and for Jeremiah to come home.

On the cot, Lydia tossed aside her paper and gave a loud huff. "There is nothing here about Jews being killed. Nothing! Wouldn't you think the murder of innocent civilians would warrant front-page coverage? Micah, I don't understand this situation at all."

"Neither do I." Micah lowered his paper to his lap. "My sincere hope is our government leaders honestly don't know the extent of Hitler's madness. If they know, and have chosen to ignore it, I'm not sure I could reconcile myself with the truth."

Her face crumpled into a grimace. "Micah, the other evening I said I didn't want you involved. I'm so sorry. You're my friend, and it frightened me to think of you being caught up in something that could bring harm to you." The genuine contrition shining in her eyes touched him deeply. She went on quietly.

"But I want you to know I'm proud of you. You and Jeremiah are risking everything to save those children. I admire you very much for what you're doing."

Micah remembered his disappointment at her initial reaction, and now pride swelled at her turnaround since she'd seen firsthand the little ones affected by the war's horror. "Thank you, Lydia. Maybe if more people came in contact with these innocent victims, more would be willin' to get involved."

She pushed off the cot, knelt, and pulled her suitcase from beneath the bed. With a flick of her fingers, she flipped it open and rummaged through it. Puzzled, Micah watched as she removed a leather pouch from the bottom of the bag and spun on her bottom to face him. Cross-legged on the floor, she cradled a flapped pouch in her hands and looked at him.

"Micah, Father gave me a significant amount of money to help in my search for Mrs. Fenwick." She extended her hands toward him, the pouch balanced on her open palms. "I want you to use it to purchase supplies for the children Jeremiah is helping."

Micah drew back. "Your father gave that to you for—"

"Father would understand, if he knew the situation. He won't ask for it back, so you don't have to worry about me talking about what you're doing." She jiggled the pouch, her fingertips nearly brushing his knees. "Take it, Micah. Let me help Jeremiah's worthy cause. Please?"

When she looked at him with her brown eyes glittering with hope, he didn't possess the strength to say no. His fingers trembling, he took the pouch. It was weighty in his hand, and his thoughts raced, considering the things this money could provide. "Thank you. I appreciate your help." He shook his head, blowing out a mighty breath. An amusing thought tripped through his mind. "You know, I have to tell you, when you were at Schofield, I thought you were spoiled and selfish." When she ducked her head, toying with a loose thread at the toe of one of her socks, he caught her chin with his fingers and lifted her face. "I'm glad I've had the chance to get to know you now. You're a wonderful person, Lydia. I'm glad you're my friend."

Warmth glowed in her eyes. She leaned back slightly, removing herself from his light touch. "I'm glad we're friends, too. One can't have too many of those, you know." She rested her weight on her palms, her head tipped to the side as she continued to fix her steady gaze on him. "You know, Micah, if I've changed, it's thanks to you and my roommate at Schofield. Yours and Callie's prayers, and your Christian witness, helped me find my way to God's Son. Having Him in my life has made such a difference." She paused, a scowl creasing her forehead. "But I must not be as good a witness as you two were. I can't seem to get through to my parents."

Micah set the pouch aside, crisscrossed his legs, and leaned his elbows on his knees. "What do you mean?"

"When I talk about God, or praying, or religion in any way, Father dismisses me. Mother listens, and I think if Father weren't so adamant against it, she would go to church with Nicky and me. But Father . . ." Sadness tinged her tone.

With what little Micah knew of her father, he could understand Lydia's frustration. Allan Eldredge wasn't a man who listened—he was a man who gave orders. How difficult it would be to witness to a man like that.

Lydia continued in a soft voice heavy with sorrow. "I told him we needed to pray about the situation with Nicky, and he turned off his light to go to sleep without addressing it. Then, when we discovered Mrs. Fenwick was no longer in Boston, Father acted as if it were my fault. He said something like, 'See how much your prayers helped?'" She licked her lips, her forehead puckering. "But if we'd found Mrs. Fenwick right away, I wouldn't have come to New York, and I wouldn't have met those little children. They touched me, Micah, deep inside, and that night after we came back—" She stopped and turned her face away.

Micah waited in silence, admiring the sweet turn of her jaw and full sweep of her thick lashes. Her chin trembled, and it took all of his self-control not to brush his hand across her shoulder in a gesture of comfort. After several seconds ticked by, he prodded gently, "What about that night, Lydia?"

Slowly she brought her gaze around. Two bright tears hovered on her eyelashes. "That night, when I prayed for those children and asked to do more to help, God . . . He answered me." She looked deeply into his eyes as if waiting for him to refute her claim. When he remained silent, she repeated, "God answered me, Micah."

Micah lifted his shoulders. "What did He say?"

She blinked rapidly, her lips parting in surprise. "You believe me?"

"Certainly. What did He say?"

Lydia leaned forward, eager and intense. "He said, 'Be patient and wait.' He said I'd know in time—be patient and wait." She lifted her chin, a hint of defensiveness appearing. "You don't think I was hearing things?"

Micah took a deep breath and linked his fingers together. "To my way of thinking, prayer goes two ways. Most people stop at one way. They pour everything out to God, and then they're done. But prayer is like a conversation. Takes two people talking to have a conversation. Why shouldn't God speak, too?"

"He's spoken to you?"

Micah nodded, allowing his mind to drift backward. "Sure He has. In a variety of ways. In a calmness I feel deep inside, in an idea I know didn't come from my own head, in an opportunity that leads me to places I wouldn't have gone otherwise . . ."

"But I heard a voice, Micah. A *voice*." Her dark eyes sparkled with fervor. "Have you ever heard His voice?"

Micah shook his head slowly, a disappointment settling in his stomach. "No, to be honest, I haven't. But God spoke to people in the Bible in a voice that could be heard. So I believe it can happen. It just hasn't happened to me."

Lydia ruffled her hair once more, leaving it lying in beguiling little feathered ridges. "It was so *real*, Micah. I felt so . . . so special when I heard it. I think God needed me to meet those children, needed me to know what you were doing. I think He led me here."

Micah smiled. "Tell your father about your experience—just like you told it to me—when you get home."

She burst out with a short laugh. "He'd say I've lost my mind!"

"Then convince him you haven't. Let him know what you heard, and then when God reveals His plan in His timing, you can prove God's existence to your father."

Lydia shook her head, the humor fading from her expression. "You don't know my father. It will take a miracle to change his mind about God. He thinks God is for women, children, and weaklings—and he is none of those things."

Micah took Lydia's hand. "I'll pray for your father. You keep praying for him, too. God can work miracles. I've witnessed it many times over in my lifetime. God will find the way to reach your father. Hang on to faith. Just believe."

"I want to believe. Nicky so needs a Christian man in his life. I'm sure I'll never marry—"

"Whoa, back up." Micah gave her hand a little tug. "Why wouldn't you ever marry?"

Lydia made a sour face. "Micah, think about it. Everyone believes I bore Nicky out of wedlock. No decent man is going to pursue a relationship with me. Why, as far as the community is concerned, I'm merely a fallen woman and Nicky is a—"

Anger flashed through Micah's middle. "Don't say it. Don't even think it!" How could she see herself in that manner? Allan Eldredge had done tremendous harm with his misguided lies. "You and I both know you are not a 'fallen woman,' and Nicky is very legitimate. Someday you're going to meet a man who will see you for what you really are—a beautiful, loving, giving person. And if he chooses to walk away from you, he's a bigger fool than your father."

Unshed tears glittered in Lydia's eyes. "Do you really mean that?"

"Of course I do. Any man would be lucky to claim you and Nicky as his family." If only Micah could claim them right now. But then what? Ask her to abandon her parents and drag Nicky away from everything familiar? Expect her to wait up while he delivered packages, wondering if something would go wrong? Offer her a small apartment in a brownstone instead of a house in the country where Nicky could run and play? No, the timing was all wrong. He couldn't express his feelings for her now. But he could offer his assistance as a friend, and he could pray for her.

Setting aside his own desires, he spoke a vow. "I . . . I will pray for you to find the man who will love and accept Nicky as his son when he chooses to love and accept you as his wife."

Lydia's eyes filled, and she nodded a thank-you. Then, unexpectedly, she yawned behind her hand. She glanced at the watch on Micah's wrist. "Gracious! Look at the time. We'll be dragging tomorrow."

Micah checked his watch and grimaced. "You're right. I'd better get across the hall and into bed." He stood, scooped up the pouch she'd given him, and headed toward the door. "Tomorrow morning, we'll start calling these numbers. Hopefully Mrs. Fenwick will answer on one of them."

"Thanks again, Micah, for all your help." She stood in the middle of the room, the light bulb over her head bringing out the highlights in her dark hair and gilding her eyelashes in gold.

Micah placed his hand on the doorknob to keep from wrapping his arms around her and kissing her breathless. He patted the leather pouch against his thigh. "Thank *you* for the help. I'll come get you in the morning." And he scurried out before temptation took control.

17

Shortly after eight thirty the next morning, Micah tapped on Lydia's door. He expected to find her dressed in the familiar coveralls, but instead she wore a light green suit similar to the yellow one. He whistled, arrested by the sight. "Don't you look nice. I guess this means you aren't going to do any work at the clinic today?" No smile appeared on her face, raising tingles of apprehension. Micah frowned. "Is something wrong?"

She reached beside the door and retrieved her suitcase. "Micah, I'm not going with you to the clinic. I'm going to the train station so I can go home. After talking last night about Father and Nicky, I found myself so homesick I could hardly sleep." She heaved a huge sigh, tears flooding her eyes. "I have the numbers we found in the newspapers in my purse and I can call them from Boston as easily as I can from here. When I find Mrs. Fenwick, Father can make travel arrangements for her by telephone. So I'm going home."

Micah took a backward step, a rock of dread filling his stomach. "Oh. Well . . ." He shoved his hands into his pockets and lifted his shoulders. "I see."

She slumped, tears spilling down her cheeks. "Please don't be angry with me. I . . . I just miss Nicky so, and I—"

Her dismal pose stirred sympathy. He reached out and chafed her upper arms, forcing his lips into a grin. "Hey, it's okay, Lydia. I understand. You just caught me off guard." Not until that moment did he realize how much he'd come to enjoy her presence. Saying good-bye would be harder than he'd imagined. He gave her arms one more quick squeeze, then reached for her suitcase. "Let me carry that down for you, and I'll help you find a cab."

She swept away her tears with her fingertips and offered a wobbly smile. "Thank you."

They descended the stairs in silence, and when they reached the street corner, Micah flagged down a cab. He swung Lydia's suitcase into the backseat, then held out his hand. "Let me have that list. I'll add my telephone number at the clinic. Then you can let me know when you make it home, and also when you've found Mrs. Fenwick."

Lydia withdrew the crumpled pages from her purse and Micah wrote his telephone number in bold numbers. He pressed the papers into her hand. "You take care. Give Nicky a hug for me, okay?"

Lydia nodded, her eyes shining with unshed tears. "I will. Thank you again, Micah, for everything."

"You're welcome."

They stood for a moment, two feet apart and staring past each other's shoulders. Then, instantaneously, they seemed to make the same choice, because two pairs of arms lifted, two right feet stepped forward, and Micah found himself holding her against his chest in a warm embrace.

He tipped his head to rest his cheek against her hair, breathing deeply of her scent. Her muscles convulsed once, and he suspected she battled sobs. His arms tightened. How quickly his affection for her had blossomed. *God, find a worthy man for this woman. She deserves someone special.*

The cab driver hit his horn in one short blast. "Hey, could ya hurry up? I got a livin' to make, ya know."

Reluctantly they separated, and Micah brushed a single tear from Lydia's cheek with his thumb. He opened the door for her. "Go on now, and Godspeed."

Without a word, she slid into the backseat of the cab next to her suitcase. Micah closed the door and watched the taxi pull away with Lydia's face framed in the window. He watched until the taxi turned the corner and disappeared from sight. He watched for a few more moments, remembering the feel of her in his arms, the scent of her hair in his nostrils, the shudder of her shoulders as she fought tears.

He repeated his internal prayer. *Find a worthy man for this woman.* And then, his shoulders sagging, he turned his steps toward the clinic.

⁂

Lydia drew on every ounce of strength she possessed and gained control of her emotions. She kept control while she checked train schedules, purchased her ticket, waited for the number thirty-four to arrive, and settled herself in a private berth. But when the door slid shut on her own personal cubby-hole, she gave vent to heartache and allowed herself the luxury of a cry. A full-blown, full-of-self-pity, sobbing-as-if-her-lungs-would-collapse cry. A cry the likes of which she hadn't allowed herself since the day she'd learned of Eleanor's death, when the midwife had placed little Nicky in her arms.

Her tears then had been for Eleanor, who wouldn't know the joy of mothering Nicky, and for Nicky, who wouldn't know the joy of being mothered by Eleanor. These tears, though the sound and body-aching fury was the same, were for herself. She recognized the selfishness, but she still allowed it.

The train was well across New York by the time she finished crying. Raising her head from her soggy lap, she cleaned her face with a handkerchief, then blew her nose until she could breathe again. She considered ringing the bell and requesting a cool cloth for her neck—her head throbbed horribly from the force of her tears—but she decided she didn't want anyone to see her in her sodden state. Instead, she closed her swollen eyes and brought up her feet to curl on the tufted bench cushion, allowing her mind to ponder the reason behind the wild crying.

Last night as she and Micah had sat on the floor of her apartment and Micah vowed to pray for her to find a man who would love her and Nicky, her heart had welled up and ached for him to be that man. Back at Schofield when she'd set her sights on Micah, it had been his handsome face and status as a doctor that had attracted her attention. But it was so much more now. Yes, he was still handsome—perhaps even more so as time had honed the boyish edges away and he had developed a mature bearing—and he was still a doctor, but such a caring, unselfish doctor—spending his days in a clinic with patients who couldn't afford to offer payment, caring for them as tenderly and willingly as if they all were the upper crust of Manhattan. Such a giving heart Micah possessed.

Then there was his willingness to assist those little Jewish children, to find sanctuary for them when no one else seemed to care. He was placing himself in danger by reaching out, yet he did it unhesitatingly. And if Lydia had found the teasing, sparkling Micah from Schofield attractive, this new mature, steadfast Micah was entrancing. She had seen the perfect Christian husband and father sitting before her with warmth shining in his blue eyes, and all she had wanted was to embrace him and claim him as her own.

But she couldn't.

Micah's heart belonged to the immigrants of New York and Jeremiah's orphans. Those two responsibilities were more than enough for any man.

Lydia's heart belonged to Nicky and her parents. She couldn't allow her friendship with Micah to flourish, let alone allow love to blossom and grow. Longing for Micah was as foolish now as it had been back at Schofield. Micah was where God had planted him, and Lydia was on her way to where she was needed. As much as it hurt, that was the way it had to be.

She sniffled, rubbing a fist under her nose, and pulled tighter into a ball. *God, please take Micah out of my heart so I can focus on Nicky. Micah said he'd pray for a good man to come into our lives. Please help me recognize him when he comes. Help me not to compare him unfavorably to Micah. Let him have Micah's heart for right, his tender spirit, and his love for You. And help me love him, because right now I can't imagine loving anyone else besides Micah Hatcher. . . .*

Lydia squeezed her eyes tight against the tears that threatened once again, and willed herself to sleep.

"Of all the foolish—" Father paced back and forth in the den, his face mottled with fury. He whirled on Lydia, who sat at his desk, her jaw set firmly against his verbal barrage. "You came home without her. You came home with a list of telephone numbers, one of which *might* be hers. What were you thinking, Lydia?"

Lydia straightened her shoulders, grateful Mother had taken Nicky to the zoo for the day so he wasn't privy to this argument. "I was thinking I wanted to get home to Nicky. I missed him, and I was worried about him." She could have added it was becoming too difficult to be in such close proximity to Micah Hatcher, but she chose to keep that to herself. "When I locate Mrs. Fenwick, I can make all the arrangements for her over the telephone—I didn't need to be there."

"And if none of those numbers turn out to be hers—then what?" Father's sharp voice cut like a whip.

Lydia refused to cower before him. "Then I contact Micah, and he finds some more numbers."

Father snorted.

Praying silently for patience, Lydia steepled her hands and assumed a beseeching tone. "Father, don't you agree it's our best chance for finding her? It's the same way you found her here in Boston. Does it not follow she would advertise her service? It's her means of supporting herself." Father stubbornly refused to answer, and Lydia threw her hands outward in frustration. "Fine, don't answer me. But the longer I stand here defending myself to you, the more time is wasted that could be spent trying to find Mrs. Fenwick."

Father chopped his hand in the direction of the telephone. "Call then." He spun and pointed his finger at Lydia's nose. "But don't come crying to me when you turn up empty and we're left with no one to tell the authorities Eleanor wanted Nicky to be yours."

Blowing out a breath of aggravation, Lydia turned and stalked back to the telephone. With her back to her father, she picked up the receiver, checked her list, and dialed the first number. While it was still ringing, she heard her father stomp out of the room, and then the front door slammed, signaling his departure. For a moment her shoulders sagged—*Lord in Heaven, help me find her*—and then she straightened as someone on the other end said, "Hello?"

⁂

Nic walked onto the factory floor, wincing at the racket of saws and hammers and boards banging together. When he'd worked here, the noise had assaulted his sensitive ears—the morphine always heightened his senses rather than dulling them—but over the past years he'd forgotten the overwhelming hubbub. He broke into a clumsy trot, eager to reach the open staircase at the back corner and climb to the loft, where the office was located. Up there, he could get behind a closed door. Although no place in the factory was completely quiet, the ruckus was at least muffled up there.

He thumped up the stairs, then twisted the knob on the office door, entering without knocking. When the door opened, sound poured through, and N. Allan Eldredge whirled around in his desk chair. Nic allowed himself a moment to enjoy the shock on the older man's face before he slammed the door and then leaned against it, just in case the owner got some idea about hollering for help. Not likely he'd be heard, what with all the commotion down below, but he wanted Eldredge's attention all to himself.

Eldredge's face went white. He rose from his chair. Slowly, like his joints were rusty. "Pankin." Even though fear pulsated from the man, his tone carried derision. "I thought I told you not to show your face at this plant ever again."

Nic shrugged, his empty sleeve bobbing with the motion. "You got something I want." Bosco'd seen a wooden airplane and blocks on the parlor floor as well as a child-sized matching cap and jacket tossed on a chair. "Comin' here's the only way I can get it."

Eldredge's hand inched toward a desk drawer.

Nic shot forward and captured the older man's wrist. "Don't

be reachin' for the pistol you keep on the grounds." Eldredge had waved that pistol around the last time they'd met, using it as leverage to chase Nic off the property. He'd scuttled away then, tail between his legs, but he'd fight to the bitter end this time. "Won't do you no good. Besides, I ain't here to hurt you. Just want what's mine."

Eldredge wrenched his arm free and then rubbed his wrist. Nic's fingerprints left red lines on the man's pale flesh. "What do you want from me?"

Nic admired the man's bravado. Thirty years older, with a belly paunch and no muscle in his arms to speak of, but he stood upright and glared into Nic's face. Only his colorless pallor told of his fear. Nic set his feet wide and glowered from his greater height. He bounced his thumb against his chest and leaned in, glaring directly into Eldredge's face. "I want my son."

18

Lydia glanced at the mantel clock and gave a little jolt. Her mother and Nicky would be back any minute, and she didn't want Nicky to overhear the phone calls. Two more numbers left. So far she hadn't found Mrs. Fenwick. Her heart beat with nervous anticipation as she dialed another number. Despite the series of negative responses, she still felt a rush of hopeful adrenaline with each turn of the telephone dial. She listened to the rings. One, two, three, and then—"Yes, hello?" A woman's voice.

Lydia pressed the receiver to her ear and began her now-familiar spiel. "Hello. I am trying to reach a midwife named Mrs. Fenwick. Is this Mrs. Fenwick?"

"No, it's not," the voice answered, and Lydia's heart fell. "I'm her sister, Norma Sweigart."

Lydia sat bolt upright, her spirits soaring.

"Did you need to make arrangements for a birthing?"

Lydia struggled to not babble with excitement. "No, Mrs. Sweigart, but I need to talk to Mrs. Fenwick. My name is Lydia Eldredge. I live in Boston—"

"You're calling from Massachusetts?" The woman sounded pleased. "Ruby lived in Boston. Are you a friend of hers?"

"No, ma'am, actually—"

"Oh, then you must be one of the mamas she assisted."

Lydia stifled the urge to reach through the line and put her hand over the other woman's mouth. She took a deep breath. "Mrs. Sweigart, may I please speak to Mrs. Fenwick?"

"She's not here right now. She went to deliver a baby. Left very early this morning. It's a first baby, so it might be a while before she's back. What did you say your name was?"

"Lydia—Lydia Eldredge." Lydia spoke slowly and carefully. Her entire body trembled with impatience, and she clamped both hands around the telephone receiver to hold it steady. "Mrs. Sweigart, it is very important that I talk to Mrs. Fenwick. Could you please have her return my call?"

"All the way to Boston? I'm sorry, miss, but we can't afford a call like that. It's all we can do to pay the bills as it is."

Lydia's mind raced. She couldn't just keep calling, waiting to connect. *Lord, help me.* An idea struck like a lightning bolt. "Mrs. Sweigart, would you be able to call a number in Queens?"

"Queens? Why, sure, I can do that."

"Good. Do you have a pencil and paper?" Lydia spoke as if she were addressing a child, but they must get every detail correct. "Here's the telephone number." She stated each number clearly, pausing in between, then had Mrs. Sweigart read it back to her. "Please, as soon as Mrs. Fenwick returns, have her call that number and ask to speak to Dr. Micah Hatcher. He will be able to give her my message. All right?"

"Certainly. I'll do it." There was a slight pause. "Are you in some sort of trouble, miss?"

Lydia's pulse skipped into hiccupping beats, yet she spoke with surety. "Nothing that Mrs. Fenwick and I can't fix. Thank you, Mrs. Sweigart." She hung up, waited a few seconds, then picked up the phone again to dial the clinic.

"Queens Clinic. Dr. Hatcher speaking."

Just the sound of his voice made Lydia's heart flutter. She clung to the receiver in lieu of clinging to the man.

"Hello, is someone there?" Micah's voice held a hint of worry.

"Yes. Micah, it's me. L-Lydia." She pressed one hand to her chest in an attempt to calm her erratic heartbeat. Goodness, the effect he had on her!

"Lydia!" She felt the warmth of his smile from two hundred miles away. "So good to hear your voice. I hope you're calling with good news. . . ."

"Oh, Micah, the best news! Your idea worked. I found Mrs. Fenwick's sister." She quickly explained the woman's hesitance to make a long-distance telephone call and Lydia's instructions to call Micah's clinic instead. "Will you please let her know the situation when she calls?"

"Of course I will. That was good thinking." Lydia imagined him leaning against the desk, his smock in place, one hand in his pocket as he spoke. "If she needs to speak to you directly, I'll let her use this phone. And I can help her arrange for travel, if you'd like."

Grateful tears blurred Lydia's vision. "Micah, I appreciate you so much."

There was a slight pause—and then Micah's deep voice. "That's what friends are for, right?"

Lydia smiled, her cheek pressing against the mouthpiece. How wonderful having Micah Hatcher for a friend. "Well, you are a friend who goes above and beyond the call of duty. Thank you."

"Now stop that thankin' me nonsense." The teasing twang crept through, causing Lydia's heart to sing. "An' let's free up this line so Mrs. Fenwick can reach me. Take care of yourself, and give Nicky a hug for me."

"I will. Good-bye, Micah."

"Good-bye, Lydia."

"I love you." The phone line went dead before she said the words. But they slipped out so effortlessly, Lydia knew they had to be true. She loved Micah. She loved him as more than a friend. Yet a friendship—a limited, miles-apart friendship—was all they could have.

She sighed, trying to press down the feelings that had swelled at the sound of his voice. When she'd regained control of her emotions, she picked up the telephone again. She had one more call to make—to tell her father she'd found Mrs. Fenwick. But she would be very careful not to say "I told you so."

The office telephone at Eldredge Crating Company rang twice, then Father's voice answered. "Eldredge Crating." He sounded strained.

"Father, this is Lydia," she said, her heart lighter than it had been in weeks. "I have wonderful news. I located Mrs. Fenwick."

"Is she on her way?"

No "that's wonderful" or "I'm happy"—just a brusque question. Lydia stifled a sigh of disappointment. "No, Father, she was away from her apartment, delivering a baby. Her sister will have her get in touch with Micah, then he'll direct her to us." She waited, but no response came, and Lydia's impatience boiled over. "Say something! I found her! Within days she'll be on her way to Boston! Aren't you pleased?" She cringed in shame when she heard her tone, as harsh and unfeeling as her father's, yet she seemed powerless to change it. He so infuriated her with his stubborn pride.

"That's good, Lydia." This time when Father spoke, the brusqueness was gone, and instead Lydia heard an element of brokenness. "Because I had a visitor a short while ago."

A chill crept up Lydia's spine. "A . . . a visitor? Was it—"

"Yes." The clipped word cut her off. "He knows we have

Nicky. He demanded the boy. Two workers came in while he was here and escorted him out, but he'll be back. I know he will. We're on borrowed time, Lydia."

Lydia's knees went weak. She collapsed into Father's chair, feeling as though a great fog swirled around her. "Oh, Father . . ."

The front door swung open, little feet clattered through the foyer, and Nicky's cheerful voice called, "Mama! I'm home! Mama, where are you?"

Lydia cupped her hand around the mouthpiece and whispered, "Father, Nicky is here. I need to get off the telephone."

"Whatever you do, keep him in the house. Don't answer the door if the bell rings. I'll be home as soon as I can." Father's stern voice cut through the fog of fear.

"Yes, Father." She replaced the receiver in its cradle, clasped her hands together briefly with a silent, simple prayer, *Oh, please, God . . .* Then she rose, pasted on a smile, and went to find her son.

For two days, Micah waited for Mrs. Fenwick's call. Each time the clinic telephone jangled, he snatched it up, ready to gain Mrs. Fenwick's assistance. And each time it was someone else on the other end, his shoulders sagged in disappointment. He felt as jumpy as the lone hen at a fox party, and he kicked himself a dozen times for not asking Lydia for Mrs. Fenwick's number so he could call her himself. What could be taking the woman so long?

Every time he thought of Mrs. Fenwick, he thought of Lydia. Her voice had sounded so melodious as it came through the telephone line, the sweet tone pulling at his heart. He thought of little Nicky, too, and prayed for his safety. How heartbreaking to think of that boy being hauled away by a man whose only motivation was to use the child for his own selfish gains. The longer it took to locate Mrs. Fenwick, the more likely it became that Nicky would be removed from Lydia's care, and remembering how much Lydia loved Nicky increased his worry. Would the woman never call?

As he cleaned up late on Wednesday afternoon, planning where he would grab some quick supper on the way to church, the phone rang. Distracted, his mind on other things, he picked up the phone and answered, "Yes, Dr. Hatcher here."

"This is Mrs. Ruby Fenwick. I have a message to contact you?"

Micah nearly dropped the telephone. He sat on the edge of the desk and his voice rose in eagerness. "Yes, Mrs. Fenwick, thank you so much for calling. I need to ask for your help. I know you left Boston because a man was bothering you—"

"He did more than bother me, young man! He harassed me. Scared me right out of my home and my livelihood!"

Micah cringed. Given Mrs. Fenwick's bitterness, he feared it would be difficult to convince her to go back. "Yes, Mrs. Fenwick, I'm very sorry you faced such a frightening situation. The man is a menace, and he needs to be stopped. That's part of why I asked you to call." She hadn't hung up on him yet, so Micah bravely forged ahead. "Do you remember the mother of the child the man is looking for? Her name was Eleanor."

"Oh yes, I remember." Mrs. Fenwick's fiery tone turned melancholy. "The poor little thing was so upset. She stayed with me while awaiting the birth of her son—she was scared of that man, too. She had a difficult time. I was nearly inconsolable when she died. I gave the baby to a friend of hers." Her tone changed, picking up a hint of anger again. "And all the better for him! The father showed up after the birth demanding that sweet baby, wanting to sell him. I tried to tell him the baby had died, but I'm not a convincing liar. He just kept coming back. . . ."

Micah hoped he'd be able to use her indignation in his favor. "I'm friends with the woman to whom you gave the baby. Her name is Lydia Eldredge, and now the father is bothering her."

An odd *tick-tick-tick* came through the line—Mrs. Fenwick apparently clicked her tongue against her teeth. "I'm so sorry to hear that. I hope she's able to keep the baby with her. That awful man sure doesn't deserve his little boy."

Micah took encouragement from the woman's sympathy. If she cared about Nicky's well-being, surely she'd be willing to help Lydia. "The boy's name is Nicky. He's a fine, sunny little fellow, very bright and personable—and he calls Lydia his mama. But you and I both know she isn't Nicky's real mother, and unfortunately so does the boy's father. Lydia wants to gain full custody of Nicky. Nicky's father is trying to get him back, and the courts will surely hand the boy over unless they can be convinced the birth mother wanted the baby to go with Lydia. Do you have records, or perhaps a letter, that would prove Eleanor's desire?"

"I do keep a journal of all the births. Have that little boy's birth date recorded in it—was August of 1940, as I recall—but a letter from the birth mother?" A long, thoughtful pause followed. Micah nearly held his breath. "No, that poor girl wasn't in any shape to be writing letters when she knew she was soon heading on to glory. But I surely remember how she begged me to give the baby to her friend. I could tell somebody so."

Micah's heart soared. "Would you be willing to travel back to Boston and visit with a judge personally?"

"Back to Boston? Oh, I don't know. I'm not sure I'm up to that journey. Besides, I'm finally getting the chance to deliver babies here. That's why I couldn't get back to you right away. I've delivered three babies this week—two girls and a boy, all healthy and doing well." Pride carried clearly through the line. "I'd hate to be away and lose business again."

Micah chewed the inside of his mouth. How could he convince her? Before he had a chance to formulate an idea, she asked, "Could I write it all down—everything I remember—and sign my name to it and then send it with my birth journal for you to show the judge? Would that help?"

"That would be better than what they have right now, Mrs. Fenwick. I appreciate your willingness to help. A little boy's future rests on your testimony." Micah heard the fervency in his own voice and tears pressed behind his eyes, proving just how emotionally involved he had become with Lydia and Nicky.

"All right, Dr. Hatcher. I'll get started right now writing down what I remember, and get my journal from 1940 out for you. When will you pick it up?"

"Is tomorrow morning too soon?"

"No, I'll have it ready by tomorrow morning."

Micah asked for her address and recorded it. "Thank you, Mrs. Fenwick."

"You're welcome. Hope your friend gets to keep that little boy. His father surely doesn't deserve a sweet boy like you described."

He hung up, clapped his hands once, and announced to the empty room, "Thank you, Lord!" Then he dialed Lydia's number. He let it ring twelve times before hanging up, disappointed. Well, he'd try again. After collecting the written testimony and birth journal from Mrs. Fenwick, he'd check out train schedules and deliver the items himself to Lydia.

He'd barely finished formulating his plans when someone banged on the locked clinic door. Micah crossed to the door and pulled up the shade. He recognized one of the members of Rabbi Jacowicz's synagogue. His heart thumped in a rush of worry—could one of the children be ill? Swinging the door wide, he waved his hand in invitation. "Come in. What can I do for you?"

"Rabbi Jacowicz asked me to come share news with you of which he learned."

Micah crossed his arms. "News?'

The man nodded, his thick beard bobbing. "Jewish refugees have been granted asylum in New York. In Oswego, at Fort Ontario. Rabbi's sources tell him nearly a thousand of our people are on a ship called *Henry Gibbons* along with wounded American soldiers. The Jewish people will remain at Fort Ontario. Rabbi thought you would be interested in providing medical care to the people."

Micah uncrossed his arms, eagerness swelling in his chest. "A thousand people? Are they all children?"

The man shook his head. "Rabbi's source says it is families. Will you help?"

Micah didn't hesitate. "Of course I will help. When will the ship arrive?"

The man frowned and scratched his beard. "Early August. A day is not known by Rabbi."

Early August. Within days. But what of Lydia and the delivery of the journal and testimonial letter from Mrs. Fenwick? Micah sorted through possible solutions. He couldn't be in two places at once. The most logical solution would be to ship the information to Lydia, but he'd anticipated seeing her and Nicky personally.

Micah shook himself loose from his musings to address the man awaiting an answer. "Tell Rabbi Jacowicz I will do whatever I can for the Jewish refugees. Have him let me know when the ship arrives. I'll provide whatever medical care they need."

The man clasped his hands against his chest and smiled. He bobbed forward twice, then silently stepped back out the door.

Micah closed and locked it behind him, then leaned against it, his eyes closed.

I won't lie and say I'm not disappointed, God. You placed the plight of the Jewish people on my heart, and I will do whatever I can do help them, even if it means remaining here rather than going to Boston to help Lydia. But Lydia and Nicky are also in my heart. Help me find a way to put those feelings where You want them to be. Please show me Your will concerning Lydia and Nicky.

19

Nicky looked up at Lydia from his spot on the floor where he constructed a block tower, his face creased in puzzlement. "Mama, aren't you gonna answer the telephone?"

She tapped the end of his nose with one finger, forcing a smile to her lips. The phone blared again, and she cringed. She leaned close to his ear. "Want to play a game with Mama?"

Nicky's eyes lit with interest. "What kind of game?"

"An I-can't-hear-it game. Every time we hear a bell—a telephone ring, or a doorbell, we'll pretend we can't hear it. Does that sound like fun?" Lydia grasped at straws. Somehow they had to keep themselves hidden until Micah and Mrs. Fenwick arrived.

The telephone's persistent ring sounded again. Nicky grinned, his dimpled cheeks rounding with the upthrust of his sweet lips. "I didn't hear that, did you, Mama?"

Lydia rolled her eyes and flipped her hands outward. "Didn't hear what?"

Nicky giggled with delight. "Nothing! I didn't hear nothing!"

"Me either." Lydia and Nicky kept up their nonsense dialogue until finally the phone stopped and silence reigned.

Nicky threw himself into her lap. "That was fun, Mama. Will we play it again?"

"Oh yes. Every time we hear a bell, we'll play the I-can't-hear-it game, okay?"

"Okay!"

Nicky's enthusiasm nearly broke Lydia's heart. He was so innocent. And somehow he must remain so. She gathered him tightly against her breast and kissed his soft curls. Lydia couldn't allow him to sense her fear, to understand that until the arrival of Mrs. Fenwick they were prisoners in their own home. The thought led her to Micah and the children he and Jeremiah had brought to freedom. Her heart had ached at the fearful, miserable conditions those little ones suffered. Now, in a way, her own child had been forced into hiding.

If Nic Pankin came before Mrs. Fenwick, Lydia would surely face separation from Nicky. The courts always favored blood relatives when deciding custody. Tears spurted into her eyes, and she wrapped both arms around Nicky and held tight, delivering a hug that bordered on desperate. How horrible it must be for Jewish mothers to be separated from their children! Her heart ached with empathy for those women, and as she held her son in her embrace, she sent up a prayer for the faceless, nameless throng of mothers whose children were not in their arms.

Her mind drifted backward to the night in New York when she had asked God to allow her to help. She'd so clearly heard His voice telling her to be patient and wait, in time she would know. Her arms coiled ever tighter, fear writhing through her belly. How could she help those other mothers and children when she couldn't even keep her own child safe?

"Mama, you're squishing me!"

Nicky's protest awakened her to reality. She forced a light laugh as she relaxed her hold. "I'm sorry, sweetheart." She kissed his cheek, smoothed his hair, and attempted a quivery smile. "Mama just loves you so much, she almost squeezed the stuffing out of you."

Nicky's dark eyes peered up at her, round and serious. "I need my stuffing. It holds my outsides apart."

Lydia burst into laughter. Real, heart-lifting, soul-cleansing laughter. "Oh, Nicky . . ." She hugged him again, but gently this time, rocking him from side to side as she buried her face against his moist neck. How she loved this child.

God, please let me always be Nicky's mama, and let me find a daddy for him—a man who will treasure him for the gift he is. Together, let us keep him safe and happy, the way he is right now, always.

Without warning, Micah's face appeared behind her closed lids. Her breath caught. She must stop looking at Micah as an answer to her problems. Allowing herself to fantasize about creating a family with him could lead only to further heartbreak. Her prayer continued, nearly begging.

Take these whimsical ideas about Micah out of my heart, God. But please bring him to Boston with Mrs. Fenwick quickly.

The morning of August fourth, Nic put on his cleanest pair of trousers and a plaid shirt that had all its buttons and no frayed spots. Using a safety pin, he secured his empty sleeve to the shoulder so it wouldn't flap around his waist. Most days he didn't let the dangling sleeve bother him, but today he didn't want anything to give the impression of slovenliness. The day a man added five thousand dollars to his pocket was a day worthy of a little spiffing up.

He grunted as he tucked in the tails of his shirt—always a challenge with only one hand. But if he couldn't tuck shirttails as neatly as a two-handed man, he could still swing a hammer, cut a steak when he was able to afford one, and even drive his old truck one-handed. He'd figured out that for most things, he didn't need his left arm. But not having it sure left him needing something else. The familiar hunger rolled through his gut. A growl escaped his clenched lips. Fool doctors anyway, pumping him full of a medicine that left him aching and wanting and always short on cash.

But thanks to his arrangement with Mrs. Darwin Thaddeus Bachman, he'd have cash for a good long while.

Crossing to the small cracked mirror hanging above his bachelor chest, he examined his reflection. Rosy cheeks from a fresh shave. Hair too long—thick blond curls lay across his collar—but clean and combed. Presentable. He took a step backward and glanced down his front, scowling when his gaze encountered the scuffed toes of his old brown boots. Maybe he'd splurge and get a shoe shine before picking up the kid.

His head bounced up and he caught a glimpse of his satisfied smile in the mirror. Another hour—maybe two if he had trouble finding a shoeshine man, and then . . . He released a low whistle, turning toward the door. "Then I'm gonna be rich."

Micah cleared out the storage cabinet and then reorganized it. Normally he delegated cleaning assignments to a volunteer, but the mindless task was a welcome respite from his worries. Every day for the past week, he'd called Lydia's home morning, noon, and evening. Each time, the phone rang incessantly, but no one answered. Where could she be? A constant prayer for her safety played in the recesses of his heart.

He'd placed the journal and Mrs. Fenwick's letter in the mail the morning after visiting with Mrs. Fenwick, sending it on its way with a prayer for speedy delivery. With mail now being delivered by train, it should have taken only a couple of days for the bulky envelope to reach Lydia's home. He hoped when she read the letter he'd also enclosed, she would understand why the package came by postal service rather than hand delivery. He twisted his face in frustration as he stacked rolled bandages on the cabinet's middle shelf. If only he'd known trying to help the Jewish refugees was pointless—he could be with Lydia right now.

On the first day of August, he'd left the clinic in the hands of volunteers and traveled to Fort Ontario at Oswego, his trunk filled with first-aid supplies, only to be informed by a uniformed guard that arrangements had already been made for medical care. Micah had tried to persuade the man in charge that one more doctor would be a help rather than a hindrance with so many people, but the man had remained firm. Micah was not allowed in. Irritated, Micah had been forced to turn around and head home.

But he'd received a glimpse of the thin, sallow-faced people in ragged clothing, and his chest had tightened with desire to help them. According to the man at the gate, the people would stay at Fort Ontario until the war was over. Micah huffed in aggravation. They'd merely traded one prison for another, as far as he was concerned. But at least they were no longer under threat of death. Those nine hundred eighty-two people were safe and receiving help, even if they were confined behind barbed wire.

Micah paused in his work, pondering anew why the government wasn't doing more. Of course there were those who protested immigration generally and Jewish immigration specifically. They spouted things like "keep America for Americans." He scoffed at their attitude. If such an attitude had existed a hundred years ago, his own family would have been banned from entering the country. The same applied to countless others, many of whom now screamed the ridiculous litany. What made an American, anyway? Was it birthright, or was it devotion? Micah preferred to believe it was the latter. He'd worked with so many immigrants who embraced this country as their own—immigrants who gladly sent their sons to war to defend it.

He closed the cabinet, scooped up the empty boxes, and headed to the trash bin behind the building. One thing he knew for sure—God had called him to work with the immigrants. Serving them was his ministry, just as standing behind a pulpit and delivering sermons was Jeremiah's ministry. Jeremiah had been tugged in a different direction with the war raging, but as soon as peace reigned, he'd return to preaching. Until God told Micah otherwise, he'd be right here in this clinic, serving the people in Queens.

Tossing the boxes into the trash bin, he wrinkled his nose at the foul smell in the alleyway. He squinted upward and watched a wispy cloud float through the slice of sky exposed between the tall buildings. Longing for Texas swept over him and he released that longing with a sigh. What he wouldn't give to lay his gaze once more on its open spaces and on his family—Mama and Pop, his brothers. He hadn't seen his older brothers in over three years, even longer for Jeremiah. In that time, two nieces and one nephew had joined the family, and he still hadn't been introduced to them.

He turned back toward the interior of the clinic, making a promise to himself that as soon as the war ended, he'd get somebody to fill in for him so he could make a journey home and spend time with his family. Maybe start a family of his own.

His feet came to an abrupt halt. He'd been considering his lack of a family ever since the letter from Allan Eldredge had arrived. Being accused of paternity, then meeting Nicky and reacquainting himself with Lydia had caused him to reconsider his bachelor status. There was a ready-made family waiting to be adopted.

He plunked down in the chair behind his battered desk, propped his elbows on the wooden top, then rested his chin in his hands, allowing his thoughts to roam. He'd dated his fair share of women as a young man, but the thought of settling down with one of them had never appealed to him. Yet lately, when he was too busy to date, matrimony constantly played in the corner of his mind.

With the thought of marriage came an image of Lydia, and beside her stood Nicky with his bright eyes and stubborn curls. What would his folks think if he brought the two of them home as his new family? A smile tugged at his cheek. He knew what Mama would say—"If you prayed about it, son, and your heart said 'yes,' then I'm celebratin' with you."

Well, his heart sure seemed to be wrestling him in Lydia's direction, but his head knew better. Better to keep praying for Lydia to marry someone else, so he could stay focused on his work here. Heaven knew he had plenty to keep himself busy without adding a wife and son to the list.

His chest gave a painful lurch, but before Micah could fully examine the reason, the clinic door opened, and a woman and two children entered. He bounded around the desk to help them in any way he could. He was needed once more.

20

Lydia pulled back one curtain just a bit and peeked out in both directions. No sign of Nic Pankin. Relief flooded her frame, followed closely by a rush of frustration. No sign of Micah and Mrs. Fenwick, either. Father's lawyer had paperwork ready to petition the courts to make Nicky's placement with them permanent, but they couldn't proceed without Mrs. Fenwick's testimony. When would the woman finally come and bring an end to this living in concealment? The constant worry ate a hole through her stomach. And the walls were starting to close in on her.

Not once in the past week had she, Mother, or Nicky ventured out of the house. Father crept out the back door, a pistol in his pocket, at the crack of dawn, drove to the factory, and completed whatever work he deemed absolutely necessary, then returned well before lunch. The unfamiliar routine—and the loaded pistol always at the ready—had them all on tenterhooks. They'd taken to snapping at one another, the tension too much to bear.

Fingers descended on Lydia's shoulder, and she released a squawk of surprise. She spun as her mother leaped backward, her eyes wide. Lydia let out a huge breath of relief. "Goodness, Mother, you scared me out of a year's growth."

Mother's face creased in remorse. "I didn't intend to startle you. I just wanted to let you know your father took Nicky for a short drive."

Fear attacked, creating a metallic taste on Lydia's tongue. "Is that wise?"

"I asked the same question, but Allan insisted he'd stay away from the city, where Nic might spot him." Mother shook her head, a soft smile tipping up the corners of her lips. "Nicky needs to get out, the poor little boy. He's so restless. Allowing him to take a drive with his poppy is the least we could do, since his birthday had to slide by largely unnoticed."

They'd celebrated Nicky's fourth birthday very quietly two days ago with a cake and a few presents. He had asked to go to the zoo, but they couldn't risk taking him out in public. His acute disappointment had pierced Lydia, and she wished they could explain everything to him in a way he could understand without frightening him. But all they could do was wait and hope to have it all settled without alarming him.

Lydia gave a reluctant nod. "I suppose you're right."

Mother stepped forward and glanced surreptitiously up and down the street. "We haven't emptied our mailbox all week. Should I go see to it? The street appears very quiet."

Even considering stepping outside raised a prickle of apprehension after their days behind locked doors and pulled window shades. But the postal deliveryman would begin to worry if they left the items uncollected much longer. Lydia held up her hand. "You stay here and watch. I'll fetch it."

Her heart pounding like a bass drum in a Sousa march, she cracked the front door and looked left and right. Nothing appeared amiss. She sucked in a breath and raced to the mailbox at the end of the walk. She turned the key, removed several small envelopes and one large brown packet, then dashed back to the house. After slamming and locking the door, she leaned against the sturdy wood, her chest heaving.

Mother plucked the items from Lydia's hands and riffled through them. Her eyebrows rose when she reached the larger packet. "This is from Micah Hatcher."

At the mention of Micah's name, Lydia's stomach fluttered. She wanted to snatch the packet back—to examine his penmanship and imagine his blunt-tipped fingers holding a pen—but her trembling hands refused to cooperate. "What is it?"

"Let's go sit down and see." Mother headed for the kitchen, and Lydia followed. Sliding into a chair, Mother used a butter knife left on the table from breakfast to slit the top of the packet. She spilled the contents onto the table. A bound leather book of some sort, a sealed envelope with the words "Mrs. Fenwick's testimony" printed in block letters on its front, and a folded lined sheet of paper slid across the smooth tabletop.

Lydia reached for the book first. She flipped it open and scanned its entries. She let out a little gasp of surprise. "Mother, look, this is Mrs. Fenwick's records of births for the year 1940." She leafed forward until she found August. A smile tugged at her lips when she spotted Nicky's. "See? Here's Nicky's birth information. Eleanor's name, the time of birth, and also a record of Eleanor's death." Her face clouded. "How sad that Nicky won't ever know Eleanor."

Mother touched Lydia's hand. "He will, darling, through you. You'll tell him someday."

Lydia nodded, blinking against tears. She would need an extra dose of courage the day she told Nicky she wasn't his real mother. She hoped it wouldn't change his feelings toward her. She fingered the sealed envelope, frowning. "Do you suppose this means Mrs. Fenwick isn't coming?"

Mother shrugged, her narrow shoulders barely lifting. "I . . . I don't know. Does the other paper say anything about her travel plans?"

Lydia picked up the last item and unfolded it. Micah's bold script filled the page. She quickly scanned the letter, her hopes fading with each line of print. She relayed the news to her mother. "Mrs. Fenwick is reluctant to leave New York because she is just beginning to work again, and she's fearful about facing Nic." The next paragraphs explained Micah's reason for being unable to make the trip, but she shouldn't share the information with anyone. Not even Mother. She remained focused on the section involving Mrs. Fenwick. "So he sent the journal and Mrs. Fenwick's testimony in the hopes it would be enough. He advises us to leave the envelope sealed until it's handed to a judge."

Although Lydia understood and fully supported Micah's reasons for not coming—of course he'd want to be available to the misplaced Jewish people—she couldn't put aside the immense disappointment of receiving only a letter in place of seeing him. Loneliness for him created a physical ache in the center of her chest.

Mother rested her palms on the table, leaning sideways a bit to peek at the page. "Does he say anything else?"

Lydia quickly folded the sheet. "Nothing important." Not even anything of a personal nature. The absence of an "I miss you" or "I wish I could come" increased the sharp pain of longing. She pressed the brief missive to her chest and battled tears. "Oh, Mother, I can't wait for Father to get home. We should go to the lawyer's office immediately."

"And now that we have the journal and signed testimony, we shall, the very moment your father returns." The sound of a slamming car door carried from outside, and Mother brightened. "That must be your father now."

"Oh, thank the Lord!" Lydia pushed Micah's letter into her pocket. "Odd that he parked out front, though. I locked the door when I returned with the mail—I'll go let him and Nicky in." She trotted through the hallway to the vestibule and swung the door open, words of welcome on her lips. "Father, Nicky, guess what came in the—" Her voice stilled, her tongue losing its ability to function. Instead of her father and Nicky on the doorstep, Nic Pankin filled the entrance.

He offered a leering grin. "Well, Lydia Eldredge, lookit you." His gaze roved slowly from her face to her feet and back again. He let out a low whistle. "Been a long time, hasn't it, honey? But I gotta tell ya, you're pretty as you ever was."

Her frozen muscles thawed. She grabbed the door to slam it in his face. But he reached out with his one good hand—the hand that was stronger than most men's—and held it open. "Now, now, is that any way to greet a long-lost friend? An' you was askin' a question. 'Guess what came,' you said. I can answer it—I came!" He laughed, causing Lydia's skin to crawl.

Mother scurried up behind Lydia's shoulder, her face pinched and white. "Nic Pankin, you are not welcome here. I demand that you leave."

Nic laughed again. "Demand all you want to, lady, but I ain't goin' nowhere. Not 'til I get what I come for. I know he's here." He barged past the women and into the hallway, peeking first into the sitting room and then the den. "Kid? Where are ya, kid? Come meet your daddy!" His booming voice filled the house. As he called, he ambled toward the kitchen.

He'd made it halfway down the hall before the shock of his arrival faded enough for Lydia to move. She charged directly into his path. Inwardly she quaked in fear, but she forced a fierce scowl on her face and planted her palm on his chest. "He isn't here. He's out."

Nic lifted his shoulders in an unconcerned shrug. The empty sleeve moving up and down gave Lydia a sick feeling in the pit of her stomach. "Then I guess I'll wait 'til he gets back."

"You'll do no such thing. You will leave at once or I will call the police!"

Nic leaned on the doorframe leading to the den and looked down at her from his impressive height. A knowing grin creased his face. "Yeah, I think I'd like that, Lydia. Call the police and explain to them why you been keepin' my kid hid away from me all these years. Denyin' a father access to his son. You want to explain it, go right ahead." He slid an insolent glance into Father's den and bobbed his chin at the telephone on the desk. "There's a phone right there. What's stoppin' ya?"

Micah's voice rang through Lydia's memory—*"In the eyes of the law, what you've done up to this point is kidnap Nicky."* Even Father's lawyer had intimated the same truth. Lydia couldn't call the police.

Nic laughed again, showing surprisingly white, even teeth. "That's what I thought. Your old man threatened the same thing, but he never lifted a finger to dial. 'Cause you know I'm right." He jabbed a thumb against his broad chest, his grin taunting her. "'Cause I'm that boy's daddy."

"You're not!" Mother rushed forward and stopped a few feet from Nic, wringing her hands. "You're not his daddy. A daddy is a man who loves and cares for his child. You've done none of those things!"

Nic pushed off the doorframe, his face blotching scarlet. "I couldn't do none of those things 'cause you had my kid!" He waited until Mother skittered backward a step before nodding, the victory won. "But I aim to change that today. I ain't leavin' this house 'til you've handed over my kid."

Indignation at Nic's callous way of speaking about Nicky

filled Lydia's middle and spilled from her lips. "Your *kid* has a name." Nic advanced one step toward her, but she held her ground. "Don't you even care what it is?"

"Yeah." He stuffed his hand into his pocket and scowled down at Lydia. "What'd Eleanor name him?"

"Eleanor didn't name him. I named him. I named him because Eleanor gave him to me." Lydia threw her shoulders back, daring Nic to contradict her. "We call him Nicky."

"Nicky, huh?" Nic popped out his lower lip in contemplation. He nodded. "Named for his papa."

"No, named for his poppy." At Nic's puzzled expression, Lydia explained, "That's what he calls his grandfather."

Nic's thick brows formed a sharp V. "He's never met his grandfather."

"I'm referring to my father. Nicky knows him as his grandfather."

"An' I aim to fix that misconception."

"Nic, please listen." Lydia heard the pleading in her tone and hated herself for the weakness it showed, but she'd do anything for Nicky. Even get down on her hands and knees and beg if it would convince Nic to leave them alone. "What good will it do to tell Nicky I'm not his mother? He's just a little boy—only four years old. You'll hurt him if you tell him his mother is dead."

A cunning look crossed Nic's face, sending a chill down Lydia's spine. "Well, I reckon if you want Nicky to go on thinkin' you're his mama, it's all right with me."

Her heart leaped. "You . . . you mean it?"

"Why, sure. Seems I recall you favored me once." He removed his hand from his pocket and slowly traced his finger from her temple to her chin and left it there, the pressure possessive. "He could've been yours, I s'pose, had things turned out different. But we could still get married, and that'd make you his mama."

Revulsion turned her stomach, and Lydia started to lurch away from his touch. But might playing along with him earn his trust? If Nic believed she was willing to go with him, to continue being Nicky's mama, perhaps she could talk him into letting her adopt Nicky. Then, later, she and Nicky could escape him. *Help me, God! Help me know what to do!*

She hesitated a moment too long. Mother forced her way between them. "Keep your filthy hands off my daughter. She wants nothing to do with you."

Nic's lips contorted into a snarl of rage. For a moment Lydia feared he might actually strike Mother, but then he whirled on his heel and marched into the den. He plopped onto the sofa and sat, grinning, his eyelids at half-mast. "You forget somethin', lady."

Mother slipped her arm around Lydia's waist, and they hovered in the wide doorway, listening.

"I hold all the winning cards. That kid is legally mine, an' you all want what I got. So if Miss Eldredge there wants to keep playin' mama, she's gonna hafta do it with my blessin'." He winked. "Keep that in mind." He scooted down, crossed his ankle over his knee, and closed his eyes.

Mother pressed her fist to her mouth, her eyes flooding with tears. She locked gazes with Lydia, her expression anguished, and Lydia nodded in silent agreement. There was no escape now. Nic Pankin was there to stay.

21

Micah sent the mother and her sons out the door, each boy proudly sporting new bandages. Micah couldn't resist an indulgent chuckle. Children were the same everywhere—a bandage was a badge of courage. He closed the door behind them, the same prickle of awareness that had plagued him an hour ago bothering him again. He couldn't get Nicky out of his mind. The whole time he had cleaned and bandaged the skinned knees and elbows of the boys, who had rolled down a graveled alleyway after tumbling from a homemade scooter, his mind had been on Nicky. Why did a child miles away pull his attention from those at arm's length?

With no one in the clinic except a volunteer cleaning the examination room, he had time to spare. He crossed to the telephone and dialed Lydia's home number, which he now knew by heart. As it had on all previous occasions, the ringing went on and on without an answer.

His dread increased. He should have been able to reach her before now. Something must be wrong. Deep inside, awareness dawned. Nicky and Lydia needed him. Without another thought, he flipped open the small book he kept in his desk drawer and located the number of Dr. Stanford, the Manhattan physician who offered the greatest amount of support to the clinic. He dialed, the *rat-a-tat-tat* of the finger plate keeping beat with his pounding pulse.

A receptionist answered on the first ring. Micah sucked in a deep breath and blurted, "This is Dr. Micah Hatcher of the Queens Clinic. I need Dr. Stanford to assign an intern to cover my clinic for several days, and I need it arranged as quickly as possible. Please have him return my call at his earliest convenience. Thank you." He hung up as soon as the receptionist acknowledged the message, then hurried to the exam room to talk to his volunteer. "Mark, not sure when I'll be able to leave, but I'm going to put the clinic in the hands of an intern for a week or so. Will you help him settle in—show him where we keep supplies and so forth?"

"Sure, Micah." The man gave Micah an intense look. "Is something wrong?"

Micah's stomach whirled. "I'm afraid so."

"Can I help?"

"Yes." Micah closed his eyes, steeling himself against the deep worry pinching his chest. "You can pray."

A car pulled into the driveway behind the house—certainly Father and Nicky returning from their drive. Lydia's heart fired into her throat. She glanced in Nic's direction. His eyes were closed, as they had been for the past twenty minutes. Was he asleep? Maybe she could sneak to the back door and send Father away. She signaled a silent message to her mother—upraised, open palms gesturing *stay here*. Mother nodded, and Lydia tiptoed down the corridor. Before she could reach the back door, it swung open and Nicky bolted through, his dimpled cheeks sweaty and his hair standing on end.

"Mama, Poppy let me stick my head out the window!" His high-pitched voice, full of excitement, nearly pierced her ears. She hissed in fear, throwing a frantic look over her shoulder. Boots thudded on the floor—Nic up and moving. Without another thought, she scooped Nicky into her arms and ran toward the back door, nearly colliding with her father.

"Lydia, what on earth are you—" Father's eyes drifted beyond Lydia's shoulder. His jaw dropped, and he staggered backward two steps, inadvertently blocking her passage. Defeated, Lydia turned as Nic stepped into the kitchen doorway. The same knowing grin he'd worn when he pushed his way into the house half an hour ago still rested on his face. How could she have ever thought him charming and handsome?

In her arms, Nicky shifted to look at the tall stranger. His brow puckered, and he pointed at Nic's shoulder. "That man has a bad owie."

Fearful of Nic's reaction, Lydia whispered a reprimand. "Shh, Nicky, be polite."

Nic burst out laughing. "Hey, he's sharp, isn't he?" He stepped fully into the kitchen. Father moved beside Lydia, placing a protective hand on Nicky's back. Nic kept his eyes on Nicky as he slowly advanced. Nicky watched Nic, his wide eyes holding curiosity but no fear. Nic stopped a mere three feet from Lydia and stood silent, seemingly entranced by the sight of his son.

Frozen in the kitchen doorway, Mother held both hands to her mouth. Father's heavy breathing filled Lydia's ears. Nicky's warm weight filled her arms. Senses alive yet strangely dull, Lydia felt as though she were watching a drama unfold on a stage. She was a part of it, but she didn't know her lines. A scream built in her throat, but she held it inside, determined not to frighten her son.

"Hi, mister." Nicky's innocent greeting of welcome brought tears to Lydia's eyes.

"H-hi." Amazingly, Nic's voice sounded gentle despite the deep tone. He shook his head as if to clear it. He flicked a glance at Lydia. "Didn't expect him to look so much like Eleanor."

Nicky tipped his head. "Who's Lellanor?"

Nic chuckled. "E-lea-nor," he repeated slowly. Then he shrugged. "Somebody I knew a long time ago."

"Oh." Nicky cupped Lydia's cheeks with both hands, capturing her attention. "Mama, I'm thirsty. Can I have a drink?"

"May I—" she corrected automatically, but she carried Nicky to the sink and poured a glass of water. He guzzled it, making the slurping noises parched little boys are prone to make, and all the while Nic Pankin remained rooted in place, watching them.

When Nicky finished he let out an "Ahhh" of satisfaction and handed Lydia the glass. He beamed a smile. "Thank you. Can I get down?"

Lydia tightened her hold on him.

Nicky sighed. "*May* I get down?"

"Yeah." Nic's sharp voice made Lydia jump. "Put him down. Lemme get a good look at him."

Lydia, too frightened to do otherwise, stood Nicky on the floor, but she kept a hand on his shoulder to hold him near. As usual, Nicky's socks bunched around his ankles above his brown Oxfords. His bony knees below the hem of his blue shorts seemed much more fragile to Lydia than they ever had before—perhaps because she was comparing him against such a tall, broad-shouldered man.

Very slowly, Nic went down into a crouch and extended his hand to Nicky. "C'mere, boy. Let's pull them socks up."

Nicky wriggled free of Lydia's hand and bounced forward, sticking out first one skinny leg, then the other. It took Nic a little time to tug the socks back where they belonged, working with only one hand, but he got it done.

"That better, boy?"

"I'm Nicky." Nicky stood in front of his father, hands behind his back. "Nicholas Allan Eldredge, the third, but Mama"—he gestured over his shoulder to Lydia—"calls me Nicky. You can, too."

Nic chuckled, a rumbling sound. "Oh yeah? You like that better'n 'boy,' huh?"

Lydia held her breath as Nicky worked his wiles on Nic. Her heart pounded erratically, and she inwardly prayed for strength to wrestle Nicky away when Nic tried to cart him off. Nic rose to his feet, his big hand reaching toward Nicky. Lydia's breath whooshed out, her muscles tensing, ready to leap forward. But Nic only ruffled Nicky's hair. "Okay, then, Nicky. How's that?"

Nicky nodded, his hair flopping across his forehead. He rocked in place. "What's your name?"

Nic glanced at Lydia, and for a moment she read confusion in his eyes. Then he dropped his gaze to the little boy who stood waiting, shifting from one foot to the other, and his expression changed. "My name's Nic. But you can call me Daddy."

Nicky turned around and sent Lydia a puzzled look. "Mama?" He lifted his foot as if to walk toward her. Before anyone else could move, Nic's arm snaked out and caught Nicky around the middle. He scooped the child from the floor and held him backward against his hip. Nicky, a panicked look on his face, squirmed to get down.

Father stepped forward, fists clenched. "Put him down, Pankin."

Mother reached for Nicky. "Yes, please put him down."

Nicky's wide-eyed gaze swung from his poppy to his grammy

to Lydia. He kicked his feet and pushed at Nic's arm. "You're squeezing my stuffing!"

Nic gave Nicky a little shake. "Hold still."

The gruff tone frightened Nicky into obedience, but the little boy's eyes welled with tears and he locked gazes with Lydia. He whimpered, "Mama?"

In her heart, a constant prayer repeated itself—*Help . . . Help . . . Please, help*—but she didn't know what she could do to stop Nic from taking Nicky.

"Mama-a-a-a?"

Nicky's cry prompted Lydia into action. She dashed forward and curled her hands over Nic's forearm. "Please, Nic, not like this. You're frightening him. Please put him down."

Nic scowled. "If I put him down, are ya gonna do somethin' stupid?"

"I won't do anything to endanger Nicky." Her breath came in little spurts through her nose as she locked eyes with Nic and waited for him to trust her. Nicky's arms stretched out to her, and after what seemed an eternity, Nic leaned forward slightly and deposited her son into her arms.

Nicky wrapped his arms and legs around her like a monkey clinging to a tree. He stuck out his lower lip and glowered over his shoulder at Nic. "You scared me."

"Sorry, boy. Just wanted to hold you."

"I'm Nicky." Nicky buried his face against Lydia's neck.

"Can't you see what you're doing to him?" Father thundered the question. The veins in his temples stood out. "If you care about him at all, you'll leave."

Nic clenched his teeth. "I can't do that. He's all I got, an' I want him."

Lydia cradled Nicky's head in the crook of her neck and whispered, "You won't—you won't sell him?"

Nic rocked on the heels of his boots. His gaze lingered on Nicky's hair—the dark curls so reminiscent of Eleanor's tumbling, shiny locks. A tenderness flitted through his gaze. But then he wiped his face clean of all emotion and spun on Father. "I reckon that's up to your papa here. If I'm gonna keep him, I gotta be able to provide for him. I need a decent job. You got one for me?"

Father drew back his shoulders, straightening to his full height, which was at least six inches shorter than Nic. His cheeks bore bright banners of temper. "You know very well why I let you go the first time. Has anything changed?"

Lydia drew in a sharp breath. *Oh, Father, please—just tell him yes!*

"Nope. An' it won't, either."

Nic's abrupt answer seemed to anger Father even further. "I will not have someone with your *habit* working in my plant. You're a safety hazard."

Lydia's knees went weak. She slumped against the kitchen table to keep from sagging to the floor. Why couldn't Father swallow his pride and give Nic the job? At least then they'd be able to keep track of him—and be able to keep track of Nicky.

"Then I can't make guarantees about what will happen with the boy." Nic turned to Lydia. He jerked his thumb toward the front door. "You can carry him out or give him to me here."

Tears rolled down Lydia's cheeks. "Please, Nic. Please don't do this to him." *Or to me.*

Father stepped forward, reaching into his pocket. Lydia gasped, preparing to shield Nicky if Father withdrew his pistol. But he held his money clip toward Nic. "Take it. Take all of it. But leave Nicky and don't ever come back."

Nic's eyes narrowed. "You gotta be kidding! You'd have the cops after me in a heartbeat, claimin' I stole that from you. I'm no idiot."

"I won't contact the police. All I'm asking for is your word that you won't ever come looking for Nicky again."

Nic looked at the thick wad of bills. His hand clenched and unclenched again.

Take it—please, Lord, let him take it. The prayer ran through Lydia's heart while several seconds ticked by, Mother's and Nicky's soft sobs the only sounds in the room.

Then a look of scorn crossed Nic's face, and he turned his hard gaze on Father. "That'd make it real easy on you, wouldn't it, old man? But the answer is no. You took my boy, you took my job, you took my dignity when you ran me out of your plant. You think you can buy anything with your money. Well, you can't buy me. I'm here to claim what's mine. So, Lydia"—he swung his gaze on her—"you can make this easier by carryin' him out to the truck, or I can take him here."

"Nic, please . . ." Lydia bit back a wail of distress. Where was her avenging angel? Couldn't God send one of His messengers to swoop in and save her son?

Nic bounded forward and wrapped his arm around Nicky's middle. Nicky screeched in fear as Nic pried him from Lydia's trembling arms. Father raced over and caught hold of Nicky's wrists, and the two men engaged in a fierce tug-of-war with Nicky as the rope. The little boy's cries became frantic, his fear-filled gaze boring into Lydia's with a pleading that nearly shattered her heart. She cried out, "Father! Nic! You're hurting him! Stop!"

The tussle ended so abruptly Nic staggered backward several feet, nearly dropping Nicky, who wriggled for freedom. Nic shifted his grip, allowing the boy to dangle under his arm like a sack of potatoes. He bounced a scowl across the other adults in the room and growled, "Next person who interferes is gonna get this kid dropped on his head. That what you want?"

Father clenched his fists, his body arching toward Nic. Lydia shot to his side and curled her hands around his stiff arm. "We don't want Nicky to be hurt." She spoke to Nic, but she prayed her father would heed her words.

"Smart girl." Nic turned toward the hallway, Nicky no longer writhing but continuing to whimper. "I got what I came for, so I'm leavin' now."

Lydia scuttled after him with Father on her heels. She held her hands helplessly toward Nicky, who dangled from Nic's arm like a rag doll, but Nic's brisk pace kept Nicky just out of her reach. Outside, Nic stomped to the truck, but with Nicky in his grasp, he couldn't open the door.

He spun on Lydia. "I'm gonna put him down. Don't do nothin' stupid." His glare moved past Lydia to her father, who stood bristling behind her, and lowered his voice to a whisper. "Got a gun in the truck glove box. You grab him and try to run . . ." The threat hung in the air between them.

Lydia stared hard into Nic's sullen face, her heart pounding. Was he bluffing? He could be, but she didn't dare risk it. She swallowed. "I won't."

He bent slightly, lowering Nicky's feet to the grass. The moment Nicky gained his footing, he lurched toward Lydia. But Nic grabbed the little boy's collar with a fierce yank. "Don't you move, boy."

Tears trailed down Nicky's flushed cheeks. His lower lip quivered, his dark eyes beseeched, and his arms remained outstretched, but both he and Lydia stayed obediently in place while Nic yanked the truck door open. He flapped his hand at the torn seat. "Get in."

Nicky hunched his skinny shoulders and shot a confused look in Nic's direction. "Where'm I goin'?"

"With me." Catching Nicky's shirt in a wad, Nic lifted the squirming boy and hefted him into the truck's cab.

Nicky yelped in surprise. He scrambled onto his knees as Nic slammed the door. Leaning out the open window, he whimpered, "Mama?"

Nic slapped the door. "Get back in there!"

Nicky's sobs became wild, stabbing Lydia's heart with a pain so intense she could scarcely draw a breath. She bolted forward. "Nic, let me comfort him at least! You're frightening him!"

Nic looked past her to the boy, and something in his hard expression melted. He jerked his thumb toward Nicky. "Go ahead. Make him calm down." Derision twisted his face again. "Don't wanna listen to him blubber the whole ride."

Ignoring Nic's callous reasoning, Lydia leaned into the window's opening and rubbed her son's back. Nicky's hold on her neck turned desperate, his little fingers digging into her flesh. "Nicky, sweetheart, please listen to Mama." Anguish strangled her vocal cords, putting a tremble in her voice, but she had to make this easier on Nicky. "You're going for a ride. You'll get to sit up high and look out. It will be a fun ride, Nicky."

Slowly Nicky pulled his tear-stained face from her shoulder. "I'm going for a ride?" His voice quavered.

"That's right." Lydia eased him onto the seat. She wiped his tears with her fingertips then brushed back his hair. "A ride with—" She couldn't call the monster who stood glowering at them *daddy*. "Nic."

"Can you come, too?"

She looked at Nic. He shook his head. The knife in Lydia's chest twisted. "No, sweetheart. Just you and Nic."

Fresh tears spilled down his cheeks. "But I don't wanna go without you, Mama."

Lydia sensed Nic's impatience. She shot a quick glance over her shoulder, silently begging him for time. Mother scurried across the yard with Nicky's teddy bear, which she held toward the little boy. Nic grabbed the tattered bear and started to throw the stuffed animal in the pickup's bed, but then he paused, staring at the bear for a moment with an unreadable expression on his face. He sighed, then snorted. With one gigantic step, he nudged Lydia aside and thrust the bear through the window opening. "Here. Now you aren't alone."

Nicky cuddled the bedraggled toy against his chest. "Please come, too, Mama."

Lydia's heart was surely shattered. Never had she felt such agony. "I can't, sweetheart." She took a deep breath, forcing a smile. She captured his face between her hands and kissed his forehead, his cheeks, his Cupid's lips. She breathed in the little-boy smell of him, memorizing every freckle, every scratch, every misplaced lock of hair. "Remember, though, that everywhere you go, Jesus goes, too. You're never alone, Nicky." She drew in a shuddering breath. "Y-you go now, and have fun. And you tell me all about it . . . when you see me again."

Nic grunted behind her. She swung around. Tears blurred her vision, but her voice was strong. "I will see him again, Nic. You can't keep him from me forever. He's my son."

Nic leaned forward, his face inches from hers. "He's *my* son, Lydia." He stomped around the truck, swung himself into the seat, and pumped the clutch. The engine roared to life. Nicky wrapped his fingers over the window case. Tears streamed down his pale cheeks. His mouth formed the word "Mama," but Lydia couldn't hear him over the sound of the engine. Then the truck lurched forward, sending Nicky against the back of the seat, and Nic drove away.

Lydia, her hands outstretched, took several stumbling steps after the truck. The futility of her action stilled her feet, but she stood in the road, hands reaching, staring at the top of Nicky's head in the back window. She remained there, frozen, until the truck turned the corner and disappeared from sight. Even then, she stared, praying . . . hoping . . . it might reappear.

"Lydia?" Mother touched Lydia's arm, tears streaming down her cheeks. She rasped, "I called the police. They're coming."

Hopelessness sagged Lydia's spine. "What difference does it make now? He's gone." Her gaze moved past Mother's form to the middle of the yard, where Father stood as if rooted in place. He might have been carved in stone, so still and stern was his appearance. Fury roared through Lydia's mind. Fists clenched, she staggered toward her father, her leaden feet making her clumsy. "A job. All you had to do was offer him a job, and we might have been able to stay in touch with Nicky until we could work this out."

Father's chin shot up, his eyes like granite. "I won't hire an addict."

"You won't hire—?" She clutched the hair at her temples and screeched loudly enough for the entire neighborhood to hear. "But you stood there while an addict drove away with my son!" Grief overwhelmed her. Sobbing, she fell to her knees. "My son. My baby, my baby . . ." The words groaned out in an animalistic keening. Mother knelt behind her, enclosing Lydia in her arms and rocking with her, crying with her. Together they mourned their loss, the sorrow no less for being shared.

When Lydia finally raised her face, her father was gone.

22

Nic squeezed the steering wheel and gritted his teeth. He glanced at the kid, who hugged his stuffed bear to his chest and sobbed. The wails pierced Nic's ears. If he had a free hand he'd give the boy a good whack so he'd have a reason for all that caterwauling.

"Hush your fussin' right now," Nic demanded. The truck hit a bump, and Nicky lost his seating. He let out a sharp yelp of alarm, but the shock stifled the wails. For the moment.

Scooting back and forth, the little boy wriggled his way into the corner again, as far from Nic as he could go without crawling out the window. Tears dampened his face and clung to his thick lashes, making them stand out in moist spikes. Nic turned his gaze forward, focusing on the road leading to Weston, determined to push aside the image of Eleanor that rose in his memory. But despite his efforts, the remembrance lingered, burning like coals in the center of his chest.

She'd cried so hard the day she'd told him she was expecting. For good reason. Nic'd been furious. Hadn't he told her he didn't want kids? He'd never had anything all to himself—certainly not anything that mattered. And he hadn't wanted to share Eleanor with anything or anybody. Not six months married and she'd gotten in a family way. And then she'd up and run off, choosing the baby over him.

Nic released a low growl, and the boy whimpered, hunkering over his bear. Nic shot another quick look at Eleanor's son. The little boy met his gaze, hurt and fear glittering in his eyes. The burn in Nic's middle increased in intensity. The boy's eyes—set in a heart-shaped face above a tip-tilted nose and bowed lips—stirred pictures of the sorrow he'd inflicted on the woman he'd loved and lost.

And now, if he handed the boy over to Mrs. Bachman, he'd lose his only remaining tie to Eleanor. But he had to let the Bachmans take Nicky—how else would he get money?

Confusion rolled through his mind as the strange desire to keep the little boy who resembled the woman he'd loved battled with the strong desire for money to feed his habit.

"M-mister?" The child's wavering, high-pitched voice filtered through Nic's thoughts. "I . . . I don't feel so good."

Nic took a look at Nicky's white, sweaty face, and he cursed. He jerked the steering wheel, bouncing the truck off the road and onto a grassy patch, nearly mowing down a cluster of scrub bushes. The engine died. Grinding his teeth in aggravation, Nic reached past Nicky and twisted the door handle, but the sticky latch remained caught. He wrenched the handle violently, muttering one oath after another. He needed to push the boy out of the truck before he made a mess. The latch finally released and Nic shoved the door open, but before he could grab Nicky's arm and send him onto the roadside, the contents of the boy's stomach spewed onto Nic's sleeve, Nicky's lap, and the seat. Nic cursed again and lurched backward, banging his head on his door.

Nicky wailed anew, blubbering, "I'm sorry! I'm sorry, mister! I didn't mean to."

"Shut up! Just . . . shut up!" The stench turned Nic's stomach, and the boy's shrill cries made his head pound. He cranked down his window and stuck his head out the opening, sucking humid air while Nicky sobbed on the other side of the cab. Nic pressed his fist to his forehead, his eyes crunched tight. Now what? He couldn't deposit a vomit-covered kid in the Bachmans' fine foyer. Mrs. Bachman would screw up her face in disgust. He'd have to take Nicky to his apartment, clean him up, then make the trip to Weston.

Stifling a string of profanity, he coaxed the engine to life, whirled the truck into the opposite lane, and headed back toward Boston.

Micah thanked the cab driver, grasped his suitcase, and trotted up the walk to Lydia's front door. The niggle of foreboding that had started in New York a week ago grew even stronger, the sensation of icy fingers coiled around his heart. The days of waiting for the replacement doctor had been agony, but now that Micah had reached Boston he hesitated about pressing the brass buzzer—what might he see when he looked into Lydia's eyes?

Taking a deep breath, he forced his trembling finger to connect with the button, then stepped backward. In a few moments the door opened slowly, revealing Lydia. Her face was colorless save deep smudges of purple beneath her eyes. Her hair, normally shiny and brushed back into feathery wings that framed her face, hung limp and lifeless beside sunken cheekbones. She appeared to have lost ten pounds since he'd seen her last. Concern washed over him like a tidal wave.

Her gaze met his, and then her face crumpled. Tears pooled in her bloodshot eyes. "Micah . . ." Without warning she threw herself into his arms.

Micah dropped his suitcase and held her tight. Her sobs were so harsh Micah feared she would break in two. Never had he witnessed such an outpouring of grief, and tears stung the back of his nose in response.

He lifted her and stepped over the threshold, closing the door with his foot to seal them inside the vestibule. Lydia continued to cling and weep with her arms locked around his neck. Micah rocked her, rubbing her back and smoothing her hair, whispering nonsense words to soothe her. Minutes stretched like hours as he waited for the storm to run its course, but eventually her sobs subsided to shuddering heaves and the raining tears dried to a trickle. Lowering her arms, she took a step back, but Micah kept his hands on her rib cage. He wasn't ready to let her go, and after such an emotional outpouring, he feared she might collapse.

She stood before him, her hands resting lightly on his forearms and her swollen eyes downcast. "I'm sorry, Micah. I shouldn't have fallen apart like that."

His fingers tightened and he managed a weak grin. "Don't apologize. You're entitled to a good cry now an' then—God gave us tears for a reason. You had a hurt to dispel." He paused, swallowing against the lump of worry filling his throat. "The hurt . . . It's about Nicky, isn't it?"

Lydia's eyes filled again, but she bit down on her lower lip and kept a rein on her emotions. She nodded, her hair slipping across her forehead. She reached up to brush it back with trembling fingers. "Nic took him six days ago."

"And you haven't eaten at all since he left, have you?"

Slowly, her head shifted left, right, then left again. "I can't eat, wondering if Nicky has had any dinner. Everything tastes like sawdust. I just—I just can't seem to function without him."

"Why didn't you call me?"

Her brow furrowed, and she lifted her bewildered gaze to his. "Your letter said you had a commitment . . . that you'd be away."

Micah inwardly groaned. He should have called more times. Sent a telegram. Sent someone in his stead. He'd failed her. And Nicky. He bowed his head as guilt weighed him down.

"Why did you come, Micah?"

Her raw query brought him to life. He guided her to the parlor, seated her on one end of the sofa, and settled himself at the other end. "I kept getting this feeling that something was wrong. I tried calling several times, but no one answered the telephone. My worry got the best of me, and I knew I wouldn't be able to rest until I saw for myself that you were okay."

Lydia released a huff. "I'm not okay. I'll never be okay again." She stared across the room, her expression haunted. "How do they do it, Micah? How do those mothers in Poland leave their children with strangers?"

Micah slid close and took her hand. It lay limp within his grasp. "They do it in the hope of saving their children."

She shook her head. "It's horrible, being separated from your child. Those women whose children have come to America—the children are safe, but the mothers will never see them again. Never!" She shuddered, hunching into herself. "I can't bear the thought of never seeing Nicky again. And I don't have the assurance that he's safe. With a man like Nic, he most certainly is not safe."

"Did the judge give Nicky to Pankin even with Mrs. Fenwick's letter of testimony?"

Lydia's eyes narrowed. "Nic showed up here the day we found your packet in the mail. We never got a chance to go to the judge. Nic took him before we could go."

Guilt assailed Micah. He should have gotten on a train and

delivered those documents himself the moment he had them in hand.

"Mother called the police the day Nic stormed in on us. They came nearly an hour after he'd left." Her expression hardened. "And just as Nic had said, they sided with him the moment I admitted Nic was Nicky's father. They didn't want to listen to my concerns, and they threatened me with . . . with prosecution if I tried to take Nicky away from his rightful father." Her chin quivered. "It isn't fair, Micah."

Micah agreed, but bemoaning things wouldn't help Nicky. "But you've got those papers now. And your father has a lawyer. Take the papers to a judge and fight to get back your son. Don't just roll over and play dead for Pankin."

Defensiveness flashed in Lydia's swollen eyes. "I've used up nearly all of my gas ration coupons, as well as many of Father's, driving the city in search of Nic and Nicky. But it seems hopeless. How can I fight for him when I don't know where he is?" Lydia's shoulders slumped. She hung her head. "I don't know what else to do."

Micah stared at her defeated pose. What had happened to the stubborn, determined woman he'd known before? Sorrow had taken the fight out of her. He squeezed her hand. "Where are your parents?"

"Father is at work, and Mother went to the market."

"What has your father done to try to find Nicky?"

"Nothing." Lydia's lips formed a grim line. "Father has done nothing. He acts as if there never was a child named Nicky who called him Poppy. When Mother or I cry, he leaves the room. He has no tolerance for our broken hearts."

Micah held his frustration inside, not wishing to add to Lydia's distress. But his thoughts railed against N. Allan Eldredge. What an obstinate man Lydia's father was. Micah drew in a deep breath and pushed off from the sofa. "Then I suggest we do what should have been done the day Pankin walked out the door. We'll take Mrs. Fenwick's letter and journal to the police. Not just some street cop, the chief of police. You'll tell him everything you can remember about the day Pankin came—what he was wearing, the kind of automobile he drove, anything he said that might help us find him. Then we'll take those documents from Mrs. Fenwick to your lawyer so he can arrange a meeting with a judge. We'll be ready to win custody the moment we've located Nicky."

Lydia still looked helpless. "Do you really think anyone will listen to me?"

Micah propped his hands on his hips. "I wouldn't have taken you for a quitter, Lydia. I can't believe you'd even consider giving up on your son without a fight." His words were harsh—intentionally so. But somehow he had to stir her to life, to action.

Lydia's head dropped. Her entire frame quivered, but she balled her hands into fists. Micah waited, watching her chest pump like a bellows as she sucked in great gulps of air and released them. Suddenly she jolted upright, her eyes glittering with indignation. "I'm not a quitter. And I won't give up on Nicky."

So she did have some life in her. Micah smiled. "Good." He took her hands. "We'll go, but first, let's pray." He bowed his head. "Heavenly Father, our hearts hurt because someone we love is not with us. But You know his whereabouts—Nicky is under Your watchful eye. Keep him safe. Hold Him tight in Your loving arms. And please lead us to him. In Your name we pray, amen."

"Amen," Lydia echoed. She looked up at Micah, her face still wan but her shoulders square. "Mrs. Fenwick's letter and journal are in my room. I'll get them, and then we can go."

Micah rubbed his cheek. "Lydia? Before we leave, you might want to run a brush through your hair and change your clothes."

Lydia lifted a hand to her bedraggled locks and glanced down her own length. She grimaced. "My, yes. If I go out in these rumpled clothes, the police will wonder if I'm the morphine addict." She dashed toward the stairs, but as she placed her foot on the lowest riser she paused and peered back at Micah. "Thank you for coming. I . . . I didn't realize how much I needed you."

Micah's heart turned over. He started to apologize for not coming sooner, but she clattered upstairs before Micah could form the response.

23

His name is Nicolai Pankin. His hair is dark blond—he wears it long, down to his collar—and his eyes are green. He is over six feet tall, with muscular shoulders but otherwise is fairly thin. He only has one arm—his left arm is severed just below the shoulder."

Micah stood in silence while the police chief on the other side of the cluttered desk recorded Lydia's description. Straightforward, professional, and articulate, she showed amazing strength, and Micah's admiration for her grew.

Lydia continued, "He drove away in a Ford pickup truck—an older model, rather battered—dark green in color. And he'll have a small boy with him." She swallowed, her throat visibly bobbing and her composure momentarily faltering. "At least, I hope he will." She sent a pleading look in Micah's direction.

He rested his elbow on the corner of the desk and gave the policeman Nicky's description. He watched his statements appear in pencil lead on a sheet of yellow paper: *Dark curly hair, brown eyes, age four years, approximately 38 inches tall and 34 pounds*. In his memory, Nicky's sweet voice echoed—*"I'm small for my age"*—and Micah sniffed back tears. How could a few brief lines of scribbled text possibly encapsulate the wonder of this child? He gulped and added, "He's a wonderful boy. Very bright and imaginative. And when he laughs . . ." A smile grew on Micah's face without effort. "Your heart ignites."

Lydia squeezed his hand, the shimmer in her eyes offering a silent thank-you.

Unruffled by her show of emotion, the officer asked Lydia, "And this Pankin—you say he's an addict?"

"That's right. Morphine. Which is why his wife didn't want him to have their baby. She was afraid he would harm the child."

"But he has the child now?"

"Yes, sir. He took Nicky from my care a week ago. I haven't seen either of them since."

The officer jotted another few lines, then raised his gaze to Lydia once again. "Do you have any idea where Pankin lives or works?"

Lydia pursed her lips. "He doesn't have a job, to my knowledge. As for where he lives—no idea at all. I just know he's in Boston somewhere."

"And you're sure he's still addicted to morphine?"

Lydia whisked a troubled glance at Micah before answering. "The day he took Nicky, he asked my father for a job. My father reminded him why he'd been fired from the plant four years ago—because of his habit—and asked if the situation had changed. Nic said no, and it never would."

Her grim statement chilled Micah. This man had Nicky.

"Well, thank you for coming in. I understand your concern. I'll alert the men to be watching for a man meeting this description." The officer leaned forward, his brow crunching into a scowl. "You understand . . . we can't arrest him unless he's caught performing an illegal activity. All we can do is keep an eye out."

Lydia raised her chin. "A four-year-old boy's life could very well be in danger right now because of this man's habit. I trust you will alert the men to that fact, as well."

The police chief nodded. "I will. Good luck in your custody battle, miss. Appears to me there's just cause for removing the boy from his father's care." He pushed out of his chair and strode away with the notes in hand, presumably to share them with the other officers.

Micah turned away from the desk. Lydia stood from her creaky wooden chair and looked up at him. "Now the lawyer?"

Micah waved his hand toward the double doors leading to the sidewalk. "Let's go."

As they left the police department, Lydia commented, "The law office my father uses is only a few blocks from here. We could save gasoline if we walked."

Considering the limited number of gas rations Micah had tossed into his suitcase as a last-minute thought while packing, her suggestion made sense. And a brisk walk might dispel some of their nervous energy. Micah shifted the envelope containing Mrs. Fenwick's letter and journal to his right hand and offered her his left. "That sounds fine."

Lydia slipped her hand through the bend of his elbow. They turned east and set off with a determined pace. Now that a plan was in place, Lydia seemed eager to see it through. For the first two blocks they walked in silence, eyes straight ahead. But as they waited to cross to the third block, Lydia swung her gaze to his. "Micah, how were you able to close the clinic?"

Micah looked right and left and then guided her across the street. "I asked a doctor friend to assign an intern for a few days." He grimaced. "Took longer than I'd hoped to find someone willing to fill in, which delayed my coming here, but I'd never leave it closed. Too many people rely on it."

Lydia hop-stepped onto the curb, sending a soft smile in his direction. "You love that clinic."

She'd made a statement rather than asked a question, but Micah affirmed it anyway. "I do. But more than that, it's where I'm meant to be. God put me there. I'll stay until He plants me somewhere else."

Lydia puckered her lips, her brow pinched in thought, as they wove between other pedestrians on the sidewalk. Finally she sighed. "I wish I knew where God wanted me planted. I feel . . . rootless. Especially now with Nicky gone. I feel as though my purpose for living has been ripped out and tossed aside."

Micah drew her to a stop. "Lydia, I know you're hurting. I know you miss Nicky. But I want you to remember something. Jeremiah—the book in the Bible, not my brother—says that God's thoughts are in place for every life, and His thoughts are for peace, not evil. That applies to Nicky, too. Somehow God will use this situation for good one day. We just have to trust."

"I want to trust. I've felt so much closer to God since I was in New York and I heard His voice. I know He's there. I just miss my son." Tears quivered on her lashes, but she roughly brushed them away with her fingertips and began moving forward again, her steps purposeful. "Eleanor wanted Nicky with me. I believe that's best for Nicky, too. We'll find him. We have to find him." She stopped in front of an ostentatiously carved building.

Micah looked up and spoke the name carved into the limestone cap on the building. "Claiborne and Mitchell."

Lydia nodded briskly. "This is the place. Let's go." Steely resolve colored her tone.

Micah opened the door and Lydia marched directly to the long, carved desk in the center of a massive reception area. He followed, resisting the urge to release an awe-filled whistle. Obviously these two lawyers did very well. A hallway divided the back half of the building, and ornately carved, paneled doors sprung off in both directions. Micah envisioned the rooms behind those doors—probably all wood-paneled and bedecked with thick Persian rugs, original oil paintings, and brass light fixtures just like the lobby. Suddenly he felt self-conscious in his tan dungarees, button-up shirt with the collar open, and scuffed Oxfords.

Lydia, however, was not cowed in the least. She moved directly to the receptionist, who sat like a king on his throne behind the glossy desk. "I need to speak to Mr. Claiborne immediately. It is a matter of great importance."

The thick glasses enlarged the receptionist's eyes, giving him the appearance of an owl. "Do you have an appointment, miss?"

"No, I do not. However, I'm certain Mr. Claiborne will be willing to see me."

"Mr. Claiborne rarely sees anyone without an appointment." The man set his lips in a firm line.

Lydia squared her shoulders. "I don't recall it being necessary for my father to make an appointment in the past."

"And your father would be—?"

"Nicholas Allan Eldredge."

The receptionist's ears turned red. "Please stay here, Miss Eldredge. I'll see if Mr. Claiborne is available." He disappeared down the hallway.

Lydia turned to face Micah, a wry grin on her face. "He'll be available. Father's money opens doors."

"Do you want me to come back with you?"

"It isn't necessary, Micah, but thank you." She took the envelope from him and lightly slapped her thigh with it.

The receptionist returned quickly, a tense smile on his narrow face. "Right this way, Miss Eldredge. I'm sorry to have kept you waiting."

Lydia clicked across the marble floor behind the receptionist, and a booming voice carried from the first room on the left. "Why, little Lydia, how good to see you!" The receptionist closed the door, sealing off the lawyer's voice.

Micah crossed to a grouping of leather chairs and seated himself, the leather squeaking as his weight pressed against it. He picked up the most recent *Life* magazine and thumbed through it while he waited for Lydia, silently praying that things would go well. Barely fifteen minutes passed before Lydia emerged. Her cheeks sported bright splashes of pink, and her eyes shone with determination.

Micah rose and met her halfway across the floor. "What did you find out?"

Lydia pointed toward the doors, and they headed outside. "Just as Father was told earlier, it will be hard to declare Nic as unfit, but it can be done with some effort. We're going to need to find people willing to testify that they have seen Nic use morphine—and it needs to be recent use. We also need a record of his employment and why he left each job. Father fired him when he came to work under the influence, so it's possible other employers have released him for the same reason. That will need to be verified. His home will require a thorough examination to determine if it is safe for a child, and it will also help to have a record of his places of residence—see if there's a pattern of moving because of his addiction. Mrs. Fenwick's accurate accounting of Eleanor's last wishes is a benefit but by itself isn't enough for me to win custody. We've got a lot of work ahead of us."

He liked the way she said "we," including him in the effort. He also liked her enthusiastic attitude. She glanced up and must have caught his smile because she paused. "What's amusing?"

"I'm not amused, Lydia. I'm pleased by the change. You

scared me when you opened the door and fell apart. You didn't seem to have any life left in you. Yet here you are, armed for battle and charging out, determined to win."

Lydia smiled sheepishly. "I was feeling sorry for myself—and overwhelmed. Honestly, Micah, all Mother has done is cry since Nicky left, and Father . . ." She shook her head, sighing. "Well, Father shows no emotion at all. I've been caught between them. But not anymore! My little boy is out there somewhere, and with God's help, I'm going to find him and bring him home."

"Good girl." Micah's chest swelled with pride, and he impulsively wrapped her in a quick hug. "That's the Lydia I know and love."

The moment the last word escaped, both of them froze. The air seemed to sizzle between them. The bustling city—the blaring automobile horns, the odor of exhaust, the towering buildings—slipped away, and Micah and Lydia were all that existed in a patch of sunlight, breath held tight, eyes wide and seeking, blood pumping, incredibly aware of what Micah had just admitted.

A car horn honked as tires squealed, and Micah jolted. His breath whooshed from his lungs. Lydia shifted her gaze away, her shoulders wilting. Micah's heart rate slowed, his breathing regulated, the city rushed back, and reality surrounded them once more. He opened his mouth to tell her—what? That he didn't mean what he'd said? He couldn't honestly deny it. He did love her. But to have allowed it to slip out in that way, at this time, was all wrong. How could he take it back without hurting her?

Before he could form any kind of speech at all, her dark eyes suddenly widened and she pointed frantically to something behind him, spluttering, "Look! Look!"

Micah spun and looked, but he saw nothing more than a

ramshackle pickup truck turning off Market Street. Then his heart lurched. He reached for Lydia, who caught his arm and tugged at it.

"That's Nic's truck! I'll get my car and we'll follow him! Watch the truck!"

And off she ran, leaving Micah straining to keep the pickup in his sights.

24

Lydia squealed the car to a stop next to the curb where Micah stood waiting. As he climbed into the car, she asked, "Which way did he go?"

Micah pointed. "The pickup turned south—I think about three blocks off of Market. Let's try to catch him. I think your Hudson will be more reliable than that thing he's driving."

Lydia lunged into traffic. Two cars swerved and honked at her, but Lydia merely gritted her teeth. She drove as recklessly as she dared, following Nic's trail. Finally, they caught a glimpse of Nic's pickup a few cars ahead.

"Yes! There it is! We've got him in sight now." Micah touched Lydia's shoulder. "Settle down and drive safely."

She risked a quick grin in his direction. "Am I scaring you?"

"No, but your driving is."

Lydia laughed, amazed at how good it felt. Her heart still raced—she might soon be reunited with Nicky!—but she slowed enough to avoid riding the bumper of the car ahead of her.

She sat as high in the seat as possible, trying to peer around traffic to get a clear view of Nic's back window. "Does Nic have Nicky with him? Can you tell?"

Micah grabbed the dashboard, squinting ahead. "I think he's by himself."

"That means he's left Nicky somewhere." Now her heart pounded in fear. "Oh, Micah, you don't think he's sold Nicky, do you?"

Micah snorted. "If he'd recently come into money, I don't think he'd be driving that old heap."

Lydia prayed he was right. They followed Nic's pickup as it left the downtown area, passed through several middle-class neighborhoods, and finally wove its way into an area Lydia had never visited before. She grasped the steering wheel tightly as her nervous gaze scanned the area. "This looks like a rough place to live." Her voice trembled with nervousness. "And he left Nicky here somewhere, alone."

"Not alone," Micah said, his tone firm. "Nicky is never alone."

"That's exactly what I told Nicky the day Nic took him away. And I know Jesus is with him, but—" She yelped as a taxicab careened from a side street, narrowly missing her. She slammed her brakes and downshifted. The Hudson jumped a curb before shuddering and then heaving into silence. Two blocks ahead, Nic's truck rumbled around a corner and disappeared.

"No! No!" Lydia pounded on the steering wheel, then viciously twisted the key, willing the car to life. A whine vibrated from beneath the hood, but the engine refused to engage.

Micah hopped out. "Release the hood's latch."

Lydia gave the silver latch a firm yank, and Micah lifted the hood. He leaned in, then knelt on the glass-strewn pavement and peeked beneath the car. After a few seconds, he stood, brushed his hands together, and sent a dismayed look in her direction.

Gooseflesh broke out across Lydia arms. She slid out and joined Micah. "What is it?"

"When you went over the curb, something pierced the oil pan." He pointed to a thin flow forming a shiny black puddle under the car. "You flattened a tire, and I think the wheel might be bent. This car won't be going anywhere anytime soon."

Panic clawed at her heart. "What do we do?"

"We'll have to see if someone who lives around here will let us use their telephone to call for help—either your father or a towing company."

Lydia gaped at him. "But what about Nic? He's getting away!"

Sympathy creased Micah's brow. He cupped her shoulders. "Lydia, you can't chase after him on foot. Look around."

She did, taking in the dilapidated houses with broken windows and rotting porch floors. People peered from behind shredded curtains, their faces somehow menacing. She shivered despite the sun's heat.

Micah nodded grimly. "We can't leave the vehicle here unattended, and we shouldn't go traipsing around. I don't think it's safe."

A lump filled Lydia's throat. She swallowed, but the knot remained there, a ball of frustration and worry. "But Nicky might be here somewhere, Micah. How can I think of my car before him?"

Micah massaged her shoulders briefly before lowering his hands. "As difficult as it is, you've got to see to your car first. Without it, we can't seek Nicky." Slipping his arm around her waist, he guided her to the gaping driver's door. "Get in there, roll up the windows, and set the locks. I'm going to"—he flicked an uncertain glance at the closest house—"see if anyone has a telephone I can use. If not, I'll walk until I find a telephone booth. But no matter how long I'm gone, stay inside the car. Don't open your door for anyone but a policeman or me. Do you understand?"

Lydia recognized the deep concern in his voice. As much as she ached to run down the street in search of Nicky, she understood the importance of safety. "All right." She climbed behind the wheel and pulled the door closed behind her. Reaching through the open window, she caught Micah's sleeve. "Please hurry."

He leaned down and offered a reassuring smile. "I will. And don't worry. We asked God to lead us to Nicky, and He brought us this far. He won't fail us now. Sit tight—I'll be back as quickly as possible. While I'm gone, pray."

He waited while she rolled up the windows and pushed the lock buttons. Then, with another smile and wink—the sweet gesture bringing the sting of tears to Lydia's eyes—he strode up the block.

Nic parked behind a car with two missing wheels and the back window broken out. When would the landlord make the owners haul the thing away? Cats had taken up residence in it and they yowled all night, disrupting his sleep. Besides, with that hunk of junk filling space, he couldn't even get close to his own apartment building. He'd lodge another complaint if it wouldn't require a face-to-face with the building's owner. Since he was behind on his rent, he needed to keep his distance.

He skirted patches of broken glass as he strode across the weed-infested yard where a squealing passel of dirty-faced kids kicked an empty coffee tin back and forth in place of a ball. A rolled-top paper bag clutched in his hand, he stepped off the yard onto the chipped concrete slab fronting his building. The door had long been stripped of its doorknob and it hung on loose hinges. He hooked the bottom edge with his boot toe, sending the warped door bouncing against the brick wall, and entered the hallway. No sunlight reached inside, and deep shadows shrouded the filthy space. Nic poked the button for the overhead light. The bulb on a length of twisted wires brightened, fizzled, then popped. Darkness fell around him. He snorted. Burned out. Again.

He stood for a few moments, allowing his eyes to adjust to the gloom, and then he aimed himself for the narrow stairway leading to the upper floors. Two kids plowed out of an apartment door on his left and dashed past him while their mother hollered after them to get themselves right back inside. The pair didn't even pause—just laughed like a couple of hyenas and kept going. Nic shook his head in disgust and moved onward. Fool kids anyway.

He'd wanted a first-floor apartment when he'd moved in. Tough hauling belongings up flights of stairs with only one hand. And on his weak days—the ones when he couldn't get ahold of any magic dust—he had trouble just getting himself up the stairs. But people with kids lived in most of the first-floor apartments. And he'd always wanted to avoid kids.

Until now.

He paused midway up the staircase, his knuckles resting on the banister and one foot on a higher riser than the other. His gaze lifted, and he envisioned his one-room apartment where Eleanor's son—*his* son—probably cowered in a corner. The kid had spent every day so far hunkered in the corner, as far from Nic as he could get and still be in the same room. Nic berated himself. Why hadn't he delivered the boy to the Bachmans yet? His August fourth deadline had long passed. And he needed money. Needed it bad. The hubcaps and leather coat he'd taken from a fancy car uptown hadn't fetched nearly enough at the pawn shop. So he oughta take the boy to Weston and get his promised five thousand dollars.

But he remained rooted on the stairway like a garden statue, his face aimed toward the second floor and his stomach pinching. If only the kid didn't look so much like Eleanor. If he had his father's coloring instead, Nic would be able to dump him in a heartbeat. He'd never cared for his own appearance. Too much like his old man's face looking back from the mirror. He'd had no trouble walking away from his parents, but walking away from Nicky . . . He couldn't do it. Not when the kid looked at him with Eleanor's eyes.

Need scratched his flesh, giving him the sense of bugs crawling beneath his skin. Nic sighed and forced himself to continue upward. He'd get to his apartment, take his medicine—or his candy, as he now called it for Nicky's sake—and maybe, just maybe, if there were any luck in the world at all for Nicolai Pankin, the morphine would dull his pain and give him enough courage to make that trip to Weston after all.

Nic plodded up the remaining stairs, rounded the curve at the landing, and scuffed the short distance to his apartment. He unlocked the door and pushed it open with his shoulder, stumbling over the threshold. He waved the paper sack. "Hey, kid. Gotcha some bananas." He scanned the room, looking in each corner first. No crouching boy with a teddy bear locked in his arms. Kid must've found a new hiding place.

He roamed the small space, peeking behind furniture and in cubbies. "Remember yesterday, you said you wanted one? Well, c'mon and get it." Nic kicked at a heap of discarded clothing, but the boy hadn't burrowed beneath it. He frowned, turning a slow circle while apprehension prickled his scalp. "Nicky?"

Nic plopped the sack on the little table in the kitchen area of the apartment and then darted out the door and down the hallway to the bathroom. The door was closed. The lock never held, so closed was supposed to mean occupied—knock first.

Nic didn't bother to knock. He threw the door open, bellowing, "Nicky, you in here?"

"Ain't nobody here but me!" a crotchety voice rasped from behind a stall wall—old Mr. Tinker from Apartment 4B.

"You seen a little boy—dark hair, 'bout waist high?" Nic's heart thumped as he waited for a reply.

"Seen a little dark-haired feller scuttlin' down the stairs near an hour ago. Had a teddy bear under his arm." The old man's voice took on a sharp edge. "Now get outta here an' let a man have some privacy, why don'tcha?!"

Nic backed out, leaving the door wide open. Tinker hollered in indignation, but Nic ignored him. That boy could be anywhere by now, and he'd better find him. Five thousand dollars—and his own peace of mind—rested on it.

Nic searched until dusk, exploring the gaps between close-set houses, behind trash bins and abandoned appliances, and under parked cars. He stopped every person he encountered and asked if they'd seen a little kid carting a teddy bear. Most just shrugged, but twice someone pointed him in the direction Nicky had gone. But even with their hints, Nic came up empty. With night approaching and his ability to see hindered—as well as his need to consume his magic powder making every muscle in his body twitch—he reluctantly aimed himself for the apartment building once more.

He growled under his breath as he stomped back home. The itch beneath his skin tormented him, and he dug at his flesh with his chipped fingernails while he walked, his frustration growing with every step. Blamed kid. What'd gotten into him to take off like that? Didn't he know danger lurked in this neighborhood? Nicky would be like a lamb in a wolves' den with the rough kids who lived around here. And all beat up and bloodied, no way Mrs. Bachman would pay full price for him.

His steps faltered as he envisioned Nicky covered in bruises, maybe lying hurt and alone somewhere. Something akin to protectiveness welled within him, and the feeling had nothing to do with losing money. He paused and examined his own thoughts. Had he grown attached to the kid? He released a derisive snort and forced his feet into motion. His need for morphine was muddling his brain. As soon as he steadied his system with his magic dust, he'd borrow—or steal—a lantern and go searching again. He'd find that boy if he had to turn over every stone between here and the county line.

He entered his building and pawed his way to the second floor, the lack of light making him dizzy. When he rounded the bend on the foyer, his gaze fell on a small lump in the hallway right outside his door. He squinted, trying to make out the shape in the shadows. Realization dawned, and within his chest his heart seemed to turn a somersault.

"Nicky?"

The lump shifted, Nicky's head lifting from his sunk-low pose. His white face nearly glowed in the gray hallway. "M-mister?"

Nic stumbled forward, anger mingling with relief in his mind. He grabbed Nicky's arm and tugged him to his feet. "Where you been, boy?"

Tears winked in the child's eyes. "I . . . I wanted to go home. I want Mama. But I couldn't find my way."

Blowing out a mighty breath, Nic gave Nicky's skinny arm a shake and then released him. He fumbled for his key. "'Course you couldn't. We ain't anywhere near your old house. Plain stupid for you to even try to find it."

Tears slipped down Nicky's cheeks. He began to whimper.

Nic unlocked the door and pushed Nicky inside. The little boy scuttled to the closest corner and sank down, burying his face in his teddy bear's stomach. Sobs wracked his little body. Nic stood just inside the door, staring at the child. An unfamiliar yearning—the desire to offer comfort—rolled through the back of his mind. But he didn't have any idea what to say. What to do.

The prickle of need pulled his attention from the distraught little boy in the corner. He strode to the kitchen table and opened the sack. In the bottom, below the pair of overripe bananas, his packet of magic dust beckoned. He'd see to himself. Satisfy the demons that clawed at his flesh. And tomorrow he'd bundle the kid in his pickup and take him to the Bachmans. No more delays. He had no place in his life for a child. Especially not Eleanor's child. Because Eleanor's child deserved more than he could give.

25

Micah listened with interest as Lydia faced her father across the kitchen table where she, Micah, and Allan Eldredge sipped Postum while Lavinia washed dishes.

"Father, I'm not asking for your ration coupons. I'm asking for the use of your car until mine is available again."

"But the mechanic indicated it might be several days before the Hudson is operational." Allan flicked a frown in Lavinia's direction. "Is there any of that pie left? I'd like a piece to go with my Postum."

Without a word, Lavinia crossed to the refrigerator and removed a small plate holding the remaining slice of strawberry-rhubarb pie. Micah held back the question hovering on the end of his tongue. How could Allan Eldredge behave as if nothing were amiss? Lavinia had prepared a fine meal, but no one had an appetite except Allan. He'd consumed every bit of his pork roast, peas, carrots, and potatoes, seemingly oblivious to the cloud of worry hanging over the table. His unconcerned, uncooperative attitude puzzled Micah. Didn't he care at all about the child he'd previously claimed as his grandson?

Lydia put her hand over her father's wrist, preventing him

from stabbing a fork into the pie. "Do you understand we spotted Nic today? We found the area of town in which he apparently lives. Nicky could very well be there with him, and—"

Allan jerked his hand free and rose at the same time, sending his chair clattering to the floor. Fury blazed in his eyes. "You honestly believe the man still has Nicky? He's an addict, Lydia. He'd sell his own soul to feed his repugnant habit. The very day he carted Nicky out of this house, he disposed of him the same way any of us would dispose of an unwanted litter of kittens. The boy is gone, and I will not have you encouraging me to cling to a hope that doesn't exist!"

Lydia pushed to her feet, reaching her hand toward her father. "Father, I—"

He slapped her hand aside. "No! I will not listen to another word. Nicky is dead to us, Lydia. It's best for all of us to accept it, bury him in our minds, and move on." He stomped out of the room and then his feet pounded on the stairs. Moments later a door slammed overhead.

Lydia turned slowly toward her mother, who looked at the ceiling with her lips pursed tight. "Should I . . . ?"

Lavinia shook her head. "Let him be. I'll go up in a bit and talk to him." Her sympathetic gaze rested on Lydia's face. "He's proud. Too proud to admit he was wrong the day Nic came and asked for a job. He blames himself."

Lydia's expression hardened. "He should."

Lavinia sighed. "Yes. But we can't change what's past." She angled her head to look at Micah. "Dr. Hatcher, you don't have an emotional investment in this situation, which allows you to look at things more logically. May I ask you a question?"

Micah could have argued with her assumption he had no emotional investment. His heart ached for Nicky, for Lydia, and even for the stubborn man who sealed himself away from everyone upstairs out of his heavy burden of guilt. But instead, he said, "Of course."

Unshed tears brightened the older woman's eyes. "Do you really believe there's a chance Nic hasn't . . . disposed of Nicky in some reprehensible manner?"

Micah wouldn't offer false hope, but he would answer honestly. "When Lydia and I spotted Pankin today, he was driving his dilapidated truck into a very unsavory neighborhood. My gut tells me if he'd sold Nicky, he'd be long gone. Or at least have used the money to purchase a decent automobile or a better apartment." He swallowed, his heart pounding in trepidation. "We can't know for sure without talking to him, but I do believe there's still reason to hope."

Lavinia offered a thoughtful nod, her lower lip caught between her teeth. Her movements so slow Micah almost thought he imagined them, she turned to face her daughter. "Lydia, you know I never go against your father's wishes." Her whisper held evidence of deep turmoil. "But my heart is breaking. And even though he won't admit it, so is his. We have to keep seeking, no matter what he says." She gripped Lydia's hand and looked at Micah. "Take Allan's car and go tonight. Find Nic. Find Nicky. Allan stores a loaded pistol under the driver's seat. Do whatever you must to bring my grandson home again." She scurried for the stairway.

Lydia watched her mother depart, then turned to Micah. Her face was white, but her eyes held determination. "Are you ready?"

Micah's pulse galloped. "You bet," he said. Then he followed Lydia out the back door, a prayer rising from his heart. *Lord, guide us and keep us—all of us, including Nic—safe.*

❧

"Look . . . isn't that Nic's truck?" Micah's voice was croaky but carried a note of excitement.

Lydia gripped the steering wheel and leaned forward, searching the shadows in the direction Micah had pointed. The car's hooded headlights showed trash-strewn streets, weed-speckled yards, and run-down apartments. As much as she wanted to find Nicky, she almost hoped Micah was wrong about the truck. The idea of Nicky being trapped in such a dismal place made her shudder.

She rolled to a stop next to the truck, and recognition exploded in her mind. "It's his. So this is it." Immediately, within her stomach, butterflies whirled into a wild dance of both apprehension and anticipation. "I'll park, and we'll go in."

A trio of rough-looking young men leaned against a nearby building, scowling in Lydia's direction as she pulled up to the curb. She gulped. "Do you think it's safe to get out?"

"We'll be all right. Grab the flashlight, will you?"

Lydia retrieved the battery-operated Streamlight her father kept in the glove box while Micah pawed under the driver's seat. She pushed the switch on the brass flashlight and its beam fell on the pistol's barrel as he slipped the weapon into his waistband. A band of fear wrapped around Lydia's chest, impeding her breathing. How she prayed he'd have no need to utilize the pistol.

He twisted the door handle. "All right. Let's go."

Micah caught her hand when she rounded the Studebaker's hood. Shivers ran like spiders up and down her spine. Clinging tight to Micah's hand, she aimed the flashlight's beam forward and kept one eye on the young men. They fell silent and stared at her and Micah, but none of them approached. Relieved, she watched her feet as Micah guided her toward the apartment building closest to Nic's truck.

The three risers leading to a square concrete stoop hosted

a jagged crack climbing from bottom to top, its erratic pattern reminding Lydia of the part a little girl might make in her doll's hair. Crumpled newspapers and broken bottles hugged the foundation of the building in lieu of flowers or bushes. Faded red bricks and crumbling mortar formed the outside façade, and paint-chipped shutters hung haphazardly from window casings. The entire structure held a weary, hapless appearance that created an ache in the center of Lydia's chest.

She glanced at Micah. "This is where my Nicky lives?"

Micah's lips formed a grim line. "He won't be here for long."

They climbed the steps, one on either side of the crack, and entered the dark, foul-smelling building. Lydia bounced the flashlight beam across the walls, illuminating numbers and slots holding little paper cards with names scrawled in faded black ink on every door. She nearly sighed in relief. If those names indicated each apartment's occupant, they'd be able to locate the one belonging to Nic without knocking on doors.

After checking all eight doors on the first floor, Micah nudged Lydia to the stairs. Their feet moved in unison, the light slap of their soles on the wooden risers echoing in the narrow staircase. A slight turn awaited at the top, and Lydia aimed the flashlight's beam at the first door. Before she could read the name, however, a familiar voice, raised in anger, erupted from behind the second door and sent her stomach into spasms of fear.

"Listen, boy, I've had it. Stop that snivelin' an' let me sleep!"

Her heart lodged in her throat. Nic was such an intimidating man, and to holler so—Nicky must be terrified. But at least she knew Nicky was still with his father.

She thrust the flashlight at Micah and darted on quivering legs to the door bearing the little card that read "Pankin." Unconcerned about other occupants in the building, she banged her fist against the unpainted wood as hard as she could. The *bam! bam! bam! bam! bam!* reverberated in the hallway, and up and down the corridor mutters rose from behind closed doors.

One bellowed above the others. "Go away!" Nic's voice again, somewhat slurred. Was he drunk? Sobs also carried from the apartment. Fear made Lydia queasy, and she pounded a second time as Micah stepped up behind her, his warm palm on the small of her back a reassuring pressure. Footsteps thumped, drawing near. Then the door swung wide.

Nic, wild-eyed and red-faced, gripped the doorjamb and glared out at them. When his gaze fell on Lydia, he shook his head and grimaced. "*You*. Shoulda known you'd show up."

"Where's Nicky?" Lydia nearly danced in place, eagerness to hold her son making her light-headed. "Is he all right?"

Nic growled. "Yeah, yeah, he's fine. Stubborn cuss. Won't eat nothin'. But he's got enough wherewithal to keep me awake with his *waah-waah*. All he does is cry."

The thought of her ever-happy little boy reduced to constant tears crushed what was left of Lydia's injured heart. Tears clouded her vision. "May I see him?"

Nic grimaced again, sweat beading across his forehead. "Might as well. Maybe you can shut him up. He doesn't listen to me." He stepped aside and allowed Lydia and Micah to enter.

Lydia's gaze swept the gloomy, grimy room. Nicky crouched on a tattered, bare mattress in the corner. He sat with his knees pulled under his chin and his hands covering his ears, his eyes squeezed tight. His tear-stained face appeared chalk-white in the dim light. She rushed over and knelt before him. Her voice broke as she touched his arm. "Nicky?"

The little boy cracked open one eye, then both eyes flew wide and he catapulted into her arms. "Mama! I prayed to Jesus to bring you an' He did it!"

From the middle of the room, Nic stood with his weight on

one hip, his expression dour. "All that kid does is whimper an' talk to Jesus. Startin' to think he's half-witted." The muscle in his left cheek twitched.

"This child is far from half-witted, Nic." Lydia sat on the mattress and cradled Nicky. He clung to her as though he'd never let go. She swallowed her agony and addressed Nic. "He needs care beyond what you're giving. You can't keep a child locked up in a room like this and expect him to be happy." Her stomach writhed in disgust at the stained furniture, the food rotting on the counter, and the trash littering the scuffed wood floor. "You can't holler at him and expect him to listen. How would you like to be treated that way?"

"Well, I'm his daddy!" Nic staggered across the room and pointed an accusing finger at Nicky, who burrowed deeper into Lydia's neck. "I don't much care for bein' treated like he hates me!"

Micah stepped between Nic and Lydia, his hand resting on the handle of the pistol. He spoke in a reasonable tone. "We all realize you are Nicky's . . . daddy." It appeared to take some effort for Micah to say the word. "But since Nicky has grown up not knowing you, it will take some time for him to accept that relationship. He can't know you any better than you know him right now."

Nic turned his narrowed gaze on Micah. "Who're you?"

Micah smiled and held out his hand as if he were at a social event making the rounds. "I'm Micah Hatcher, a friend of Lydia and Nicky's. It's nice to meet you."

Nic looked at the hand, hesitated, then finally gave it two pumps before pulling away. He turned back to Lydia, swaying slightly with the motion. "Kid's gonna hafta accept it. First, I figured on stickin' him with a family. I got connections." He smiled, but it looked more like a sneer. "Had folks interested—willin' to give me five thousand dollars to adopt him." He jammed his open hand in the air, wonder blooming across his face. "Five thousand dollars. Can you believe that? Coulda got myself outta this dump and into somethin' nice with that kind of money."

He shook his head, scratching his whiskery chin. "Every day, been puttin' the kid in the truck, headin' out to make the deal"—Lydia cringed at the way he equated the sale of a child with a simple business deal—"but he kept lookin' at me with Eleanor's eyes. An' I kept thinkin' about Eleanor . . . what she'd want me to do." Nic's voice softened, a tenderness creeping in. "An' I couldn't do it. Couldn't make the deal. So I brought him back here." The tenderness disappeared as he straightened and blustered, "But I can't do nothin' to please him. So tomorrow, I'm gonna follow through." Nic's swaying became more pronounced, and sweat beaded on his forehead and temples.

Micah's brow creased in concern. "Are you okay, Nic? You don't look so well."

Nic snorted with humorless laughter. "I'll be okay. Just need some o' my . . . candy. Been waitin' for the boy to go to sleep before I took care o' myself." Lydia clutched Nicky tighter as Nic stumbled to a decrepit table and reached into a rumpled paper bag. He turned with a small square packet in his hand. "I'll be fine an' dandy here in no time." Micah followed and reached for the packet, but Nic pulled it back, his expression fierce. "Whadda ya think you're doin'?"

Micah shrugged. "Just curious. What kind of candy makes you feel better?"

Nic grinned and shook the packet in Micah's face. A small amount of white powder drifted downward. "This kind. An' I need it *now*."

"Is that morphine?"

Nic drew back, his brows coming down in a sharp V. "You some kind of cop?"

Micah chuckled. "Nah. Not even close."

Nic scowled at Micah for a moment, as if measuring him. Then he released another snort. "Yeah. It's morphine. Now get outta my way so I can take it. Already got the sweats an' shakes. I gotta get this in my gut." Nic started to push past Micah, heading for the sink.

Micah took one step, blocking Nic's pathway. "No. You don't have to take it."

Nic gawked at Micah, his jaw hanging slack. "Are you trying to be funny, mister? 'Course I gotta take it." Nic grimaced, rubbing his withered shoulder. "You don't know the pain that comes when I don't take it. I got no other choice."

Micah inched closer to Nic. "Listen, I'm a doctor, and—"

Nic swore. "Oh, just what I need. Another doctor. It was a doctor got me hooked on this stuff! Said, 'Take it, Nic, it'll ease your pain.' So I done what he said, an' I been battlin' pain ever since!"

Micah nodded, his expression kind. "You've had a rough go, there's no denying it, but I can help you beat this addiction if you'll let me."

Nic sank against the edge of the counter, the little packet pinched between his fingers. He stared at it with watery eyes, his face drooping. "What's the use? I ain't worth nothin'. Even my old man told me so—what good's a one-armed farmhand? Tried to prove him wrong, but I can't get beyond needin' this stuff to get through the weeks. All I do anymore is find ways to get it. It's no life, but it's all I got. . . ."

"It can be better, Nic." Micah's voice grew more intense. "If you want it to be better, then we can make it so. We'll work together to help you beat this addiction."

"The only way I'll ever beat it is to die."

The words emerged on a strangled groan. Despite the man's deplorable behavior, sympathy rose in Lydia's chest. How awful to be held in such tight clutches. Nic was in prison—a prison of his own making. She struggled upright, carrying Nicky, and crossed to the men. Although everything within her desired to race out the door with Nicky and never come back, she knew they'd never be free of Nic unless they did what they could to help him beat his addiction.

Gathering up every bit of gumption she possessed, she spoke directly into Nic's drawn, whisker-dotted, hateful face. "Listen to me, Nic Pankin, you said you wanted to be Nicky's daddy. You chose not to sell him so you'd have the chance to be his daddy. But you know Eleanor wouldn't want Nicky's daddy to be addicted to that . . . that foul drug. So get yourself clean! Trust yourself to Micah. He's a fine doctor, and he can help you because he has a Higher Power on his side."

"Higher power?" Nic's bleary gaze roved in Micah's direction, then swerved back. "You mean opium?"

"No, I mean God."

Nic threw back his head and laughed, ending with a vicious cough that doubled him over. "God? Did you say God?"

Lydia held her chin high, refusing to be cowed by his ridicule. "Yes. *God*. Don't for one minute question His power. Micah and I prayed to find you, and we did—before you could do something stupid." With a burst of bravado she snatched the packet out of Nic's hand. "God knows exactly where you are, and He knows what you need. He sent Micah here to help you. So stop being so disagreeable and let him help you."

Nic stared at Lydia, and even Micah gazed at her in open-mouthed surprise. She took a step backward, replaying her statements in her mind. Had she really demanded Nic accept

Micah's assistance? How many times in the past week had she wished ill on the despicable man? Yet in those minutes she realized that even more than she wanted him to suffer, she wanted him to live, to find freedom from the chains that had held him in bondage for so many years, and for him to find his way to God. How different his life would be—Nicky's life would be—if Nic changed.

Her body quivering in hopefulness, she repeated, "Let Micah help you." She held her breath, waiting for Nic's response.

Nic's face was deathly white, the sweat causing his pale flesh to glisten as if he ran a high fever. His cheek twitched, and he brought up his trembling hand to press against the quivering muscle. His watery gaze darted from Lydia, to Micah, and then settled on Nicky. For a few brief seconds, Lydia glimpsed a tenderness in his eyes, and her heart expanded. Somewhere underneath this hard, unyielding man was a kind heart trying to break free. For Nicky's sake, Lydia prayed Nic's kind side would finally emerge.

"What do you say, Nic?" Micah took Nicky from Lydia's arms. He held the boy on one broad arm, angling Nicky toward his father. "Will you try, for Nicky?"

Nic locked eyes on Nicky, and it seemed he drew strength from the little boy's presence. After a long, tension-filled moment, he finally gave one brief nod of his head, his shaggy hair flopping. "I'll try." He released a shuddering breath, his body slumping forward. "I'll try."

Lydia reached for Nicky, and the little boy tumbled against her. She spoke quietly to Micah. "I'll take Nicky to the house, gather up some decent food and clean sheets, then—"

Nic lurched upright. "You ain't takin' him nowhere. I never said that."

Lydia started to argue, but Micah's hand on her back stopped her. "Nic, what you're going to face in the next few days is a battle. It won't be easy. You're a strong man—you can face it without crumbling. But Nicky is just a little boy. He shouldn't have to watch. Let Lydia's parents take care of him for a few days. As soon as you're better, you ask for him, and I promise I'll bring him."

Nic pressed his lips together, his narrowed gaze pinned on Micah's face. Then he shuddered as if struck with a chill. Fresh sweat broke out across his forehead. "Okay. Okay, take him outta here." He swung on Lydia. "But he promised!" He waved his hand at Micah. "You heard him. He promised to bring 'im back."

"And Micah keeps his promises." Her gaze collided with Micah's, and Micah's warm smile embraced her as tenderly as the gentlest hug.

Nic spun and propped his hand on the filthy counter. "Go now before I change my mind."

With one last look at Micah, Lydia scurried out the door, carrying Nicky. Not until she put Nicky on the seat did she realize she still clutched Nic's packet of morphine. She wouldn't bring that vile substance into her vehicle. Tearing the packet open, she emptied the contents into a puddle of dirty water along the curb. She watched the powder dissolve in the murky water and then, satisfied it could bring harm to no one, she slid behind the steering wheel next to Nicky. She took his small hand. The sight of his pale, thin cheeks pained her. "Are you okay, sweetheart?"

Nicky nodded, the familiar lock of hair falling across his forehead. He tugged at the corner of his mouth with a grimy finger. "I didn't like it there, Mama. Do I have to come back?"

There was a very good chance, unless a judge acted quickly on her motion to assume legal custody of Nicky, he would have to return to Nic's apartment. Emotion clogged her throat as she answered truthfully. "Yes, Nicky, but hopefully not for long.

Mama is trying to arrange it so you can live with Mama and Grammy and Poppy again. We'll have to pray real hard."

Nicky nodded, his eyes solemn. "I prayed while I was with . . . *him*. I prayed you would come and get me." A small smile crept up his cheek, one dimple appearing. "And you came."

Lydia leaned forward to kiss the end of his nose. "Yes, I did. I prayed I'd find you, and I did. Jesus answered both of us."

"Then I'm gonna pray that I can live with you forever and ever. And Jesus will answer." Nicky's confidence increased Lydia's belief.

"Come on, sweetheart. Let's get you home." She started the engine, and as she pulled into the empty street, an unpleasant thought struck. They were counting on a morphine addict being seen as an unfit parent. If Nic was clean, would the judge side with him?

26

Micah sat in one of the kitchen chairs and watched Nic pace the room, restless as a caged tiger. The tall man hadn't ceased his erratic movements since Lydia and Nicky's departure nearly three hours ago. "How many days has it been since you had a hit, Nic?"

Nic's foot swung out to kick at discarded clothing and trash in the way. He shrugged his good shoulder. "Not sure. Kinda lost track of time. No job to go to messes the days up in my mind. I know I've had a couple hits since I got the boy."

Micah nodded. "Must've been hard to get when you had Nicky to take care of."

Nic spun, his eyes narrowing. "Everything's harder when you got a kid around." He resumed pacing, muttering almost to himself. "But there's somethin' about that kid . . . Couldn't go through on the deal . . ."

Micah sat quietly and allowed Nic to pace. He knew in time Nic wouldn't have the energy or the desire to be on his feet. Might as well allow him the luxury of storming around the room while he still could. He was encouraged by the fact that Nic was taken by Nicky. Especially since it sounded like Nicky'd been weepy rather than friendly. Nic's inability to discard his son indicated an element of goodness buried deep in the man's soul. Micah sincerely hoped they'd be able to unearth that goodness when he was freed from his desire for morphine.

A light knock sounded on the door. Nic looked toward it but made no move in its direction, so Micah crossed the floor and opened it. Lydia stood in the hallway, her arms filled with several bundles. Micah took all but one and she followed him into the room. Her nose wrinkled in disgust as she placed her bag on the grime-encrusted counter. Micah hid a smile. No doubt somewhere in these bundles were cleaning supplies that would soon be put to use.

"I brought everything I could think of that we might need for the next few days." Lydia kept her voice low, speaking only to Micah as they untied bundles. She began unloading items and organizing them on the table. Micah was glad he had run a rag over the table earlier so they had one clean surface to use. She named the items as she unloaded. "Clean sheets. Food staples—I'll shop for fresh vegetables and meat each day since Nic doesn't have an icebox. Towels and washrags. Aspirin." She turned and watched Nic in his frenetic pacing for a moment, then brought her gaze back to Micah. "Is he all right?"

Micah shrugged. "He's in the restless stage. It will be much worse than this before it gets better."

Lydia shivered. "It makes me nervous, having him march around this way."

Nic suddenly stormed to the table. His scowl swept across the items Lydia had brought, and he turned to her with a sneer curling his lip. "You think I'm some kind of charity case?"

"Not at all." Lydia maintained a calm, even tone. "If Micah is going to stay here, he'll need these things to see him through the week. He's got to eat, and he'll need something on which to sleep."

Nic scratched his chin. His scowl faded. "Okay. Okay. I gotcha." He swiped his hand across his brow to remove the perspiration, then resumed his pacing. A muscle in his cheek twitched, and he repeatedly rubbed the spot.

Lydia leaned forward, her voice barely above a whisper. "How long until the morphine is out of his system?"

Micah dropped his voice, too. He didn't want Nic to know exactly what could happen over the next few days or the man might change his mind about getting clean. "At least a week, Lydia. I don't know when he last had some—he doesn't remember—but he knows he's had it twice since he took Nicky, so I'm guessing it hasn't been more than two days."

"He actually took that stuff in Nicky's presence?" Lydia's face reflected her horror.

Micah nodded, his own heart twisting at what Nicky must have witnessed. "But whatever Nicky saw while Nic was on morphine would be better than watching Nic trying to clear his system. The suffering will be intense. The symptoms will reach their peak in two or three days and run at that level for another two or three days before lessening. Nic's got a rough row to hoe."

Lydia glanced at him again, and her expression softened. She shook her head. "I've been so angry with him, but right now I feel sorry for him. He got started on this pathway quite by accident, and now he's trapped."

"Well, we're going to untrap him," Micah said. "I hope you brought my suitcase."

Lydia nodded. "It's in the car, as well as cleaning supplies and some blankets to make a couple pallets on the floor." She wrinkled her nose again. "But before I put my clean blankets on this floor, it's going to get a good scrubbing. Do you think you can convince Nic to pace in the corner long enough for me to clean everywhere else?"

"I'll see if I can get him to help me carry in the rest of the things from your car, then I'll try to keep him occupied while you scrub." He balled his hands on his hips and frowned at her. "But you said a couple of pallets. We only need one. You're not spending the night."

Lydia's eyebrows rose. "Oh?" Her challenging tone sent a clear message. He'd have his hands full trying to persuade her to leave. But he wouldn't argue with her now. He turned to Nic. "Hey, Nic, can you give me a hand?"

"A hand . . ." Nic released a snort. "That's all I got to offer."

Micah was exhausted. He'd been with Nic for three days and knew the man must be worn out, as well, because he never slept for more than an hour at a time. Even when he did appear to be sleeping, he thrashed and groaned, keeping Micah from resting fully. Nic went from hot to cold, throwing off his covers and flailing, completely drenched in sweat. Then minutes later he'd wrap himself in the same covers and shiver as if he'd turned to ice. He complained of muscle cramps, and Micah rubbed his back or legs to help relieve the cramping. Even though he ate little, nausea frequently overtook him and he retched until Micah feared he'd turn his stomach inside out. Watching was awful. But experiencing it had to be worse.

He'd managed to convince Lydia to spend part of her day and all night at her own house by reminding her Nicky needed her. Even then she'd wavered, arguing that Micah would require assistance with Nic. But in the end she'd agreed, for which Micah was grateful—she wasn't constantly exposed to Nic's suffering. However, as Micah's mouth stretched into a wide yawn, he realized he might need her to spell him one night soon or he'd be useless to Nic.

He would give Nic credit for one thing—as often as he cried out in misery from the powerful effects of cleaning the morphine from his body, not once did he ask for the drug. The man shook and twitched and kicked his legs uncontrollably, but he gritted his teeth and didn't resort to begging.

In one of Nic's more lucid moments, Micah had asked what made him decide to try to end the habit. Nic looked at Micah with eyes so dilated the irises were nearly swallowed by his pupils and choked out two words—"My kid." Micah squeezed Nic's healthy shoulder in understanding. Nicky had given Nic the motivation to come clean. And, Micah suspected, when all was said and done, the man would fight tooth and nail to keep the boy. He ached for Lydia's certain loss, yet he admired the man for his determination.

A gentle creak intruded. The door to the apartment opened slowly, signaling Lydia's return. She didn't knock anymore—the sudden noise aggravated Nic—so she just crept in as quietly as possible. Her brown eyes swept the room until she spotted Nic, bundled in his blanket, snoring in the corner, then found Micah at the table. She crossed to him. He admired the trim fit of her brown trousers and simple white blouse. Lydia looked stunning no matter what she wore.

He shook his head, clearing those thoughts, then turned his attention to the small cloth-covered basket in her hand.

"I brought your supper," she whispered, seating herself across from him. "Are you hungry?" Her gaze turned sympathetic. "You look awful."

Micah chuckled. "Thanks for your honesty." He flipped back the cloth napkin to reveal thick sandwiches and shiny apples.

"Well, you do. You look as if you haven't had a wink of sleep."

"I've had a few winks," he said, succumbing to another yawn. "I'll be fine."

Lydia shifted sideways in the chair and watched Nic for several silent seconds. He shivered in his sleep, his feet moving back and forth as if running a race. "What about him?"

"He'll be fine, too." Micah offered a silent prayer of thanks and then bit into a sandwich. The roast beef tasted wonderful. He bobbed his head in Nic's direction. "I'm proud of him, Lydia. By now most men would be writhing in agony and begging me to give them something to put them out of their misery. But not Nic. He writhes, but he doesn't beg. I've never met an addict who has worked so hard to come clean."

Lydia bit down on her lower lip. "And he's not doing it for himself, is he?"

Micah slowly shook his head, his appetite fleeing as tears pooled in Lydia's eyes.

"I thought about it the day I took Nicky home. If Nic is clean, he'll be able to hold a job, and he'll probably move into a better place, and then he'll be able to keep Nicky. A judge would let him keep Nicky." She blinked rapidly, removing the glimmer of tears. "Yet I've been praying for him, that he'd be able to be clean. I can't wish otherwise. It's so hard, Micah." Her voice turned hoarse with emotion.

Micah placed his hand over hers, wishing he could embrace her instead. "I know."

She sighed. "Father thinks I'm crazy for helping him. He says Nic deserves whatever he gets for forcing Eleanor into hiding and misusing a drug all these years." Lydia looked again at the slumbering form in the corner. "But I saw something in his eyes when he looked at Nicky. I truly believe, deep down, he wants things to be different, but he's caught."

"Oh, he's definitely caught. But he's fighting for his freedom now. And I believe he's going to win." Micah paused, then asked, "How's Nicky doing?"

A small smile teased the corner of Lydia's lips, her eyes taking on a glow. "Nicky is doing well. He's so happy to be back with us. I've never gotten so many hugs. At first I was afraid he would be angry with me for allowing Nic to take him, but he's forgiven all of us and is our little ray of sunshine, like he's always been." She clouded for a moment. "He does ask each morning if this is the day he has to go back to 'him'—he doesn't use Nic's name or the title 'daddy.' I told him he'd probably have to return here for a while, but that I would try to make it so he could come back and live with me always. Every night, I tuck him in and listen to him pray, 'Jesus, let me live with Mama forever and ever. Amen.'"

She pinched the bridge of her nose, obviously fighting tears. "Oh, Micah, what happens if Nic takes him permanently? What will happen to Nicky's faith? He's so young and so trusting. I can't bear to think of him being brokenhearted. . . ."

Micah got up, rubbed his achy hips, and went to his suitcase. He bent over stiffly and removed his Bible, then returned to the table. "Lydia, let me share something with you." He flipped to Psalms, the sixty-first chapter. "I've been reading to Nic. It seems to calm him. Let me read you what I shared with him early this morning." He put his finger underneath the words to focus his bleary vision and then read aloud, "'Hear my cry, O God; attend unto my prayer. From the end of the earth will I cry unto thee, when my heart is overwhelmed: lead me to the rock that is higher than I.'"

He looked up, meeting Lydia's gaze. "No matter where we are, Lydia, God hears our cries. Our prayers are never so far away that God can't hear them and respond. Right now your heart is overwhelmed with worry. Nicky's heart will be overwhelmed with sorrow if he's forced to separate from you. But both of you can find your strength in the Rock of Christ Jesus. *He* is the rock that is higher than you or I. When we stand on His strong foundation, we have the strength to face whatever comes along. Teach Nicky to stand firm in Jesus' strength, Lydia."

Lydia held his gaze. "When Nic took him the first time, I told Nicky to remember Jesus was with him. He said he prayed every day for me to come, and that Jesus answered."

Warmth flooded Micah's soul. The faith of a little child. "Then he knows Jesus is there and He cares. He'll be okay, Lydia. Remember? God's thoughts for Nicky are for peace and not evil. Trust. Everything will turn out for the good of all of you. You have to believe."

Lydia opened her mouth to respond, but a wild thrashing from Nic's corner interrupted. Both Micah and Lydia jumped up and rushed to his side. Micah rolled Nic onto his back. Tears and mucus ran like rivers down his face. Micah pulled his handkerchief from his pocket and cleaned Nic's nose and cheeks. Nic trembled from head to toe, the shaking so severe his teeth rattled.

"It's b-bad, Doc. It's r-real b-bad." He crossed his arm over his chest and moaned. "Oh, the pain . . . my b-back . . . m-my legs . . . hurts . . ."

"Massage his legs, Lydia." Micah lifted Nic into a sitting position and began rubbing his shoulders.

Nic grasped his midsection with his good arm and retched, the spasms bringing up nothing from his empty stomach.

Micah encouraged, "Deep breaths, Nic. Take deep breaths and fight it off."

Nic tried to comply, rocking forward, his head thrown back. Lydia knelt beside Nic's legs, working his muscles like a baker works bread dough. Her face was a study in concentration, her focus solely on Nic. Micah's heart swelled with pride for her—reaching out to this man who'd so wronged her closest friend.

The retching ended, and Nic's spine straightened, his whole body shaking as his legs began to kick spasmodically. "Uh-uh-uh-uh . . ." The repetitive sound seemed to fire from his throat without Nic's conscious effort.

Micah assumed an authoritative tone and spoke directly into Nic's ear as he continued to massage the tense muscles of his back. "Nic, remember what I read to you? Remember the words? God is your refuge, your strength. Lean on Him now. Ask Him to lift you to the higher place. Call on Him to help you through this."

"H-help me, G-G-God." Nic's eyes closed and his face twisted in agony. "P-please . . . help me . . ."

Lydia began praying aloud, her strong tone carrying over Nic's rasping voice. "God, touch Nic's back. Relieve his pain. Touch his legs. Take the pain from his legs, Lord. Give him rest—healing rest. Lift him from this prison of addiction. Please, Lord, heal his body. Help Nic, Lord."

For long minutes they continued their ministrations, alternately praying for an end to Nic's suffering, while Nic clenched his jaw and uttered moans for relief. Eventually the cramps seemed to subside. His muscles relaxed. His whole body wilted as he rolled away from Micah's touch. He flopped onto his side and panted with relief. "Better . . . It's better . . . Thank You, God." His eyelids fluttered, his jaw went slack, and he slept once more.

Micah slumped against the wall. He wiped beads of perspiration from his upper lip and forehead. "That's the worst I've seen. I think we're reaching the end."

Lydia touched his arm. "Micah, I'll stay here tonight. You've got to get some rest."

He looked at her, battling to keep his eyelids open. "No, Lydia, I'll be all right." His argument sounded weak even to his own ears.

She stood and moved to the roll of blankets stowed next to the door. She flipped them out in the open space between the table and Nic's mattress, then covered them with a sheet. She pointed an imperious finger. "Lie down."

Micah pushed himself to his feet, using the wall as a brace. The fatigue pressed at him, making him light-headed. He stumbled.

Lydia darted to his side and slung her arm around his waist. "Stubborn man," she scolded as she led him across the room. "What else do you expect when you eat next to nothing and only grab snatches of sleep? God gave you good sense—use it and get some rest. I can rub Nic's legs and keep him warm or cold, as the need may arise. You've got to rest."

Micah wanted to argue, but his head was fuzzy. He couldn't find the right words. He sank onto the pallet and covered his eyes with his forearm. Ah, such a relief to lie down. Something drifted across his chest, and he cracked his eyes open to see Lydia covering him with another blanket. A grin tugged at his lips. "Thanks, Ma."

"Don't get smart," she said, but he heard the smile in her voice.

"Thanks, Lydia." He let his eyes drift closed.

"Now sleep."

Without argument, he followed her gentle order.

27

Micah awakened to the sound of pots and pans clanging. And Lydia's laughter.

"How do you light this thing, Nic? I've wasted four matches already."

Micah opened one eye and peeked sideways. The sight snapped both his eyes open and brought him up on his elbows. Nic stood beside Lydia, twisting the dials of the gas range and instructing her on where to hold the match so the burner would light. Micah huffed in surprise, and the pair at the stove turned in unison to look at him.

Lydia's face broke into a smile. She brought her hands to her hips. "Well, good morning, sleepyhead. Sorry if we woke you, but Nic requested pancakes and eggs for breakfast, and he wasn't willing to wait any longer."

Pancakes? And eggs? *Nic?* Micah shook his head. Was he dreaming?

Nic ambled to the edge of Micah's pallet and grinned down at him. The man's face was clean-shaven, his eyes clear, and his skin held a healthy pallor. Nic's grin widened. "Pancakes okay with you, Doc?" He held out his good hand.

"Pancakes? Sure." Micah allowed Nic to tug him to his feet, then stood uncertainly, his gaze drifting from one amused face to the other. He blinked at Nic. "You must be feeling better." He realized how foolish it sounded, but he couldn't find anything else to say.

Nic laughed—a genuine laugh. His eyes twinkled. "Yeah, Doc, I do. Better than I've felt in years. An' I owe it all to you an' that Higher Power of yours. You make quite a team." He held out his hand again, his green eyes brimming with unshed tears. "Thank you, Micah."

Micah shook Nic's wide, dry hand, his heart filling with gratefulness. "You're welcome, Nic."

"Okay, you two, I'll have breakfast on the table in five minutes. Micah, go wash up. Nic, set the table." Lydia's mild orders broke the tension of the moment.

Nic chuckled, giving a sheepish shrug. "You heard the boss."

Micah shrugged, too. "That I did." He scuffed to the sink, still a little fuzzy from his deep sleep. As he soaped his hands, he winged a silent prayer heavenward, thanking God for the miracle he'd been privileged to witness. This morning, Nicolai Pankin was a new man. Both inside and out.

Lydia couldn't eat much of the breakfast she'd made—she was too entranced by Nic sitting straight and tall in his chair, carrying bites of pancake dripping with butter and syrup to his mouth. His thick hair, freshly washed and combed, glistened in the sunlight spilling through the window. During his battle, they'd kept the shades drawn, shielding his eyes from the glare. But the sunbeam of a fresh day landed on Nic's form and seemed to announce a fresh start to his life.

Looking into Nic's clear eyes, examining his erect frame and steady hand, Lydia imagined how a judge would see him. Thin, yes, but strong. Capable of working and earning an honest wage. Capable of parenting a child.

I can't let Nicky go, God. I can't!

Micah's advice whispered in her memory. "*When we stand on His strong foundation, we have the strength to face whatever comes along.*" Closing her eyes, she sent up a frantic, silent prayer for God's strength to uphold her if the judge gave custody of Nicky to his father.

"Lydia?"

Nic's voice broke through her internal reflections. She opened her eyes and found him holding out his plate, his lips tipped in a hopeful grin.

"Can I have another pancake?"

Quirking one brow, her thoughts still on Nicky, she responded automatically. "May I . . . ?"

His lips twisted for a moment, a scowl marring his face, but then he gave an amused snort. He sent a smirk in Micah's direction. "Is she always this bossy?"

Micah placed his fork on his plate and draped his arm over the back of the chair, his eyes twinkling. "Yep."

Lydia huffed. "You two! Honestly . . ." She grabbed Nic's plate and marched to the stove, where she'd left a covered plate of pancakes warming. She flipped a cake onto Nic's plate and then clunked the plate on the table before him.

"Nothing ever tasted as good as these pancakes," Nic declared, drowning the flapjack in syrup. He lifted his head and met her gaze. "Thanks, Lydia."

As she looked into his sincere, open face, she received a beautiful glimpse of how he must have appeared before his accident, before securing morphine became the driving force of his life. She wanted to remain indignant, but something in his expression—something good and alive and warm—melted her resolve. Yanking out her chair and plopping into it, she forced a terse reply. "You're welcome, but that's the last one you're getting. Your stomach might rebel if you put too much in it at once."

Nic's lips twitched. "Yes, ma'am."

He went on eating, his satisfied "mmms" between bites both elating and stinging Lydia. Unable to watch him any longer, she shifted her head and discovered Micah examining her. The serious expression on his face sent a shaft of apprehension through her middle. She licked her lips. "Micah?"

He cleared his throat, flicking a glance at Nic. He rose. "Lydia, while Nic finishes his breakfast, could I speak with you . . . outside?"

Nic looked up, his fork midway between his plate and his mouth. "Somethin' wrong?"

Micah chuckled, but the tense set of his shoulders juxtaposed the lighthearted sound. "Yeah. Feelin' penned in after so many days in this apartment tending to your stubborn hide."

Nic blasted a laugh. "Well, go on, then." He waggled his brows. "While you've got her outdoors, I can sneak into the rest of them pancakes."

Lydia supposed she should play along and tease back, but her tongue felt stuck to the roof of her mouth. She managed to offer Nic a weak grin, then followed Micah down the stairs and into the grassless yard. A crowd of rowdy kids ran back and forth, chasing one another with sticks in some sort of wild sword-fighting game, so Micah guided her between the tall buildings. An unpleasant odor permeated the area, but the children's voices were muffled, giving them an opportunity to visit without shouting at each other.

Micah leaned against the brick wall and slipped his hands into his pockets. He heaved a huge sigh. His pants and shirt were rumpled, his hair stood up in untidy tufts, his cheeks sported at least three days' worth of whiskers, and dark circles marred his striking blue eyes. Yet despite his disheveled appearance, Lydia found him attractive. Longing to settle herself securely against his muscular frame and rest in the strength he radiated nearly overwhelmed her. She'd never known a more appealing man than Dr. Micah Hatcher.

Dropping her gaze to the discarded tin cans around their feet, she pushed her errant thoughts aside. "What did you want to say to me?" She braced herself, certain another heartache was about to be forced upon her.

"I didn't want to say anything in front of Nic—didn't want to discourage him—but he's still got a big fight ahead of him."

Lydia braved lifting her face to look into Micah's tired eyes. "Isn't his system clear?"

"Sure it is. For the first time in years." Micah freed one hand and ran his fingers through his hair. He grimaced. "But he's spent the past eight years using morphine to make himself feel good. It's been his crutch to ease his pain, to bolster his moods, to calm his temper. Sure, he's been addicted, but he's also developed a habit of relying on morphine. Just because he's clean now doesn't mean the habit's been eradicated. There will still be times—lots of times, I'm afraid—he's going to want to reach for a packet of white powder."

Lydia's heart took up a mighty caroming in her chest. Once again, her emotions teeter-tottered between wanting Nic whole and wanting him to be found unstable so she could have Nicky to herself. She stifled a groan. *Father, help me do what honors You!*

Micah tapped a rusty can with the toe of his shoe. "As much as I hate leaving the clinic in someone else's hands any longer, I think I'll make a few calls and see if I can stick around for another week. Help Nic establish healthy habits to replace the bad one. Had to do that with a few fellows in Oahu after the bombing—they got too reliant on morphine, too. It happens." He fell silent for a moment, his brow crinkled in contemplation. Finally, he added, with a gentle hesitance, "I want to make sure Nic's on good footing before I leave him alone."

"That's very good of you." Despite Lydia's efforts to maintain an even tone, her words snapped out on a sarcastic note.

Micah arched a brow. His disapproval, although he spoke not a word, was as easily heard as the angry argument between the children on the lawn.

Lydia bit her lower lip, battling tears. Shame washed over her, making her body tremble. "I'm sorry. It's just . . ." How could she explain something she didn't understand herself?

He pushed off from the wall, lifting his hand to cup her cheek. Tenderness glowed in his eyes. "Lydia, you're bound to be apprehensive about Nic's recovery. I know what you stand to lose."

Tears distorted her vision. One escaped and dribbled down her cheek to her chin. She brushed it away and nodded miserably, her tight throat prohibiting speech.

Micah caught her by the upper arms and dipped his knees slightly to peer directly into her face. "Listen to me. My mama has a little plaque hanging above her kitchen sink. Says something like, 'Only one life will soon be past; only what's done for Christ will last.'" He rubbed her arms, the touch gentle and rough at the same time. The Texas twang crept into his voice. "What'd we do here? We helped Nic. Bein' set free of his addiction's done him worlds of good. And it stands to do Nicky some good, too, to have a daddy who isn't a threat. But mostly what we did, Lydia, we did out of love. Not out of love for Nic—truth be told, I don't even like him all that much."

A short, unexpected snort of laughter escaped Lydia's nose.

Micah grinned and continued. "But love for Nicky, 'cause

we want what's best for him. And mostly—at least for me—for love of Christ. Doin' right because He's called us to reach out to the lowly and downtrodden."

Lowly and downtrodden. Micah's description certainly fit Nicolai Pankin. Lydia sniffled. "I know. And I . . . I want to honor Christ. That's what I kept praying when we were in Nic's apartment—'Father, let me honor You.' But inside . . . in here . . ." She placed her trembling fingertips against her chest. "I'm so afraid of losing m-my son."

Micah swept her into his arms, cradling the back of her head with one strong hand and rubbing her shoulders with the other. She shook with silent sobs, her face buried in the curve of his neck.

"I know. I know." His sweet Texas accent eased out like honey on an oven-warm biscuit. "But what you gotta remember, darlin', is that when we do what's right for Christ, especially when it goes against our human wants, we open up doors to blessing beyond anything we could possibly imagine. Trust, Lydia."

He gave her a tight squeeze and then set her aside. Hands still gently gripping her arms, he smiled his Micah-smile—crinkled eyes, lips crooked slightly higher on the left—and winked. "Wait an' see. Things'll work out for you an' for Nicky. Remember that higher ground I read about to Nic? You got your own higher ground, Lydia, where Jesus is waitin' to give you everything you need. You just gotta trust."

28

Although Lydia didn't visit Nic's apartment the week following his first morning of clarity, she stayed up-to-date on his progress thanks to Micah. He made use of a phone booth a few blocks from Nic's apartment building and called her each day promptly at three o'clock. After sharing about Nic, he always asked about Nicky, then prayed with her before disconnecting and returning to Nic.

As the week progressed, Lydia greater understood Micah's worry about Nic replacing his habit of using morphine. Each day, she became increasingly aware of the hour hand on the clock creeping toward three. With what would she replace her newly formed habit of standing beside the telephone at 2:59, heart racing in anticipation, steepled fingers pressed to her lips, when Micah deemed Nic capable of forging forward on his own and returned to New York?

Nicky had settled back into his routine, acting as if he'd never been carted away by a strange man who daily threatened to sell him to an unknown family. Lydia marveled at his resilience, and in the back of her mind mulled the thought that perhaps—just perhaps—Nicky would adjust to living with Nic when the time came. A prayer winged heavenward numerous times both day and night for God to work His perfect will in their situation. She wouldn't allow herself to hope Nicky could stay with her, knowing her heart would surely shatter if the hope was dashed. Instead of hoping, she did as Micah advised. She trusted.

And she discovered, as the days slipped by, an indescribable sense of peace taking root in the center of her being. The peace was still there on the morning Nic had indicated he would come for Nicky. She and Micah had prayed extra long the afternoon before, and she'd shed tears. Yet, with God's strength bolstering her, she maintained a smile as she laid out a pair of clean shorts, a bright red shirt with a sailboat embroidered on its front, and blue socks for Nicky.

She watched the little boy scramble into his clothes, biting back a chuckle as he grunted in aggravation while searching for his shirt sleeves and blinked away tears when he began to hum as he wriggled his feet into his socks. When he'd finished dressing, she sat on the edge of his bed and stood him before her to comb his wayward curls into place. His little hands rested on her knees, his trusting face tipped upward, and she offered another prayer for strength before speaking in a calm voice.

"Sweetheart, today is a special day. Today you'll get to see your new place to live."

Nicky's dark eyes grew wide with alarm. "But, Mama, I don't want to go away again!"

Lydia hugged him close and kissed his hair. Then she lifted him into her lap, taking his quivering chin between her fingers. "I don't want you to go away, either, Nicky. But you see, Nic Pankin is your real daddy. He couldn't take care of you when you were a baby because he was sick, so I took care of you. But now he's better, and he wants to get to know you. He wants you to live with him."

Nicky poked out his lower lip and bounced off her lap. He marched to the corner and stood with his back to her and his arms folded tightly over his skinny chest. "No. I don't want to. I don't like him. He yells, an' he won't let me play. He calls me 'kid.'"

"Nicky, sweetheart, please listen to Mama." The little boy hunched further into the corner. Lydia's heart ached so badly tears pricked once again. How could she share this information in a way that would make sense? Nicky was still so young.

Oh, God, please help me.

She drew a deep breath. "Nicky, Nic is sorry for yelling. You see, he had a bad sickness that made him yell. He didn't like yelling, but inside he hurt all the time. You know how when your tummy is upset, you get grumpy?"

Nicky didn't turn around, but he peeked at her over his shoulder. A lock of hair fell across his thick eyelashes, rising and falling as he blinked. He gave a very slight nod.

"Well, because Nic didn't feel good, he was very grumpy and he yelled. But, Nicky, Micah and I prayed to God for help, and Nic prayed to God for help. Now Nic isn't sick anymore, and he really, really wants to be a good daddy to you. He loves you, Nicky." Lydia had no doubt that love for Nicky had given Nic the will to battle the monster of morphine addiction. She clung to the knowledge, trusting it as proof Nic would treat his son kindly in the future.

Nicky's lower lip trembled, and tears began to splash down his cheeks. "But I love *you,* Mama, an' I wanna be with *you.*"

"Oh, sweetheart, I know." Lydia held her arms open, and with a little sob Nicky raced to her. She swept him into her embrace, pressing her nose into his hair as he nuzzled into her shoulder, crying quietly. "But no matter where you are, my love goes with you. It won't ever leave you any more than Jesus will leave you. You believe me, don't you?"

Nicky's head bobbed against her neck. She kissed his temple and rocked him, much the way she had when he was a baby suffering a touch of colic. "You're a very lucky boy. So many people love you. Jesus, Mama, Grammy, Poppy, Micah, and now Daddy." She remained in Nicky's room, holding him, singing to him, and praying for him, until a doorbell announced Nic's arrival.

Nicky refused to release her neck, so she carried him down the stairs and encountered Mother and Father standing stiffly side by side in the foyer with Nic framed in the vestibule doorway. He looked up as Lydia descended the stairs, and she gave a jolt of surprise at his appearance.

His clothes fit loosely—he'd lost even more weight during his ordeal—but he wore clean trousers and a tucked-in plaid shirt buttoned clear to the collar. He, too, was clean—the coarse whiskers gone from his chin, his hair neatly combed into a thick wave that swept from his forehead to the nape of his neck. He was once again the handsome man who had caught Lydia's eye five years ago.

Nic's gaze had seemed to memorize Nicky as Lydia approached, but when she reached the bottom riser and set Nicky on the floor, Nic shifted to face her parents. For a moment, his lips pressed together, but then his face relaxed, as if something had whispered an assurance in his ear. He offered his hand to Father.

Father's cheeks mottled red, and he harrumphed. But he gave Nic a brief handshake of greeting before jamming his hand into his trouser pocket. He fixed Nic with a steely glare. "Lydia tells me you're clean." There was no mistaking the sarcasm in his tone, and Lydia held her breath, anticipating an outburst from Nic.

But instead, a slow smile crept up Nic's smooth-shaven cheek.

"Yes, sir, I sure am. And it goes deeper than my skin." His gaze drifted to Nicky, who stood half behind Lydia with his arm wrapped around her leg. Tenderness bloomed across his face. "Hi." The single-word greeting drifted out as softly as a feather floating on a breeze.

Nicky's hold tightened. Lydia cupped the back of his head with her hand and gently urged him forward. "Say hello, sweetheart."

Nicky shrank back. He flicked a worried glance upward and whispered, "Dunno what to call him."

Nic went down on one knee before the boy and traced the sailboat on Nicky's shirt with his finger. "Well, most folks call me Nic, 'cause that's my name. But, ya know, other folks are just folks. None of 'em are my son." He scratched his chin, giving the impression of deep thought. "Since you're my son, you could call me somethin' different than other folks do, if you wanted to."

Nicky tipped his head sideways, and he brought up his hand to scratch his chin, a perfect imitation of Nic's gesture. "You mean, I could call you Daddy?"

Tears appeared in Nic's eyes, and Lydia found herself battling them, as well. Nic swallowed, the sound loud in the deathly quiet of the foyer. "Yeah. You could. If . . . if you wanted to."

"Okay." Nicky reached out and placed his hand on Nic's knee. "But you call me Nicky, 'cause that's my name."

"That's a deal, Nicky." Nic held out his hand to seal the bargain, and father and son shook hands. Nic continued to hold Nicky's small hand as he stood upright and turned his unwavering gaze on Lydia's father. "Mr. Eldredge, if I'm going to take proper care of my son, I've got to have a job. I know you've turned me down before, and I understand why. But, sir, that reason no longer exists. I'm clean, an' I aim to stay that way. So I'm askin' you for another chance."

Father's chin jutted arrogantly. "How do I know you won't go back to it?"

Nic raised his chin also, but instead of arrogance, the gesture gave an appearance of certainty. "'Cause I'm not fightin' it alone anymore. Micah warned me I'd still want it for a good long while, an' I already found out he's right on that. But I got God on my side now. An' His strength is bigger than mine could ever be. Together, we're gonna keep me clean. When I want that stuff, I ask God for strength to resist. I get an answer, too. I won't go back to it." He glanced down at Nicky, and he gently swung the little boy's hand. "I got a good reason right here to stay clean." His gaze rose, meeting Father's head-on. "I won't let Nicky down, sir. An' I won't let you down, either."

Father stood in silent contemplation for long seconds while Lydia held her breath and Nic held his gaze. Finally Father pointed at Nic. "All right. I'll give you another chance. But I'm telling you, Pankin, I'll be watching. One slip up, and you're gone."

Nic beamed. "Thank you, sir. You won't regret this. I promise." He turned to Mother, his smile twitching into a sheepish grin. "I have a favor to ask of you, ma'am. While I'm workin'"—pride squared his shoulders as he stated the word—"I'll need someone to watch Nicky. I can't leave him alone. I can find a sitter, if it don't suit you, but I thought since he already knows you, maybe—"

Mother gave a little delighted gasp. "Oh no! A sitter isn't necessary. I'd be pleased to keep Nicky for you while you're working." She caught Father's arm and hugged it to her ribs.

Lydia's heart thumped double-time as Nic finally aimed his gaze in her direction. He released his hold on Nicky and held out his hand to her. She took it in both of hers, stepping forward slightly to shorten the distance between them.

"Lydia, after all I put you through, you didn't have to help me. But you did, an' I thank you for it. You an' Micah—you showed me the kind of person I want to be from now on. With God's help, I'm gonna be better. I'm gonna work hard to make God . . . and Eleanor . . . proud of me."

Lydia gave him a smile, but she couldn't find her voice.

Nic continued, his hand still between hers. "You've been Nicky's mama ever since his birth, an' you've been a good one. Thank you for takin' such good care of him for Eleanor. I was wrong to want to pull him away from you. He's gonna need you, too, so I want us to find a way for him to be with you as much as you both like. Can we—can we maybe meet after work one evenin' soon and talk about how to make that happen?"

Warm tears—tears of joy unspeakable—spilled down her cheeks. She had trusted, and God had answered the prayer of her heart. Inwardly she rejoiced as she forced her emotion-filled throat to form an answer. "Of course, Nic. And thank you."

He nodded, then pulled his hand from her grasp and placed it on Nicky's head. The little boy stood beneath Nic's touch, his little face turned upward. Nic smiled at his son before addressing Lydia again. "Will you see Micah today?"

His simple question removed a bit of the joy that had flooded her frame moments earlier. She offered a stiff nod. "He's leaving early this afternoon for New York, but he'll come by beforehand to tell us all good-bye."

"Tell him—" Nic cleared his throat, swallowing tears. "Tell him thank you for helpin' me get my life back. Tell him I'll hold on to God an' keep standin' on that higher place we talked about. I won't ever forget."

Lydia nodded, Nic's form blurring through the tears clouding her vision. "I'll tell him."

Nic bent down to Nicky. "Son, I got to go now, so you stay

here with your grammy. I got an errand to run. . . ." He paused and worried his lower lip between his teeth. Leaning toward Lydia, he confided in a raspy whisper, "Gotta go cancel a deal." Lydia's heart skipped a beat as she read the meaning behind his statement. Nic turned his attention back to Nicky. "I'll come by this evenin' so I can show you an' your mama our new apartment." He straightened, talking to Lydia again. "Ain't goin' back to that other place. No place to raise a kid."

"No place to raise a Nicky," Nicky corrected.

Nic laughed. "That's right. Thanks for remindin' me." He swung his gaze across each of the adults. "I best be goin' now." He leaned down and kissed the top of Nicky's head. "'Bye, son. See you later."

Lydia and Nicky followed Nic to the door and watched as he headed down the stairs. The moment his foot reached the lowest riser, Nicky called out, "'Bye, Daddy!"

Nic froze in place for the length of three seconds. Slowly, he turned and sent Nicky a glimmering smile. He raised his hand in good-bye, then spun and trotted to his waiting pickup, his steps so light Lydia thought it appeared his feet hovered a couple inches above the ground.

29

Micah took a taxi to the Eldredge house and arrived mid-morning. Buggy, in his cage, swung from a hook under the porch eaves. The canary's cheerful song drifted through the cab's open windows. Lydia and Lavinia knelt beside the flower plot, trowels in hand, and Nicky galloped in circles in the sunshine. Micah couldn't stop a smile from growing at the pleasant picture they created.

He tapped the cab driver on the shoulder. "I'll only be a few minutes. Please wait for me." The man nodded.

The moment he climbed out of the cab, Nicky came running, arms outstretched. Micah captured him in a giant hug. "Hey, partner, I didn't expect to see you here." He swung the giggling boy to his shoulders and walked toward Lydia, who met him halfway across the yard.

Dirt smudged her chin and decorated the knees of her trousers. Wisps of hair clung to her sweaty temples, and beads of perspiration dotted her nose. She was adorable. Micah gripped Nicky's ankles to keep from capturing her face between his palms and kissing her breathless. He asked, "Hasn't Pankin been here yet?"

Lydia's eyes shone with happiness. "He's been and gone. He said Nicky needs time with us, too, so we're going to work out the means to share in raising him. And he asked Mother to keep Nicky for him while he's at work."

Micah raised his eyebrows. "Work?"

Lydia rocked on her heels, her hands clasped tightly as if reining herself in. "Yes, work. Father gave him a job."

From his perch, Nicky added, "Poppy's gonna watch him."

Lydia flicked a smile at the boy. "That's right, Nicky." Her gaze met Micah's, and she spoke softly. "Father was apprehensive about trusting him, but I believe he's going to do okay, Micah."

Micah gave a firm nod. "I believe it, too. 'I can do all things through Christ which strengtheneth me'—he must have repeated the Scripture a dozen times last night. As long as he relies on the strength of Jesus, he'll make it."

Nicky wiggled, so Micah swung him to the ground and the boy scampered off, waving his arms and blowing air through his lips to make engine noises.

Lydia watched Nicky for a moment, a fond smile playing on her lips, and then she turned back to Micah. "Nic asked me to thank you for helping him get his life back and to tell you he wouldn't forget the 'higher place' you talked about."

Micah shrugged, pushing his hands into his pockets. "He did the hard part. I just offered some support."

Lydia laughed—a sweet, melodious trickle of happiness. "Sometimes you're too modest, Dr. Hatcher. Not many people would be willing to reach out to someone like Nic Pankin. What you did was work a miracle."

"Huh-uh. Not me." Micah pointed skyward. "God performs the miracles. All we can do, as Christians, is be willing instruments of His service, ready to be used whenever He calls. I'm privileged to have been used. It's pretty special, witnessing a miracle."

"And it is miraculous, the change in his heart." Lydia's eyes widened, the velvety irises shining. "I kept staring at him when he was here, hardly able to believe this was the same man who barged into my home, wild-eyed and snarling, and snatched my son out from under my nose."

Micah offered a lopsided smile. "The touch of God does amazing things."

Her face pinched, the joyful glimmer leaving her eyes. "I wish Eleanor had lived to see it. She loved Nic so much. This change would have made her so happy."

They fell silent, the sun hot on their heads, Nicky's cheerful chatter competing with Buggy's raucous song, while Micah relived the past days in his memory. Had he been here only two weeks? So much had happened—so much good had been achieved—it hardly seemed possible such a short amount of time had passed. He wished he could stay longer. To bask in the glory of Nic's transformation, to take walks with Nicky, to sit across a table and admire Lydia in candlelight. But his clinic—and his brother's mission—required him in New York.

Releasing a regret-filled sigh, he gestured to the waiting cab. "I should go so I don't miss my train."

Her forehead puckered. She dipped her head, silky strands of deepest brown slipping to frame her rose-splashed cheeks. "I wish you could stay longer."

Me too. "Oughta be another package arriving soon."

Lydia's head lowered even more. "I understand." Her shoulders lifted, then fell in a deep sigh, and she looked up, unspeaking, her attentive gaze unreadable. Micah's heart began a clamor he felt certain Lavinia Eldredge could hear from fifteen feet away. He licked his lips, seeking a proper way to tell this woman farewell.

But she spoke first, her businesslike tone a direct contrast to the silent pleading in her eyes. "Thank you for everything. It looks as if things are going to work out between Nic and Nicky."

"I'm glad." Micah's heart *kawumped* wildly as he turned toward the cab. "I'll be praying for all of you."

Lydia moved along beside him, her stride perfectly matching his. "I'll pray for you and Jeremiah, and for your 'packages.'" Her chin quivered, and soon tears winked in her eyes. Softly—so softly he might have imagined it—she said, "I'll miss you, Micah."

Oh, how he yearned to pull her against his chest and feel her arms wind around his neck. The longing to kiss her temples, her cheeks, her lips nearly turned him inside out. If only he could reach out and lose himself in the beauty of the woman she'd become. But if he embraced her now, he'd never let go.

Hands firmly at his sides, he teased, "I'll miss you, too, my bossy little nurse."

She laughed, a ragged laugh that fell short of real humor but managed to erase her tears. She waved Nicky over. "Micah is leaving. Come say good-bye."

Nicky loped across the lawn, swatting his own backside with one hand. He reined in his imaginary horse, intoning, "Whoa, Squirrel." Micah swallowed a chuckle. Only Nicky would name a horse Squirrel. The little boy swung his leg as if dismounting, his face set in a serious scowl. He took two swaggering steps in Micah's direction and finally broke free of his play to launch himself into Micah's arms.

"Bye, Micah-my-friend! Come again soon!"

Micah hugged the sweaty little boy close, gratitude for the miracle of God's hand of healing once again filling him. No more would Nicky live beneath a cloud of fear or entangled in a web of lies. And no more did Nicky require Micah's presence. A knot of sorrow filled his throat, and his arms tightened around the boy's body as he battled a wave of sadness. Delivering a quick kiss on Nicky's tousled curls, he set him down.

Micah swiped his hand beneath his nose, assuming his drawl to cover his melancholy. "Best mount up an' get to ridin', pardner."

"Giddyup, Squirrel!" Nicky swung his leg over his pretend horse, fisted invisible reins, and bounced away. He waved one hand over his head. "'Bye, Micah! I love you!"

Micah swallowed hard and turned to Lydia. If only he could make the same declaration Nicky had just shouted so matter-of-factly. But to do so now would only create more heartache. He pushed the declaration of love deep inside and offered a simple farewell. "'Bye, Lydia. Take care."

She tipped her head, and tears once again flooded her eyes. "You, too, Micah. Good-bye."

He climbed into the cab and slammed the door. "Let's go." The cab pulled away from the curb, and Micah turned backward in the seat and memorized the scene shrinking behind him. Lydia at the curb, her wistful face aimed at the departing vehicle, Nicky prancing on the lawn behind her. He willed himself to remember every detail of it.

The cab turned a corner, and Micah crunched his eyes closed, holding his breath, hoping. A relieved sigh heaved from his chest. Yes, the image of those two special people remained imprinted in his mind's eye.

Satisfied, he leaned forward and caught the driver's attention. "Can you hurry? I gotta get home."

The cab driver chuckled, shooting Micah a quick smirk over his shoulder. "'Peared to me you had plenty back there to stick around for." He waggled his eyebrows.

Micah slouched in the seat without answering. Already his

heart ached for Lydia, but what good would it do to dwell on his affection for her? With Nic's situation settled, she didn't need Micah anymore. He deliberately turned his thoughts to Jeremiah. *I'm here for you now, brother—only you. No more distractions.*

Yet the entire way to the train station, and every mile of the long, rocking ride to New York, the distracting image of Lydia standing still and sorrowful on the curb replayed in his memory.

Nic arrived at work fifteen minutes early on Monday morning and was first in line to punch his brand-new time card. In the past, he'd ambled in just as the shift-change buzzer blared, but his promise to Allan Eldredge—to make sure the man didn't regret hiring him—meant developing a better habit.

Habit. He toyed with the word as he watched the big clock tick by the minutes. Micah had told him habits weren't healed. He'd have to work to overcome his habit of relying on morphine. "It'll leave a hole that needs fillin', Nic," the doctor had advised, his Texas drawl making him sound relaxed even when talking about something serious. "So you gotta look for good things to plug that hole." At Micah's suggestion, Nic relied on Bible reading and prayer first, and relearning whittling second.

When he was younger, before the auger stole his arm, he'd been real clever with a pocketknife. Birds, dogs, horses, even roses emerged from a scrap of wood. His father'd never seen much use in whittling, but it had pleased Nic to make something pretty out of something plain. By rigging a clamp on the edge of the table to serve as a hand, he'd spent hours of the past week peeling away the excess on a chunk of pine in search of the bird underneath. When he finished, he'd paint it yellow. Canary yellow. And he'd give it to Nicky.

He hoped Nicky would like the little apartment he'd located. Nothing fancy, but in a cleaner part of town, away from the morphine alleys and beer halls. They'd have to share a bedroom, but one of the other tenants had already offered Nic the use of a little iron bed her son had outgrown. When he got his first paycheck, he'd buy sheets and a coverlet for it—blue ones, the color Nicky said was his favorite—as a surprise. He imagined his first night tucking Nicky between blue sheets, maybe kneeling beside the bed to say nighttime prayers with him, the way the boy said Lydia did. The idea settled comfortably on his shoulders.

An unfamiliar but welcome warmth flooded his chest as he thought of his son. Guilt smote him as he recalled demanding Eleanor visit one of those backstreet doctors who emptied a woman's womb before the babe could thrive. He fidgeted in place, the memory stinging. He'd been wrong, so wrong, to make such a command. He'd been wrong to want to sell Eleanor's child. Mrs. Bachman had called him all sorts of names—liar, thief, swindler—and she was right on every count. In the end, she couldn't press charges without admitting her intention to purchase a child, but she hadn't let that stop her from flaying him with accusations.

The sins of his past crept from the recesses of his soul and left him feeling stained and ugly and sore. A groan hovered in his throat. He needed comfort. He needed to forget. He needed—Second Corinthians 5:17, one of the verses Micah had insisted he memorize—*"Hidin' God's Word in your heart'll send bad thoughts runnin' for cover,"* Micah had declared—ran through Nic's mind. *"Therefore if any man be in Christ, he is a new creature: old things are passed away; behold, all things are become new."* Just as Micah had indicated, the sin reminder scuttled into the shadows. Nic heaved a sigh and offered a silent prayer of gratitude as the shift buzzer blasted.

The line of workers nudged him forward. Nic squared his shoulders and poked his time card into the slot. The solid *per-clunk* raised a wave of satisfaction. He was no longer the man he'd been. The old was gone. Nicolai Pankin, a new creation, was saved by God to live better now. He'd been given a second chance, and he wouldn't waste it.

He marched onto the factory floor, his head held high.

30

For the third night in a row, Micah waited by the dock at Dartmouth Harbor. A Red Cross ship was due in, and Jeremiah had indicated a package would be aboard. He needed to be ready. He yawned and tapped his thigh with the folded copy of the *New York Times.* The waiting became tiresome when the sun slipped too low to read. He had hoped to finish the article on the U.S. forces' infiltration of Germany. According to the reporter, soldiers had forged across the Siegfried line on September thirteenth—only two days ago. The thought of American soldiers pressing into Germany caused blood to pound in Micah's ears. If America conquered Germany, surely the war would end.

Lord, let it be soon.

When the war ended, Micah hoped Jeremiah would come home—or at least limit his work to the Russian church. No more dangerous escapades for Jeremiah. No more retrieving packages for Micah. No more *reason* to retrieve packages. That would be the best part—an end to worrying about children being hunted or hurt or killed. With this responsibility set aside, his life would be much simpler. Only the clinic to care for. And if he had only the one responsibility, then perhaps there would be time to develop personal relationships.

An image of Lydia immediately appeared in his memory.

She wrote daily, and receiving her letters had become the highlight of Micah's day. Not as good as being with her, talking to her, but for now it had to suffice. She and Nic Pankin had come to an amicable agreement concerning Nicky's upbringing. Nic kept Nicky during the week, with Lavinia watching him during Nic's working hours. Every other weekend, Nicky stayed with Lydia. On Sundays, Nic brought Nicky to church, and Lydia had begun inviting Nic to dinner with her family. Micah's heart leaped as he recalled the exciting news in her last letter—Lavinia had begun attending church with Lydia and Nicky. Allan Eldredge still held himself aloof from the idea of a relationship with God, but Lydia expressed confidence they would eventually win him over. She'd written, *"I'm trusting, Micah."*

Micah smiled, happy about how well things were going for Lydia, but a stab of jealousy melted the smile. Thoughts of Nic and Lydia spending so much time together rankled. He reminded himself once again he had no claim on Lydia. Hadn't he been praying for her to find a Christian man to love, a man who would also love Nicky? Maybe Nic was that man. By Lydia's account, Nic was growing daily in his Christian walk, and he certainly loved Nicky. Maybe one day soon he would declare his love to Lydia, as well, and they could become a real family.

Hard as Micah tried, he couldn't conjure up so much as an ounce of satisfaction at the thought.

He blew out a breath, smacking his thigh with the paper. It'd be good for Lydia and Nicky if they formed a family with Nic as the husband and father, but how would he handle it, if the day came? Weeks had passed since he'd seen Lydia, and she still haunted his dreams and sneaked into his thoughts during daylight hours. Despite his efforts to avoid it, his love for her had blossomed with the same tenacity as the dandelions growing in his childhood yard. Pa had done almost everything to rid the grass of those stubborn weeds, yet they cropped up year after year, proudly waving their yellow heads all summer long.

The mournful tone of a foghorn sounded. Micah straightened, peering outward. A ship approached, its lights sending ribbons of white across the choppy ocean waves. He tossed his unfinished newspaper into the nearest wire bin and then trotted halfway down the pier, squinting across the water. When the ship was within a hundred yards of the dock, he recognized Jonesy standing on the deck, and relief washed over him. He could finally collect his package. "Maybe," he muttered as hope rose in his chest, "this'll be the last one necessary."

He waited until the ship pulled in and the stevedores secured the mooring lines to the bollards before he walked to the edge of the dock. One worker—Jonesy—leaned against the railing and raised his hand in a wave. "Hey, Micah!"

They hadn't lowered the gangplank yet, so Micah caught hold of a rope and pulled himself hand over hand onto the deck. "Hey, Jonesy. Welcome home."

Jonesy shook Micah's hand, leaning close. "Two li'l 'uns this time. Girl an' a boy. Little girl cried a lot, hardly ate. Boy did okay, though."

Micah glanced across the deck. "Where are they?"

"Got 'em in my cabin." The wiry sailor shrugged. "Easier to take care of 'em that way. Captain didn't mind. Stay here—I'll git 'em for ya."

Jonesy clattered down a narrow staircase, disappearing from view. Micah breathed the sea scent and stayed out of the way of the sailors carrying cargo to the gangplank. In a few minutes, Jonesy returned with the children, who clung to his rough hands as if they were lifelines. Micah approached slowly, unwilling to frighten the pair, his eyes bouncing from the boy to the girl. Jonesy was right—these two certainly were little ones, and as wide-eyed and thin-cheeked as all the others had been.

"Here they be, Micah."

Micah withdrew a few bills from his shirt pocket and offered them to Jonesy, but the man took a backward step. "Nah. Use that to buy somethin' nice—some new American clothes or play pretties. These li'l 'uns need the money worse'n me."

Micah's heart warmed toward the crusty sailor. With his weather-roughened skin and three-day growth of beard, the man looked as grizzled as an old bear, but underneath he possessed a tender soul. "Are you sure?"

"Sure I'm sure. Don't say nothin' I don't mean." The man tugged loose of the children's grips. Regret pinched his features as he shoved his hands into his pockets. "Gotta tell ya, got myself kinda attached to these two. Might have to git hitched an' have some young'uns of my own."

"Maybe you should, Jonesy." Micah went down on one knee and held his hands out to the children. They leaned against Jonesy's legs, fear on their faces.

"When the war's over. Couldn't stand to raise kids durin' a war." He put his hands on the backs of the children's heads and propelled them toward Micah. "Take 'em. Find good homes for 'em. Give 'em a good dose o' happy. They deserve it."

"Thanks, Jonesy." Micah, still on his knee, smiled at the somber pair and gave his welcome message. "*Powitanie, dzieci.*"

They looked up at Jonesy, and he waved at them. "Go with Micah. I'm done with ya now." He rubbed his finger beneath his nose and turned away.

"*Wy jesteście bezpieczni.*" Micah assured the little ones they were safe.

As others had done before them, they stepped forward and took his hands. Micah walked them to his coupe, tempering his stride to match their much shorter ones. He judged the boy to be five or six years old, and the little girl couldn't be more than three. She was smaller than Nicky, but he'd glimpsed cotton drawers under her ragged dress, which indicated she was toilet trained. Still, so very, very young to be on her own. He hoped Rabbi Jacowicz had a wonderful family in mind for this little one.

Micah helped the children into the backseat of the coupe, then fired up the engine. He drove the quiet streets to the synagogue and pulled into the alley. Rabbi Jacowicz hurried out to meet him.

"You look tired, my friend," the rabbi said.

Micah chuckled ruefully. "I'll get some rest after we've seen to the needs of these new arrivals. A boy and a girl this time—neither of them bigger than nubbins." He opened the back door to reveal the children. The two had coiled themselves into a ball and were sound asleep, with the little girl's head resting on the boy's hip. Micah smiled. They reminded him of two puppies in a basket. He turned to the rabbi to share his thought, but the older man's frown silenced Micah's whimsical comment.

"This child . . ." Rabbi Jacowicz pointed an arthritic finger at the little girl. "She has blond hair."

Micah peered in again. In the pale glow of the car's dome light, he could see the child's hair was an ash blond color. He turned a confused look on the rabbi. "Does it matter?"

The rabbi shook his head, his beard swaying. "I cannot take a blond child."

Micah furrowed his brow. "Why not?"

The older man clicked his tongue against his teeth. "The Jewish family which I have chosen has all dark hair and eyes. This child would not fit in." Micah continued to stare at him stupidly, and the man's tone deepened as he struggled to explain. "She does not look Jewish. She looks of the German coloring. She would not fit in."

Anger rolled in Micah's belly. "You mean this child was forced to leave her homeland because she *is* Jewish, but a Jewish family will reject her because she doesn't *look* Jewish?"

The rabbi's sad gaze fixed on Micah's. "I know it sounds unreasonable, but it is true. All members of this sect are dark-haired. This child would be ridiculed by other children. She would not be accepted by her adoptive parents. I cannot take her."

"Nor would I leave her, knowing she wouldn't be treated well." Indignation colored Micah's tone.

"There are other places for orphaned children in the city," the rabbi said. "You should take this child and leave her there. She would find a home."

But what kind of home? Micah trusted the rabbi to place the children with loving families. If he simply dumped the little girl at one of the orphanages or foundling homes, he'd have no control at all over where she went.

Their voices must have roused the children. Both sat up, rubbed their eyes with dirty fists, and then peered at the two men with wide, uncertain eyes. Micah looked into the face of the little girl. Her blond hair tumbled around her thin cheeks in disarray. Her big blue eyes fixed on him, the long lashes throwing a shadow on her pale skin. She tipped her head, blinked twice, then held out her little arms toward Micah. "Papa?"

Micah's heart dropped into his stomach. He reached into

the car and lifted her out. She weighed next to nothing, her bones as fragile as a baby bird's. As he held her against his chest, she brought up a tiny hand and touched his cheek. "Papa?"

Tears gathered in the rabbi's eyes. "She thinks you are her father."

Micah nodded. He didn't have the language to tell her otherwise, and he discovered he didn't want to correct her. *Lord, let me do more.* The prayer he'd offered months ago whispered through his memory, and peace flooded him. He wouldn't hand this precious little girl to strangers in some orphanage. The child would come home with him.

He turned to the rabbi. "Take the little boy. I'll be responsible for the girl."

"I thank you, Micah. And I am sorry I cannot take her."

Micah opened the front passenger door and placed the child on the seat. "Stay there, sweetheart." He held up both palms, hoping she would understand. To his relief, she leaned back, her little legs straight out in front of her, her skirt riding up to expose filthy knees.

Micah opened the trunk and removed a bundle of donated clothing, which he gave to the rabbi. The two men said their good-byes in the alleyway, and then Micah slid behind the steering wheel. He looked at the little girl. For a moment, panic struck. What was he thinking? Could he really keep this child? Then she turned her chin to look at him, her little hands clasped in her lap, her expression wary. Her uncertainty pained him. He must reassure her. But how?

Micah offered a hesitant smile.

She tipped her head, her fine brows coming together.

Micah winked.

Her face puckered. She stared hard at his eyes.

He winked again, and she carefully closed both eyes in a tight squint, then popped them open.

Micah clapped his hands. "Good job, sweetheart!"

She hunched her skinny shoulders and a hesitant grin creased her face.

Smiling broadly, Micah started the coupe's engine. The little girl scooted next to his hip, rested her head against his ribs, and fell asleep.

31

By the time Micah reached his apartment, the midnight chimes from the big Catholic church had already sung their greet-the-new-day song. He carried the girl upstairs, her little head snug against his shoulder. Once inside the apartment, he looked around. Had he lost his mind? He had no bed for her, no toys. But he did have clothes. Boxes of clothes, all stored along the back wall of his living area, waiting to be shared with Jeremiah's packages.

Very gently, he laid the sleeping child on the sofa and then began opening boxes. In the third one he found a nightgown that appeared to be the right size. A little more digging turned up several ridiculously tiny pairs of white cotton underpants. When he turned, items in hand, he discovered the child had awakened and was sitting up, watching him.

"Well, hello, sweetheart. I'm glad you're awake." Micah knew the little girl couldn't understand anything he said, but it felt natural to talk to her, so he did. He moved to the sofa and held out the gown. "Look what I found. We can get you dressed for bed."

The little girl touched the white flannel with a grubby finger.

Micah frowned. If she was as dirty all over as her hands and knees indicated, she needed a bath. But he'd probably scare her to death if he plopped her in a tub. Deciding one more night of filth wouldn't be a catastrophe, he whisked her tattered dress over her head and reached for the nightgown. But his hands stilled as he caught sight of her ribs clearly protruding. Her arms and legs seemed to be skin stretched over bone. Her rounded belly stuck out, but Micah knew it wasn't food creating the fullness—such swelling indicated a lack of proper nutrition. Tears threatened, and he slipped the nightgown into place before they took control.

When she was dressed, she wriggled off the couch and scurried to the kitchen. She paused beside a chair, tipped her head, and babbled something unrecognizable. Micah didn't need to understand Polish to know what she wanted. "Okay, sweetheart, I'll get you a snack."

Micah helped her into a chair, then placed a plate with two pieces of buttered bread in front of her. She gobbled the first piece so quickly he feared she would throw it up. Then, as Micah watched in puzzlement, she got down from the table with the second piece of bread in her fist. Cradling the bread against her stomach, she scurried to the corner and buried it between the folds of the dirty dress Micah had discarded.

He feared his heart would break. "Oh, sweetheart, how will I make you understand that you will have enough to eat now?" He knelt beside her, intending to retrieve the bread and carry her back to the table. But she squawked in alarm, slapping at his hand. She'd need time to realize she needn't hide food. He wouldn't upset her now. He put his hands behind his back. "Okay, sweetheart, I won't take your bread. It's all right."

She glared at him, her blue eyes clearly expressing fear and fury for a few minutes. But when he made no further attempt to take the bread, she seemed to understand it was safe. She pushed the dress farther into the corner, then sat down beside it. A wide yawn squeezed her eyes closed, and she coiled into a ball with the wadded clothes and the hidden piece of bread wrapped tight in her arms.

Micah crouched near, gazing at her tiny frame in its protective pose. "Oh, my poor little sweetheart . . ." He whispered the words, crooning them like a lullaby. "It will take some time for you to be a regular little girl, won't it?" He waited until he was sure she slept, then he removed the soiled items from her grasp and lifted her into his arms. She made a soft mewling sound as he laid her on the sofa but didn't rouse. Curling onto her side, she brought up her little fists beneath her chin, and he covered her with the afghan that lay across the back of the sofa. He paused, frowning. Would she roll off during the night?

He searched the room for a better place for her to sleep, and when he spotted the kitchen chairs, an idea struck. He placed two chairs against the front of the sofa, their high ladder backs forming a makeshift crib. Then he stood, looking down at her as she slept. Her fine hair was matted into snarls. He hoped he'd be able to get a comb through it in the morning, or he might be forced to cut it short.

"I'd hate to shear your locks, sweetheart," he whispered, enjoying talking to her, even though she slept through the conversation. He stroked her tangled curls, his heart lifting in his chest. She looked like a little angel. "Lord, I hope I did the right thing. I hardly stopped to think about it. When she called me Papa . . ." He closed his eyes for a moment, remembering the rush of emotion the simple word had evoked. He gazed at her again, affection flooding his heart. "Having her here feels right. Help me give her a good home."

He yawned. What a night it had been! He longed to drop into his own bed, but he shouldn't leave her alone her first night in a strange place. Instead, he retrieved the blanket from his bed and stretched out as best he could in the overstuffed armchair across from the sofa. He kicked off his shoes, flipped the blanket over himself, and within minutes, drifted off to sleep.

It seemed he'd barely closed his eyes when something—not a sound or anything he could pinpoint—jarred him into wakefulness. A soft glow from the single bulb he'd left burning above the kitchen sink bathed the room. Micah sat up, confused. Why was he in the chair? Then, remembering, he looked around. And he saw what must have brought him so abruptly out of sleep.

The little girl sat straight up, staring at him from between the crossbars on the back of one of the wooden kitchen chairs. Her pale face and golden hair appeared almost ghostlike in the dim room.

"What's wrong, sweetheart?" Micah rose and took two steps toward her. She cowered against the back of the sofa. Although she made no sound, the fear in her taut body and wide eyes spoke more loudly than words. "It's okay." Micah kept his voice low, soothing. His movements became as slow as if he were slogging through molasses. He reached one hand toward her. She allowed him to touch her hair, but her breath puffed in little spurts of terror. His heart melted. How must she feel, waking up in a strange place?

Lord, help me show her she's safe now. The prayer helped calm his own rapidly beating heart. Micah pulled away the chairs and sat on the sofa. Very gently, he slipped his hands beneath her armpits and lifted her onto his lap. She sat as stiffly as if she were carved of stone. Her hands and feet were icy even though the room was warm. He draped the afghan around her and cradled her against his chest. When her hair brushed his chin, he remembered the feel of Lydia's silky locks, and he wished Lydia were here right now to help him with this little girl.

Holding her close, Micah began to rock gently back and forth. He sang the lullaby his mother had sung to soothe him to sleep when he'd been roused by a bad dream as a boy. He sang and rocked and stroked her hair, murmuring in between, "It's okay, sweetheart. *Wy jesteście bezpieczni.*" Over and over he assured her she was safe.

Eventually she relaxed in his arms, leaning fully into his embrace. Her eyelids quivered shut, and she slipped back into sleep. Micah sang the lullaby once more to her sleeping form, his chest tight with emotion. Even when he was positive she slept soundly, he didn't lay her on the sofa. If she wakened again, he wanted her to know the security of his arms. He prayed his touch would assure her no harm would come.

He slid downward, seeking a more comfortable position. *Please don't let me drop her, God.* Then Micah, too, slept.

32

Lydia sat at the foreman's desk, which was set at an angle on the loft so the person seated in the creaky wooden, wheeled chair could easily survey the work floor of the Eldredge Crating Company. Pounding hammers, buzzing saws, and muffled thuds of wooden boxes being stacked together mingled with the voices of the workers, creating a familiar thunder in her ears. The only difference from her childhood remembrances was the number of female voices in the throng—the women far outnumbered the men. And among the men, one stood head and shoulders above the rest.

Resting her chin in her hand, she watched Nic grab a three-foot-square slatted box and swing it into place on the stack, his movements as smooth as if he were performing in a ballet. Just as he had been five years ago, Nic Pankin was a man who garnered notice. A smile pulled at her lips. Nic was still handsome. Still strong. Still commanding. But now he glowed. His eyes sparkled with an inner light. He carried himself with his shoulders held back and his chin held high as if he had the world by the tail.

From shift start to end, he never slowed. When things got hectic, Lydia counted on Nic to keep an even temper and a sensible head. She found herself depending on him more and more as Father relinquished responsibility to her. Although he never verbalized it, Father was priming her to take over the company. Before the war, Father probably never would have considered allowing a *woman* to run the plant—not even his own daughter—but having so many trustworthy, hardworking women on the floor had altered Father's viewpoint.

She doodled in the margin of the work order on the desk as she thought about last Sunday's dinner. For the first time, Father had addressed Nic in conversation. On previous occasions, he'd tolerated his presence but studiously ignored him. But suddenly, in the midst of consuming his roasted potatoes and boiled carrots, Father had looked directly at Nic and asked what he thought about changing the wood in their largest crates from pine to cedar. Lydia could still remember the startled look on Nic's face and the way his gaze darted around as if to ascertain Father was asking him. Then he leaned back and expressed not only his opinion but the reason for it. Although Father hadn't disputed or agreed with Nic's words, Lydia had seen it as a turning point.

"Lydia, is that order finished?" Father's voice behind her shoulder startled her into dropping the pencil.

"Almost." She snatched it up, her cheeks flaming, and quickly turned it to the eraser side to remove the incriminating squiggles. Father moved to the railing and scowled down at the floor. Lydia shook her head, releasing a soft huff of amusement. "He's doing fine, Father. You needn't drill holes through him."

Father sent Lydia a chastising look. "I'm hardly drilling holes through him. I told him I would watch him." He shifted his gaze to the work floor again. "If he looks up, I want him to see it still holds true."

Lydia pushed from her chair and joined her father. Below,

Nic strode from the stacking area to the scrap pile, conversing with one of the other workers. He picked up a length of wood and gestured toward the saws, his forehead creased in concentration. Even from this distance, she noted his skin glistened with perspiration, the muscles beneath the sleeve of his work shirt bulging. Why couldn't Father see how hard Nic worked?

"It's been almost three months, and he hasn't made one error."

"Not yet." Father's tone was grim.

Awareness dawned in Lydia's mind. She spun on Father. "You want him to fail, don't you?"

Father's scowl deepened. "What do you mean by that?"

Lydia placed her hand over her father's and spoke gently. "Nic tells everyone his change is due to his relationship with God. If you acknowledge Nic is no longer the man he used to be, then you have to acknowledge God makes a difference. And you can't bear to admit you might be wrong about God."

"Nonsense." Father yanked his hand free. "Hanson's Shipping is awaiting confirmation of their order. Make sure it's taken care of this morning." He stomped across the loft and slammed himself into his private office.

Lydia sighed. Had she really thought Father was softening? *God, what will it take to help Father see You? So many of the people I love have embraced Your Son—Mother, Nicky, and even Nic. But the circle won't be complete without Father. Help me find a way to break through his hard shell and open his eyes to Your love and grace.*

A shout from the floor captured her attention. She looked over the railing. Nic cupped his hand beside his mouth and hollered over the general din. "Lydia, the truck from Manahan Orchards is here—bring down their packing list, would ya? Gotta get it loaded!"

Lydia waved in acknowledgment, retrieved the list from the file on her desk, and turned. She ran smack into Father, who had stepped behind her again. "Uff!"

Without apologizing, he snatched the list from her hand. "I'll take care of this. Finish your paperwork."

Lydia stood at the railing and watched her father thump down the wooden staircase that led to the floor. He flapped the order list in the direction of the wide doorway at the opposite side of the floor, and Nic fell in step with him. The pair exited the building together.

She sank back into her chair, dropped her chin to her hand, and released a long sigh. Sometimes when she looked down from this angle and watched Nic going about his business with a determined stride, shoulders held square, her heart skipped a beat. Not because it was Nic, but because it reminded her of another man who moved with such confidence. Micah.

Closing her eyes, she pushed the sights and sounds of the factory aside and allowed herself to relive moments with him. The feel of his arms around her back, the scent of his aftershave caught in the fabric of his shirt, the pressure of his cheek against her hair . . . Three months had passed since she'd seen him, yet the remembrances were as crisp and clear as the reality had been. Her heart began its familiar ache. How she missed him.

Of course, she'd received letters from him, although he didn't write as frequently as she did. Receiving one was a treat, and when she held his scripted pages, she imagined his hand—the slight curl of the coarse hairs on his knuckles, the curve of his tapered fingers around the pen, his blunt-cut fingernails, the movements of the tendons on the back of the hand shifting as he penned the words.

She gave herself a little shake and popped her eyes open.

If the vision of his hand could send her stomach into flutters of pleasure, she was badly smitten. But she must set wistful daydreams of Micah aside. He was caught up in his work. She was caught up in hers. However, his work was ordained by God and hers was assigned by her father. Although earning Father's trust gave her a sense of satisfaction, it wasn't the same type of satisfaction Micah must experience in his work. When would she discover what God planned for her?

The words she'd heard uttered that night in New York whispered through her mind again. *"You'll know in time. Be patient and wait."* She lifted her gaze to the thick overhead beams. "Lord, I've been waiting. When are you going to tell me the rest?" Impatience sharpened her tone, and she hoped God would forgive her. But an urgency rested in her chest—the desire to be doing more, to be helping more. She believed God had a plan. She only wished she knew what it was.

The squeal of tires followed by a truck's blaring horn sounded from outside and brought an abrupt end to her ponderings. An explosion of voices—some outside, some from the factory floor—immediately followed. Concerned, Lydia hurried to the railing and peered down. Machines wheezed into silence as workers left their posts and raced to the doorway leading to the loading area. Their jabber filled the air, nearly as loud as the saws had been moments ago. The noise became confused and disordered, prompting the bitter flavor of fear on the back of Lydia's tongue. And then an uneasy quiet settled over the group clustered at the doors.

A truck's engine still rumbled, but it was as if every other sound—machinery, voices, even the shuffling of feet—had been silenced. Lydia stared at the workers. Some held their hands over their mouths. Others clung to a neighbor. Their shocked, stiff poses made Lydia's blood run cold. She knew she should go down and investigate, but her rubbery legs refused to cooperate. The blood pounded in her ears, and waves of gooseflesh attacked her body.

Then one of the women nearest the door leaned forward, the knotted kerchief on her head bobbing with the movement. "Is . . . is he dead?"

Although she'd spoken in a raspy whisper, her words carried to the loft and penetrated Lydia's fear-muddled brain, spurring her to action. She dashed down the wooden stairway, her heels clattering in a deafening beat. In her haste, she missed the bottom riser and fell, scuffing the heels of her hands and banging her knees. Unmindful of the pain, she leaped up and rushed toward the doors. *Who is "he"?* The question echoed in her mind, but she couldn't find the courage to speak the words. Contemplating the answer was too frightening.

Heart pounding so hard she feared she might collapse, she pushed through the workers, her voice shrill in her own ears. "Step aside, please. Let me through." They shifted, creating a path, and Lydia staggered into the graveled yard. A scream formed in her throat, but she clamped both hands over her mouth and held it inside. There, on the hard ground below the back fender of the rumbling truck, lay two crumpled forms resembling rag dolls tossed aside by a child after play.

The truck driver leaned over them, partially hiding them from view. Lydia gasped, and the driver turned, his face a ghostly white. He fluttered his hands toward the fallen men. "It . . . it was an accident. I swear to you, I didn't see 'em." He lurched toward the building and slumped against the wall, allowing Lydia a full view of the men on the ground.

Her knees went weak. Her hands stretched toward her father and the man Nicky now trustingly called Daddy. A moan rose from her chest. "Oh, God, please . . . no . . ."

33

Miss Eldredge?" One of the floor workers shook Lydia's arm. The woman's pale face and wide eyes reflected the terror spinning through Lydia's stomach. "What should we do?"

Lydia glanced across the sea of shocked faces. *Oh, dear Lord, please help me.* Even while her knees trembled and her stomach rolled so violently she feared she might become ill, she drew upon the strength that was so much greater than her own. She commanded, "Call for an ambulance!" The woman scurried away, and Lydia forced her wobbly legs to carry her to her father and Nic.

She dropped to her knees beside their still forms. Dust rose, clinging to Nic's hair. Father lay on his back with Nic sprawled facedown across him with his head nestled in the crook of Father's right arm. Two workers approached and reached in as if to lift Nic off Father, but Lydia yelped, "Get back!"

Snippets of her nursing training flitted through her mind. No matter how ungainly the two appeared, stacked together like discarded lumber, they shouldn't move them. The wrong movement could cause more damage. If they were still alive. Lydia gulped.

The truck driver inched forward, wringing his hands. "Miss, I'm so sorry . . ."

Lydia barely glanced at him, her focus on Father and Nic. "What happened?"

His voice shook as he replied. "I . . . I'm not altogether sure. I was backin' up so the crates could be loaded from the loading ramp, and I heard a shout. I thought I hit my brakes, but I must've hit the gas, 'cause the truck lurched backward and . . . I must've hit 'em."

Bile filled the back of Lydia's throat. She pressed her fingers to Nic's neck. A faint pulse. Hope ignited in her breast. She shifted her attention to Father and, after a moment of fearful hesitance, placed her fingers against his carotid artery. "Oh, praise the Lord!" The prayer whooshed out with the breath she'd been holding. She addressed the workers who remained motionless in the doorway. "Did any of you see what happened?"

A woman in stained blue coveralls and short red hair scuttled forward. "I saw, Miss Eldredge. Mr. Eldredge was standin' there"—she pointed to the spot of ground in front of the loading ramp—"when the truck started backin'. He went to move out of the way, but it looked like he got caught on somethin'. He was pullin' his foot, but it wouldn't move. Nic looked over an' gave a shout to the driver, then he dived at Mr. Eldredge to knock him out of the way."

Lydia clutched her chest. "Did the truck hit them?"

The woman's eyes flooded with tears. "I'm sorry, Miss Eldredge. I got so scared, I closed my eyes. But I guess it did."

The woman Lydia had directed to call for help ran from the plant. "I called the hospital, miss. They're sending an ambulance." She knelt beside Lydia, her presence comforting. "We're all praying for your father and for Nic."

Lydia shifted her attention to the gathered workers. Each

stood with clasped hands, closed eyes, mouths moving in silent petition. Tears gathered in her eyes. She grasped the woman's hand. "Thank you." Then she bowed her head and added her prayers to those being uttered by the workers.

Micah awakened midmorning, stiff from his awkward position. Very carefully, he slid the little girl onto the sofa cushions and stood. He enjoyed a lengthy stretch before padding to the telephone and calling the clinic. Stan answered on the second ring.

"Stan, I've got a conflict today and can't come in. Can you manage things there?"

"Sure, Micah. Pretty quiet so far—only person to come in was an old geezer with pink eye."

Micah chuckled. "Well, if anything requiring more than a bandage or an aspirin crops up, give me a call. Otherwise, I'll see you tomorrow." He set the receiver back in its cradle, nibbling the inside of his cheek. His gaze fell on the sleeping child. Sunlight flowing through the window showcased the grime crusting her skin. Oh, how she needed a bath. But cleanliness could be met much easier than the other aspects of her daily care. What would he do with her while he was working? The clinic was no place for a little girl to spend the day. He flicked a glance toward the ceiling, silently requesting suggestions from the heavens. No answer came.

With a sigh, he scuffed to the refrigerator and pulled out a bowl containing three eggs. By the time he'd scrambled the eggs and toasted the bread in the oven, the little girl was sitting up, rubbing her eyes and looking around in confusion.

"Good morning, sweetheart," Micah greeted.

The child jabbered something in Polish and trotted to the

table. She climbed into a chair and gave him a look of expectation. *"Jedzą?"*

"Yes, we'll eat," Micah responded, grateful for his understanding of her simple query. He scooped half the eggs and a piece of toast onto a plate and set it in front of her. Before he'd even served himself, she'd wolfed down every bit. His appetite fled. He dumped his eggs and toast onto her plate. Without hesitation, she began shoving food into her mouth.

He clicked his tongue on his teeth. "We're going to have to learn manners, but that can wait for another day. Right now, it's more important to let you eat your fill."

She curled her arm around the plate, her furtive gaze fixed on him.

Micah held up both hands in a sign of surrender. "I'm not taking it. Go ahead and eat. *Jedzą.*"

Hunkering over the plate, she followed his directive. While she ate, he returned to the telephone and called Mrs. Flannigan.

"Good morning, me darlin'," Micah singsonged, and his landlord chuckled in response. "Might you be willin' to come up to my apartment for a few minutes? I need your assistance with something." The little girl would probably take to a woman bathing her more readily than a strange man. He only hoped Mrs. Flannigan wouldn't mind performing the task.

"Lemme finish my morning tea, an' then I'll be up," she said.

Micah thanked her and disconnected the call, then dug through the clothing boxes. The little girl, apparently full at last, climbed down from the chair and pattered over to watch him. Her face lit when he removed a pink-checked dress and ruffled pinafore from a box. She reached for it, her fingers wiggling, but Micah shook his head. "Not yet."

Micah led her to the bathroom and turned on the tub spigots. She pinched her fine brows as the water spattered against the porcelain, but by the time Mrs. Flannigan knocked on the door, the child was sticking her fingers in the water and giggling. Micah quickly explained what needed done, and to his relief Mrs. Flannigan didn't ask questions. She bustled into the bathroom, closing the door behind her with a firm *click*. A half hour later, she emerged with the shiny-faced little girl, who wore the pink-checked frock. It fit her loosely, the hem hanging well below her knees, but the pastel color was perfect for her golden hair and blue eyes.

Mrs. Flannigan plunked her fists on her hips. "I'm supposin' she's one o' the immigrant urchins you're so fond of." Although the woman's words were brusque, the look she aimed at the child held tenderness.

Micah wished he could tell her the whole story, but he didn't dare. He drew in a deep breath. "Yes. But this one . . . she's mine."

His landlady's jaw dropped. She spluttered for a few seconds. "Y-yours?" Wagging her finger in his face, she scolded, "Micah Hatcher, you scalawag, I—"

Micah held up both hands. "No, no! Not . . . what you're thinking." Heat seared his face. Mrs. Flannigan fell silent but her scowl didn't melt. Micah explained, "She was abandoned. And she needs a home. So . . ." He looked down at the little girl who stood beside him, damp tangled curls framing her sweet face. Her big blue eyes—so wide and innocent—held confusion. He placed one hand on her head and sent Mrs. Flannigan a sheepish grimace. "You think I've lost my mind, don't you?"

The older woman's eyes twinkled. "Micah, Micah . . . you are full of surprises, aren't you?" She stepped forward and put her wrinkled fingers beneath the little girl's chin. Her lips puckering, she examined the child's face for long seconds. "Takin' on one so young . . . especially you bein' a single man an' all . . ."

Lydia's face flashed in Micah's memory. He swallowed hard.

"But if any man's got the wherewithal to do it, you'd be my first choice." She clicked her tongue on her teeth and stepped back, folding her arms over her ample chest. "I'd have a hard time resistin' this'n meself, an' that's a fact." She reached for the doorknob. "Be lettin' me know if you're needin' anything else. Me an' my mister never had the pleasure of raisin' young'uns, but I reckon I can still lend a hand. If you're desperate." She breezed out the door.

Micah chuckled. He shifted his gaze to the child. "Mrs. Flannigan's a nice lady, yes?" The little girl blinked in reply. He sighed. "All right, sweetheart. We've got to get something figured out here." He led her to the sofa and lifted her onto his knee. He bounced his thumb against his chest. "I'm Papa. Papa."

She nodded somberly. "Papa."

Micah gave her a quick hug. "That's right. I am Papa. My name is Papa."

"Papa," she repeated.

Sucking in a hopeful breath, Micah lightly tapped his finger to the center of her chest and raised his eyebrows. "What's your name?" He searched his memory, then blurted, "*Imię*."

Her little shoulders jolted. Her eyes flew wide. A string of Polish spilled from her rosebud mouth, ending with, "Shustina."

Micah's heart skipped a beat. "Justina? Your name is Justina?"

She nodded.

Micah swept her into another hug. "Well, hello, Justina!" She snuggled into his neck, her little fingers coiling in his hair. He repeated her name several times, and with each utterance her little-girl giggle rang in his ear.

Finally he set her on his knee again and tweaked the end of her nose. "You are Justina," he said, "and I am . . . ?"

A smile lit her face. "Sweet-heart!"

With one word, she wrapped herself completely around his heart. Micah burst out laughing. He hugged her again, rocking side to side as he laughed. She laughed, too, her infectious giggle warming Micah to the center of his soul. Rising, he scooped her up to ride on his forearm and crossed to the telephone.

"I have to tell Lydia about you, sweetheart. She'll be at work right now, but I bet she won't mind a short interruption." A stamp cost much less than a call, but sometimes expense shouldn't matter. He set the telephone receiver aside and dialed the factory number. With Justina balanced on one arm, flicking his earlobe with her fingers, he held the receiver to his other ear and listened to the rings. After the eighth ring he hung up with a sigh of disappointment.

He caught Justina's hand and pulled it away from his ear, wrinkling his nose at her when she grunted in protest. "I guess she's away from her desk right now. We'll call her later. For now, let's go see Mrs. Flannigan again." The woman had indicated a willingness to help, and there was something else he needed.

Lydia perched beside Mother on a hard bench outside the examination rooms. The sterile smell of the hospital made her nose itch, and she sneezed. At the sudden noise, Mother gasped, and Lydia took her hand in apology.

Mother leaned forward and peered down the hallway. "What could be taking so long?"

Lydia wished to scream in impatience, but she squelched the urge. Screaming wouldn't help the situation. "There's a lot going on here, Mother. Father and Nic aren't the only patients." She frowned. "I hope Nicky is okay with the neighbor. He must be scared."

"He's not the only one." Mother's voice sounded tight with

controlled emotion. "If something happens, and your father doesn't make it, I—"

"Mother, don't talk that way! Of course Father will be fine!" Lydia injected as much confidence as she could muster into her tone. The image of Father and Nic lying white and still on the ground haunted her memory. She pushed the ugly image aside and focused on a different one. "You should have seen all the workers praying. They were storming Heaven. We must trust that Father and Nic will be all right."

Mother leaned her head against the wall and closed her eyes. Lydia leaned back, as well. How she longed for Micah's wise, unflappable presence. If he were caring for Father and Nic, she wouldn't feel half as anxious.

The door beside Lydia swung open and a nurse peeked out. "Mrs. Eldredge?"

Mother bolted to her feet. "Yes?"

"Your husband would like to see you."

Lydia grabbed Mother's hand, joy rising in her heart. "He's awake?"

The nurse nodded. "A bit groggy, quite grouchy, but ready for company."

Lydia followed Mother to the door, but the nurse pursed her lips into a sympathetic pout. "I'm sorry, miss. The doctor will only allow one visitor at a time."

"Oh." Lydia sank back onto the bench, tears of disappointment stinging her eyes. "All right."

The nurse and Mother disappeared into the room. Lydia stared at the clock ticking on the wall across the hall. The minutes passed more slowly without her mother by her side, and she grew restless. She rose and crossed to the information desk. "Excuse me." She waited until the white-uniformed woman behind the desk looked up. "Could you please give me an update on Nicolai Pankin? He was brought in about an hour ago from the Eldredge Crating Company."

"Your name, please?"

"Lydia Eldredge."

"Are you a relative?"

"No, I'm—" Lydia hesitated. How should she identify herself? As Nic's friend? His child's surrogate mother? She finished lamely, "His boss."

"Let me check with the doctor. Wait here." The woman moved silently through the hallway and stepped into the room just beyond Father's. In a few minutes she returned, her face unreadable. She crossed directly to Lydia and spoke in an emotionless voice that frightened Lydia. "The doctor has asked me to locate Mr. Pankin's next of kin. Mr. Pankin is unable to offer any information. Who might I contact?"

Lydia searched her memory. "He was raised on a farm near Captain's Bluff, but I don't know if his parents are still living. I've always assumed he was an only child, since he's never mentioned siblings. He has a son, but the boy is only four years old."

The woman's brows came together briefly. "I see."

An unwelcome thought filled Lydia's mind. Clasping her icy hands together, she took a deep breath to calm herself before speaking. "Ma'am, I'm the closest thing to family Nic has. I've known him for several years, he married my best friend, and I've been his son's surrogate mother since his wife's death. We're all he has. If he's in there dying . . ." Her voice broke. She took several shuddering breaths, then straightened her shoulders, lifted her chin, and gave the woman her most determined look. "I don't want him to die alone."

The woman's expression softened. "I'll tell the doctor." She emerged from Nic's room only a few minutes later, beckoning Lydia with a crooked finger. "The doctor says you may come in."

Relieved, Lydia hurried to the room. Nic lay on a railed bed, his arm in a cast and his head wrapped in a turban-like bandage. The doctor stood at his side, two fingers pressed to Nic's wrist, his eyes on his watch. Lydia waited quietly while he wrote something on the clipboard lying on the bed. The doctor flicked a brief look in her direction.

"How is he?"

The man scribbled something else on the clipboard, his gaze on the paper. "He's unconscious. He hasn't roused once since he arrived. His arm is fractured below the elbow—it looks as if he sustained a heavy blow that broke the bone all the way through. We've set it, and it should heal in time. He also has a sizable knot with significant swelling on the side of his head. There's the possibility it's putting pressure on his brain."

The doctor's clinical tone grated on Lydia's raw nerves. Why couldn't he exhibit some compassion? Micah would employ a tone intended to offer a small measure of comfort. If only all doctors were like Micah Hatcher. She swallowed her resentment and asked another question. "If the brain receives pressure, what could happen?"

"If he lives, he could experience loss of speech, limited mobility, inability to reason, and more." Finally he looked up from the clipboard and offered a poor imitation of a smile. "Let's not borrow trouble, Miss Eldredge. You may remain here as long as you are quiet. He needs to rest."

He departed, leaving Lydia alone in the room without even a chair on which to sit. She moved to Nic's bedside and took his hand, stroking the row of calluses on his palm with her thumb. He lay as still as he had on the ground behind the truck. To her confusion, a wave of anger rose from her middle. How dare he simply lie there and give up when he had so many reasons to live?

Leaning close to his ear, she gave his cheek a light pat. "Come on, Nic. Fight." She goaded him with her terse commands. "Show Nicky his daddy isn't a quitter. Open your eyes and tell me how you got yourself into this mess."

She stared into his face, waiting. No response. Not even a quiver of his eyelids. She huffed and stood upright, hands on her hips. "All right. Don't talk to me now. But don't think that means I'll leave you alone. I'm a fighter, too, and I won't let you slip away."

She didn't trust the expressionless doctor. He seemed to care little about Nic. However, she knew a doctor who would care. Leaning down, she spoke directly into Nic's ear. "If you haven't opened your eyes by the end of the week, I'll call Micah. He'll know how to wake you." The thought of speaking to Micah sped her pulse. She gave Nic's hand another pat and whispered, "Hang on, Nic. Help is on the way. Just hang on."

34

Something pinched his nose. Micah jerked beneath his sheets. His eyes flew open, and he found himself face-to-face with Justina, whose short-cropped blond curls shone like a halo in the morning sun. He chuckled, stretching. "Good morning, sweetheart. You woke up before Papa today."

Justina broke into a wide smile, and she grabbed his nose again. He didn't understand her fascination with his nose, but she loved to grab it. Their second morning together, she'd wakened him with a pinch on the nose, and she'd done it every morning since. Most mornings he awoke before she roused, but when he heard her small feet pattering into his room, he closed his eyes and pretended to sleep so she could surprise him. This morning, however, she'd given him a genuine surprise.

Still holding his nose in her small fingers, Justina spoke her favorite English word. "Sweet-heart."

Micah laughed and held out his arms. She climbed onto the bed and sat on his chest. He chuckled again, bouncing her with the vibrations of his belly. She added her high-pitched giggles to his low-toned chuckles. The melody pleased Micah's ears. He could spend the entire day listening to this child's bubbling laughter.

The ring of the telephone interrupted. She turned her head, looking toward the sound. "Sweet-heart?"

"Nope, telephone." He swooped her through the air and set her down, then trotted into the living area. He snatched up the receiver. "Hello." His voice emerged a little croaky from sleep.

"Good morning. Did I wake you?"

The female voice at the other end brought Micah to attention. "Lydia?"

"That's right. You sound groggy. Should I call back later?"

Justina tugged at his pajama leg and pointed to the table. He put his hand over the mouthpiece. "Yes, sweetheart, breakfast in a minute." Then he said to Lydia, "No, no, this is fine. Actually, I've been trying to reach you for almost a week, but you never answer your phone." He laughed lightly so she'd know he wasn't scolding. "How are you?"

"Is someone with you?"

Micah glanced at Justina, who stood near the window, playing with the dust motes dancing on a sunbeam. "I'm in the company of a very special little lady."

Silence fell on the other end. Micah pulled the phone from his ear for a moment. Had they been disconnected? He pressed it close again and said, "Lydia? Did you hear me?"

"Yes. Yes, I heard you. Perhaps I should let you go."

"Don't be silly! I have something important to tell you. But you first. You must have called for a reason. What can I do for you?"

He heard her sigh, as if debating with herself, and worry prickled his scalp. Something was wrong or she'd be chattering away about Nicky. Finally she spoke again, but the warmth that he'd come to expect was missing.

"Actually, Micah, I need your advice as a doctor. A few days ago, Father and Nic were in an accident. A truck at the plant was backing up, Father was in the pathway, and Nic tried to push him out of the way. They both were hit. Father suffered a slight concussion and some bumps and bruises, but Nic broke his arm and the bumper of the truck struck his head."

Micah sank down on a chair. He pulled Justina into his lap. "How is Nic now?"

"He's still in the hospital. He's been unconscious since the accident. They're calling it a coma. The doctors here keep telling me to leave him alone, not to stimulate him for fear of agitating him. But, Micah, I trust your judgment. If you were here, what would you do?"

Justina toyed with the buttons on his pajama top while he answered. "If he's in a coma, my advice would be the opposite. Talk to him, bring Nicky in to talk to him, give him good reasons to wake up. His brain needs to be stimulated. Are they working his legs for him, doing any kind of physical therapy?"

"Nothing. After all, he's only a one-armed laborer with no family of which to speak. Why should they waste their time with him?" Lydia's frustration carried through the line. " I . . . I could really use your assistance."

Micah's first impulse was to volunteer to come to Boston and check on Nic himself. But the little one in his lap reminded him that he couldn't just pick up and go. Mrs. Flannigan had been a jewel, taking care of Justina while he worked at the clinic, but he couldn't expect the dear woman to keep the active little girl day and night for an indeterminate length of time.

Apparently he hesitated too long, because Lydia's voice cut into his thoughts with uncharacteristic harshness. "Never mind, Micah. I'll take your advice and deal with this situation myself."

"It isn't that I don't want to come, it's just that—"

"Your 'little lady' has precedence. I understand."

No, she didn't understand. "Lydia, I—"

"I'm sorry I bothered you." The phone went dead.

"Lydia!" Frustrated, he plunked the receiver into its cradle and ran a hand through his hair.

Justina blinked at him, her eyes wide and innocent. "Sweetheart?"

"No, that was definitely *not* a sweetheart." Micah absently stroked Justina's silky curls as he stared at the phone, trying to understand Lydia's rudeness. Her worry over Nic, combined with his hesitance, must have forced her into behaving differently than he had come to expect. He picked up the telephone and dialed her home number. The jangle blared several times but there was no answer. She apparently had called from the hospital, but which one? There were several in Boston, and he didn't have time to call all of them. Frustrated, he muttered, "Now what?"

Justina crawled down from his lap and pointed to the table.

Micah nodded, setting aside thoughts of Lydia and Nic for the moment. "Breakfast it is." He lifted Justina into a kitchen chair and listened to her jabber to herself while he scrambled a couple of eggs and buttered slices of bread.

To his relief, after the first couple of days, Justina had stopped hiding food around the apartment. By the third night, she slept peacefully in her own bed. The little girl had settled into her new home as if she'd never lived anywhere else. Yet, despite Micah's and Mrs. Flannigan's best efforts to add to her vocabulary, she made use of only two English words—"Papa" for Micah, and "sweetheart" for everything else. Eventually, she would need to learn, and Micah hoped she wouldn't be school age before it happened. In the meantime, he enjoyed his new role as papa, and fully understood Lydia's love for a child who wasn't hers by birth. His love for little Justina went as deep as anything he could imagine.

His heart panged as he recalled Lydia's obvious distress. As soon as he settled Justina with Mrs. Flannigan and reached the clinic, he'd try calling her again. And he'd keep calling until he caught her at home.

He placed a plate and fork in front of Justina and then took her small hands between his. As had become their custom, they bent their heads and Micah asked a blessing for the food. Today, however, his prayer was longer than usual.

"Lord, bless this food to nourish our bodies. Touch Nic's body and bring healing to him. And please help me reach Lydia so I can be of more help to her. And so I can tell her about Justina. Amen."

Justina picked up her fork. "Sweet-heart!"

After Lydia offered the woman at the reception desk a nod of thanks for the use of the telephone, she hurried to the washroom. She managed to hold the tears at bay until she locked herself in the tiny cubicle. But the moment she had privacy, she allowed the tears to flow.

"A special little lady," Micah had said. The "little lady" was in his apartment first thing in the morning. Knowing Micah's character, there could be only one explanation. Micah was married. Sorrow stabbed like a knife through her chest. He'd gotten married without saying a word to her. Didn't their friendship mean anything to him?

Yesterday, when she and Mother had taken Father home, her father had made an absurd proposition as he'd settled himself gingerly on the sofa in the den. "Lydia, when Nic comes out of this, you should marry him."

Lydia had stared in openmouthed surprise. Had the accident affected his ability to think clearly? "Marry—? Father, what on earth would make you suggest such a thing?"

"He's a good man. I've been watching him. He's changed. You could do far worse."

"I'm sure that's true, but—"

Father continued as if she hadn't spoken. "You both love Nicky. You've already formed a family of sorts in raising the boy together. I know you care for Nic. So marry him."

Lydia sat beside her father and spoke calmly, unwilling to upset him. "Father, Nic is in a coma. There are no guarantees he'll wake up again."

"Oh, he'll wake up." Father flopped an afghan across his lap while Mother fluffed a pillow and placed it behind his head. "That God of his seems to be working well for him."

Lydia's hopes lifted. "You . . . you really believe God has been helping Nic?"

"*He* believes God has been helping him. He talks about it often enough." Father huffed, rolling his eyes. "He's nearly driven me to distraction with his God talk. I'm not ready to take it on for myself, but I will concede it's put Nic's feet on the right track." He shifted slightly, grimacing with the movement. He set his gaze on Lydia once more. "I tell you what—I'll give you the plant as a wedding gift. You will be the owner, and he will be the foreman—"

Lydia placed her hand on his arm. "Father, I can't marry Nic."

"Why not?"

"Because I don't love him."

Father waved his arm, shaking her hand loose. "Love can come later. It isn't as if anyone else is in the running for your hand."

Lydia looked him in the eyes and admitted, "Father, I already love someone else. I love Micah."

How wonderful it had felt to say the words aloud, to share the wondrous secret. But it hurt, too. She ached more fiercely than she had the day Nic took Nicky from the house, when she'd been certain her heart would never beat again. Because if Micah had married, he was lost to her forever.

In the little hospital bathroom, Lydia sobbed into her hands, giving full vent to her sorrow. And anger. How could he not tell her? After all they'd been through, after the way he'd looked at her and held her and led her to believe he saw her as someone special?

"No more of this." Lydia raised her face and spoke firmly to her tear-stained reflection in the mirror. "Crying won't change a thing. Micah never promised anything to me other than friendship, and he's been a good friend. Be thankful for his friendship and go on."

She splashed cold water on her face, diminishing the swelling around her red-rimmed eyes. Powder and lipstick, liberally applied, revived her even more. Convinced she'd made herself presentable once again, she headed with a determined stride to Nic's room. Micah had advised her to give Nic a reason to wake up. An uneasy question formed in the back of her mind. Would the prospect of the three of them—Nic, herself, and Nicky—forming a family be a strong enough reason for him to rouse?

35

Lydia, much to the chagrin of the nurses on duty, took up residence in Nic's room. For the next several days, she monitored his treatments and added her own regimen of muscle massages, exercises, and verbal stimulation. When she ran out of things to say, she read to him. Chapter after chapter of the Bible.

On the twelfth morning, while Lydia read aloud from Psalms, Nic's eyelids fluttered. That evening, at Lydia's prodding, he squeezed her fingers. The next day he opened his eyes and gave her a funny lopsided grin that set her heart to pattering because it resembled the Micah-grin she remembered. But she forced herself to smile at Nic rather than the memory of Micah.

Two days after Nic awakened, Allan Eldredge checked him out of the hospital, paid his bill in full, and brought him home to stay in the family's guest room until he had completely recovered. He remained with them through Christmas, giving Lydia an opportunity to deepen her friendship with him. Although they drove to work together, ate supper together, and visited every evening, she never summoned the courage to broach the subject her father had introduced concerning a permanent relationship with Nic.

On Christmas Eve, a card arrived in the mail from New York. Lydia crept into the front room to open it in private. Her hands shook as she removed the brightly colored card from its envelope, and when she read the signature—"Love, Micah & Justina"—the breath squeezed from her lungs. Pain stabbed, and she crushed the card to her chest.

Nic ambled around the corner. His brow furrowed when he caught sight of her, frozen in front of the fireplace. "You all right?"

Unable to speak, Lydia shook her head. She opened the card and gave it to Nic.

He squinted at the writing. "Who is Justina?"

Lydia forced a reply past her tight throat. "Micah's wife."

Nic's eyes widened. "He got married to someone besides—?" He stopped without adding the word "you," but it hung in the air between them.

Tossing her head, Lydia assumed a cavalier attitude. "It's okay. Really. It's been months since I've seen Micah. And how could anything develop between us when we live in separate states? He was never meant to be more than a friend."

Sympathy softened Nic's gaze, but he didn't argue with her. As their eyes locked in understanding, she couldn't help but wonder if God was thinking of Nic when He'd told her to be patient and wait. Was Nic's the life she was meant to touch?

She looked deeper into Nic's eyes, hoping to find the answer there, but then Nicky galloped around the corner, straddling a hobby horse Father had given him several days ago. Directly following Nicky's entrance, Mother stuck her head around the corner.

"Nicky, put Squirrel in her stall. It's dinnertime. Come along, Lydia and Nic."

Both reluctant and relieved, Lydia pushed away thoughts of Micah.

Mother had prepared a succulent beef stew thickened with barley and seasoned with garlic and basil. Served with fresh biscuits dripping with honey, the meal should have pleased everyone's palates. But midway through their meal, Father pushed his plate away and growled, "I can't eat. I wish I hadn't read the newspaper."

"What is it? Bad news?" Lydia cleaned Nicky's face with a napkin and sent him upstairs to play.

Father's cheeks flushed with indignation. "Over eighty American prisoners of war were massacred a week ago near Malmedy, Belgium. The SS men in charge didn't want to be burdened with feeding them, so they just shot them—slaughtered them like animals."

The words reminded her of the story Micah had told her about the Jews, and she swallowed against the bile rising in her throat. "Oh, Father . . ."

Father slammed his hand on the table hard enough to rattle the teacups. "I don't understand. It's Christmastime—a time when people spout peace and goodwill to men, but look what's happening. Peace? Bah! The world's gone mad!"

Nic placed his arm carefully on the edge of the table. The doctor had removed his cast a few days earlier, but he still treated the arm gingerly. "The world needs to recognize the Savior who came on Christmas Day. His goal was to bring peace. I read the Christmas story to Nicky last night. Then I did some readin' on my own. Found a verse in John—John 14, I think—that spoke of peace. I don't remember it word for word, but it was Jesus talking and it said somethin' like, 'Peace I leave with you, my peace I give unto you. . . .'"

He shook his head, his expression sad. "All that fightin' goin' on, all those failed attempts to win peace—the ones who refuse to embrace God's ways are the ones who create this madness."

Lydia expected Father to roll his eyes and bluster at Nic, but to her surprise her father's eyes took on the sheen of unshed tears. "What else does it say?"

Nic closed his eyes for a moment, his lips pressed tight in deep thought. "The end of the verse seems particularly fitting. It says, 'Let not your heart be troubled, neither let it be afraid.' That's a good thought to hold on to while so many things are goin' wrong around the world."

Father sat quietly for a few moments, seemingly absorbing Nic's words. Lydia's chest puffed with appreciation for the message Nic had shared. Why Father accepted this kind of teaching from Nic when he refused it from anyone else confounded her, but it seemed Nic's words were impacting her hardheaded father.

One of Micah's favorite verses flitted through her mind—*"And we know that all things work together for good to them that love God, to them who are the called according to his purpose."* She'd been so frightened when Nic located Nicky, forcing his presence into her life. Oh, how she'd fought against his intrusion. Now she welcomed him. God had used this big one-armed ex-morphine addict as a tool to reach her father.

She glanced at Nic, who picked up his spoon and lifted a bite of stew. How at ease he appeared, sitting at her table as if he'd always belonged here. Was Nic meant to be more than a friend to her in the future? She replayed his final words to Father—*"Let not your heart be troubled, neither let it be afraid."*

Right there at the table, she winged up a prayer. *Lord, remove these troubling thoughts from my heart, and let me find Your peace. Show me where I belong. Show me where I'm meant to make a difference.*

Micah's face appeared in her mind's eye, but she steeled her heart against the remembrance. Micah was another troubling thought that must be dispelled. The sooner the better.

January 1945 passed in a blur for Micah. An outbreak of influenza wreaked havoc among the Italian immigrants, and he spent much of his time visiting quarantined apartments, providing treatment and teaching mothers how to care for their ailing children. The wind blew strong in the city, cutting off his breath as he moved through the streets, and he longed for springtime and an end to this illness.

He also longed for an end to the war. He hadn't heard from Jeremiah since early November, and his worry increased daily with the newspaper reports of German attacks on Allied airfields in France, Belgium, and Holland in what the German leaders called The Great Blow. It was, indeed, a great blow, destroying over one hundred fifty British and American aircraft. Hitler had also launched attacks in the south near Strasburg, attempting to overtake the American Seventh Army.

Although Jeremiah wasn't in any of those areas, Micah worried that Germans were also busy in places too small to warrant coverage. Fear for his brother's safety as well as for Jeremiah's health became his constant companion. The winter months had always been hard on Jeremiah—his polio-weakened legs ached terribly in the cold—and each time an icy blast blew Micah's coat away from his own legs, he sent up a prayer for his brother.

As the month continued, reports showed Allied forces fighting fiercely to keep Hitler's army on the run. Airplanes bombed Berlin almost daily, and on the streets of New York people cheered the loss of life in the German city. He couldn't understand their pleasure. Maybe it was his vow as a doctor to preserve life—all lives, even Germans—that made his heart cry when he heard others celebrating the death of German civilians.

His daytime hours were filled with doctoring the immigrant population, caring for Justina, and tracking the war. But nighttime. Ah, nighttime. Those hours stretched long and empty.

As he settled beneath his covers, his thoughts carried him once again to Boston. Since Lydia's telephone call asking his advice concerning Nic's care, he'd only received one communication from her—a Christmas card. She'd enclosed a brief note informing him her father was home and recovering well, Nic had been released from the hospital and was staying with the family, and Nicky was happy and healthy. She'd closed with, "Nicky sends his love." But there was nothing personal to him from her. It had disappointed him.

He rolled over in his bed and snapped on his bedside light. Lydia's card lay next to his Bible, and he lifted it, smoothing his fingers over the embossed cardinal on the card's face. Bright. Cheerful. In direct contrast to the emotionless note inside. He read her words again. Slowly. Hoping maybe he'd missed something. But no—the stilted message was the same. He flumped onto his pillow and sighed at the ceiling, the card still in his hand.

Lydia . . . If he closed his eyes, he could picture her on the curb, the sun shining on her hair, her eyes bright as she blinked back tears, a smile quavering on her lips. Behind her, Nicky loped around the yard, hard at play, riding an imaginary horse named Squirrel. He'd sent the boy a hobby horse for Christmas, but she hadn't acknowledged it. Maybe it hadn't gotten through. He propped himself up on one elbow and punched his pillow, then folded it in half before lying down again.

He wanted to visit her. He wanted to see her. He wanted to see her *now*. But he had to wait until he wasn't so busy. Then he'd have time. Time to visit. Time to court. Time to . . . propose. His heart thumped erratically at the thought of asking

Lydia to be his wife. He couldn't imagine spending the rest of his life with anyone else. He smiled in the dusky room, considering how quickly his love for her had blossomed. It must be a God-given love. What else could explain it? War and busyness and distance hadn't changed his feelings for her. If anything, his affection had deepened, becoming so rooted in his heart nothing could pluck it out. And he'd been certain she held affection for him, too.

So why did she remain so aloof? Why hadn't she called to ask who Justina was? Might she be avoiding him because her heart had changed? Maybe having Nicky's father under her roof had turned her heart elsewhere. It would be good for Nicky to have his daddy and the woman he called mama truly united.

Give me a chance to talk to her again, Lord, to settle these feelings that wage like a personal war inside of me.

The patter of little feet interrupted his prayer. A small shadow slid across the floor and then the little girl followed. She padded directly to the side of the bed and reached out a small hand. The hand stilled midway to his nose as she looked into his open eyes. She blinked twice, her expression innocent. "Papa?"

"Do you want to come up?" He patted the bed beside him. "Up? Come up?"

Justina smiled her beaming smile that lit the room and then clambered onto the bed. She curled herself against his side, resting her head on his shoulder. "Papa. Sweet-heart." A contented sigh whisked from her lips.

Micah brought up the edge of the blanket to cover her. He let his thoughts continue, but he spoke them aloud, sharing them with the little girl who snuggled beneath his arm. "Yes, I love Lydia. And I love you, too, sweetheart." Justina nodded, tipping her head to peer attentively into Micah's face. He went on, as if telling a bedtime story. "I wish I'd had a chance to tell

Lydia about you when she called. I think she'd love you, too. She has a little boy named Nicky, and he's just about your age. You two would get along great, I reckon. He's very articulate, and with your wide vocabulary"—he released a quick chortle at his own joke—"Lydia and I would probably never get a word in."

Justina's big blue eyes locked on Micah's. "Sweet-heart."

He patted her little back. "That's right. I'm surprised she hasn't written to ask about you. I signed your name to the Christmas card I sent her. Lydia's usually full of questions."

He slapped a hand to his forehead as understanding smote him like a club landing on his head. Justina sat up, stared at his hand for a moment, and then imitated his gesture.

Micah groaned, gently pulling her against his shoulder. "Yes, sweetheart, Papa did a dumb thing." How could he have been so foolish? He'd signed the card "Micah & Justina"—with no explanation of who Justina was. It had seemed so natural he hadn't given it a second thought. The signature painted a clear picture in his mind of himself and this beautiful little blond-haired girl. But what must Lydia have thought?

"I know what she thought," Micah railed aloud, shaking his head. Beside him, Justina shook her head, making her curls bounce. Micah hugged her, laughing at the ludicrous idea that must be planted in Lydia's mind. "She thinks I married someone named Justina!"

"Sweet-heart!" Justina crowed.

Micah pressed his nose to Justina's. "Well, I'll just have to set her straight, won't I? And when I tell her the truth about you, I'll tell her the truth about me at the same time. I'll come right out an' tell her I love her. Is that a good idea?"

Justina grabbed Micah's nose. He shifted his chin, trying to catch her fingers between his lips. She giggled wildly and then began bouncing on the bed. Realizing she was getting wound up, he scooped her into his arms and carried her back to her bed. "It's nighttime. You need to sleep. No"—he gently pressed her back against her pillow and kept his hand on her chest, shaking his head—"not play, sleep."

He closed his eyes and let his head flop to the side, pretending to snore. One more little giggle escaped. Opening his eyes again, he leaned down and kissed her forehead. "Sleep now, darling girl. And in the morning, I'll call Lydia and set things right."

36

The next morning, while Justina sat at the table munching her breakfast toast, Micah crossed to the telephone, ready to call Lydia. A clamor on the street captured his attention. Brow furrowed, he moved to the window and pushed it open, allowing in a cold blast of air that swept the curtains out on either side of him. A newsboy stood on the sidewalk, waving a paper and bellowing at the top of his lungs.

"German atrocities exposed! Death camp liberated by Russian army! Jewish victims of German cruelty set free!"

Micah cupped his hands beside his mouth. "Boy! What are you talking about?"

The youth looked up. His wind-chapped cheeks glowed red. "Someplace called Auschwitz—the Russians released a bunch of Jews who'd been kept prisoner there. They tell some awful things."

Micah gasped. Exactly what Jeremiah had described! And it had become front-page news? He hollered to the boy, "Stay there. I'm coming down." He turned to Justina and held up his palms, a signal she had learned. "Sit still, sweetheart. Papa will be back." Micah ran down the stairs and onto the frigid porch. Frost stung the bare soles of his feet, and he danced in place while he traded a dime for a newspaper. Back in his apartment, he read the article so many times he nearly memorized it, and certain passages painted images in his head that pierced his heart.

For the next week, everyone who entered the clinic buzzed about the place called Auschwitz. "Can you imagine?" one woman gasped. "I would never have thought such things possible in this civilized world!"

Of course, Micah knew Auschwitz was just the tip of the iceberg, but he kept the knowledge to himself. The nations' leaders would need to fully divulge the horrors inflicted on innocent people during this terrible war. He wondered if any article would incite greater indignation in his neighborhood than the one about Auschwitz.

And then, almost a month later, the news turned to Yalta. Although the information was kept hushed, rumors spread that the three Allied leaders—President Roosevelt, Winston Churchill, and Joseph Stalin—were meeting to discuss Europe's postwar reorganization. Though no one knew the details of this meeting, it seemed clear to Micah that if agreements were being made for a postwar time period, then the war must surely be coming to an end. The idea almost made him giddy.

Every day from the morning the news article of Auschwitz hit the front page, Micah dialed Lydia's number first thing in the morning. But each time, Allan Eldredge answered and agreed to ask Lydia to return the call. Yet she never called. Micah could only assume she was refusing to speak to him, and his frustration grew. But he didn't give up. He wouldn't give up. He couldn't.

Valentine's Day arrived—a day for cupids and romance. And someone had sent Lydia a dozen red roses. Nic paused in the office doorway, absorbing the sight of Lydia seated behind her father's massive desk. She knew the business—she'd grown up around it and she handled things as well as her father ever had, in his opinion—but somehow she just didn't look comfortable in Allan Eldredge's chair.

He watched her pinch a rose petal between her fingers, her brow puckered in either confusion or disapproval. He couldn't be certain which. Or maybe the crunch of her brow had something to do with her reason for calling him to her office. He wouldn't know until he asked.

Clearing his throat, he took a forward step. She spun toward him, the wooden chair creaking noisily with the sudden movement. He chuckled. "Sorry. Didn't mean to scare you." He bobbed his chin at the roses. "Somebody thinks you're special."

"And you just confirmed for me that it isn't you."

Nic drew back in surprise. "Me?"

Lydia sighed. She rocked back in the massive wood chair, the spring popping, and crossed her arms. "I'm fairly certain these came from Father, but the fact that there's no card tells me he wants to keep it a secret."

Nic smirked, shaking his head. "You know, I've come to like your old man. Cagey. Knows how to get things done."

Lydia scowled. "If he'd limit himself to business dealings I'd admire his caginess a bit more. But I resent his intrusion into my personal life." She gestured toward one of the chairs along the wall, assuming a professional air. "Thank you for coming up. Sit down for a minute, would you, Nic?"

Nic settled himself in the chair closest to the desk and peered at Lydia. "You look awful serious. Are we talkin' boss to employee, or is it somethin' else?"

"I realize we're on company time, but this is important. And it's something else." Lydia leaned forward, cringing when the chair released another loud pop. "Now that the office is officially mine"—did unhappiness flash in her eyes with the statement?—"I intend to shop for a new chair." She drew in a deep breath, blew it out, then pinned him with a frown. "Nic, do you love me?"

Nic jolted. "*Love* you?" He whistled through his teeth. "Whew, Lydia, you're right. That *is* somethin' else!"

Her expression remained serious. "Answer me, please."

Nic scratched his chin, stretching his lips into a nervous grimace. Did she realize how much she was putting him on the spot? "Well, now . . . you mean a lot to me, Lydia. You've taken care of my son, taken care of me, helped me get my feet back under me so I can live a halfway decent life. All of that matters a lot. A whole lot. So naturally I have feelings for you. . . ."

Lydia snorted. "You're very good at tiptoeing around the issue. I'm going to take your ambiguous evasion as a no. Would my assessment be accurate?"

Nic shrugged. "Yeah. I s'pose it would be."

Finally she smiled. "Good. That puts us on even footing."

He couldn't resist teasing, "Awww, you mean you don't love me?"

Her eyes flashed. "Careful there. We could have this turn into a boss-employee conversation."

He laughed, not at all threatened. "Why are you askin' me this?"

"Father has been after me to marry you ever since you knocked him out of the way of that truck."

Nic threw back his head and laughed—one brief, raucous blast of laughter. Then he brought his chin down and wiped his hand across his face, trying to remove the humor. "Well, you know, Lydia, there are some cultures where you offer yourself as a slave to a person who saved your life. Maybe Allan figures I'd rather have you."

"Nic, it isn't funny."

The look on her face let him know the conversation wasn't an easy one for her. He tried to curb his amusement.

She went on. "I feel as if I'm being thrown out as a . . . a sacrificial offering! I've done everything I can think of to convince him neither of us is interested in making such a commitment, but he insists I'm not looking at the situation logically. He reasons we've developed a good working relationship, so therefore—to his way of thinking—we'd also make an excellent married couple."

Nic snatched his hat from his head, bounced it twice on his knee, then set it back in place. "I can see his point, Lydia. I mean, we get along good. We both love Nicky. From a logical standpoint, it would make sense for us to marry. We'd probably do just fine together."

Lydia dropped her jaw. "Are you suggesting—?"

"No!" He held up his palm. "'Course not! I'm just tryin' to help you see it from your father's way of thinkin'."

"Well, what I need from you is some help making my father see it from *our* way of thinking." She tipped her head, giving him a pleading look. "Will you come to dinner this evening and talk to him? I've given up on making headway on my own."

Nic shrugged. "Sure. I'll try to set him straight. Besides . . ." He winked. "I've been meanin' to talk to you about somebody. You know Myrna Todd, the new gal you hired a couple weeks ago?"

A slow grin crept up her cheek.

Heat filled his face, but he continued. "I've been thinkin' about askin' her out for dinner Saturday night, but it's my weekend with Nicky. Do you suppose . . . ?"

Lydia laughed. "No, I won't babysit. Ask my father. Maybe it'll give him a strong message that you aren't interested in me."

He grinned and pushed to his feet. "You got it, boss. Oh, and by the way, I'll find some oil and fix that chair for you." He paused, frowning. "Funny. It never popped when Allan sat in it."

The remainder of the day, Nic's comment about the chair rolled in the back of Lydia's mind, taunting her. No, the chair hadn't popped for Father. But he hadn't wiggled in it as much as she did because he was comfortable in it. Why couldn't she settle in?

She understood the business. She was good at running it. The employees accepted her as their new leader without question. Father savored his newfound freedom. Everyone seemed happy with this arrangement. Everyone except Lydia.

As she drove home, a prayer rose from the center of her being. *Lord, I long for my place of service. If I'm meant to operate the plant, will You please give me peace?*

When she entered the front door, Nicky came sliding down the hardwood hallway in his stocking feet and collided with her thighs. She caught her balance on the doorjamb. "Nicholas Allan Eldredge, you are as wild as a March hare!" Laughing, she bent down to bestow a hug.

Mother appeared at the opposite end of the long hallway, her hands on her hips. "He's been a mischief-maker *all day.* I told him if he didn't settle down, he'd have to sit in his room."

Nicky stuck out his lower lip. "Grammy's been grumpy."

"Sounds like she has good reason." Lydia took Nicky by the hand and sat on the bottom riser of the staircase. "Why have you been naughty today, Nicky?"

The little boy blew out a mighty breath. "Nobody will play with me. Poppy went to town. Grammy had to clean. Buggy flied away from me when I took him out to play."

"You took him out?" No wonder Mother was frustrated. Lydia drew Nicky beside her and put her arm around his narrow shoulders. "Nicky, sweetheart, it isn't safe for Buggy to be outside of his cage. You shouldn't take him out."

Nicky propped his elbows on his knees and rested his chin in his hands. "I know. Grammy told me." He peered at her with sad brown eyes. "She told me, an' told me, an' told me . . ."

Lydia gave him a quick squeeze. "Did Buggy make messes?"

"Yes. Seeds and feathers and"—he dropped his voice to a barely discernible whisper—"poop. But Buggy didn't mean to."

Lydia swallowed a smile. "I'm sure he didn't."

Nicky dropped his arms, sitting up straight, his expression brightening. "But can you play with me now?"

Lydia slumped against the railing. "Oh, I've just worked so hard today, I don't know if I have the energy to play."

Nicky recognized the teasing in her voice. He bumped her with his shoulder. "Mama-a-a-a-a . . ."

She grinned. "I bet I have time for a quick game before supper. Daddy is coming over to eat, so maybe he'll play horsey with you then."

"Goody." Nicky stood and grabbed her hand. "C'mon, Mama, let's go play."

Lydia rose to follow Nicky upstairs, but the telephone rang. Mother called from the kitchen. "Lydia, my hands are dirty. Could you answer that?"

"Yes, Mother." She turned to Nicky, who flopped down with a disgruntled sigh, and ruffled his hair. "When I'm done on the telephone, we'll play, okay?" She hurried into the den and picked up the telephone receiver. "Hello?" From the other end came a series of soft scuffling noises followed by whispers. And then a small child's voice uttered the most unexpected word.

"Sweet-heart!"

37

When Lydia answered the phone, Micah could hardly believe his luck. After weeks of calling, he finally heard her voice. But instead of answering her "hello," he quickly put the receiver in Justina's hand and whispered, "Talk, Justina! Talk, sweetheart!"

As expected, Justina chirped her favorite word. "Sweet-heart!"

"Good girl!" Micah took the receiver back in time to hear Lydia ask, "Who is this?" Confusion colored her tone. Micah's heart pounded so hard he felt short-winded. "It's me—Micah."

Her sharp intake of breath carried from across the miles, and he imagined her at the other end with a delicate hand on her chest, her hair falling sweetly around her high cheekbones. "M-Micah?" She sounded as out of breath as he felt. "But who was that a moment ago?"

"My little girl, Justina." The tremble in his hands threatened to dislodge the receiver from his ear. He took a two-handed grip on it. "Lydia, I have so much to tell you." Justina picked up her rag doll and toddled to the sofa, where she put the "baby" to bed. He smiled, watching her. But his smile faded when Lydia spoke again.

"Yes, I imagine so. It's been several months."

Her chilly tone stirred defensiveness in Micah's chest. "It isn't as if I haven't tried to speak to you. You wouldn't return my calls." Nic Pankin flashed through his mind, and the defensiveness melted, replaced by anxiety. "Is it . . . is it because you were . . . otherwise engaged . . . with someone else?"

"What do you mean I wouldn't return your calls?" Although she still spoke sharply, he sensed a hint of bewilderment beneath her bluster. "Micah, the only contact I've had from you since I telephoned you to talk about Nic is a Christmas card that had your name coupled with some woman's."

"But that's what you need to understand. It wasn't 'some woman.'" He released a frustrated sigh. If only they could have this conversation face-to-face. Long-distance telephone calls were a marvelous invention, but some things needed to be said while holding the hand and looking into the eyes of the listener. "Lydia, Justina is three years old. She's one of Jeremiah's packages. I took her to Rabbi Jacowicz, but he refused to place her because she's got blond hair and blue eyes. He said she wouldn't be accepted in the Jewish community."

"You must be joking."

"I assure you I am not joking. Ludicrous, isn't it? She's been with me since September."

"Why haven't you told me about her?"

"I told you, I've been trying to reach you by telephone. I've tried dozens of times and left messages each time."

"With whom?"

Micah paused. A thread of anger wavered in her voice, and he didn't want to create problems.

"Micah, who took the messages?"

Micah ran a hand through his hair. "Your father, Lydia."

"I see." A pause. "I think I understand." Her voice had lost its edge. Micah sighed with relief.

Justina scampered over and handed Micah her doll. He pretended to rock the baby as he continued his conversation. "I have more to say, but I don't want to say it over the telephone. Would it be possible . . . I don't want to intrude, but . . . If I arranged for someone to fill in for me at the clinic, could I bring Justina to meet you?" Micah held his breath, waiting for Lydia's reply. She hadn't answered his question about her time being filled by someone else. His heart raced as he waited to find out whether his attention would be unwelcome.

Finally, her soft voice came through the line, as tender as a kiss. "Yes, Micah, I would like that very much. I—" He heard her throat catch. "I've missed you."

He wished he could reach through the lines and embrace her. His voice turned husky as he admitted, "I've missed you, too." He grasped the receiver tightly, willing his pulse to slow. "I'll call you tomorrow when I know what I can arrange at this end. Until then, give Nicky a hug for me, and I'll talk to you again soon."

"I'll be here."

"Oh! And, Lydia?" He swallowed, gathering his courage. "I love you."

Lydia nearly reeled. Three little words. Just three little words. But what an impact they made on her heart. Her head spun, her pulse pounded, her smile nearly split her face. She found enough voice to whisper, "Oh, Micah, I love you, too. Good-bye."

Nicky appeared in the doorway. He plunked one hand on his hip. "Mama, are we gonna play a game or not?"

"What?" She felt as if she floated somewhere near the ceiling. She blinked twice at Nicky's disgruntled expression. Reality returned. "Oh, Nicky. Thank you for waiting so patiently. Yes, we can play now."

Upstairs, Nicky and Lydia sat cross-legged on the floor and Nicky laid out the checkerboard, but Lydia found it difficult to concentrate. Now that the sweetness of Micah's words was wearing off, she found herself battling a mighty anger. How dare Father keep secret Micah's calls? She thumped the checkers across the board—*clack! clack!* Father and his infernal interference would have to stop immediately. He might think he had her best interests at heart, but he had no right to manipulate her life. At supper, the minute after Nic made his announcement about wanting to date the new girl at work—what was her name? Myrna?—Lydia would make it very clear that her father was to allow her to make her own choices concerning her future.

Nicky looked up expectantly. "Your turn, Mama."

"Oh. Thank you, sweetheart."

The voice of the child speaking the word "sweetheart" replayed in her memory. Micah had said she had blond hair and blue eyes. The opposite of Nicky, she realized, reaching out to brush Nicky's dark hair away from his eyes. Why had the child said "sweetheart" instead of "hello"? Imagined images of the little girl forming in her mind, Lydia inwardly applauded Micah for giving her a home. What a difference he was making in one small life.

It's time. You'll soon know.

She recognized the Voice, so she didn't startle as she had the first time she'd heard it, but she lifted her gaze to the ceiling. "It's time?"

"It's time for what, Mama?"

She didn't realize she'd spoken aloud until Nicky asked the question. The doorbell chimed. Lydia smiled, rising to her feet. "It's time to wash up for supper. Daddy's here."

"Daddy!" Nicky leaped up and raced down the stairs.

Lydia followed more slowly, pondering the miraculous relationship that had developed between Nic and Nicky after their shaky start. God knew Nicky needed a dad, and He'd provided a very loving one. What joy to see God's plan for Nic and Nicky fall into place. Her heart sang as she thought about the message she'd been given. God's plan for her was about to be revealed.

"I was wonderin' . . ."

The note of teasing in Nic's voice alerted Lydia. She looked up from her bowl of beans and bacon in time to catch the wink Nic aimed in her direction. Then he turned to Father, his handsome face innocent. "Would you folks keep Nicky this weekend instead of next? Then I can take this girl I know on a proper date."

Father's smile turned smug. He looked from Nic to Lydia to Nic again. "A proper date, hmm? Sounds serious."

"Oh, not yet." Nic chuckled. "I think she's nice. Pretty, too. Might not amount to anything. But there's no harm in askin', right?"

Father nearly beamed—more jovial than Lydia could remember seeing him in ages. "No harm at all."

From the other end of the table, Mother smiled sweetly. "Who is she, Nic?"

"Myrna. Myrna Todd."

Father gave a jolt. "Did you say Myrna?"

"That's right. She's new at the plant. The boss here"—he bounced a smirk at Lydia—"hired her a couple weeks ago. I trained her. She's a nice girl."

"But—but—" Father's fork dropped to the table with a clatter.

"What's wrong, Father?" Lydia knew the answer, but she asked the question anyway. She supposed she should feel guilty about making Father uncomfortable, but after what he'd done, he deserved a bit of discomfiture.

Father took a grip on his fork. "Nothing."

Lydia curled her hand over her father's wrist, preventing him from dipping into his plate. "I understand what you were trying to do. But you can't control people's hearts." She waited until Father raised his head and met her gaze. "Nic and I care about each other. We've become good friends, and I think we always will be." She sent a soft smile in Nic's direction, and he answered with one of his own. Then she turned her attention to Father. "But it would be wrong to try to manufacture more than friendship just for Nicky's sake. Neither of us would be happy." She leaned forward, tipping her head. "You *do* want me to be happy, don't you, Father?"

A bit of Father's old bluster returned. "Of course I do. You're my daughter." He clamped his lips together for several tense seconds, and then he sighed. "I only did it because . . . I love you."

Tears welled in Lydia's eyes. Father so seldom spoke tenderly. She savored the sound of those words from his lips. "And I love you. But when you push me into places I'm not comfortable going, or hide things from me— things that should be shared—I don't feel loved. I feel manipulated."

Mother looked at Father with lowered brows. "What is she talking about?"

Lydia sat up straight and shook her head. "It isn't important, Mother. Father knows."

Father flushed crimson. "I suppose you're speaking of the telephone calls from Dr. Hatcher."

Mother interrupted again. "Dr. Hatcher? From New York? Has he been calling?"

"Micah-my-friend!" Nicky twirled his spoon through the smear of gravy left on his plate. Nic captured Nicky's hand before he made a mess.

Father glared across the table at his wife. "Yes, that doctor from New York has been calling and asking for Lydia. Almost every day! But Lydia's been busy learning how to manage the plant. She didn't need the distraction."

Mother plunked her fork on the tabletop. "Allan! I'm shocked. Keeping messages from Lydia? What were you thinking?"

Lydia gawked in amazement. Across the table, Nic and Nicky fell silent. She'd never heard her mother challenge Father. For reasons she couldn't understand, she rushed to Father's defense. "It won't happen again, Mother." She slanted a look at Father. "Right?"

Father lowered his head. The defeated slump of his shoulders pierced Lydia, sending any hint of anger far away. "I suppose I'm just a foolish old man. I thought by giving you the plant, finding you a man who was interested in working at the plant with you, I'd keep you . . . and Nicky . . . close by." He sighed, lifting his gaze slightly to look into her eyes. "I . . . I like having you near."

Tears flooded her eyes, distorting her vision. "Oh, Father . . ." She rose and crossed behind his chair. Wrapping her arms around his neck, she rested her cheek against his. "I like being near you, too. But I have to grow up sometime." She moved to his side, knelt, and placed her hand on his shoulder. "Father, you're a wonderful businessman, and you have wonderful ideas for making things work. But there are some things we have to allow the hand of God to control."

She glanced at Nic, who was using his napkin to wipe the remainder of gravy from Nicky's chin. A smile grew on her face without effort. She turned to Father again. "Do you remember how we tried to keep Nicky away from Nic? God's plan was different. Whose was better? I don't want to consider what might have happened the day of your accident if Nic hadn't been there."

Father's face twisted into a brief, embarrassed grimace.

Lydia continued softly. "I'm pleased you care enough about me to want to keep me near and to worry about my well-being, and I'm so proud you've entrusted the plant to me." She drew a sharp breath. What would Father do if she refused to take over the business? He had no other children. As quickly as the worry rose, it departed. She would trust God to meet her father's needs. She finished in a whisper-soft voice, "But God might have something else in store for me, and if He does, I'll follow His leading. Even if it means someday moving away."

"Mama, you're not movin' away from me, are you?"

Nicky's worried query captured her attention. She reached past Nic to tap the end of Nicky's nose. "Remember what Mama told you? I love you forever. My love will never move away from you."

Nicky nodded, satisfied.

She turned back to her father and squeezed his shoulder. "That goes for you, too."

He grimaced again. "All right, all right. Now sit down and eat. A cold supper gives me indigestion."

Lydia laughed. She returned to her seat and picked up her fork. Conversation moved to other topics, but she only half listened. Her mind was miles away. In New York. In a little apartment where a dark-haired man and a blond-haired little girl made plans to travel across the distance.

You'll soon know.

Lydia let her eyes slide closed. Whatever the Lord willed for her, she was ready.

38

Lydia held tight to Nicky's hand. Twice he'd tried to run out onto the boarding ramps, fascinated by the trains. A thorough scolding left him pouting, but at least he wasn't trying to get away from her anymore. She understood his eagerness. More than a month had slipped by since Micah's telephone call, and now that the hour of his arrival was upon her, she could barely contain her excitement.

So much had happened in the past weeks sometimes Lydia had a hard time absorbing it all. Nic's date with Myrna hadn't gone well, but Myrna had introduced him to her sister, Eliza. Nic and Eliza announced their engagement only four weeks later. Eliza was a sweet young woman who loved the Lord, adored Nic, and accepted without resentment that Nicky would still call Lydia "Mama."

Things across the ocean were exploding. Only this morning the newspaper headline had shouted of an encirclement of German troops by the Americans in the Ruhr. Every time the Germans suffered another setback, Lydia's heart raced in anticipation of the day Hitler's madness would come to an end. Standing behind a fence, waiting for the train that carried

Micah and Justina to Boston, Lydia offered another prayer for a speedy end to the war. *First the Germans, then the Japanese, Lord. Please bring it to a close.*

"Mama! There's another one!" Nicky pointed with his free hand, dancing in excitement beside her. "Will Micah-my-friend be on that one?"

"We'll have to wait and see, Nicky. The time is right." She wanted to dance, too. Tingles of anticipation climbed up and down her spine like dozens of ambitious spiders, and a tightness unrelated to the powerful engine chugging the train into the station built in her chest.

The ground trembled, the vibration tickling the soles of her feet. Nicky strained toward the ramp, pulling at Lydia's hand, but her quivering knees refused to carry her forward. *Oh, Micah, it's been so long. . . .*

The train heaved to a stop, and a suited porter leaped from the closest landing. He dropped a small stepstool into place, then held out his hand to descending passengers. Lydia scanned the faces as people emerged, her heart pounding.

"Micah-my-friend! It's Micah!" Nicky bolted toward the train, nearly jerking Lydia's arm from its socket. She released his hand, allowing him to wriggle between the legs of others while she followed as quickly as she could, peering over shoulders and around bobbing heads, trying to keep Micah in sight. She had yet to spot little Justina—the crowd in front of her blocked her view.

"Micah! Micah!" Nicky's shout carried over everything else, and Lydia fought tears as Micah went down on one knee, arms outstretched, to capture Nicky in a hug. Fortunately, people began spreading out along the boardwalk, greetings and laughter ringing from all areas, and Lydia was able to break through. She picked up her pace, running the last few feet as Micah released

Nicky and rose to meet her. He, too, stepped forward at the last minute, his arms opening wide, and without compunction she threw herself against him as exuberantly as Nicky had.

He laughingly swept her off her feet with the hug, and she clung to his neck, her cheek pressed to his, feeling as if her smile would never fade. The heart-lifting, joyful feel of being held in Micah's arms! Would she ever tire of it?

He set her on the ground, and she leaned back slightly, her arms still looped around his neck, his arms secure around her waist. Her gaze locked on his, and the busy spiders climbing her spine began a footrace. His head tipped slightly, his face moved closer, and she closed her eyes, lifting her chin in anticipation of the moment when his lips would finally touch hers in a kiss.

"Hey!"

Nicky's exclamation startled Lydia's eyelids open. She discovered Micah's wide blue eyes mere inches away. Still locked in the embrace, they swung their heads in the direction of the cry. Nicky stood with one hand on his hip, the other hand flipped palm outward in the direction of a darling little girl with curly blond hair, clear blue eyes, and a cherubic expression.

"She keeps calling me sweetheart." Nicky's voice held disgust. "Micah, would you tell her I'm Nicky?"

Micah threw back his head and laughed. Lydia's hands slipped to his chest, where she felt the vibration of his merriment through the fabric of his shirt.

"We'll discuss that sweetheart business later, partner." His gaze returned to Lydia, and although the laughter faded away, a sparkle remained in his dear eyes of blue. "Right now, I have to kiss your mama."

And Lydia discovered the engine of the mighty Union Pacific locomotive was less powerful than the effect of Micah Hatcher's lips when they met hers for the first time. It was a short kiss out of respect for their watching audience, but length didn't seem to matter where emotion was concerned. Lydia's feet felt no longer grounded. Surely she was floating as high as the steam above the engine's huffing stack.

Slowly, Micah's hand drifted from her back to her waist. "Lydia, I'd like you to meet someone very important in my life." He placed his other hand on Justina's cap of light hair. "This is my little sweetheart, Justina."

Lydia crouched before the child and held out her hand. Justina put her small fingers flat against Lydia's palm and offered a shy smile.

"Micah, she's adorable!"

"Adorable, and a real responsibility." The little girl raised her arms to Micah, and he picked her up, settling her on his hip. Lydia reached for Nicky's hand, and they fell into step together, moving to retrieve Micah's luggage from the baggage car. His eyes searched hers. "Would you be opposed to raising a child of Jewish origin?"

Lydia's heart hiccuped into thrilled double beats. Was he insinuating he would ask her to share in the upbringing of this child or simply seeking her opinion on such a venture? She allowed her heart to answer. "It would be an honor to raise a child of Jewish origin—a child of God's chosen race."

The tenderness in his smile warmed Lydia all the way to her toes.

Nicky, skipping along beside Lydia, smiled up at Micah and entered the conversation. "She's neat, Micah. Where did you get her?"

Micah chuckled. "From a big ship, Nicky." His gaze returned to Lydia. "But there won't be any more."

Lydia felt her brows lower as trepidation tickled her middle. "No more packages?"

Micah shook his head. She hoped he might elaborate, but instead he put Justina down and selected his brown case from the jumble of luggage waiting on the boardwalk. Lydia held out her hand to Justina and the child took it without hesitation. With Nicky holding her other hand, she led Micah toward her waiting Hudson. She longed for private moments with Micah, to discuss what he'd meant by his last comment, to perhaps experience the joy of another kiss. But the small pair of feet skipping along beside her reminded her they wouldn't be alone on this visit.

Micah almost pinched himself. Surely this was a dream. Sitting beside Lydia as she drove expertly through Boston's streets with Nicky and Justina together in the backseat, a feeling of family settled comfortably around his shoulders. He wanted to memorize every detail—the delicate turn of Lydia's jaw, the unruly curl in Nicky's hair, the steam on the window from their combined breaths, the clang of trolley bells drifting to their ears.

Justina seemed entranced by the trolleys. She bounced on her bottom, pointing out the window. At every clang of a bell, she yelled, "Sweetheart! Sweetheart!"

Nicky leaned over the seat and tapped Micah's shoulder. "This girl has a problem. She thinks everything's a sweetheart. Why doesn't she know anything?"

Micah laughed and turned sideways so he could face Nicky. "Justina knows a great deal. But she was born in another country. Her language is Polish. Listen. I'll ask her name." He stretched his arm across the back of the seat. *"Co jest wasze imię?"*

Justina spun from the window. "Justina."

Nicky's eyes widened into perfect circles. He tipped close to her. "What's your name?"

"Sweetheart."

The little boy sighed. "Maybe you better teach me that Pole-ush language so I can talk to her."

"I wish I could, but I don't know very much of it myself."

Nicky tossed a sour look at Micah. "Then we have a problem."

Micah laughed again, sharing a grin with Lydia, who peeked at him and shrugged. "Tell you what, partner, maybe you can help Justina. The only English word I've been able to teach her is sweetheart, probably because I call her that so much."

Nicky nodded solemnly. "Mama calls me sweetheart, too."

"I'm not surprised. But maybe, since you're closer to Justina's size, she'd be more willing to learn English words from you. Do you think you could try?"

Nicky's eyes blazed with interest. "What do you want me to teach her? I know lots of words, like Buggy, and flower, and trolley car, and cake . . ."

Lydia released a snort of humor. "Oh, Micah, you've opened a can of worms now."

Micah chuckled. "Don't be so helpful." She smirked. He turned his attention to Nicky. "Well, when children are learning to talk, most parents teach them the names of their family members, the parts of their body like nose and eyes, and words that will help them communicate."

Nicky shifted his gaze and examined Justina.

"Sweetheart!" Justina cried, pointing at the passing buildings.

Nicky's face puckered. "How long do I have?"

Micah grazed Lydia's shoulder with his fingertips. "Three days." She nodded.

From the backseat, Justina squealed, "Sweetheart!"

Nicky shook his head. "I hope that's enough."

Micah sighed, his gaze returning to Lydia's profile. He hoped so, too.

39

Supper that evening turned into a raucous affair, with Nicky and Justina sitting side by side and decorating each other with smashed peas. Although Lydia usually required better manners from Nicky, she didn't have the heart to scold. Watching him make friends with Justina gave her heart a lift.

When they'd finished eating, Mother took the children upstairs for a bath, and Father joined Micah and Lydia in the front room. Lydia preferred to have Micah to herself, but how could she tactfully tell her father to vacate his own front room? She needed to find her own home. In the past when she'd mentioned moving out, her mother had insisted Lydia needed help with Nicky, and Father had insisted she'd be stymied by Boston's housing shortages. So she'd stayed put. But it was time to make the change.

Father stretched his arm across the arched back of the sofa and pinned Micah with his dark eyes. "Dr. Hatcher, I'm interested in your future plans."

Micah cleared his throat. He glanced in Lydia's direction—she offered a discreet wink—and then he gave his full attention to Father. "Well, Mr. Eldredge, I've been hesitant to look too far ahead. I think most people feel as though they need to put plans in limbo until the war is over. But"—he scratched his head—"I know my future will involve providing medical care to low-income families, and specifically to immigrant families."

"I see."

Micah's face reflected the passion Lydia had come to expect when he spoke of his work. She longed for the day the same fire ignited in her heart, and her pulse sped as she remembered God's message.

"When immigrants arrive here," Micah told Father, "they look different and act different than most. Because of those differences, some people are hesitant to spend time with them, so the immigrants feel isolated. Except, of course, with others who are like them. I enjoy showing them they don't have to feel alone—that an *American* really cares about them."

He leaned forward slightly, his voice gaining strength as Father tipped his head, listening intently. "They usually have limited funds—traveling to America is costly—but health care is so important. They hesitate to go to the hospitals because doctors charge fees they can't afford. And they don't understand the terminology used there. Unfortunately some doctors treat the immigrants as if they're stupid just because they don't understand the language. By providing medical care for them at the clinic, I can ensure they receive care at a price they can afford. Plus I take the time to ascertain they understand what kind of treatment is needed." He leaned into the sofa's cushions, smiling. "I love my work. I can't imagine ever leaving it."

Lydia's heart thrilled to his words. She so admired his willingness to answer the calling God placed on his heart.

"And you chose New York because . . . ?"

Micah finished Father's lead-in. "Because a soldier who was injured in the Pearl Harbor attack mentioned the people of

New York to me. The idea wouldn't go away, and I came to believe God planted the seed in my heart to go there. After I finished my duty at Schofield, I made some inquiries, and I learned that a doctor who had opened a clinic in Queens was looking for someone to replace him. We talked, and he offered me the clinic the same day. Once I was settled, I knew I was where God wanted me to be. Other things"—he sent Lydia a secretive smile—"happened that convinced me I was in the center of God's plan for my life."

"Mm-hmm." Father crossed his legs and drummed his fingers on his knee. "Well, it seems as if you've decided to make New York your home."

Micah gave Lydia a lingering look. "Yes. For now."

Her heart leaped, but before she could question Micah's cryptic statement, Father's fingers stilled, and he said sharply, "For now?"

Micah shifted his attention to Father, lifting his shoulder in a brief shrug. "Well, sir, plans can change. God may need to plant me elsewhere. If that happens, I'll be willing to go where He leads." He smiled, and his Texas twang crept in, a sign that he was completely at ease with what he shared. "One thing I've learned, sir—if I aim my feet where God wants me to go, I stay on higher ground, out of the miry clay where the travel is hard and unhappy. Doesn't necessarily mean things always go perfectly, 'cause life isn't a perfect proposition, but it does mean my feet are secure. Can't imagine a better place to be."

Father's face pursed into a thoughtful frown. "Nic and Lydia have spoken of this 'higher ground.'" He sighed, shaking his head. "To be honest, I've always seen God as a baby carriage for those too weak to function without help. But lately . . ." His eyes took on a sheen. He dropped his foot to the floor and leaned toward Micah. "Dr. Hatcher, will you tell me how to find that higher ground for myself? I'd like to place my feet there, too."

Lydia froze. N. Allan Eldredge had just *asked* Micah to tell him about God! Her soul sang as she listened to Micah present the salvation message in simple, clear terms. And when her proud, self-important father bent on one knee next to the sofa, bowed his head, and folded his large hands in prayer for the first time, she wept tears of pure joy. When he rose, the light of Christ shone in his eyes.

Lydia flew across the room and enveloped him in a hug as tears continued to roll down her cheeks, the words from Romans 8:28 playing through her mind. Micah, Nicky, Nic—all had played a role in helping Father find his Savior. Her happiness knew no bounds.

She turned to Micah to thank him, and the light in his eyes immediately opened her heart to the answer she'd been seeking. She knew her purpose. God's plan was revealed so clearly she envisioned an ornate gate swinging wide for her entrance. Her heart winged in awe and glory of the moment, her soul praising, *Thank You, God. Thank You for leading me to Your higher ground!*

Micah stepped silently aside, allowing Lydia and her Father to celebrate. Their hug was long, tight, and laden with happy tears. When they finally pulled apart, the smile on Lydia's face sent a shaft of joy through his soul.

While Lydia dried her eyes, he placed his hand on Allan's shoulder. "Mr. Eldredge, I'm proud of the decision you just made. I know Lydia, Nic, and your wife will be pleased, because they've been praying for you. Go tell your wife what you've done. You've been reborn. Give her the chance to celebrate with you."

Allan blew his nose into his handkerchief, then gave a brisk nod. "I will. Thank you." He shook Micah's hand firmly, and although he held his head high, the aura of arrogance had melted.

The moment her father turned the corner, Lydia flew into Micah's arms. Her hair tickled his cheek and the scent of her perfume filled his nostrils. "Oh, Micah, thank you!"

He chuckled, reminding himself of the purpose for this embrace. "All I did was help him jump the finish line. You and Nic brought him to the point of acçeptance."

She wriggled loose from his grasp and gazed at him in awe. "My father reborn . . . I never thought it possible."

"Now, now." Micah teasingly tapped the end of her nose with his finger. "*All* things are possible with God, remember?"

"I know." She sighed, lifting her shoulders and swinging her arms outward. "Oh, I'm too keyed up to sit still. Let's take a walk. We can talk as we wander the neighborhood, okay? Mother will get Nicky and Justina into bed."

"Sounds good to me." Micah opened the door, and they stepped into the early spring evening. The moment they reached the bottom of the porch steps, Lydia slipped her hand into his. It felt good—right—to hold her hand. He linked fingers with her, giving a gentle squeeze, and she beamed up at him. They walked in contented silence, swinging their hands slightly between them. Their steps matched perfectly as they ambled along the sidewalk. Overhead, the sky was fading from cerulean to cornflower, with a hint of pink lighting the west. A hint of pink brightened Lydia's cheeks, as well.

The air smelled fresh and clean. And when the breeze moved right, Lydia's floral perfume wafted to his nose. He pulled her closer to fully enjoy the delightful aroma that spoke *Lydia* to him. A contented chuckle rose from his chest. "You know, Lydia, you look like you just caught a leprechaun and all your wishes are comin' true."

"Micah, I *feel* that way." She stopped and turned to face him. She appeared ready to burst from eagerness. "I have to share something with you."

He grinned. "Share."

Her eyes still danced, but her expression became serious. "Do you remember when God spoke to me in New York? I wanted to do something to help, remember?" He gave a nod, and she continued. "He said to be patient and wait—I would know in time. After you and Father finished praying, and I looked at you, there was something in your eyes, and . . ." She closed her eyes and drew in a slow breath, as if savoring something sweet. "Now I know." She peered up at him, eyes shining with unshed tears, a smile gracing her beautiful face.

He gave an impatient huff of laughter. "Are you goin' to tell me the plan?"

"Oh!" She laughed, the sound of music to Micah's ears, then released his hands to hug herself. "I'm to help your immigrants. With their language, so they can understand." She threw her arms wide. "I know medical terms, thanks to my Red Cross training, and if needed, I can also do some nursing, but God wants me to share language with them."

Impish dimples appearing in her cheeks, she caught his hands once more. "I'm going to start with Justina. We can't have her going through life calling everything 'sweetheart,' now can we?" She spun a circle, involving him in a quick do-si-do of happiness that aimed them toward her house. "Oh, it feels so wonderful to know what God wants me to do!"

She walked quickly, dragging him with her. Her animation knew no bounds, and it was all he could do to keep from sweeping her into his arms and kissing her until the stars exploded overhead. She'd never seemed more beautiful.

"It isn't as if I haven't been doing things that were useful. Being Mama to Nicky, caring for Nic, helping Father run the plant . . . All of these gave me pleasure, but not a true sense of fulfillment. But now—uncovering the special plan God made just for me—gives me a deep-down fulfillment. And I feel so full I might pop!" She laughed and swung his hand as they continued their buoyant stroll along the sidewalk.

Micah understood her elation. The peace he found working with the immigrants and assisting Jeremiah could only come from God. And now Lydia's happy announcement had made clear to him that God had planted another desire in his heart. What would she say when he shared the desire with her?

He drew her to a stop, ready to speak, but the sudden change in her expression raised a prickle of concern and stilled his planned words. He cupped her cheek. "Hey, why so glum?"

Lydia ducked her head for a moment, blinking rapidly. "Just thinking. It will be hard to leave Boston and my parents." A brave smile quivered on her lips. "But they could visit me. I'm not sure what will happen with Nicky, though—Nic will certainly want him to stay here. Nic recently became engaged to a wonderful girl—he'll probably bring her by to meet you."

Her hand in his, she guided him forward, now with slow, plodding steps. Although she spoke aloud, Micah believed she was reassuring herself rather than addressing him. "Eliza will be good to Nicky. He won't want for a mama. Spending time with your little Justina and the immigrant children I'm sure to meet will keep me from being *too* lonesome for Nicky. And of course he can visit if Mother and Father come. As for the plant, Father could probably find a manager. Maybe even Nic. And eventually the plant will still go to Nicky, just as Father intended." Her progress slowed to a crawl while she thought out loud, and then she stopped right there on the sidewalk.

Micah stood beside her, waiting. Had she finished her musings? He counted off a few seconds to be certain she had nothing left to say, then he took her chin in his hand and tipped her face toward his. "Do you have everything arranged to your satisfaction, Miss Eldredge?"

She pursed her lips, her brow crinkling. Finally she gave a brief nod.

He gave her skin a gentle caress before lowering his hand. "Good. Now may I share my thoughts with you?"

40

Lydia's skin tingled where Micah's fingers had just rested. The tenderness of his touch and the intensity of his gaze stole her ability to speak. He'd asked a question, and she wanted to hear his thoughts—wanted to listen to his sweet Texas drawl. But her tongue refused to function. So she offered a slow, single bob of her head in reply.

His lips quirked into the lopsided Micah-grin she so loved, and then he slipped her hand into the bend of his elbow and set off in a lazy, easy pace that matched his relaxed tone. "Lydia, you know I've been called to serve our country's immigrants, and I love it. Which means, of course, in all likelihood, I'll never be wealthy. Not in a monetary sense."

They reached her home, and he guided her to the porch steps. "Shall we sit?" She nodded, and he waited until they were situated before he continued speaking. "You've been raised in a much different environment than what I perceive for my future. Would you . . . would you be happy in a simpler dwelling, with fewer luxuries?"

Lydia's stomach clenched. Was he asking out of idle curiosity, or did a deeper meaning hide beneath his casual query? She angled herself on the riser and allowed her gaze to rove from the cinder-block foundation, up the brown brick façade, and on to the gabled cedar-shake roof. Her inspection complete, she looked directly into Micah's deep blue eyes—eyes the same color as the pounding surf of Oahu—and answered honestly. "A house is a shell for the home inside. And home is the people."

Something—approval and something more—flashed in his eyes. He lifted her hand, brushed a sweet kiss across her knuckles, and then lowered their clasped hands to his knee. "When I've come to visit you, I've needed to find someone to fill in for me at the clinic. The last replacement—a Dr. Springfield—was particularly good. He speaks fluent Italian and German. How often I've wished I had those talents!" He shrugged. "But somehow I've always managed to communicate, in spite of the language gaps."

Lydia couldn't hold back a spurt of laughter. "Oh yes, I've seen how you taught Justina to communicate . . . *sweetheart!*"

He laughed, too, his eyes crinkling in merriment. He shook his head and squeezed her hand. "Oh, I think my little sweetheart enjoys keepin' me on my toes. If I'd stop responding to it, she'd quit doing it, but I haven't found the wherewithal to be that firm with her yet. However, the time is coming. She's going to have to make some changes." His fingers tightened on her hand. "And so am I."

Awareness tiptoed across Lydia's scalp. "Changes?"

Micah shifted to look her full in the face. All humor left his expression. "I've been praying about it a lot lately. Ever since I was here last, and we worked with Nic. On my way to the train station, I passed the areas where Boston's immigrant population lives, and my heart went out to those people. I made some inquiries, and I discovered there's only one small medical clinic servicing all of your city's immigrants. It's not nearly enough."

Lydia gasped as understanding dawned. "Are . . . are you considering moving to Boston?"

He twisted his face into a comical, apologetic pout. "Will that mess up all the plans you were makin' while we walked?"

She yanked her hand free and playfully shoved his leg. "You're not funny! Answer me—is that what you're thinking?"

He slipped his arm around her shoulders, pulling her snug to his side. "It wouldn't be right away. Dr. Springfield is interested in taking over the clinic, but I need to ease him into the position. Many of the immigrants have come to depend on me, and I can't just abandon them."

Lydia's mind raced ahead, imagining the joy of Micah living here in Boston. What bliss to see him on a regular basis, to enjoy leisurely strolls in the evening or go to concerts and attend worship services together every Sunday. Caught up in her plans, she gave a little jolt when he began speaking again.

"Of course, lots must happen here before I can make the move. I need to find financial support and a building to use as a clinic, not to mention a place to live. I'd really like to find a facility that can be both clinic and home. Then I'd always be available to those who need me."

She patted his knee. "Micah, Father can assist you. He has connections everywhere in the city. Let's go talk to him now!" She bounced up, but Micah caught her hands and pulled her back beside him.

"Later. I just want time with you for now, okay?"

She wouldn't argue about spending Lydia-and-Micah time. She sat beside him, relishing the strong feel of his fingers linked with hers.

"I also need to stay in New York until Jeremiah returns. His last letter indicated he will be on the next Red Cross ship, but that could be the end of May." Micah shook his head, frowning.

"He had a rough winter, and he's not able to work any longer. The church in Russia is sending him back. He's terribly disappointed and feels as if he failed to finish his task."

Lydia squeezed his hand. "You and Jeremiah both need to think about the children you brought to safety. God would be telling him, 'Well done.'"

Micah smiled, tipping forward to plant a light kiss on her forehead. "I'll tell him you said so." He slipped his arm around her waist, resting his chin against her temple. "Ah, Lydia, I wish I could make definite promises to you right now, but this war . . . So many things are uncertain."

But her feelings for him were far from uncertain. His nearness sent her heart into flutters of pleasure. Her senses drank in the scent and sight and strength of this man. No matter how long it took, she would wait for him. He was meant for her. And she for him.

Pressing more snugly against his chest, she released a contented sigh. "I understand, Micah. Our time might not be now, but it will come . . . in God's timing."

He captured her jaw between his palms and tilted her face to him. The sun had slipped below the rooftops, draping them in long shadows, but his lips found hers, the kiss soft and lingering and flavored by the cherry pie they'd eaten for dessert. When he opened his eyes, she glimpsed the reflection of stars in his irises. He sighed, his breath drifting across her cheek. "I love you, Lydia Eldredge."

The dearest words ever spoken. For a moment she held her breath, savoring their meaning. Then she brought up her hands to clasp his wrists. "And I love you."

His thumbs traced the line of her jaw. "I want to marry you. As soon as I'm settled here. Will you be my wife?"

Lydia melted into his arms. "Being your wife would bring me more pleasure than I deserve."

"Ah, Lydia . . ." His husky tone told her everything she needed to hear. One hand at her waist, the other weaving itself into the hair at the nape of her neck, he drew her upward. She closed her eyes, anticipating another kiss.

The porch light snapped on and the door flew open. "There you are!" Nicky—excited as always.

Micah released her by increments, his fingertips sliding the length of her arm and along her rib cage as he gazed into her eyes with that secretive smile playing on his lips.

"Mama! Micah! Listen to this!" Nicky clomped down the stairs, pulling Justina by the hand. He guided her past Lydia and Micah and stopped at the base of the stairs. His face crunching in concentration, he caught Justina's shoulders and positioned her just so. He raised his fine brows and clenched his fists, resembling a pint-sized football coach. "Okay, Justina. Tell the names." He put a finger against her tummy. "Who are you?"

"Justina."

Micah and Lydia clapped. Nicky poked his own belly. "Who am I?"

Justina smiled. "Nicky!" She clapped, too, this time.

Nicky pointed to Micah. "Who is that?"

Justina tipped her head and rocked back and forth. "Papa." Her tone was knowing. Micah tweaked her nose and she giggled.

Nicky took a deep breath and sent Lydia a worried look. "This is the hard one, 'cause you weren't here. But we're gonna try it." Nicky touched Justina's hand and then pointed at Lydia. "Who . . . is . . . that?" He sucked in his lips and hunched his shoulders.

Justina looked skyward, brought her gaze back to Lydia, and offered a shy smile. "Mama?"

Nicky let out a whoop, jumped in the air, then hugged Justina with such exuberance he nearly knocked her off her feet. "She did it!" He beamed at the little girl. "Good job! You know your family!"

Lydia found herself watching the children through a mist of happy tears. "Family . . ." She whispered the beautiful word.

Micah squeezed her hand and then held out his arms. Nicky plowed against him, settling himself on Micah's knee. Justina slid into the slice of space between Micah and Lydia. She placed her little hand on Lydia's knee, and Lydia covered it with her own. They sat beneath a canopy of twinkling stars while a night bird sang its evening song and a delicate breeze tossed Justina's soft curls.

Lydia swallowed the lump that filled her throat, Nicky's joyous proclamation ringing through her heart. *"You know your family!"* It was true. They were family, just as God intended them to be.

Micah stretched his arm behind the two youngsters to caress Lydia's shoulder. She tipped her head and smiled at him, a smile intended to communicate the joy flooding her soul. He offered a gentle nod in response, and in his eyes she read the same message repeating itself with every beat of her heart.

God's higher purpose is fulfilled.

A Note From the Author

Dear Reader,

During the Second World War, a number of people worked tirelessly to rescue Jews from Hitler's systematic annihilation. Among them were ministers, farmers, housewives, and business owners. (You can read more at *www.ushmm.org*.) Being caught assisting Jews meant a death sentence, so these people literally risked their lives for the sake of another. Although Micah and Jeremiah Hatcher are fictional characters, they are inspired by the many selfless individuals who sacrificed all in reaching out to a persecuted people with compassion.

To my knowledge, no Red Cross ships were used to transport Jewish children from war-torn Europe to the safety of the United States. However, the Red Cross did work to bring food and other supplies to our own soldiers held in captivity by enemy forces, as well as to others affected by the war. And who knows? Maybe unbeknownst to the history-recorders, a child or two might have been whisked to safety by sympathetic sailors. Truth is often stranger than fiction.

As a mom and grandma, I frequently petition my Heavenly Father to keep my children safe. Just as Lydia told Nicky, regardless of what transpires in this fallen world, we can always find a refuge in the arms of Jesus. I pray you've discovered that place of security, as well.

May God bless you muchly as you journey with Him,

Kim

ACKNOWLEDGMENTS

I am deeply grateful to those who enrich my life and my writing ministry:

Mom and Daddy, who taught me to seek Jesus and modeled relying on His strength. I am so thankful you are mine.

Don, who shares this journey with me.

Kristian, Kaitlyn, and Kamryn, who bless me and challenge me and who reside deeply in my heart.

Connor, Ethan, Rylin, Jacob, Cole, Adrianna, Alana, Logan, and Kaisyn, who give Gramma so many reasons to smile.

Connie, Margie, Eileen, Darlene, and Donna, who not only critique my work but have befriended me and lift me in prayer. We're more than critique partners—we are sisters.

Sabra, Kathy, Bev and Jim, and Bonnie and Lanny, who encourage me and also keep me grounded. Your friendship is precious to me.

Charlene, David, Steve, Debra, Noelle, Carra, and the rest of the amazing team at Bethany House, who partner with me in sharing the truth of God's love through story. God's blessings to each of you.

Finally and most importantly, *God,* who lifted me from the miry clay, set my feet on a firm foundation, and gave me an opportunity to serve Him. There are no words to express what You mean to me. May any praise or glory be reflected directly back to You.

Kim Vogel Sawyer is a bestselling, award-winning author highly acclaimed for her gentle stories of hope. She has more than one million copies of her books in print. Kim lives in central Kansas, where she and her husband, Don, run a bed-and-breakfast and enjoy spending time with their three daughters and nine grandchildren. To find out more about Kim and her books, please visit the sites listed below.

www.kimvogelsawyer.com
writespassage.blogspot.com
www.TheKingsInnBnB.com

More Heartwarming Romance From Kim Vogel Sawyer

To learn more about Kim and her books, visit kimvogelsawyer.com.

When tragedy strikes on the grueling journey west, throwing Tarsie and Joss into an unexpected partnership, can they trust God with their dreams for the future?

A Home in Drayton Valley

When Amy Knackstedt and her children move in next door, Tim Roper's tentative relationship with them stirs memories of the Mennonite faith he left years ago. Can their unlikely friendship blossom into something more?

When Hope Blossoms

When the lovely young singer who has stolen his heart appears to be part of the very crimes Thad is investigating, can their budding relationship survive the scrutiny—and the truth?

Song of My Heart

BETHANYHOUSE

Stay up-to-date on your favorite books and authors with our *free* e-newsletters. Sign up today at bethanyhouse.com.

Find us on Facebook.

Free exclusive resources for your book group! bethanyhouse.com/anopenbook

Historical Romance From Kim Vogel Sawyer

When a single minister comes to her mountain town, can he help Lizzie find the peace she desires or will he only confuse her heart further?

A Whisper of Peace

Miss Amsel is ready for her first teaching assignment: a one-room schoolhouse in Walnut Hill, Nebraska. But with her modern ideas and fancy language, is this little prairie town ready for her?

Courting Miss Amsel